VALOROUS
BOOK ONE: AGE OF HONOR

TAMARA LEIGH

TAMARA LEIGH

THE WULFRITHS. FIRST. IN BETWEEN. IN THE END.

The late middle ages. England's king seeks to recover the French lands of his ancestor William the Conqueror and claim the continental throne. France's king aspires to seize the remainder of his royal vassal's lands and retain his throne. So begins the Hundred Years' War, the backdrop against which the formidable Wulfriths of the AGE OF CONQUEST and AGE OF FAITH series continue their tale.

THE HONOR OF HECTOR WULFRITH

Pale rider. For all the wives lost to him, it is what some call England's renowned trainer of knights, a name that reaches beyond those losses to the plague come out of the east. Believing it God's will he not wed again, Hector Wulfrith resists being drawn to the courageous lady who enters a country at war with her own and, disguised as a man, trespasses on his home. However, when her resolve to obtain training for a boy she claims is Wulfrith kin drags him into her mess of murder and thievery, mutual attraction becomes something more. If he can save her, dare he risk gaining her for himself knowing her fate could prove the same as his doomed wives'? Would it not be better to encourage her to return the affections of his heir—a brother wronged for what Hector stole from him?

THE MESS OF SÉVERINE DE BARRA

INTRODUCTION

Since the surrender of her town to English forces, the greatest kindness shown Séverine is that of an enemy of silvered dark hair who saved her from his own when she sought to protect her cousin. Years later, she crosses the channel to keep her word to the boy's departed sire to place him with distant kin for knighthood training. But the trouble awaiting them in England follows them to Baron Wulfrith whom she must deceive to gain an audience—one that comes to naught though he proves her former savior. Desperate to secure her cousin's future before the fugitive made of her endangers him, Séverine furthers her deception to obtain the baron's aid and finds her heart turning to him. But to what lengths will one of fortified emotions go to save a French lady destined for imprisonment in the Tower of London—and possibly death?

From USA Today Bestselling author Tamara Leigh, the first book in a new medieval romance series set in the 14th century during The Hundred Years' War. Watch for BEAUTEOUS, the second book in Summer 2022.

For new releases and special promotions, subscribe to Tamara Leigh's mailing list: www.tamaraleigh.com

VALOROUS: Book One (Age of Honor) Copyright © 2022 by Tammy Schmanski, P.O. Box 1298 Goodlettsville, TN 37070
tamaraleightenn@gmail.com

This novel is a work of fiction. Names, characters, places, incidents, and dialogues are either the product of the author's imagination or are used fictitiously. Any resemblance to actual events, locales, organizations, or persons, living or dead, is entirely coincidental and beyond the intent of the author.

All rights reserved. This book is a copyrighted work and no part of it may be reproduced, stored, or transmitted in any form or by any means (electronic, mechanical, photographic, audio recording, or any information storage and retrieval system) without permission in writing from the author. The scanning, uploading, and distribution of this book via the Internet or any other means without the author's permission is illegal and punishable by law. Thank you for supporting authors' rights by purchasing only authorized editions.

Cover Design: Ravven

Ebook ISBN-13: 978-1-942326-56-4

Paperback ISBN-13: 978-1-942326-57-1

"As far as the east is from the west, so far hath he removed our transgressions from us." ~ Psalm 103:12 KJV

CHAPTER 1

Crécy-en-Pointhieu, France
August 26, 1346

L*et not that conniving woman turn you from your purpose, Hector of the Wulfriths. Honor your name! Do your duty to king and country! Protect the prince!*

No easy thing with the sixteen-year-old abandoning his position to attack forces that sought to prevent the English army from reclaiming French ancestral lands that belonged to King Edward by way of William the Conqueror. Of course, now there was another matter of contention between the English and French kings—the former's claim to the throne of France by way of his mother.

As Hector and the prince's standard-bearer forged a bloody path on the ridge for others coming to aid Edward the younger who was being surrounded by the French, once more someone rallied the English with, "God is our side!"

So it seemed though they numbered half their opponent. The first portent of French defeat occurred when King Philip's forces began a disorderly advance into the valley and crows flew before them, the next when the sky darkened, thunder rolled, and lightning preceded heavy rainfall.

Then as if backhanded by God, the clouds had fled and the setting sun shone in the eyes of the French. With dusk approaching and the ground over which they must pass muddied, the English had expected them to withdraw and make camp for the night, but as if pride usurped reason, King Philip of France had unfurled the Oriflamme.

As his crossbowmen plodded forward, the immense red banner with its golden sun was loosed upon the breeze to strike fear in the English nobility who knew what it signified. Until lowered, no quarter would be given, those otherwise taken prisoner for ransoming slaughtered. However, it was the French crossbowmen who were slain when, urged on by trumpets and pressed forward by foot soldiers, they shot bolts before they were in range—though they were well within range of the superior longbows of the English.

"Wulfrith!" Sir Richard FitzSimon shouted as he gripped the standard that must not be lost to the enemy and with his other hand thrust his sword into the belly of a warrior between him and King Edward's son. "The prince is down!"

As Hector felled another chevalier, he saw what remained of the young man's bodyguard struggled to give him time to regain his feet, which he absolutely must lest the French claim one priceless spoil of war.

Though Prince Edward had not received his knight's training at Wulfen Castle for which Hector's family was renowned, a moment later he showed the superiority of his education in all things warrior. He shot upright, lunged past his guards, and thrust his sword in an opponent. As that one dropped, he whose build was not yet fully developed set himself at another and once more dealt a killing blow. It was then the knight guarding his back was put through, providing a clear path to King Edward's heir.

The prince pivoted and arced his blade high, but the strength of his opponent's blow spun him to the side and his knees hit ground again.

"His left flank, Wulfrith!" FitzSimon bellowed.

As already Hector moved that direction, he arrived well ahead of the one under whom he had served during the campaign. Thus, it was his sword that pierced the enemy seeking to take the prince.

Forced to relinquish his hold on young Edward, the Frenchman swept up his blade to avert his opponent's next swing. When Hector leapt to the side, the tip of that one's blade sliced the back of his hand and skimmed his armor-clad shoulder. He felt the sting, but the hand yet functioned, allowing him to land his blade against knees lacking protective armor.

As the man toppled, FitzSimon gained the ground in front of the prince and dropped the standard. Setting a foot atop it to keep it out of enemy hands, he shouted to fellow warriors fighting their way forward, "To the king's son!" Then he and what remained of the bodyguard fended off the French who continued to advance.

As Hector moved toward Edward the younger, the prince pushed up and came around with sword in hand. Despite a bloodied temple, his eyes were bright and teeth flashed. "Much gratitude for aiding your prince while he came right of head, Sir Hector!"

Hector was not surprised the young man knew the identity of FitzSimon's knight, not only for the renown of the Wulfriths but this one's prematurely silvered hair. However, he had not expected him to be acquainted with his Christian name.

That Hector of twenty-two summers had achieved such

notice made him feel esteemed as if he were more than six years the prince's senior.

As expected when the Wulfrith heir had answered the king's summons to join his campaign, Hector's reputation grew. He knew it was a small part of his purpose in fighting for his sovereign, but the indulgent pride mostly excised by his trainers—foremost his sire and his uncle—was stitching itself back into place.

More he should resist since it could render a warrior vulnerable in a world partial to breaking its fast on the weak, but it was balm and distraction to what was of greater detriment—anger over his wife's betrayal. If a warrior's emotions were to be greatly moved, surely better by pride that aided in swinging a sword harder than anger that made him want to thrust his blade in the ground, raise his face, and roar.

Assured the prince was firm on his feet, Hector said, "Sir Richard dispatched word to your father you are in great straits, but I see no reason we cannot finish these Frenchmen ere relief arrives. Do you, my prince?"

As his sire's cannons fired more projectiles, Edward the younger shouted, "I see no reason at all!"

When a score of the king's bodyguard arrived minutes later, including Hector's relation, Sir Achard Roche, they were not needed. Those seeking to capture the heir were in retreat, FitzSimon had raised the standard, and the prince, two of his guards, and Hector leaned on their swords amid the slain.

As expected, the reprieve was short-lived, but allowing them to catch their breath ahead of the next onslaught. And it was needed since it would be nearly midnight before the last of the enemy retreated. Not only had the English killed two horses out from under King Philip, but an archer had put an arrow in his jaw, forcing him to flee. As for his sacred battle standard, its bearer had been of special interest to English bowmen who struck him down.

Just as the King of England's unequivocal victory was unexpected, so were his losses numbering in the hundreds. Just as the humiliation dealt the King of France shocked, so did his losses numbering in the thousands.

Beneath a sky ink-black but for a quarter moon torn into that canvas and punched through with stars, the windmill atop the hill that had served as King Edward's command post was filled with brushwood. Set alight, it allowed the English to move among the fallen and more easily locate their own, whether for burial or delivery to a physician.

This past hour, still arrayed in armor and displaying the Oriflamme draped over his destrier's back with the saddle strapped atop it, King Edward had ridden among his men, praising them as he kept order to ensure none let down their guard lest the French returned. Having reached the forces that withstood the first attack and seeing his son, he reined in, removed his helmet, and dismounted. Garments more bloodied and tattered than the prince's, he embraced the youth.

It surprised how long the sire held the son and the son the sire. When finally King Edward drew back, he considered his heir's disarray that evidenced how courageously he had fought. "Prince Edward of the revered Plantagenets, most loyal son, you acquitted yourself well and nobly, honoring king and country," he proclaimed.

"As due my lord father and our people." The youth bowed. "I serve."

"You are worthy to keep a realm," his sire said and set a hand atop the prince's head, closed his eyes in prayer, then raised him up. "Though many proclaim our reign the Golden Age, with you at our side, better it is called the Age of Honor."

The young man stood taller, jerked his chin.

As done throughout the king's progress, England's ruler addressed those here, commanding that none boast of victory, all give thanks to God, and to remain on guard lest an enemy relief force attack in the night. Then England's present and future king crossed to FitzSimon and Hector, the former yet possessing the prince's muddied and bloodied banner.

"Well done, FitzSimon." The king clapped him on the shoulder, looked to Hector. "We are told much is owed you, young Wulfrith."

It was hard not to take offense at being made to sound a youth, but Hector reminded himself he had far fewer years than King Edward who was more experienced in life and battle—though since Hector's arrival in France, by leaps he gained greater experience in both. *Including the private side of my life,* he thought, then questioned if he would still have a wife upon his return home.

"'Tis told you were valorous," King Edward said. "Worthy of your name."

As he embraced the praise, the prince inserted, "Greatly he aided, and for it nearly lost his sword hand." As his sire looked to what was bandaged, he continued, "I am confident I would have escaped capture, but with this knight's aid, sooner we slew a good number and set others to flight."

Again Hector struggled not to take offense, and easier it was to overcome for the smile cornering the king's mouth. Edward knew his son exaggerated, though not *overly*. And he was proud as Hector expected one day to be proud of his own son.

Do I gain one, his thoughts returned to the missive that alluded to him being incapable of siring children.

"A reward is due you, Wulfrith," King Edward said.

Might you appeal to the papacy on my behalf? hope slipped in only to be dealt two swift kicks. The first was the reminder the French pope, unashamed in advancing the interests of his countrymen, would be further ill-disposed toward England's king after the humiliating defeat of King Philip. The second kick came from sound reasoning. If the lady with whom Hector had been pleased for her gentility outside the bedchamber and ardency inside it did not want him, he would be foolish to try to hold to her. Far better he place his hope in Pope Clement bending to her family's influence, the lies of their physician, and financial incentive. Once the marriage was annulled...

The bitter of Hector longed to forswear wedding again, but if he wished a son—and to prove he was capable of siring children—a search must begin for his third wife who would be his fourth had the girl to whom he was first betrothed lived long enough to wed.

Determining this time he would not leave the decision to his grandmother and sire that had allowed him to devote himself to his training and that of others, he returned his attention to the king and found he was watched.

"We all wear many hours and shall wear more ere dawn, Wulfrith," Edward said sympathetically. "God willing, afterward it will be safe to gain our rest."

Hoping the warmth in his face was not visible with the great torch made of the windmill behind, Hector said, "I shall not lower my guard."

"And we shall think on your reward." Edward turned away. "Come, worthy prince, see how well the banner of he who calls himself King of France serves as a saddle cloth. It makes our seat no more comfortable, but we are convinced red and gold look fine beneath us."

His son laughed, and as he matched his stride to his sire's and FitzSimon followed, King Edward commanded his bodyguard to dismount and walk the stiff out of their legs.

Sir Achard, who hours past had returned to guarding the king when he and others sent to aid the prince appeared, led his destrier to Hector. Being of good size, this relation wore well the marks of battle—so minor the damage to armor and garments there was no doubt the blood upon him was mostly of the enemy.

Golden hair and face lit by the burning windmill, he swept his gaze down Hector, paused on the bandaged hand, then with forced lightness said, "All your limbs appear intact, little cousin."

Little only because Achard was two years older and had aided with Hector's training at Wulfen during the completion of his own. Proof of that was had when they stood before each other, there being little difference in height nor breadth between cousins so far removed that marriage to Achard's sister had been a consideration before the deceitful one was chosen for the Wulfrith heir.

"Your brother?" Achard asked after Warin who had been knighted and wed a sennight before joining King Edward's army.

"Injuries the same as many who fought in the front ranks, but nothing serious," Hector said and silently thanked the Lord. He had wanted Warin at his side during his brother's first real battle and FitzSimon had agreed, but the second born had declined. Eager to prove himself, almost single-handedly he had shored up a hole the enemy made in the English's right flank.

"I am glad to see you are whole as well, old man Roche," Hector said.

His chuckle flat, Achard closed mismatched eyes of brown and blue said to have been passed to him by the Saxon woman who wed one of Hector's Norman kin following the Battle of

Hastings. "Not even twenty and five, and yet I feel old this day." He looked around.

Hector followed his regard to the battlefield with its hillocks of bodies. When the sun rose, further the senses would be assaulted as the heat of day warmed away the cool of night. Blessedly, few if any of those trained at Wulfen would number among the dead. From all Hector had seen, young and old—some of blood relation, most not—had acquitted themselves admirably, honoring the Wulfrith dagger worn to further attest to superior training.

"I know our king was pushed to this, Philip's confiscation of the Duchy of Aquitaine a declaration of war," Achard said, "and I am grateful our prayers were answered, but this is a vile business." He moved his regard to the king and prince who stood alongside the destrier cloaked in the Oriflamme. "When Philip hears of the fate of his sacred banner, it will further his humiliation. Though Edward believes it a good thing if it tempts his adversary to come out of the rabbit hole he is fond of going into headfirst and sooner settle this dispute whether by negotiation or battle, I am not as certain."

Is it a good thing? Hector wondered. *Will Philip cease his attacks on English shipping, its ports, and the Channel Islands? Will he withdraw his support from England's Scottish enemies? Or will he return to striking from out of the shadows and be more resistant to relinquishing his claim on lands to which King Edward owes him homage and naught else?*

Hector wavered then went the way of Achard. Had he to guess, this war was the beginning of what could take years to resolve. And as long as his aging sire retained his title and oversaw the training of warriors, Hector would serve their king in whatever capacity was required of him.

Or nearly so, he silently amended, determined not to compromise the honor of the Wulfriths as Achard believed he himself had dishonored the name of Roche during the capture of the city of Caen—both aware their resolve could be tested at Calais where next they journeyed to take the coastal town that would give access to the channel for receipt of English reinforcements and supplies.

Since against all odds King Edward had gained a victory at Crécy, greatly elevating his spirits, hopefully he would be better disposed to keeping control of his forces at Calais should that city resist.

What neither cousin could know was those spirits would be further bolstered when thousands of French arrived late to the battle. And amid the morning mists, the English dispatched them atop those already fallen and rode to ground others who fled.

CHAPTER 2

Port of Calais, France
August 3, 1347

Annus mirabilis—year of marvels. That was what the English were calling the period from their king's forces landing in France in 1346 to the Battle of Crécy weeks later to the submission of Calais this day of 1347.

It offended the French, but who could dispute it? Not the inhabitants of Calais whose town had been under siege nearly a year and were on the verge of surrender when their governor smuggled a missive to his sovereign. He had warned the King of France that unless relief was given as pledged, the survivors would march out and fight since it was better to die with honor than be reduced to eating human flesh.

At last, their sovereign had brought an army, causing rejoicing inside the walls. However, after discovering how entrenched the English were with siege defenses and a town built outside the walls that included shops, homes for its leaders, and a palace for their king, King Philip had withdrawn.

Twice it had made Séverine de Barra curse him and heave up what was little more than bile—once when she stood atop the battlements watching Calais' saviors-turned-cowards go from sight, and this morn when the bell rang to assemble the garrison and citizens who had suffered in holding the town against the English.

After rinsing her mouth and wiping her face, she had tied a knot in oil-tarnished hair to secure it at her nape. Next, she had donned a mantle, covering a gown months without benefit of soap and water, supply of the first long depleted and the second more precious than the last of the food rationed out on the day past.

Now with the little one on her hip and aching for his whimpering over a belly nearly as empty as hers, Séverine stood behind those gathered in the marketplace before the governor and trembled over what was told of his meeting with King Edward's man, Sir Walter Manny.

Though merciful terms of surrender were sought, since the English ruler was deprived of the opportunity to best King Philip, he was in no mood to guarantee the lives of those who had resisted him. Hence, the people of Calais could remain inside and starve to death or come out and chance being put to the blade.

The whimpers of the boy of nearly two years becoming cries, Séverine swayed to soothe him to sleep as more he was given to the weaker he grew.

"Hung-y, Mama," Mace bemoaned.

The fifteen-year-old Séverine was not his mother, but his cousin on the side of the lady who had died a month before the siege commenced. However, as she had been his most constant caregiver for a year and his sole caregiver these three months since his sire and others stole outside the walls to forage for supplies and not returned, she supposed she was the mother he named her.

"Hung-y," he said more loudly, causing townsfolk to turn sorrowful eyes on him.

"Forgive me for not better protecting you," the commander of Calais said tearfully. "On this fourth day of August, exactly eleven months since the siege began, the decision between opening the gates to what *could* prove a swift, merciful end and remaining inside to what *will* prove a slow, merciless end is made."

As Mace resumed whimpering, evidencing not even Séverine's last portion of food was enough to nourish him, she prayed the gates would be opened since it seemed their only hope. Shortly after the siege began, the governor had expelled seventeen hundred poor women and children to preserve supplies that would ensure the well-being of those who were to hold the town until relief arrived.

Séverine and other noblewomen had wept, aware those set outside would likely be slain before the walls or left to starve in sight of those within. And more likely it seemed after what the English had done at Caen. However, King Edward had been merciful, allowing the women and children to pass and providing food and drink for their journey. Though it was doubtful he would do so again after all these months, she had to believe it was possible.

"Please, Father mine," she whispered. "If not the women, preserve the children." Of which there were scores as weakened as Mace though their mothers also sacrificed to keep the little ones alive, as evidenced by figures as gaunt as Séverine's.

Amid the silence complete but for the pitiful noises of children, the one raised above the gathering cleared his throat. "It is decided—"

"Governor!" someone shouted. "Sir Walter Manny returns!"

Rising to her toes to gain what should not be a dizzying height, Séverine saw the soldier who entered the marketplace from the direction of the gatehouse.

"Mayhap God be merciful!" the governor cried, then with a stagger that evidenced his rations were as meager as the others', he descended the platform and commanded all to pray.

It could not have been a quarter hour before his return, but to Séverine whose body ached and emotions strained, it felt hours.

The man remained grim, but his chin was high. "Reprieve, people of Calais! Not for all, but nearly."

The cries of women and men resounded through the marketplace, and many embraced.

"Hear me!" he shouted, and like fearful children, they quieted. "Sir Walter Manny and others have persuaded King Edward to pardon all save six of our principal citizens."

Gasps. And Séverine knew among those expressing relief were ones previously envious of Calais' wealthiest inhabitants.

"Here the terms—the six shall march to the King of England with bare heads, bare feet, and ropes around their necks. Having delivered the keys of the town and castle, these men will be at his absolute disposal. Once he metes out justice as he pleases, all others will depart Calais without impunity."

"As he pleases," muttered a nearby merchant. "Has he any patience left, he will hang them from the walls. Has he not, he will lop off their heads then and there."

"You know who you are, fine men of Calais," the governor continued. "Now which of you will preserve the lives of his countrymen?"

It was wrong to think it good Mace's sire had not returned, but Séverine did, certain Amaury de Chanson would have been the first to step forward. Not only had he been among the most successful merchants but noble in birth and deed—excepting during his younger years. Hence, were he here, death would have been delayed three months with much suffering in between.

The wealthiest citizen was the first to answer the call. Gaining the platform, he said, "Gentlemen, as I have faith and trust in being shown God's grace should I die, I take my place."

His courage set many to weeping and others began moving toward the platform. However, only four more were needed, the governor announcing he would be the sixth humbled and fit for hanging, lead the others, and yield his sword ahead of delivering the keys. As more tears bathed faces long without a proper washing, he said, "We go now—men at the fore, women and children at the rear."

"Now?" many exclaimed.

"Those are the terms. As for the sick unable to assemble, we must accept the King of England's assurance they will be loaded on carts and reunited with their families in the western valley where all will make camp this eve and be given two days' supply of food and drink."

Praising the Lord, Séverine hugged Mace tighter and, jolted by his unresponsiveness, shot her gaze to his head on her shoulder. Though his lids were closed, breath flared his nostrils. "God willing, when you awaken I will have food for your pained belly and milk for your dry mouth," she whispered.

"What of my jewelry and gowns?" cried an elderly woman.

"King Edward's pardon is for those who come out with the six. As we have only a quarter hour, whatever you now carry on your persons is all you shall take."

"He thinks to lay hold of our possessions!" a man cried.

"The prerogative of the victor!" the governor snapped. "But

do you value your chattel more than your life, make haste, for the rest of us will appear at the appointed hour."

Fools, Séverine scorned those scurrying opposite. After all their suffering, how pitiful they risked the lives returned to them.

Lay up for yourselves treasures in heaven, she recalled last eve's Scripture as she joined the majority leaving behind worldly goods to gather at the gatehouse where the doomed men bared their heads and feet and fit their necks with nooses.

Tears welling, once more she scorned those absent for having more regard for their possessions than salvation offered by these courageous citizens.

Only four had reappeared when the governor commanded, "Open the gates!"

"Lord," Séverine breathed, and as hinges ground, looked behind.

Here came a woman who had gone for her goods. From her laborious stride, much was beneath her mantle. Hopefully, the others would reach the gatehouse before the last of the garrison and citizens exited.

Gasps and cries turned Séverine forward again. Though she pushed to her toes to peer beyond the opening gates, the townspeople were too packed to see much past them. Doubtless, in front of the siege defenses erected between the town of Calais and that which the English had raised and tauntingly named Villeneuve-le-Hardi—Brave New Town—the English gathered. And most terrible of all would be their king.

Returning to her heels, Séverine awaited instructions sure to be forthcoming once the six delivered themselves—and hoped for as much time as possible so those gone to their homes could rejoin the townspeople.

"Fools," she rasped. "What could be more important than

—?" So great her gasp, she would have swallowed her tongue were it not anchored.

Though inwardly she recoiled, her conscience reminded, *Now Mace is as fatherless as motherless, there his future. If you leave it behind, it will be lost to the one with whom you are entrusted. And render you a liar.*

Recalling the word given her uncle, she considered the little one who would make her arms ache more had he not lost so much weight. She had no choice. However, it was one thing to risk herself, unacceptable to risk him.

"It is Sir Walter Manny who leads them to that dread king," reported one ahead.

"Dread or not," said another, "if only he were the one owed our fealty. He would not have deserted us." The voice was that of the robust woman who provided Calais with the best fruits and vegetables and now looked a sack of produce emptied of half its contents.

Séverine stepped alongside her. "I need your help."

She of middling years looked around. "Oui, Lady?"

"There is one thing I must gain from our home, and sooner I can go and return if you hold Sir Amaury de Chanson's son."

"But do you not return in time—"

"It is important."

Hesitantly, the woman accepted the little one. "Be quick, Lady. A poor mother I would make this child."

So weak was Séverine, she would not have thought it possible to run, but she did. Fortunately, her home was this side of town, and halfway there she passed another she had judged a fool.

"There is no time, Lady!" he called.

She continued forward, certain what she retrieved would protect Mace regardless of whether or not the English took

France's crown just as once the Norman-French had taken England's crown.

The well-appointed house was as she had left it—lovely and orderly despite neglect inherent in being under siege. By day's end, the English would claim its valuables.

"Not all," she rasped and ascended the stairs to enter the bedchamber of the one who had become her uncle through marriage. Except for two pots on the floor to catch rain come through the ceiling last month, the room was the same as Sir Amaury had left it.

His bed was heavy, requiring much effort to move it aside, but finally she was on her knees prying at joined planks. After freeing the panel, she reached into the cavity and pushed aside a box of jewelry, leather-bound books, and silver candlesticks, then withdrew a purse of coins. All were token treasures with which it was hoped thieves would be so content they would not further explore the space Sir Amaury had revealed to her.

On four sides, vertical planks were set back from the opening, but the one to the left was not permanent. Séverine lowered to her belly to extend her reach, felt her hand up the support, and hooked a finger through a notch. Meeting resistance as if the piece was nailed, she wrenched, straining her finger and beginning to sob as the time remaining to her was eaten away.

Gaining only slight movement of the plank, she cried, "Lord!" and dropped onto her back. As she flapped her hand, her eyes landed on the culprits—ceiling stains evidencing water had entered here, what her pots had not captured causing the floor to swell.

"You are more the fool than any other this day," she rebuked. "It is not enough to think you need more pots. You must *get* more pots."

With the townspeople soon to depart, she began searching

the chamber. What was needed was found at the bottom of Sir Amaury's trunk—an old sword alongside a nondescript dagger. After concealing the latter in her hose, she hefted the great blade and, recalling King Philip turning his back on his people, hacked at the planks until she broke through.

After putting the cask and purse of coins in a sack, she fastened the makeshift pack to her back beneath her mantle and departed the home she would not likely enter again.

Séverine came so close to making it to the gatehouse her knees nearly failed when, between two buildings, she glimpsed English soldiers entering the walls behind the last of those expelled from Calais. It was terrible enough to be caught inside without the excuse of great illness, but to have required but a minute more to bring up the rear...

She should have hacked harder at the floor, she told herself, should have stretched her legs longer. Now what? Ravishment? Death? First one, then the other?

Hide and pray for an opening, she counseled. But if an opening could be found, it must be soon since her only chance of getting back to Mace was to reach the many dragging their feet as they moved toward the enemy.

"See there!" someone shouted in her language, though not with the strength of her accent. His was of the Norman-French who conquered England so long ago their accents were diluted by those of the Saxons they subjugated—and wed.

When Séverine looked around and saw she was the one brought to the notice of another besieger, she fled. As she wove among the streets, she berated herself for not drawing her hood over blond hair that surely rendered her more visible.

I know the places here as they do not, she tried to assure herself—and failed. If these two did not uproot her, others quick to familiarize themselves with the formerly impregnable Calais would.

Hopelessness tempting her to concede defeat, she reminded herself what thumped against her back would be taken and managed to stay ahead of her pursuers. Still, they gained on her.

She turned a corner, and when she came around the next, the forge was before her. A year past, she had become acquainted with it after yielding to the flirtations of a young iron worker who assured her he could satisfy her curiosity over the operations by providing a view known only to himself. Ignoring the sense she should decline, she had followed him into the rafters, a small portion of which were floored.

She had liked learning about the forging of iron, but his kisses were pleasing as well. Had the two stayed back from the edge, they would not have come to his sire's notice. After their descent, the man had scolded Séverine for not behaving a lady, then entreated her not to tell her uncle—and told silence would preserve her reputation.

Shamed, she had held close her first kisses. Now more good might come of that shaming and the thrashing it was rumored his beloved son received.

Certain she was out of sight of her pursuers, Séverine made for the forge, but as she entered, a shout came from a different direction. Her pursuers were joined by others, but had they caught sight of her?

Lightheaded, she walked hands up the walls of the concealed stairs she ascended, and hardly was she tucked into the back corner of the flooring than the voice of a pursuer sounded beyond the door. *"I* will deal with her. As tasked, aid with loading the sick onto carts!"

Not being so naive to believe it a good thing that Englishman would alone rectify the problem of her, Séverine shuddered. Even if what had befallen many women at Caen did not occur here, it could happen to this one who had gone for worldly goods.

When the enemy entered, his advance was not marked by the ring of armor but the scrape of boots. But then, as English victory was assured, likely he believed a sword sufficient protection against any who lay in wait.

Drawing slow breaths in the still that had been clamorous the last time she was here, Séverine lowered her gaze to cracks between the planks and watched for movement.

Nearer he came, then she glimpsed him. Looking down upon the warrior, it was difficult to know his height, and as her window on him was exceedingly narrow, neither could she determine his breadth, but there was no mistaking his dark hair was shot with silver. As he was no young man, it should increase her chance of escape were she discovered.

He halted directly below, called, "Girl! Be content with what you gained in delaying your departure and go while still you have a chance of pardon."

Two things stopped her breath, the first that though his voice was the deep of a man, it seemed no match for the silver woven amid black. Might he be like Mace's sire whose hair had silvered long ere its time? Or did he merely retain a youthful voice?

The second thing—and of greater import—was his offer for her to depart unmolested. Was it but a means of coaxing her out? Likely since, unless he was quite observant, this raised floor had not drawn his notice. And were he observant, he would not believe it possible one lacking wings could ascend here since the stairs were built between the walls.

"Make haste! Once my king has treated with the six, the townspeople outside the gate depart, and it will be impossible for you to join them without being searched—at best."

Praying her belly did not resume its groanings, she waited

for him to conclude the one seen entering here had departed another way.

But then he turned his face up, as told by a glimpse of tanned brow before she snapped back her head.

"You will have to accept the word I give to keep the way clear for you."

She wished she could believe him.

"Girl! I have duties to which I must attend and soon your people will be on the move. Hence, take your treasures and leave now, else fall into the hands of those of less honor." With that, he started back across the forge.

"Hold!" She scrambled for the stairs and, gaining the ground floor, found it empty. However, when she peered into the street, he stood at the end with his back to her.

Tall and broad, silvered hair skimming shoulders, hips girded with sword, he turned an ear toward her, revealing a stubbled jaw. Then setting a hand to the side, he motioned her forward.

She whipped the mantle's hood over her head and closed the distance, though not so much she lacked space in which to flee.

As if this man did seek to keep her out of sight of his countrymen, twice he paused and veered from the course she would have taken. When the open gates were before her, she saw the people of Calais had begun to advance outside the walls, meaning the English king had received the six and their bloody sacrifice was complete.

As she swallowed convulsively, the man called across his shoulder, "Go!" This time when he motioned her forward, she was near enough to see a scar on the back of his hand—its color evidencing fairly recent acquisition.

Impulse opened her mouth to thank him. Resentment swallowed the words. Gripping the hood closed at her neck, she ran. Once past him, she was tempted to look back to know his face and age but resisted.

When she exited and English soldiers stationed outside the gatehouse shouted for her to halt, she ignored them and released the hood so her arms could aid in propelling her forward. Shortly, she inserted herself in a gap opened by those who had looked behind.

Once her fellow exiles closed around her and others drew her forward, she peered across her shoulder and thanked the Lord no bodies hung from the wall—and no soldiers gave chase.

As the townspeople moved past rows of well-fed and impressively arrayed English archers and men-at-arms, Séverine went to her toes to seek their king. There he was—the ground before him absent the bodies she expected to be there.

Astride a massive destrier, a crown on his brow, Edward III sat at the fore of hundreds of beautifully armored knights and was bounded both sides by persons of note. The one to his right had to be his son and heir of the same name, the one to his left his queen, making truth of the rumor she had joined her husband in Villeneuve-le-Hardi.

Also crowned, the skirt of her cream and gold gown draping her horse from back to tail, she looked at the remnants of those her husband had terrorized eleven months. And when it seemed her gaze fell on the young woman come late to the exodus, Séverine startled—and again when a hand closed over her arm.

"I feared for you, Lady!" said the woman entrusted with Amaury de Chanson's son.

"I thank you for keeping him safe," Séverine said as she took the sleeping boy and settled him against her chest. "What of the governor and the others?"

"King Edward ordered them beheaded." At Séverine's gasp, the woman shook her head. "His wife saved them."

"What say you?"

"Though Sir Walter Manny beseeched his liege to have mercy, Queen Philippa gained what he could not." She jutted her chin. "The six lead us."

"Merciful Lord!" If not for the woman's steadying hand, relief might have dropped Séverine.

The following morn, all having survived the night despite fear English treachery would see a mass grave made of them, the former inhabitants of Calais dispersed with their sick in carts and twice the supply of food and drink promised—hopeful beings all, none aware within months the pestilence come out of the east would make starvation seem a merciful death.

CHAPTER 3

Wulfen Castle, England
Spring, 1352

Since when did the Baron of Wulfen, trainer of the worthiest defenders of England, and one whom backbiters gave the abhorrent—albeit fitting—title *Pale Rider,* indulge such requests?

He had no time for this, and yet after glancing over the dagger shown him that appeared nearly identical to the Wulfrith dagger and commanding it returned to the young man's belt, he had accepted the parchment.

Once more, Hector considered the foreigners who stood on the other side of the high table and, wondering why he did not eject them from his hall, lowered his gaze to inked words.

My love, my heart, the half and whole of me, soon I leave you. Forgive me for being absent from you in all the years I pray to come as you welcome the first of our children's grandchildren into this unlovely world you made beautiful for me. As my light flick-

ers, soon dims, becomes smoke wending heavenward, hold my hand, kiss my brow, and let me go knowing this is not our end but a space between the life we made and when we shall hold each other again.

In parting, I have a request, beloved Mercia, though you ought honor it only if it speaks well to you. As ever, the missive you wished never to look upon resides in my clothes chest. If even in my absence still you care not for its tale, I would not have you read it. I would have you give it into the keeping of our eldest son with instructions it be passed through our line lest there come a day he or any other wishes to know more of the woman who helped me find the heart lost to me. Certes, what your grandmother wrote is not you, but be it truth or lie in the black of her ink, it is part of you for having made your light shine brighter. There my argument, and now I return to our bed and pray I awaken beside you come morn. Do I not, open wide our window, look out across the land, and there you will find what feels me flying free of these walls. Waiting for you. ~ Your Maël, in the year of our Lord, 1111

Hector considered the writing that had been no easy thing to read. Not only did it appear penned by an unsteady hand, evidencing the author's many years, but numerous misspellings indicated he was ill-schooled in written English. Either little effort was given his studies, else the language was not native to him. The latter, he guessed, as much due to the parchment being delivered by these foreigners as the intellect required to write something so near poetry it tugged at a warrior mostly immune to tugs.

Lowering the aged scroll, he settled back in his chair and looked to the tallest of those opposite. The sooner to be understood and rid of these *visitors*, this time he spoke in French which, following the Crécy victory six years past, this kingdom's nobility had begun eschewing in favor of English. "This is supposed to mean something to me, boy?"

The one who spoke for both, much strain in his accented voice to sound nearer a man, said with disappointment, "The names Maël and Mercia are unknown to you?"

Though the first stirred his memory, he was too worn from a dozen hours on the training field to delve it. Of greater reason to ignore what might be familiar was the futility of such claims of kinship. Though King Edward decreed only those of English birth train at Wulfen, this boy was not the first to come across the sea and profess kinship with the Wulfriths through one or another line of Normans who aided the Duke of Normandy in conquering England three hundred years ago.

"Both unknown to me," he said.

The youth nodded at the parchment. "As told, that is only a beginning." Moistening his lips, once more he raised the lid of the cask at the table's edge.

Something about the nervous show of tongue disturbing, more thoroughly Hector searched the young man's face, then the boy's. Upon returning to the first, he was certain of what poor lighting and impatience made him overlook.

Though more angered with himself, were the perpetrators grown men they would be fortunate to suffer mere bruises for their trespass. As for the temptation to send them away with harsh words, one of numerous lessons taught the stubborn of him slammed to mind.

Allow not wrath to command your actions nor words, young Hector, Uncle Owen had instructed, *else never will you prove worthy of your great commission—indeed, may be denied it altogether.*

Hector *would* honor his name and the great commission he had jeopardized, but he had another incentive for remaining in control—that this ruse caused what had barely interested to beg interest. He would set these two aright, but after he knew the whole tale.

He looked to Squire Gwayn who stood across the hall with his back to the fire. The young man who should have sought permission to grant these two admittance to Wulfen raised his eyebrows. The lessons due him would have to wait.

"My Lord," ventured the one who claimed to be the boy's cousin and gave the name Sévère, "here not only further proof Mace is Wulfrith kin but descended from Saxon royalty."

Hector considered the slender hand that once more offered a parchment drawn from the cask, next that one's face framed by a woolen cap, then the boy of seven or eight years. Though there was no silver in that one's dark hair, it did not disqualify him since it was uncommon more than one child of each generation present thus and more rare for the silver to appear before the age of ten.

He shifted to the boy's eyes. They were bright, it seemed as much due to the intense green as the steel in their depths.

As of one torn from childhood, Hector reflected and wondered which of his trainers would best set him on the path to knighthood. In the next instant, he stifled disgust. Even absent deception, there could be no place for him here.

"My lord?" Sévère handed the parchment nearer, providing an opportunity to look closer on that one's face.

After further verifying what was known, Hector reached his scarred hand forward and took the parchment that was either not as well preserved as the first or older. Though once what was now brittle and deeply discolored had been a scroll, it was creased from being folded flat as parchment ought not.

It was good his near vision was sharp. The words written here were well drawn but exceedingly small and of great number.

"It is dated forty years ere the one written by Maël to

Mercia," Sévère said. "It would—" That one's voice cracked, requiring throat clearing to once more sound near a man. "It would benefit to look first to its author's name."

He lowered his gaze to the final lines that read,

By God's grace, Countess Gytha, wife of Godwine, mother of King Harold, grandmother of Lady Mercia, great- grandmother of England's future king, here sets these words in the year of our Lord, 1070.

A reaction was expected, and so deeply was it felt, control was required to withhold it from those who watched. Were this parchment genuine, and that was questionable considering how false the one who passed it to him, perhaps training reserved for the English was more the boy's due than other claimants. But as for kinship with the Wulfriths…

He scrutinized Mace again, and those green eyes peered into ones less bright for the grey shot through as with nearly all those of Wulfrith blood.

"As Maël requested of his wife," Sévère said, "that has been in the possession of Mace's family for nearly three hundred years—its words as true now as then. Pray, attend to it, Lord Wulfrith."

With a grunt, he angled the parchment toward torchlight to read what was inked by the mother of the last Anglo-Saxon king of England and addressed to her granddaughter.

Blood of my blood, if this you read, you have done your duty. You, Mercia, are a Saxon strong of mind, body, and spirit. True to the blood, the bone, the marrow. More, you are a Godwine.

That was how it began, and over the next several minutes Hector read the remainder of what Lady Mercia had not wished to look upon and, perhaps, never had. Sown with bitter observations and the names of those who held power upon this island kingdom before Duke William of Normandy crossed from France and slew King Harold to claim the English crown, it was almost ponderous. However, there was much of relevance amid the words.

Believing Mercia had done her duty in wedding the son of the King of Denmark, the countess assured her granddaughter she had secured a place in her affections, then kept the promise to reveal the truth of Mercia's birth and which son sired her.

The lady was not illegitimate as believed. Though the Church looked ill upon the custom of handfasting to make husband and wife, in that way Mercia was the legitimate issue of the departed King Harold. Thus, great the countess' hope the King of Denmark's son not only succeeded his sire but, through marriage to Mercia, became King of England when the conquered Saxons supported Harold's daughter in overthrowing Duke William. Such a blow it must have been upon discovering her granddaughter had not done her duty.

Something sharp and warm, not unlike the thrill of encountering a worthy opponent, pierced Hector. The contents of this missive alongside the words written by a husband that death would soon part from a much-loved wife seemed to fit another tale told him long ago, which was the reason the name, Maël, was distantly familiar. And now Mercia.

The Book of Wulfrith begun by Sir Elias de Morville in the twelfth century, chronicling their family beginning with the sire of the eleventh-century Saxon lady of the House of Wulfrith who wed a Norman knight of the House of D'Argent, included a narrative titled *Tale of the Lost D'Argent*. Hector's grandmother, tale-giver and keeper of the book, had warned it could be more imagination than truth since it was not written until a century after its events. Still, she believed its every word —*except for the unicorn,* she had added with a wink at the boy who sat at her feet.

So was this proof the D'Argent cousin who disappeared from England had done so with the woman who, rather than aid in overthrowing King William, escaped marriage to the King of Denmark's son and wed Maël D'Argent of the conquering Normans? If so, was it also proof the boy standing before him was not only a D'Argent descendant but blood of the last Anglo-Saxon king?

Hector set the second parchment alongside the first and returned his regard to Sévère whose lips were so tight one would not know there had been fullness about them earlier. "Intriguing." He nodded at the cask. "What else have you?"

Once more the lid was raised. This time something wrapped in black cloth was removed.

Hector offered his hand and, feeling soft fingertips as the object was set in his palm, glanced at Sévère and paused over eyes averted above flushed cheeks. Not a youth, he amended. One or two steps up from twenty the same as—

Freeing himself of remembrance of the one he had laid in the ground, he turned back cloth fine enough to be a remnant of a lady's gown. Center of it was a silver and gold brooch of fine workmanship—the letter G impaled on a sword whose point was tipped with a ruby.

"You wish me to believe the *G* signifies Godwine," Hector said. "That it was given to this Mercia as proof of her birth."

"After what you have read and for how valuable the brooch, you must agree there is no other conclusion."

"Nay, I must not agree." He folded the cloth over the brooch. "Though if I did, it would change naught."

"But—" Sévère startled at the scrape of Hector's chair.

He straightened. "Whether or not this boy is of the family

D'Argent that wed into the family Wulfrith, whether or not royal blood courses his veins, he is not of England."

As Sévère's jaw worked over further argument, Hector retrieved the parchments and strode the back of the dais.

"Baron Wulfrith," that one appealed as he came around the table, "surely an exception can be made—"

"Only if you gain an audience with King Edward and persuade him to believe what you would have me believe. Both highly unlikely." Nearing, he noted the cask closed following each extraction was left open the last time. Another item was within, and the one who followed his gaze gasped and dropped the lid on an opal set in an expanse of silver.

As Hector halted, Sévère fully turned to him and stepped forward as if to shield both boy and cask.

He extended the parchments and brooch.

Surely interpreting that as an end to their audience, anger leapt in Sévère's eyes and convulsed a jaw that would never be hard or broad enough to command the respect of warriors. Then that one scooped up the brooch and snatched away the parchments. "You know not what you—"

A yelp interrupting words that sought to cure him of ignorance, Hector watched as a thick tail of fair hair tumbled from beneath the cap plucked off, then glanced from stricken eyes to those of the boy, next Squire Gwayn. "I *do* know what I do, Sévère." Mockingly, he frowned. "Or is it Séverine?"

Gripping the items returned to her, the young woman splayed her arms as if to further shield the boy. Fear where there had been anger, now in a voice strained not to sound a man but crawl past a constricted throat, she said, "Forgive me. It was done to gain your ear since women are not permitted at Wulfen, and I was certain more credence would be accorded our appeal were it not presented by one of the fairer sex."

Before he could respond, the boy said, "I told I could

present it on my own, Séverine. Now see, you have made a mess of all. Never will I be admitted—"

"Never would you be admitted regardless had *you* presented the tale," Hector growled. He had no reason to side with the woman nor feel anything less than annoyance for the time stolen from him, but it was true there was no place for the boy here. Too, he could not ignore the chill desperation fallen upon Séverine like the blackest of nights when dense clouds and stinging rain blot out moon and stars.

"I am not vengeful, Lady," he said, though he did not know if she could claim that title of nobility. "Exposing you is punishment enough for deceit. Now I have duties that need tending." He jutted his chin at the cask. "Take your treasures and go."

Her stance and wariness eased, but not trusting him enough to look away, she felt the brooch and parchments into the cask, tucked the box under an arm, and closed her mantle over it.

"Again, apologies, Baron." She glanced over her shoulder. "Come, Mace. The day grows short."

The boy shot Hector a resentful look before following her.

Now that Séverine no longer played a young man, she walked like a lady, her gait smooth and bound hair gently swaying center of her back.

"Hold!" Hector called.

Expectancy splashed across the faces of the two who spun around, he regretted they believed he gave them cause for hope. Merely, he could not have the one who entered as a young man depart as a woman in this place where the fairer sex were not permitted.

There were exceptions, as when circumstances necessitated the Lord of Wulfen extend his stay within these walls. So he not leave his wife long absent her husband where she resided at the sister castle of Stern, she would join him here, remaining out of sight of boys and young men. Over the centuries, many the Wulfrith babes conceived in this fortress and several birthed here.

Not so for the current baron, and likely never since no longer did he keep a wife. And dared not take another.

Now as he strode toward Séverine who gave him no cause to be attracted to her, he noted that lips parted by surprise and hope were once more full.

Glad she was on the plain side of pretty that, for a short time, fooled him, he halted and held out her cap. "I would not have you distract those whose minds must be on matters that will one day determine whether it is life that stands their side or death."

Hope purged, anger filling that space, she snatched the cap and thrust it on her head, shoved her hair beneath and pivoted. But she came back around. "How did you know I was not a man?"

He allowed a small smile. "You are not the first woman to enter here without permission. As your predecessor succeeded long enough to gain a measure of training, in the two hundred years since that lady humiliated my ancestor, those of Wulfen have been better trained to see beneath disguises that could endanger them."

Her eyes narrowed. "A lady, you say?"

"Annyn Bretanne, also an ancestor since later she wed the man she nearly disgraced."

Her smile was small, but it turned her prettier. "Good day, Baron."

For a time after the doors closed, Hector remained unmoving, then he called, "To the training field, Squire Gwayn. I have lessons to impart."

But first, the one who greatly trespassed imparted one to him.

Do not expect an angry woman to be compliant, he told himself when, amid the buzz of astonished boys and young men, he saw those cast out put heels to their mounts, the solid brown of which had a peculiar gait. The cap Hector had required Séverine return to her head was absent, and behind her streamed an abundance of blond tresses.

CHAPTER 4

He was the one. She knew it not by silvered dark hair, which she had been aware was possible with a Wulfrith of relatively young age, the same as other D'Argent descendants. What first alerted her the Baron of Wulfen might be her Calais savior was his voice. What drew her nearer the possibility was his hand, the scar of five years past now pale amid the tan. What firmed it in her mind was when he whose hair was now longer and jaw more bearded ended their audience by telling he had duties that needed tending and she should take her treasures and go—words nearly identical to those that coaxed her out of the rafters.

He who would have been a few years beyond twenty when she was ten and five, was the same who saved not only her and the De Chanson legacy but Mace who, without kin to make a way for him, could have been lost to poverty, neglect, or the pestilence.

Pressing down memories of that last, the worst of which her cousin had been too young to grasp, she glanced at where he rode alongside. Seeing his face remained grim, she returned her thoughts to the baron.

Already so much was owed one whose Christian name she did not know that it seemed wrong to ask more, but what choice had she? Certes, less now than before they crossed the channel and met trouble on this side.

Shivering over memories she dared not bury for the need to remain vigilant, Séverine wondered if Baron Wulfrith would have aided Mace had she revealed their encounter at Calais. Or made aware of how much he had done, might he justify doing no more, thereby salving his conscience?

Of course, that last assumed he yet possessed a sense of right over wrong. Just as Calais and all come after had changed her, he could be much altered. And considering the effects of the pestilence, turning many who lost loved ones bitter, suspect, even hostile as if others of the living were responsible, what good there had been in this Wulfrith might have gone bad.

Knowing soon Mace and she would be out of sight of the castle nearly as renowned for training warriors as the family responsible for the training, she looked behind. Through the blooming dust, she saw those practicing before the walls were back at their labors which the removal of her cap had suspended.

Had their lord seen her defiance? Anger easing, mind clearing, she acknowledged she should not have allowed him to affect her so, especially since she could not be deterred now it was just as imperative Mace gain safety as be provided training.

"You should not have doffed your cap," she rasped and, returning her gaze to the road, silently listed her laments.

If only her former savior had not been unmoved, cutting short their audience and denying her time to further her case.

If only in returning the parchments and brooch he had not drawn so near that his height, breadth, and disdain further roused anger over what seemed a threat. If only he had not made something of that threat by unveiling the woman of her, causing anger to give way to fear that made her feel fit with a noose like the six at Calais. If only he had not called Mace and her around then trampled the hope he had changed his mind.

"Father mine," she whispered, "if I cannot find a way to admit Mace to Wulfen, what am I to do?"

What little security they possessed was seriously jeopardized after they put to sea in the hope of a better life for the boy who had only her to provide for him, though increasingly he believed he could fend for both. For that, he had—

She hesitated, then looked those memories in the eye. For Mace's belief he was beyond childhood, secretly he had taken a dagger from the cask upon their arrival in England. And likely a man was now dead.

By my hand, she silently rued. *I did not mean to, but this hand played a part.*

Had the misfortune that befell them upon disembarking in Dover a sennight past happened on the continent, she might have provided a satisfactory defense, but what chance had she of being exonerated by the English who yet had cause to count the French their enemy?

The hair whipping across her face reminding her it was not only to gain access to Wulfen she had disguised herself but to mislead those hunting for the young woman said to have gutted a man, she reined in.

Though Mace also halted, he did not question what she did. As distressed as he was by her failure at Wulfen, possibly he did not care. But as ever, he would come right, though each time it took a bit longer.

And this time longer, reminded the voice within. *If he comes right at all.*

Returning to what had transpired at the stable, she saw crimson on her hands and a smear across her bodice. She saw disbelief on the man's face and the drop of his chin to look upon the hilt. She saw him fall and movement beyond him. And as that one's companion came for them, she saw horror in Mace's eyes with which a child should not be acquainted.

Having learned to survive in a world more often cruel than kind and despite errors that led to further trials, Séverine had temporarily disabled their second assailant. After getting Mace astride the horse bought by her coin—a brown palfrey with a jarring gait—she had reasoned she could be no worse a criminal and seized one of their attackers' horses to increase their chance of escape.

For hours they had ridden north, and when it felt safe to pause, she had seen that just as she trembled, so too the seven-year-old boy. And yet he had declared were they caught, he would own to being responsible for the blade in his assailant.

Séverine had named him courageous, then told she would not allow it. Though he had quieted, his silence had not been of capitulation. Thus, all the more imperative he gain a home at Wulfen, allowing her to distance herself so she not further endanger him.

A curse returning her to the present, she exclaimed, "Such is not worthy of a De Chanson, Mace! Your sire would—"

"I have only your word of what he would and would not do! And what good is it to be worthy when all the world is against you?"

That landed, though he did not aim at she who was more than a cousin. He was angry she had failed him at Wulfen, but more with himself for what he had done that caused the dust upon the wind blowing them to England to become stones.

Certain still he blamed himself for the death of his assailant that could render their quest hopeless, she said, "All the world is not against us. And were it, we would be far from alone since God—"

"Not now, Séverine!"

Her bristling was momentary. How could it be otherwise when she struggled with abandonment as well? Though loath to acknowledge it, mostly her encouragement was recitation—a means of getting the crutch of faith beneath him to keep him upright.

"Forgive me, Mace."

When he did not respond, she looked to the one remaining D'Argent dagger he had asked to display on his belt for the meeting with the baron. She had hoped it would bolster his claim to kinship. It had not, and the sooner it was returned to the cask the better.

Séverine gathered up hair given to curl—and more so in England's humidity—and donned the cap to once more become a young man whom only Baron Wulfrith had seen for a woman. Or so she hoped, no others in their northward journey daring as he had.

"Now what do we do?" the boy asked.

They had enough coin for food and occasional shelter for three months before they would have to sell one of his treasures. Séverine had seen to that by honest means despite the temptation to yield to dishonesty.

Of course, their funds would last longer if she gained employment until she found a means of persuading Baron Wulfrith training was Mace's birthright. Since the pestilence had reduced all classes wherever it spread, it should not be difficult to find work.

"Where do we go?" Mace reworded his question, tone so despairing she preferred anger.

She had an idea, and not one that leapt to mind. Last eve, their northward journey having delivered them to Wulfenshire upon which the Barony of Wulfen lay, they had secured pallets, bread, and drink in the stable of an inn. Whereas Mace had quickly fallen asleep, the disguised Séverine had sought the lad who tended the horses and needs of guests unable to afford a room.

Over games of dice, she had learned of the shire named for the family who held the greatest portion of its lands and of castles beyond Wulfen. Of particular interest was Stern where Baron Wulfrith's family resided—among them his sisters and grandmother, though no wife nor children of his own.

When she had asked after that, as if fearful of being overheard, the lad had whispered, "A widower much cursed." Then he had yawned and said he must sleep.

What she had learned had aided in forming an alternate plan should they be denied entry to Wulfen Castle. It had not been needed, though at first Squire Gwayn sought to turn them away. Blessedly, presentation of what Sir Amaury had told was nearly identical to the Wulfrith dagger had seen them escorted to the hall. But since the baron had been unmoved by that and the cask's contents, now the other plan.

Séverine urged her horse forward and set a hand on Mace's shoulder. "Be assured, we are not done here. If there is a way to get you into Wulfen, I will find it. Until then, we remain near."

CHAPTER 5

Stern Castle

A lady fallen on hard times. That she was and appeared, and having given her name in truth that in no way connected her to the Wulfriths, none could reckon her false. On those two points.

Still I deceive, she thought as she stood with hands folded at her waist and Mace behind and to the side as expected of the servant to which he was reduced to gain two positions at Stern.

On the day past, yet disguised as a young man, Séverine had inquired after employment in Ravvenborough, a large town fairly near the stone fortress. A girl encountered at the community well had confirmed there was work in the fields, and it was to that Séverine resigned herself—until the comment was made that Mace looked big enough to muck out stalls.

Séverine's cousin had glowered.

"Ho, high and mighty one," the girl had crowed, "be that

work not good enough for ye, go 'round to Stern Castle. I hear they need a wee one for lowerin' into garderobe shafts to scrape *their* muck off the walls."

Mace had been so angered he had not seen the door opening before them. Séverine had hoped to be near Stern while seeking the baron's capitulation since it could increase her leverage were she to get inside the walls and, if well received, appeal to a less heartless Wulfrith. However, she had not expected an opportunity to present so soon, certain that family would not lack laborers for seeing to their own needs ahead of those working their lands.

Having chosen her words carefully to avoid suspicion, she had learned there were other positions at Stern. Most were for men, but in addition to the mucker, a kitchen boy was needed. Though neither did Mace like that, he was acquainted with work since his fifth year. Being of noble blood, he and Séverine had not labored as hard as others in dire circumstances, but their way had not been free.

A harrumph returned Séverine to the present, though not soon enough to catch the echo of what had been spoken.

Leaning forward on an upholstered bench before an immense fireplace bounded by beautiful tapestries, the old woman of solid grey hair said, "Considering the disposition of Ondine to whom you shall answer should you be taken into our employ, it is a good thing you are not of a talkative nature."

Amid embarrassment, further curiosity was roused over the position Séverine sought of which the girl at the well had revealed little since she believed the one who probed was a young man. Whoever gained it would be companion and maid to one of Baron Wulfrith's sisters whom the girl had named *Beauty*, though this old woman called her *Ondine*.

Hence, in the hope nobility and some education would outweigh the French of her, Séverine had washed her hair and worked braids, then dressed in her least worn gown of green whose greatest extravagance was a hands' width of red around its hem. Were it only a maid sought, she would not put forth the effort, but a companion was something more.

"Forgive me, Lady Héloïse," she said. "As told your steward, my journey was fraught with sorrow since learning kin with whom I sought sanctuary are lost."

The woman averted her gaze as did many at mention of the pestilence that cruelly stole loved ones.

It was not all lie Séverine told. Her relations had been taken by the terrible sickness, but none with whom she had been close—nor had they been English as alluded. As for Mace, though she had wanted to reveal his nobility that ranked higher than hers, even he had thought it best to play the son of a departed servant lest word reach Baron Wulfrith his grandmother had hired a lady and her boy cousin. Doubtless, that one would descend and eject them before they could gain a foothold.

Thankfully, among other things learned from the girl was the baron's visits to Stern were rare. As long as they remained so, she would make good use of that time, even if all she gained was a temporary haven from those searching for her and Mace. Then…

She did not know what she would do, but they had the treasures, and that was more than most backed into tight corners.

The old woman drew breath that took some of the bend out of aged shoulders, unstacked hands from atop her cane, and returned her gaze to the two before the hearth. "Séverine de Barra and…whatever you are called."

"Mace, my lady."

She narrowed her eyes. "You will work hard for Cook

whose position is among the most important in a great household?"

As relief swept Séverine, not only for the offer of work far better than mucking out garderobes, her cousin said, "Oui, my lady."

"Oui?"

"Aye," he corrected, the steward having informed him and Séverine that though most of the nobility spoke the French of their Norman ancestors as well as native English, their king wished to set aside the former for it being the language of their enemies.

That had stung, but there was good in it with regard to gaining both positions at Stern. Since Séverine's education had included lessons in English and she had taught Mace, here another thing in their favor.

"It is decided," Lady Héloise said. "Board, lodging, and two pence a sennight, boy. Now take your pack and hie to the kitchen where you shall prove I have not made a mistake."

Mace's hesitation causing Séverine to look around, she answered the uncertainty in his eyes with a smile.

When he departed, Baron Wulfrith's grandmother once more looked the young woman up and down. "You are more qualified than hoped. Perhaps too qualified since the wages beyond board and lodging is ten pence."

"Non, my lady, I—"

She held up a hand, and Séverine expected her to correct her use of French, but she called, "Esta!"

The woman of thirty some years with her back to the fire and a wolfhound sitting alongside stepped forward, lent the old lady her ear, and strode to the stairs.

"You and I are done," Lady Héloise said.

Séverine gasped. "You will not offer the position to me?"

"Since companion and maid to my granddaughter is a job that must be taken more seriously than that of a kitchen boy, it is not for me alone to decide." She patted the dog that had moved to her chair. "Hence, I but uproot the bad, leaving it to another to determine if you make your home within our walls."

Hardly had the hope of not numbering among the bad flickered to life than it was stamped out by what was not explicitly told. The position being of import, whether her granddaughter was very young, difficult, or infirm, Baron Wulfrith would be consulted. Hence, she would have little time to win over others of his family more approachable than Lady Héloise whose severity quashed the possibility of revealing Séverine and Mace's true purpose.

"It will not be long." The old woman nodded at the stairs.

Startling at the realization the baron was in residence, Séverine's first thought was to retrieve Mace and depart. But that was all impulse.

Her second thought was she alone depart since her cousin had a position within these walls, and it was possible Baron Wulfrith would take pity on one who only appeared abandoned. But that was mostly impulse.

Her next thought was to immediately reveal the truth, chancing this forbidding Wulfrith would soften toward distant kin. But that was impulse as well.

Minutes later, descending footsteps sounded, meaning soon Lady Héloise would learn of the deceit worked on her. However, providing her grandson did not immediately cast out the offenders, this time when Séverine opened the cask, she would do so as a lady. Though quite possibly the old woman did not possess enough heart to be moved by the fate of kin several hundred years removed, there was naught to lose.

Telling herself she would be content if she could but secure

Mace's position here, ensuring those in pursuit did not lay hands on him, Séverine turned.

When the one who stepped off the stairs was the same who ascended minutes earlier, she rebuked herself for not attending to the sound of slippers far different from boots. Were the reprieve not temporary, she would have sighed.

In response to Esta's shake of the head, the old woman said, "Albeit not amazed, disappointed," then called, "And so?"

"As firmly told me," the woman said as she advanced, "this is an inconvenient time."

"And when would be convenient for the contrary one?"

It astonished she openly disparaged her grandson, but such was the privilege of the aged who had less time to make pretty out of bad.

"I was told the morrow, my lady." Esta halted. "And as I departed, it became *mayhap* the morrow."

The old woman jabbed a finger toward the ceiling. "Alone or nay?"

"Far from alone."

Quick sense was made of what caused Lady Héloise to exude more disapproval. Her widowed grandson did not abstain from sexual relations. For the sake of Mace, Séverine was grateful Baron Wulfrith refused to come belowstairs, it providing more time to decide how best to do what must be done.

"Deliver Lady Séverine abovestairs," the old woman jolted. "An answer is due her so sooner she may return to the road should she be rejected."

As Séverine's heart sank further, Esta exclaimed, "My lady! You know how—"

"I do. Now see it done."

The discomposed woman turned away.

Séverine cleared her throat. "Lady Héloise, as it is unseemly to disturb one so...occupied, I think it best I wait."

"I do not." She flicked a hand. "Accompany Esta."

Séverine set her teeth and did as told, but as she neared the stairs, recalled what she left behind and came around.

"Fear not," the old woman said, having followed her gaze to the table from which Mace had retrieved his pack and left behind Séverine's two, one of which held the cask. "Ours is an honest household. Your possessions are safe."

Were the lady not a Wulfrith and Séverine loath to offend, she would not have chanced it.

"Esta!" Lady Héloise called. "Should the answer be nay, from my lips to those ears this—your grandmother's patience nears its end. If Lady Séverine does not appeal, then the next with all her teeth shall gain the position."

Doubting the threat would be effective, Séverine ascended the stairs behind Esta and prayed the baron had barred the door and would ignore attempts to dislodge him and the woman from his bed.

Surprisingly, their destination was not the second floor where the chambers of family members were usually located, nor the third. It was the fourth which she had not realized the donjon possessed. Likely a private place for dalliances.

"I am sorry for this," Séverine said as they came off narrow stairs and started down a short corridor with a single door at its end.

"My lady is right—best done now." Esta looked around. "I apologize for how you shall be received, which may make you glad of rejection."

Séverine smiled tautly. "Since the need for employment is great, I am determined to withstand the assault and be worthy of an audience."

Which is unlikely to last long, she thought.

"Do not expect it to last long," Esta proved her thoughts ran parallel.

A moment later, a woman's laughter was heard. Though muffled by the door, Séverine was struck by its beauty and, despite dread over interrupting the baron, wondered if the face and body matched. Likely, though surely many a man would not care with such music in his ears.

"There, there! You have done it, my fine fellow. And well!" Her speech was just as exquisite, and it so distracted that Séverine was at the door before she realized what was behind those words.

The discomfort warming her displacing dread, she was certain were there any possibility of changing the baron's mind, it would be lost for what she interrupted. But as she had been commanded here by a woman of influence who, God willing, would champion Mace, she would not retreat.

"And here, darling, your reward!"

"Foul creature," Esta muttered. "Beware, he likes no one save her. Even did you offer the tastiest morsel, he would disdain it rather than eat from any other hand." As Séverine sought to fathom that, the woman knocked, opened the door, and motioned her to follow.

Séverine was shocked. She did not know Esta's place in the household, but even were she kin to the Wulfriths, surely she dare not enter without invitation, even if the baron did not keep company with a woman.

Hesitantly, Séverine stepped into a room of little note beyond its immense size directly beneath the donjon's roof and numerous covered items gathered against shadowed walls ahead and to the right. Doubtless, beneath those canvases were furnishings that had gone out of favor or fallen into disrepair.

Of further surprise, a woman with her back to them stood

in light shafting through an unshuttered window, her lithe figure clothed in layers of gossamer cloth usually reserved for hair veils, its color pale blue.

Meaning the baron lurked amid the furnishings? Though that seemed no fit for him, Séverine looked nearer upon the room.

"She should not have sent you again," spoke one whose voice was less beautiful for its rebuke, and when Séverine returned her gaze to the lone figure, she saw the woman angled her head slightly, revealing a curve of chin past dark hair falling straight to her hips. "My answer remains unchanged—on the morrow. *If* then."

Séverine was nearly staggered by the realization this was the one who would decide whether a French lady became a companion and maid. Since likely it meant the baron remained at Wulfen Castle, much praise. Since this must be the granddaughter requiring an attendant, less praise. If this Wulfrith was given to conversations with the unseen, she must suffer an infirmity of the mind. For that had the girl at the well sorrowfully named her *Beauty?*

"Forgive me, Lady Ondine, but your grandmother requires an answer now," Esta said.

A gasp sounded, and the young woman turned her face away. "You have brought her inside?"

"As ordered. Now speak with Lady Séverine who Lady Héloise believes shall serve you well."

A snort sounded, and the young woman stepped toward a box up out of which projected a pole topped by a horizontal piece of wood. "We shall resume your exercises shortly, my fine fellow," she returned to her unseemly conversation. Or so it seemed until she raised an arm to the side and something white stepped off a gloved hand onto what Séverine realized was a perch.

"That is an owl," she breathed.

"The creature she calls Sir Skyward," Esta said low. "Regretfully, his name may be all hope."

Séverine nearly laughed. What she had believed Baron Wulfrith who would eat from no hand save his lover's was a bird. And his sister was not ill of mind—at least not as feared since better she converse with a present creature than an absent one.

As the white-chested owl with tawny wings settled and swiveled its head toward the two who interrupted its exercises, its mistress removed the glove protecting her from claws and retrieved a white cloth draped over the box. After shaking out what appeared as gossamer as her gown, she draped it over her head and face.

Another peculiarity, Séverine's only acquaintance with women who covered their visages being those in mourning. Of course, perhaps for this—that she was newly widowed—Lady Ondine required more than a maid.

She turned. With graceful steps and a sway reminiscent of a willow stirred by a breeze, she crossed to her unwelcome visitors, proving though not tall, she was of good height that bettered Séverine by four fingers. However, not much more was proven, the veil and low light in the doorway concealing her features, allowing her to see through it without being seen beyond the sparkle of eyes and curves of nose, cheeks, and chin. Even with much light, it could be difficult to make out more since the exquisite veil was denser in areas where patterns of flowers were worked into the weave.

As Séverine stood unmoving, she felt every pore scrutinized, then the rest of her down to her slippers.

"How many years have you?" the lady said.

"Twenty."

"A year older than I," Ondine mused. "I was told you are a lady."

"I am."

"From France."

Hating being made to feel wares for the buying, with resentment, Séverine said, "I am."

"Your surname?"

"De Barra."

"You do not think it beneath you to be my *maid* first, companion second?"

"I do not."

"My, you are of few words."

Though her grandmother had thought it good Séverine was not talkative, perhaps Ondine did not agree. Deciding on middle ground, Séverine said, "Being fairly well educated, I can be of more words."

"And desirous of this position," the young woman said.

Feeling baited, Séverine nodded.

Ondine touched the toe of her lovely slipper to Séverine's worn one peeking from beneath the hem of her gown. "Your circumstances are much reduced."

Again Séverine nodded.

"Because of your country's war with England."

"That and the pestilence, my lady."

Ondine's breath caught, and Séverine knew she erred in speaking when a nod sufficed. That which was also called the Great Mortality had been blind to the differences between young and old, good and bad, noble and common, taking what it wanted when it wanted and so very cruelly. Had not any of the Wulfriths fallen prey, surely relatives, friends, vassals, and acquaintances.

"Aye, that monster," the young woman said. "Did you lose any dear to you?"

Séverine longed to look to Esta for direction. "I lost some for whom I had a care, but none of the heart."

"Fortunate you." Ondine sent breath up her face as told by the veil's billowing. "So I must make a decision this day—this hour."

"As your grandmother decrees," Esta said.

"I can do that." Ondine's tone sounded friendly, but since her expression was hidden, Séverine held hope at arm's length. "There are several things in your favor, Lady. I count it good you are not talkative, and I like that you are educated. When I do wish to speak, it should make for good conversation. However, there is another consideration." She touched the veil's lower edge. "As you do not look upon me pityingly, I wager none told you the reason for this."

"I assume you are in mourning. My condolences."

"Aye, mourning as well," she murmured, then set her head to the side. "The other consideration and of greater import is your constitution. Are you a fearful being?"

"When I have cause to be." *As I do now,* Séverine silently added and wondered if those who pursued she who played a part in the death of Mace's assailant yet did so. "But I do not think it a bad thing, fear being a gift from God that tells us when to run and hide."

Again Ondine's veil billowed, now with soft laughter. "Séverine de Barra *is* capable of many words—and has some wisdom about her. However, I speak of..." She shrugged. "Can you stomach the unsightly?"

"My lady!" Esta exclaimed.

The young woman raised a staying hand. "As my brother is fond of counseling—inform one's self ere making decisions of much consequence." She stepped nearer. "Brace yourself, lady of France. This makes pretty what is not."

This was the veil she raised to reveal something so unexpected Séverine caught her breath.

"Alas, she lacks the constitution required," Ondine bemoaned, then swung away, causing the veil to flutter to the floor. As she appeared to glide toward the owl who watched with black eyes set in a heart-shaped face, she called, "Regrets, Esta. The answer is nay."

CHAPTER 6

Anger. Seeking to control what she directed at herself for not considering the veil concealed more than sorrow and at Lady Héloise for giving no warning—especially since her reaction was due more to expectation than Ondine Wulfrith revealing she was a rare survivor of the pestilence—Séverine clenched her hands.

Esta leaned near. "As she did not show her face to others rejected, I did not expect that. Had I to guess, it was done because though she finds you acceptable, she prefers to accept none."

The reason being of no consequence, Séverine started to turn away.

"Lady Ondine!" Esta called. "In this event, I am instructed to deliver words you ought heed."

Standing at the perch, the young woman retrieved something from a pouch on her girdle. As she fed it to her pet, she looked around. Face and neck appearing less afflicted at a distance and a better match for her voice and movements, she said, "Deliver them, then report that despite great effort, I will not be moved."

Esta stood taller. "Your grandmother tells should this lady not appeal, the next who has all her teeth will gain the position."

Having once more reached to the pouch, the young woman faltered.

"You know she will do it, Lady Ondine."

Would she? Séverine wondered, then guessed it was so since the threat went unchallenged.

"Either Lady Séverine comes alongside you or one entirely unknown."

Moments later, the lady thrust her hand in a leather glove and reached to the owl who stepped onto her wrist.

Though no longer veiled and despite scars more discernible the nearer Ondine came, Séverine could see how beautiful she had been—so much that still she was. And with the handsome bird adding to the vision of her in a gown whose shoulders were draped with raven hair, she was so breathtaking Séverine longed to beseech her to never again cover her face.

This time she did not draw as near, likely in consideration of the owl who swiveled its head to look from Séverine to Esta.

Ondine raised her chin, providing a good view of a face surely believed ruined and drawing attention to pitted scars on her neck.

When Séverine did not react in any way to indicate aversion, the young woman said, "It seems, Lady of the De Barras, you will have to do. For now." She shifted green eyes to the owl. "He is Skyward, and cleaning his box will be among your duties."

Once more giving the lady no reason to believe this companion and maid averse, Séverine said, "I am capable."

"And yet it is a long way from France, is it not?"

"A good distance, but not as long as you think since these reduced circumstances are not newly acquired."

The young woman turned to Esta. "If Skyward is to fly again, I have more work to do. Deliver Séverine to my chamber so she may settle in and sooner perform her duties."

Which would not be pleasant. Likely there would be retaliation beyond upkeep of the owl's box, with which not even a lady's maid would be tasked. But Ondine would discover that Séverine would do whatever was needed to protect her cousin.

Even if it means blood on my hands, she thought.

"Come, Lady," Esta said.

Séverine dipped her head. "Lady Ondine," she said and followed Esta from the room.

As they started down the narrow stairs, the door closed softly behind them.

"That is encouraging," Esta said.

"What is?"

"Though she has gained control over her penchant for slamming doors, she reverts on occasion, as during her brother's last visit when he told she could not keep the owl for all the mess it makes."

Baron Wulfrith who refused to yield to one in far greater need than a sister who but wished a pet. Since he did not seem capable of fondness, likely he allowed the young woman to keep the owl because it was more expedient and must only be tolerated during infrequent visits. "Then her unseemly behavior is effective," Séverine said.

Sharply, the woman looked around, then sighed. "Only in that it gained the baron's attention and roused guilt."

"Guilt?"

"To keep the owl, Lady Ondine had to present a good argument, make habitable the uppermost room which is the only place Skyward may go untethered inside the donjon, and herself tend him. Though now she has a maid to clean the box, likely her brother will put end to that when next he comes."

Unless she slams another door, Séverine mused before it occurred it would not be necessary to forbid Ondine aid were this deceiver expelled.

Knowing it could sound self-serving, she asked, "When do you expect your liege to return home?"

"One rarely knows, there being great stretches between his visits since much of the responsibility of training warriors falls to him. As he was last here two months past, just as he might appear soon he might not."

Not, Séverine prayed. She needed time to become well regarded by those here so they side with her in providing Mace training.

As she was led down the second floor corridor, Esta said, "You have heard of the family's reputation for training England's defenders? That more nobles seek to send their sons to Wulfen Castle than there are places for them?"

"I have."

"Highly coveted since, beyond those the king sends, Baron Wulfrith has final say in who is admitted and some places he reserves for boys who, of lesser nobility—even common—possess great promise."

"Surely that includes kin," Séverine probed.

The woman halted before a door near corridor's end. "Providing they are worthy. Over these three hundred years, many the branches of the Wulfriths, including Torquays, Penderys, Boursiers, Lavonnes, and D'Arcis."

Reflecting on Mace's own kinship, Séverine thought, *And that lineage began after the last Saxon Wulfrith—a woman—wed a conquering Norman who was compelled to take her surname.* Mace's great ancestor, Maël D'Argent, had been cousin to Guarin D'Argent who became Guarin Wulfrith. Later, Maël had also taken a new surname, but not to gain the acceptance of subjugated Saxons—to disappear so he might wed the woman whose royal Saxon blood threatened the new king's reign.

Esta sighed. "Unfortunately, as with all families, the oak may be strong above and below, but the farther the branches from roots and trunk, the greater the chance acorns come to earth are bad."

Not Mace, Séverine assured herself.

Esta opened the door. "Here the chamber you shall share with Lady Ondine."

Entering first, Séverine halted so abruptly the woman bumped her heel.

"Aye, most unexpected," Esta murmured.

That was the least to be said of the room. Séverine had seen the chambers of highborn ladies. They impressed, but not like this despite some disorder that evidenced whoever temporarily served as maid had yet to do her duty—else what was earlier done had been undone.

There were finely upholstered chairs and benches, carved tables and stands, a bed draped in silken cloth and laid with a white coverlet stacked with brightly colored pillows, windows whose open shutters allowed the breeze to flirt with curtains of the same cloth the lady wore, a standing mirror that evidenced she was not averse to viewing herself—though perhaps only her clothed body.

"It pleases her to surround herself with beauty, and she is indulged," Esta said.

Because of lost beauty? Séverine wondered.

"If any can move the baron from *nay* to *aye,* it is this sister."

Then she is the one I must court above others, Séverine thought. *Blessedly, I am in a good position.* Having learned the baron's two other sisters resided here, she said, "Lady Ondine is his favorite?"

Esta hesitated. "He cares for her, but it is more than that." She pointed to a screened corner. "Your bed is behind there, as well as a small trunk where you may store your possessions which I will have delivered here."

The privacy screen surprised, as did mention of a bed rather than pallet and that Séverine would be afforded more than space on the floor to keep her belongings. Was it too much to hope the trunk possessed lock and key?

"Not only do Lady Ondine's accommodations astonish, but my own," she said.

"You gain what was due her last companion, a much removed cousin who did not also serve as maid."

"May I ask the reason she is gone?"

Sorrow crimped Esta's mouth. "Though she had just entered her middling years, one morn she did not awaken. She had been suffering a pained head, and the physician believes blood on the brain took her. A terrible loss, for she was a fine lady and given much credit for returning Lady Ondine to life after the Great Mortality sought to put her in the ground alongside her sire and others."

Séverine caught her breath.

"It is so. Even the mightiest of Wulfriths fell to that evil, though methinks the old baron welcomed it for how long he was without his second wife who died from one of her seizures eight years earlier." Esta clicked her tongue. "Though these things you should know to better serve your mistress, I leave it there ere I render myself a gossip."

Struggling against curiosity over the former baron marrying a second time, which likely meant some of his children were half-siblings, and that he had wed a woman who suffered a debility many regarded as evidence of evil possession, Séverine said, "I appreciate you preparing me. Are you also a Wulfrith?"

The woman's laugh was curt. "Not even distantly, and I would wish that on them only did I count them enemies."

There being much behind that statement, Séverine waited.

"Ten years gone," Esta continued, "Baron Wulfrith's sire awarded me my position—of which I was not worthy."

Again, Séverine waited, but when no more was forthcoming, said, "I shall strive to prove as worthy."

Esta's brow rumpled. "Were you to remain as long as I, that would be possible, but I do not think your place is here."

Séverine stiffened. "Because I am French?"

The woman turned thoughtful. "I was desperate when I arrived at Stern. Though there is desperation about you, it cannot be of the strength that afflicted me."

Surely I am more desperate, Séverine thought.

"Thus, as you are a lady and have youth about you, there is a good chance your stay will be short-lived."

Esta was right, though not as believed. Even were Mace admitted to Wulfen, there were two things that would prevent Séverine from remaining here. The first was the lie of omission to gain employment. The second was that she was hunted. Whether or not she secured training for her cousin, she must return to France to escape punishment for what the English would deem murder.

"It may prove temporary," Séverine said, "but as long as I serve Lady Ondine, I shall perform my duties well."

"Just be patient with her. Though once she possessed inner and outer beauty... Well, are not all greatly changed by suffering?"

"Almost as if we knew no other life," Séverine said.

Esta's brow rumpled. "I am guessing yours is quite the tale."

Séverine shrugged. "One's own emotions being first hand,

they can be more deeply felt, but be assured I will be sensitive to Lady Ondine's suffering."

Esta smiled. "Supper is served a half hour past sundown. If Lady Ondine has not returned to her chamber, come to the hall so you may be known to others of the family and the castle folk."

"Then my mistress may remain in the upper room?"

"Possible, just as it is possible she will take the bird to the wood to determine if it has healed sufficiently to be released, order her mount saddled for a ride, or visit with one of her sisters." Esta sighed. "For how intentionally it appears Lady Ondine moves, one might think her idle, but it is deception—like a swan on a lake, gliding at her leisure above while below it is all fierce churning lest a current take her where she refuses to go."

"I am sorry for her," Séverine said.

"Best not speak it, my lady." Esta turned away.

When her footsteps faded, Séverine closed the door. "I am closer, Uncle Amaury," she whispered. "God willing, soon I fulfill what was entrusted to me—your son in the care of kin, his future assured as much as possible."

She was accustomed to the bustle of a great hall, most landed nobles presiding over communal meals that included relations, retainers, and dogs rooting for scraps fallen to the rushes. It was the same at Stern—and yet different.

At least early on, Séverine thought where she paused in coming off the stairs. Once those politely seated turned their bellies into slopping vessels, the restrained din would become less so, and the dogs beneath the tables would make nuisances of themselves. Alcohol mixed with contentment or discontent transformed many, though she would be surprised if those of the family Wulfrith easily succumbed to the depth of excess that led to poor behavior.

Moving into the shadow of a pillar, Séverine studied those at the table erected on a dais that provided an unobstructed view of the gathering.

Sitting center was the old woman, to her right a priest, and beyond him a knight who might be a Wulfrith though his hair lacked an early show of silver. Uncle Amaury having told that mark of D'Argent blood in the De Chansons was much less prevalent than once it had been, it followed it was the same for the Wulfriths.

But there *was* one of unnaturally silvered dark hair. To the left of Lady Héloise sat a woman of perhaps a score and five, on her lap a small boy. Though a veil draped her hair, the braids coursing her breasts were shot through with so much silver it was as if a ribbon of that color was woven through them. And for how tall she sat, likely she was of good height. As there was space beside her for two more diners, Séverine guessed when Ondine appeared she would join this one who must be an older sister.

If she appeared, the young lady having remained absent from her chamber. And blessed that, allowing Séverine to organize her possessions in a trunk equipped with lock and key and straighten the room as was her duty.

Knowing she must make her way forward before the meal commenced, she searched the lower tables for Esta.

"Well come to Stern Castle," someone addressed her back.

She turned to a freckled girl who emerged from an alcove—rather, a young woman, red-blond hair falling in disordered waves over small breasts to a tiny waist.

Her speech had been so precise and proper, Séverine had expected one of nobility. However, the girl who halted before her wore a gown of homespun cloth girded by a simple leather belt from which hung a soiled pouch. And easily visible beneath the hem of an outgrown skirt were slippers whose toes and soles evidenced a walk across wet earth.

"I thank you," Séverine said. "May I know your name?"

"Fira."

A servant, then. Had her garments spoken false, surely she would have titled herself a lady. Still, why had she lurked in the alcove? It was one thing for a noble to arrive late to meal, quite another for one of the common.

"I am pleased to meet you, Fira."

The young woman glanced past her. "We must gain our seats ere the blessing of the meal."

"I was hoping to sit with Esta, but I do not see her."

Fira jutted her chin. "The table nearest the dais."

So she was, and there appeared room beside her.

"However, as you are a lady, you ought to sit at high table," Fira said, "especially since there is room with Ondine excusing herself from supper—a not uncommon event."

Séverine would not presume to ascend the dais since she was merely one born high who had fallen low.

"I shall take my meal with Esta," she said and, as she started across the hall, saw the priest push back his chair.

When she quickened her step and Fira drew alongside, she wondered if there was bench enough for both beside Esta. Great her hope with eyes making themselves felt. Regardless of whether Stern's inhabitants were aware of the newcomer's position, for a time she would be a curiosity.

Fira touched Séverine's arm. "Fear not. We bite, but only when provoked."

One surprise after another—that she sensed Séverine's unease, now she spoke in French rather than English, it sounded she counted herself among those with teeth here, and she continued to the dais.

As Fira lowered near the lady with the boy on her lap, Esta drew Séverine down and said, "I am not surprised the ever-pondering Fira lay in wait for you."

Séverine felt a fool. "She is Lady Ondine's sister."

"Aye, the youngest, and the eldest is there as well."

Séverine looked to that sister and, finding herself watched, returned her regard to Esta. "How is she called?"

"Dangereuse."

Séverine blinked. She was aware of only one christened that—the mother of Eleanor of Aquitaine who wed England's King Henry II two hundred years past, considerably enlarging her husband's French holdings. And for which their descendant, the third King Edward, had gone to war with the now departed Philip who believed no piece of his realm should be held by a rival king, even if by force he must take his English vassal's holdings.

"An imposing name that seems fitting for one who appears tall," Séverine said.

Esta nodded. "She is taller than her departed husband, her brow on level with her eldest brother's eyes."

"*Is* her name fitting?"

"Indeed, though most would not have guessed how fitting until—" As if realizing she sounded a gossip, Esta trailed off.

"Arise!" the priest commanded.

Though disappointed over the loss of further insight into the Wulfriths, Séverine was moved by the man's blessing of the meal that was unhurried and yet not of a length those with groaning bellies would find overly uncomfortable.

After a chorus of *Amen,* they resumed their seats and youths appeared with towels and water to clean the hands, ensuring shared food remained uncontaminated by ones less given to good hygiene. Next the servers entered.

Séverine had been certain Mace would not be among those delivering platters of viands, three of which were placed on each table to allow for ease in serving one's self. Not only had her cousin no experience with such, but he lacked the build required to heft and balance ladened platters. Still, she had hoped he would be given a lesser task such as offering sauce. Instead, those spouted vessels were carried by boys attired in crisp, clean garments.

Séverine winced. She kept her cousin's clothes mended and as clean as possible, but all were either outgrown or oversized for being acquired from one who had gained height and breadth. She would have to purchase cloth and fashion a new tunic and chausses to provide him opportunities beyond whatever menial tasks he performed.

Gripped by guilt over dining here while he labored amid insufferable heat, she determined that after the meal she would confirm he fared well. Providing naught was required of this companion, as seemed likely in Ondine's absence, it should be easily accomplished.

CHAPTER 7

At meal's end, Fira intercepted Séverine as she moved among castle folk departing the hall or gathering for activities that provided servants time to transform the room into a dormitory where many would sleep on pallets and benches.

Séverine halted before the young woman who stepped into her path and accorded her the title she had not accorded herself. "Lady Fira."

Offering no mischievous smile as if pleased with fooling the newcomer, the baron's sister said, "Since Ondine has left you to your own devices, join us at hearth." She nodded to where women seated themselves on chairs and benches, among them Héloise and Dangereuse, the latter's lap no longer occupied by the boy who had misbehaved more than those partaking of drink throughout supper and wolfhounds who had neither roamed nor begged. Esta was at hearth as well, standing beside the Wulfrith matriarch.

"Ah, but first you would like to ensure all is well with the new kitchen boy," Fira said.

Séverine returned her gaze to the young woman.

Now a mischievous smile. "I do my utmost to make happenings on the barony my business in preparation for the day it is my duty."

Séverine longed to question that, but Fira turned toward the kitchen corridor. "Come."

The kitchen was a marvel. Not only was it so immense it did not seem crowded despite a dozen servants moving among cooking hearths, ovens, and tables, but there were many unshuttered windows that allowed heat to escape. Doubtless, earlier the room had been a mess as was inherent in providing food to great numbers, but much had been set aright in preparation for the morrow's meals. If one earned a living laboring in a kitchen, it would be more tolerable at Stern.

"What may I do for you, Lady Fira?" asked a short, slender woman who hastened forward, apron strings wrapped around her waist several times and knotted off center.

"Cook!" Fira halted center of the room. "Here Lady Séverine, my sister's new companion recently arrived from France."

She who was unique in holding so esteemed a position, not only for her sex but age that could not exceed thirty, swept her gaze over Séverine as smoothly as if her eyes were a knife buttering hot bread. Then she smiled. "You are well come in my kitchen—*when* we are not much occupied with preparing meals."

"I shall endeavor not to be a nuisance." Séverine glanced around. Seeing none of small stature, she said, "The boy who accompanied me—"

"You speak of Mace."

Though Séverine had expected the one who ruled the kitchen was aware of acquiring an extra pair of hands, she had not expected remembrance of his name. Surely a good thing.

"Much work to be done with the lad," the woman said,

"especially as he wears an attitude that suggests he is above common labor."

Not a good thing, Séverine amended.

"But he is young and, I believe, will adjust."

She believed wrong, Mace's future far different from that of a servant—*if* Séverine did not fail him. "I appreciate your patience, Cook. He is a good boy despite life being unkind."

"'Tis the same for many who lose their mothers young," Fira said.

As the young lady would have been about four when a violent seizure took the baron's second wife, whether that one had birthed her or the first wife, she would have felt loss. However, Fira's privileged life had continued. She had remained in her home surrounded by close family and been well provided for.

"Where is the boy?" Fira asked.

Cook jutted her chin at the door, beyond which would be a garden that supplied herbs, vegetables, and fruit. "Eating his supper with the other children."

No end to the surprise of Stern. Such consideration should be shown young ones, but most were worked as hard as adults.

"I thank you," Séverine said.

The woman and Fira turned away, the latter casting over her shoulder, "I shall see you at hearth, Lady."

Grateful to speak with Mace alone, Séverine stepped into a vast garden faintly lit by torches on distant walls. Though much was in shadow, none need tell her how beautiful its spring finery was. And as she traversed a path, more proof was had when a pole lantern lit unfurling leaves and burgeoning buds on three sides of a table around which children gathered, too intent on filling their bellies to chatter. At the nearest end, Mace sat staring into his bowl.

She halted. Though certain he wished to see her, perhaps not in view of his new peers.

A moment later, her dilemma was resolved by a girl seated across from him. "Is that your lady, Mace?"

As the other children looked up, he snapped his chin around. A smile curved his lips, but he reversed it and said in the girl's English, "No longer since now I answer to the Wulfriths the same as you."

"Still, she has come to see you."

He pushed his bowl away and stood.

The spell of satisfying hunger broken, the others watched. As Mace neared, Séverine was pleased by the return of his smile, confirmation his nonchalance was a show.

When he halted, she said low, "As you can see, I gained the position of companion and maid to Lady Ondine. Is it true you are treated well?"

"Better than expected, but it is a lot of work. If I am going to run here and there and back again, better I spend my sweat on training for knighthood."

"That is what we work toward. Hence, we must be patient and give none cause to remove us."

"This I know, but if Willa does not cease talking—*ever* talking!—I may forget she is a girl and—"

"You will do naught!" Séverine glanced at the one who had notified Mace of her presence, likely Willa. Though the others had resumed eating and some chatted between bites, not the pretty well-fed one who propped her elbows on the table and set her chin in her palms to observe the two on the path.

"I am sure she but wishes to be helpful, Mace."

"It is not helpful if one does not wish help. I am older than her and—"

"Are you?" Séverine interrupted again. She had thought Willa a year or more beyond her cousin.

"Not by much," he said defensively, doubtless aware the girl was taller and broader. "Though her aunt is small, her sire must be very big. She says he is the horse master."

Séverine frowned. "She told her aunt is small?"

"Non, that is one thing she need not speak since I am not blind."

"Cook is her aunt?"

"Oui. Willa says when her mother died, Cook brought her to help in the kitchen so she could care for her while her sire tends the horses."

"Then all the more reason you must be patient with Willa," Séverine said, it being important they make no enemies. "We are safe at Stern, and this is your greatest chance to gain a place at Wulfen."

"How long will it take?"

"I do not know, but the better we are regarded by Baron Wulfrith's family, the more difficult it will be for him to refuse you a second time."

"I shall try harder," he begrudged and returned to the table.

As Séverine started back, she heard him say, "Aye, Willa, the lady is about twenty—too young to play mother to me."

And yet I have done so since before the siege, Séverine mused.

"I think it sweet," the girl said, "and she is quite pretty."

A small laugh escaped Séverine. She could be pretty and had made an effort this day, but *quite* pretty? Were that so, she could not have fooled the squire who granted her and Mace entrance to Wulfen, and certainly not Baron Wulfrith for however long he had remained ignorant.

She passed through the kitchen and, upon entering the hall, saw Fira wave her toward the gathering.

"Fine timing, Lady Séverine." She patted the space to her left. "Grandmother was about to decide on this eve's passage."

She referred to the leather-bound book on the old woman's lap. Guessing it was of illuminated Scripture and included the Gospels, Séverine was intrigued—until struck by the sensation of being watched. Following it to Lady Dangereuse on Fira's other side, she knew it would reflect poorly on her to accept the younger woman's invitation in the absence of the one she served.

"You are kind, Lady Fira, but I should return abovestairs lest your sister has need of me."

Fira frowned. "But—"

"For that she was engaged." Lady Héloise said and looked to Séverine. "Good eve."

As Séverine started for the stairs, the old woman said, "Fira dear, though I know you are taken with the D'Argents for joining their blood with the English through marriage, it is long since we read of the Wulfriths during the time of King Henry II. Let us do that."

At the realization it was not a Holy book from which she would read, but a written record of the Wulfriths—and Fira and others were conversant with the Norman family from whom Mace was descended as well—Séverine slowed lest the voices of others in the hall cloaked those at hearth.

"You must admit that since our true beginning was when the Wulfriths' Norman ancestors aided their duke in conquering England, the best of the tales arise from that time," Fira said.

"I must admit no such thing," someone disputed.

"My words were not directed at you, Dange," the youngest sister rebuked.

Preferring the eldest sister's pet name over the ominous one and realizing she was nearly out of range of hearing, Séverine halted and bent to adjust her slipper.

"All know you prefer the tale of Annyn Bretanne," Fira added.

The name was known to Séverine, Baron Wulfrith having revealed that lady had trained at Wulfen before being unveiled for a woman—and that later she wed the deceived Wulfrith.

"As I admire the lady, I do prefer her tale," Dangereuse said, "whereas you..."

"Me?" Fira prompted.

"I do not doubt you esteem Hawisa Wulfrith who wed Guarin D'Argent, but I suspect what mostly entrenches you in the eleventh century is the bishop's ring."

As Séverine mulled that, the young woman said, "I believe 'tis still in the stream. And when I find it, I shall laugh last."

"Oh, Fira! If that tale is true—and likely not since 'tis a spotty one—the possibility of finding the ring three hundred years later is delusion."

"Enough," Lady Héloise commanded. "As you two fatigue me, let us have our reading, then to bed."

Séverine longed to remain bent over her slipper to partake of those words, but had she come to the notice of any, already they questioned what was so ill about her footwear she had yet to resolve it. Too, in Mace's cask was something she wished to look near upon.

When she entered the chamber, the light of a lantern taken from a hook in the corridor revealed naught of Lady Ondine having come or gone.

Determining if she did not soon appear she would go to the upper room and, were the lady not there, alert her grandmother, Séverine went behind the screen and pulled the trunk from beneath the narrow bed.

Shortly, she drew out the cask's smallest item. The same as the brooch shown Baron Wulfrith, it was wrapped in cloth. She turned it back and considered the wide gold band with a large, faceted ruby embraced by numerous prongs.

Could this be the bishop's ring? It was grand enough to have belonged to one in high office.

Séverine drew the small square of parchment from under it and read, "Received from the Dane by way of G.W., the Year of Our Lord, 1097."

Sir Amaury had told it was in that year, almost half a century after the conquering, numerous D'Argents and Wulfriths were summoned to Normandy by Godfroi D'Argent to honor his dying wife. Amaury's ancestor, Maël de Chanson had answered the call, arriving with his wife and their children at his aunt's bedside where he was reunited with his cousins, including the one referenced on the parchment, Guarin Wulfrith.

Séverine turned the ring. If this was what Fira sought, the Wulfriths had kept no record of it being retrieved from the stream and delivered to Sir Maël. But they did know at least some of what came before, and it could be further proof of Mace's kinship.

She returned the ring to the cask and the cask to the trunk, then lit a lantern for the bedside table and carried another from the chamber to light her way during her ascent.

When she came off the last step, dark beneath the door ahead tempted her to turn back since it was indicative of Ondine's absence and Séverine was wary to enter lest the owl was territorial. But before she alerted any the lady was missing, she must be certain Ondine was not inside.

She eased open the door and extended the lantern. The first thing of note was the box with its perch near the window. The owl was there, its eerily reflective eyes staring.

Though this seemed proof the lady was not present, Séverine advanced, causing the bird to hoot and ruffle its feathers. Hopefully, it would remain an observer, keeping its clawed feet fixed to the perch.

She did not have to venture far amid covered furnishings before she caught sight of Ondine who had not tossed back the canvas covering the bench she lay on. However, when Séverine drew alongside this Wulfrith whose face was turned opposite, she understood. Though a mantle covered most of her, its hem and that of the gossamer gown were marked with dried mud, as were slippers she had removed. Between her new companion's first visit here and supper, she had been out of doors, possibly testing her owl's wings.

Séverine considered the scarred profile. As concluded earlier, not unsightly, but it must seem so to one whom the girl at the well had named *Beauty*.

"Lady Ondine?"

The young woman breathed deep and, exhaling, turned her head. When her gaze settled on Séverine, it seemed she might smile, but her brow lined. "I need no keeper."

"This I know, but as I have not seen you all these hours, I thought it wrong to gain my rest ahead of your return to the chamber."

"Not wrong at all." The lady shifted, dropped her feet to the floor, and looked past Séverine. "Poor Skyward. We try and try, but still he cannot fly."

If he is all there is to your life, Séverine thought, *neither can you.* "You must be hungry," she said. "When you return to your chamber, I will go for viands and drink."

Ondine retrieved her slippers. "I can eat come morn," she said. Minutes later, she tossed off her gown and, clothed in a silken chemise, dropped face down on the coverlet.

Feeling remiss for not being quick enough to prepare the bed so the covers could be drawn over her, Séverine retrieved the gown, folded it, and set it on a trunk against the far wall.

After extinguishing the lanterns, she went around the screen and removed her own gown. Though her chemise was far from silken, it felt wonderful to slide beneath clean, soft bedclothes and feel safe for the night. Hopefully, Mace also rested better than he had in a long time.

"Father mine," she breathed, "help me make things right for him. Give me strength to do what is required."

CHAPTER 8

For all Ondine's resentment, serving her proved less a chore than it had been others for whom Séverine labored after the fall of Calais. These five days, the lady had remained self-sufficient, not only in tending her person but the owl despite it being among her maid's duties to clean its box.

As for the role of companion, thus far naught was required beyond accompanying her to an occasional meal where Séverine took her place beside Esta. Afterward, she joined Ondine at hearth to attend to Lady Héloise's readings from *The Book of Wulfrith* that, thus far, covered only the lives of those of the twelfth-century.

She enjoyed the passages, especially ones written in rhyming verse composed by Sir Elias de Morville who gifted the book to the family, loosely binding it so others could continue recording their history, but she was dissatisfied. What she wanted was insight into the Wulfriths following the conquering since Mace's ancestor might be found in the tale of the bishop's ring.

So great was her longing to confirm it that she pondered ways to get her hands on the book whose cover was etched with the words: *Les Wulfriths. D'abord. Entre. À la fin.*—The Wulfriths. First. In between. In the end.

The family's maxim was known to Séverine, having originated with the conquering D'Argents and adopted by the Wulfriths when the eldest son wed his Saxon bride.

However, despite much temptation to seek out the book, she dared not. Were she caught, her trespass would give the ladies cause to side with Baron Wulfrith when Séverine's true purpose was revealed.

"That is enough water, boys," Ondine returned Séverine to the present. "I thank you."

"My lady," they answered, then carried emptied buckets from the chamber and closed the door.

Seated on a bench set back from the hearth to make room for the tub, Séverine returned her attention to the damaged hem of one of several gowns that evidenced Ondine did not keep her skirts clear of debris during her outings.

Regularly, the young woman rose early and departed the castle. Though that first day Séverine had hastened from bed to assist, Ondine had told she required no aid and Séverine ought to be grateful to gain more sleep.

Each day, the lady returned well after the breaking of fast and in a mood of disappointment accompanied by mutterings over Skyward's failure to stay aloft. However, this day her angst was cut short by delivery of the tub she must have ordered before ascending to her chamber.

Movement drawing Séverine's gaze, she saw Ondine cast dried flowers and herbs across the steaming water and heard her murmur, "Ashamedly, long past due."

It was true, her raven hair weighted by oil and, as noted last eve, wafting a stale scent.

"How would you have me assist?" Séverine asked.

"Continue mending, but do so with your back to me."

Little surprise. Though rarely did Ondine wear the veil in Séverine's presence alone, never did she entirely disrobe. Modesty? Perhaps, but likely to keep eyes from traveling scars on the rest of her.

Séverine seated herself on the opposite side of the bench and once more took up her needle. Shortly after completing her stitches, she heard the displacement of water and the young woman's sigh.

For a quarter hour, Séverine mended another hem, leaving only one more gown requiring attention before she could return to the tunic she made for Mace who fared well despite the annoyance of Willa.

It was Ondine who first caught the sound of horses beyond the shuttered windows. "Visitors, and they ride to the inner bailey rather than stable their mounts. As they must be of import, pray go to the window."

Séverine was curious as well, though more fearful since just as this might be Baron Wulfrith come without warning, it could be men searching for the French woman and boy who spilled English blood.

She glanced at Ondine who, having washed hair and body, reclined with eyes closed, then crossed to the window overlooking the front of the donjon and opened the shutters. At the base of the steps, two men dismounted, both appearing of good height and one with the broad shoulders of a formidable warrior. Blessedly, neither had silvered black hair, but greater her relief could she be certain they had business here that had naught to do with Mace and her.

Remembering moisture on palm and fingers coated in crimson, she swallowed hard.

"Tell what you see," Ondine commanded.

"Two riders, both men."

"Is one young with silvered dark hair the same as Dangereuse?"

Then she also suspected her eldest brother. Looking to the lady who continued to recline, she said, "Though I believe both far from aged, one's hair is flaxen, the other's brown."

Ondine sat up, revealing scars on shoulders and collarbone. "Flaxen?"

"Oui—er, aye."

The lady thrust to her feet. Water streaming down a lovely, scarred figure, she hastened from the tub and clutched a towel to a chest more endowed than that of the one who had passed for a male. When she sprang forward, Séverine sidestepped.

Wet hair adhering to shoulders and back, Ondine looked down at those nearing the landing. When the doors closed, she smiled and said, "Warin."

She spoke of her second brother who Fira had revealed crossed the channel in 1349 to serve King Edward in holding Calais that had surrendered to the English two years earlier. That had jolted, and more when she learned that just as the eldest brother had been present during the siege, so had Warin. What she did not know was the reason the second born was remiss in visiting his family, though likely he was too busy forging his own path since he was not the heir.

Ondine's smile grew. "Though I barely glimpsed him ere he entered and his hair is shorter, I am fair certain he has come home as done only once before these three years. Pray, aid me!" She swung away and crossed to the clothes cupboard.

Pretending she did not see scarred legs beneath the fall of wet hair, Séverine complied. Not until the two stood before the full-length mirror as she laced the back of a gown of orange samite embroidered with flowers from waist to thighs did Ondine speak again. "Yet more proof you have a good constitution," she said. "After all you have seen of this body that cast off the pestilence despite death choking the moat around its sickbed, do you question why I keep mirrors?"

Séverine finished the lacing and met the lady's gaze in the mirror. "I see no reason why you should not."

Ondine snorted. "Then you are a flatterer looking for gain."

Guilt flushed Séverine. Though she did want this Wulfrith's support, her words had not been angled that direction.

"You must admit I am not whole," Ondine prompted.

"I can see you bear the marks of a horrendous battle that required courage to drag yourself off that battlefield, but that does not mean you are not whole, my lady."

Gaze holding Séverine's, Ondine said, "It was a battle, and oft I thought to hoist a white flag, but the Wulfrith of me was so disgusted with surrendering to the evil burning through my skin that I accepted physical suffering was better than self loathing though the latter would be short-lived."

"I am sorry."

Ondine set fingers on the silvered glass and shifted to her own reflection. "At first I suffered mirrors for the encouragement of seeing my afflicted skin heal—and it did with good gains from the first nauseating look to hundreds more as the months passed—but only so much healing could be had. Not since the day ere the pestilence struck has any mirror reflected what I wish—loveliness I did not appreciate." Another snort. "*Beauty*—that is what some called me ere the Great Mortality. Now only pity and mockery see me named that." She fingered scars on the right side of her face. "If anyone knew, they might say this my due."

"Knew what, my lady?"

Ondine stilled, turned. "The vain creature I am for what once I was."

Just as Séverine was certain there was more to it, she knew the lady was alarmed at discovering she had eased her guard.

Moving to the stool at her dressing table, Ondine said, "Let us towel my hair and braid it."

Séverine was pleased to aid her, especially since the relatively intimate service drew her nearer one with sway over her eldest brother whose Christian name yet eluded for the family referring to him in her presence as *Baron* and *Wulfrith*.

Once Séverine had fashioned braids with tight crossings to ensure waves when the hair was unraveled, the lady surprised by inviting her to accompany her.

Lest it was not Warin in the great hall, Séverine hesitated.

"You may finish the mending later," Ondine misunderstood, "and bathe, if you like." She nodded at the tub, snatched up a veil and set it over her face.

Silently bemoaning she had no excuse to conceal her own visage and praying it was not needed, Séverine started to follow.

Ondine came around. "I did not think! As the bath water will go cold, better I introduce you later."

Séverine nearly smiled. "Providing it does not offend, I prefer that."

"It does not, and 'tis best since it is years since last we saw Warin."

And having one nearly a stranger in their midst would disrupt the reunion, Séverine thought. Hoping it *was* the second brother come home, not only for Mace's sake and hers —and it did not sooner deliver the baron to Stern—Séverine nodded. "I shall bathe and complete the mending."

"Then the remainder of the day is yours." Ondine dipped her chin and departed.

Séverine waited until certain the lady had reached the hall before venturing to the top of the stairs.

Fira was the first to confirm the identity of one visitor. "And here is Ondine, Warin!"

As Séverine's shoulders eased, he answered in a voice whose depth was similar to the baron's, "Indeed."

"Warin!" Ondine cried, then came laughter.

Returning to the chamber, Séverine praised the Lord for His mercy, then removed her clothes and sank into a tub as she had not in years, her bathing limited to basin and cloth and quick dips in cold streams.

Using Ondine's fragrant soap, thrice she washed herself head to toe. Then she settled back, and there she stayed until the water went cold and needle and thread called her back to her duties.

Wulfen Castle

RÉMY KNEW MORE WAS ASKED of him for being a Wulfrith, just as required of his older brothers. However, it was not exceptionally beyond what was demanded of others in training. To prove worthy of the dagger awarded on attainment of knighthood, great effort and achievement were expected of all.

And yet at ten and seven, the youngest Wulfrith brother was only passably proficient in all things warriors—with the exception of archery. At this he excelled, his skill having surpassed even Wulfen's battle-tested men who trained pages into squires and squires into knights.

This day's contest between groups of five squires demonstrated that well. To simulate moving, unpredictable targets, Sir Owen released five arrows in rapid succession at whatever appealed in this stretch of the wood. As soon as his first landed, the squires sought to place their own arrows alongside

Owen's while tracking the others released with the intent of hitting those targets as well.

Whereas each of Rémy's red-shafted, perfectly fletched arrows found their mark, landing nearest Owen's and splitting one, his greatest rival landed three arrows well.

Hector was proud of his brother, but more relieved since Rémy's ill start at dawn could have spilled into the rest of the day as sometimes happened when he suffered humiliation and was denied the satisfaction of landing blows that broke noses and teeth. Since his childhood affliction had once more flared with the arrival of the pestilence in England three years past, Rémy had made good progress in controlling his temper, but more would be required to gain a Wulfrith dagger—and become Hector's heir if Warin remained incapable of enough forgiveness to take his place here.

"Collect your arrows and get to the stables to relieve the dawn patrol," Hector called, then motioned to the next group of squires who sought to master the English longbow that had served King Edward well at Crécy.

Though most warriors of hilt and blade grudgingly acknowledged the importance of the long-range weapons, few sought to acquire the skill beyond taking game to ground, deeming the primitive simplicity of wood in defending one's person beneath a knight—hence, best left to the rustics.

In Hector's youth, he had leaned that direction though his sire elevated archery from a lesser skill to an essential one. The old baron proven right, Hector had accelerated training at Wulfen and across his demesne, ensuring every able-bodied man of high birth and common was exceptionally versed in archery as King Edward wished to ensure better defense of his realm. And women who sought instruction received it as well.

Rémy was the first to return with his arrows. As expected, he who would be taller and broader than his eldest brother if he continued growing at this rate, merely inclined his head. With good reason, he was the least talkative of the Wulfriths, and on days like this, less inclined to let words pass his lips.

"Well done, Squire Rémy," Hector acknowledged the impressive display, just as he would do the others. And that praise would be honest. Though they could not match the skill of the youngest Wulfrith brother, none disappointed.

Shortly, Rémy was followed by his opponents who eagerly acknowledged the praise given them.

"Well done, Squire Paul," Hector said to the last who was the least accomplished at archery, though few of his age were better at hand-to-hand combat.

"I thank you, my lord. Be assured, next time I shall do better."

When he was past, Hector smiled. Paul having begun training at an older age, his family desperate to undo what his aged, indulgent father wrought ere his death, it had been difficult to move the youth onto a path that would render him worthy of defending England. But he made strides, the only disciplinary action in recent months dealt a sennight past following the departure of Mace de Chanson and his cousin who removed her cap to flaunt having entered where she was not welcome.

It was nearly all Paul had talked about that day, causing others to speculate on how she had fooled the guard and what she had sought from the baron.

Though Hector remained vexed over her deceit and disruption of training, whenever the woman came to mind, he was troubled over what had become of her and her cousin who were less welcome in England than other foreigners.

Not my concern, he reminded himself as Owen prepared to repeat the exercise. If what she and the boy revealed was true, it was for her to gain King Edward's permission to admit one of

French birth to Wulfen. And there was little chance of her being granted an audience.

The sound of a fast approaching horse made Hector raise a staying hand to Owen who had nocked an arrow.

The rider was one of the dawn patrol, and it had to be something of import for him to return ahead of the others.

"Tidings, my lord!" He sprang from the saddle, jerked at a tunic disarrayed from hours astride, and strode forward.

"Speak, Squire Gwayn."

"During our patrol near Abingdale, we caught sight of riders come from the direction of Broehne Castle. Naught unusual in Baron Lavonne entertaining visitors, but since one was of great note, I ventured near to confirm his identity." His smile was uncertain. "Your brother is returned to Wulfenshire and appears bound for Stern."

Despite what felt a fist around his heart, Hector kept his face impassive. Finally, Warin had returned to England and without notice though he had to know his brother would learn he was upon Wulfenshire.

Did his silence mean he did not come bearing forgiveness for what was done his wife? Possibly. Would he still refuse to take his place at Wulfen? Hopefully not. Even if the brothers could not be fully reconciled, Warin was needed here.

"You were right to investigate and return forthwith, Squire. Now go to the kitchen and see yourself refreshed."

As the young man redeemed for letting a woman into Wulfen strode opposite, Hector returned his attention to his uncle whose lined brow evidenced concern, and nodded for him to resume the exercise. Once the senior squires gathered here had demonstrated their skill, Owen would be informed of Warin's return and they would discuss how to proceed, though Hector was inclined to ride to Stern before receipt of the missive his grandmother was sure to send.

He swept his hands behind him and clasped them. As he settled into his heels, Owen's next arrow streaked toward the shell of a great oak whose upper branches had long ago toppled to the floor of the wood. Then like birds frightened to flight, other arrows flew, each seeking the same perch.

CHAPTER 9

Stern Castle

She had missed the nooning meal. For it, her reward was hair mostly dried into loose curls, passage through a hall absent all but servants, and time with Mace.

In the garden, Séverine had presented the new tunic. Her cousin had hugged her, then after assuring her he made no enemy of the attentive Willa, donned the finest tunic he had possessed in years.

Promised new chausses from the remainder of the cloth Esta had obtained for her, they had gone to the kitchen where he filled a sack with bread and cheese and a wineskin for the ride she enjoyed each afternoon.

Grateful she had her own mount and it and the one taken from Mace's assailant were tended by stable lads, Séverine slowed her horse as she neared the wood and looked to the right. On the southern road by which many traveled to Stern was a wagon noted minutes earlier, but now riders came behind it.

As ever, her heart beat faster at the sight of horsemen lest they sought Mace and her. Since her fears had not been realized thus far, she assured herself if these two paused at Stern, it would have naught to do with her cousin and her.

"Pray not," she whispered and, urging her mount toward a break in the trees, glanced opposite at the less-traveled road Mace and she had taken from Wulfen to Stern. None were on it. Hopefully, that would not change with the second brother's return. Though she must face Baron Wulfrith again, the later the better.

Séverine opened the sack tied to her saddle's pommel, and as she withdrew bread and cheese, praised the Lord her physical burden was so light she was here rather than toiling.

If not for what was due her cousin and that she dare not remain in England, she could be content serving Ondine the remainder of her years. Before the siege of Calais, she would not have considered such, but the hard years since had mostly rendered her future mere dreams and imaginings.

Lady Séverine of the destitute De Barras would wed no man of good means and cradle no sons nor daughters. She was a lady by birth only and, providing Mace gained something more, that must be enough.

"I will not fail you, Sir Amaury," she said. "Your line will continue through your son, and stronger he will be for his trials."

After a few bites of her simple meal and a drink of wine, she adjusted her course to deliver her to the stream, then firmed her feet in the stirrups and rolled back over the saddle's low cantle to settle her head atop the horse's rump.

Sunlight flashing between leaves that would become denser as spring gave unto summer, rendering much of what was brightly dappled mostly shaded, she closed her eyes. She would not have believed she dozed, passage over uneven ground more jostling for her mount's peculiar gait, but so suddenly were voices upon her, she must have.

As she pushed upright, they quieted, and she saw on the near side of the stream three figures whose horses grazed nearby. All eyes were on her—if one counted those of Ondine who wore a face veil despite being entirely in the company of family.

Séverine started to turn aside to leave the sisters and their flaxen-haired brother to their privacy, but Fira called, "Join us!" Skirts knotted up around her knees, revealing hose darkened by water, quite possibly from searching for the ring, she beckoned.

Séverine considered Ondine whose owl was perched atop a gloved hand and wondered what expression was behind the veil, then Warin Wulfrith of good resemblance to his brother in build and face. Were his hair dark and silvered, one might be mistaken for the other. Another thing they had in common was an air of brooding.

Reluctantly, she urged her horse forward, and upon drawing rein, tucked back hair she would have fashioned into a braid had she not wished stirred air to complete its drying. "Forgive me for interrupting. I but sought an afternoon ride."

"You do not interrupt," Fira said. "As Ondine introduces Skyward to our brother, now I shall introduce you. Lady Séverine, here Sir Warin finally home from France. Warin, Lady Séverine come across the sea as you know from her accent."

"My new companion and maid, engaged by grandmother," Ondine clarified.

Séverine did not know what possessed her to make light of that, but she smiled and said, "Alas, Sir Knight, it was me or the next woman in possession of all her teeth."

Was that a smile tempting his mouth? It seemed so, and

further it was confirmed when he strode forward and raised his arms. "Allow me to aid in your dismount, Lady Séverine."

She looked to Ondine in the hope she would discourage her brother, but the lady said, "Aye, join us."

Séverine drew her opposite leg over, shifted around, and felt a small thrill as this Wulfrith gripped her waist.

When he lowered her, she thought, *Not as tall as his brother, but nearly.*

"I thank you, Sir Warin."

He released her. "Whence in France do you hail, my lady?"

Seeing no reason not to be honest—indeed, honesty could aid in making an ally—she said, "Several places, but Calais was longest and best known."

As what seemed regret flashed in his eyes, Fira exclaimed, "'Tis where Warin has been these years."

That Séverine knew from talk of him and that he had been present with his brother during the siege and later returned to hold Calais for his king.

"Why never did you tell, Séverine?" Fira asked.

Though she felt the sharp of Ondine's gaze, Séverine kept her eyes on Warin. "That is a tale so tragic, it is no easy thing to speak of."

His jaw shifted. "When did you depart Calais?"

Having lost her own smile, she said, "When our governor surrendered the town to your king."

"I was there."

"As was your brother, I understand."

A shadow crossed his eyes. "You were among those provided safe passage to the valley."

"Aye. Though likely I tramped past you, had you looked upon me, you would not recognize me. I was years younger and of little figure for lack of adequate sustenance."

"I regret your suffering, my lady. It was of great import

King Edward gain Calais to defend his French lands and aid in recovering those stolen from his family."

"This I know, just as I am aware our king also bore responsibility for what befell us at Calais." *And still I cannot forgive you though you have passed,* she thought as she saw again the withdrawal of forces whose relief to the loyal would have made some of their sacrifices worthwhile, though never the loss of Mace's sire.

"Intriguing," Ondine said, stroking her owl. "It makes me question what else you have not told."

Far more than you expect, Séverine thought. *Hopefully, when the time is right, you need know only of Mace's kinship and whatever is required to admit him to Wulfen.*

"I am curious as well," Fira said.

Sir Warin took Séverine's arm and urged her toward his sisters. "I doubt the lady's duties include revelation of her private life," he said with mild rebuke. "Especially its sorrows. As you can appreciate, those are not for public consumption. One shares what they wish when and *if* they wish."

Turning back to the stream, Ondine said just loud enough to be heard, "Home not even three hours and already he takes us to task."

"So he does, but better that than he remain in that dreadful country," Fira said.

As Sir Warin halted Séverine between his sisters and released her, less mildly he rebuked, "Fira!"

The young woman smiled apologetically. "I did not mean to offend, Lady Séverine."

And yet she had, though not as greatly as believed. "All is well, Lady Fira. You cannot know my country, but it is understandable you have no good regard for it."

"And forget not, Séverine wished to trade her shores for

ours," Ondine said, then swept her arm out in front of her. "Fly, my fine fellow. Be free!"

Talons gripping the leather protecting her hand and arm, the owl opened its wings slightly, and when she bounced her arm, spread them. But a sideways list made him gather them close and hold to his perch.

A sound of distress causing Ondine's veil to billow, she drew Skyward in. Then peering up at her brother through the veil, she said, "I am certain he can do it. 'Tis just he has failed so many times he fears adding to disappointment and humiliation."

"He is not alone, Ondine. When the reaping of benefits resists persistence, oft men and women are afflicted with uncertainty at best, apathy at worst."

She stiffened, said, "'Tis the same with giving and gaining forgiveness, is it not?"

Though no longer did he hold to Séverine, his tension was felt over what was left unspoken between these two—perhaps three, she realized when Fira fiercely whispered, "Not now, Ondine."

Their brother cleared his throat. "A similar affliction, especially when what must be forgiven is nearly unforgivable and the offender—or offended—is far from sainthood."

She set a hand on his arm. "Warin—"

"If you think your owl more receptive to the commands of a fellow male," he spoke over her, "I shall don the glove and mayhap I can set him to flight."

Ondine drew a strident breath. "As he seems comfortable with you, let us try."

Suspicion. Some bred by the lone rider being a woman come from the direction of Stern. Some bred by blond hair and a familiar figure. Some bred by a horse of rich brown from head to tail. Much bred by the animal's peculiar gait first seen when the trespassers were ejected from Wulfen, its stride likely the result of a break from which few horses healed well enough to avoid being put down.

That combined with the feeling he knew the woman—and despite the boy's absence—confirmed the identity of one no longer in disguise who, approaching the wood, had been distracted by those on the southern road.

Hardly had Hector and his squire returned to the trees than she looked their direction. Though distant, her face had fit the one named Séverine, and it had taken little thought to know her purpose here. Had she revealed the boy's kinship to his family, word would have been sent him. Thus, by another means she and the boy infiltrated Stern.

What Hector had been less certain of was the reason she went to the wood alone. Considering her penchant for deception, he had decided to observe her ahead of a confrontation best done away from his home. Thus, neither confirming nor denying his squire's guess she who disappeared among the trees was the same who fooled Gwayn into admitting her to Wulfen, he had commanded the young man to continue to the castle. There he was to notify Lady Héloise, whose missive had been intercepted en route, of her eldest grandson's pending arrival.

That was ten minutes past, and since then Hector had moved his mount through the wood at a leisurely pace to ensure he happened on the woman before he came to notice. Voices had made him slow, and further when he was near enough to identify they belonged to two of his sisters and his errant brother. That had surprised, Hector certain if Séverine had arranged a meeting, it would be with one of bad account.

Now that deceiver said excitedly, "Lady Ondine is right. He is capable, Sir Warin."

A moment later, Fira bemoaned, "Too soon spoken. But after all your work with him, Ondine, he must be close to flight."

They spoke of the owl that did not belong at Stern, as neither did those of France. All must be put to flight, but more imperative the woman and boy.

Moments later, he saw the four on the stream's bank and resented the position in which he found himself. This was not how he envisioned reuniting with his brother. He had no pleasant imagining of the first step in overcoming the ill between them, but he had been confident of maintaining patience and calm. Not so now. And less so when Warin straightened from retrieving the bird and smiled at the woman whose curling hair was loose about her shoulders and bright as if recently washed. Though Warin's expression was shallow compared to what he had bestowed on his lost wife, it appeared genuine.

Despite Séverine being able to pass as a boy a short time, that she could so soon affect Hector's brother evidenced she did not want for wiles—and would use them to gain Warin as an ally.

Knowing the sooner he rectified this the sooner he could begin setting aright his relationship with his brother, Hector ceased his cautious advance.

"Though my sister tells an owl's flight is entirely silent," Warin said, "we shall have to test that another day, Lady Séverine." Once more he smiled, then turned to Ondine. "What say you? Ought we do this again on the—?"

His head came around, eyes the first to land on the brother

guiding his horse forward, face the first to reflect aversion. The woman who followed his gaze looked upon Hector much the same, then came fear.

"Brother!" Fira hastened forward, her joy somewhat stilted over a reunion for which all should be better prepared.

As Warin passed the owl to Ondine, Hector wondered over the latter's face veil usually eschewed in the presence of family alone. Since one of those present was not a Wulfrith, the veil did not surprise, but as Ondine had been averse to showing her scars to Warin when last he was here, perhaps she wore it for him as well.

Hector reined in. "I did not expect to happen on my brother and sisters in the wood." He moved his regard to Séverine. "My prey was of a different sort."

As that one's lips parted with caught breath, Fira halted alongside his stirrup. "Then you but hunt? Did not intend to visit us?"

He lowered his gaze to her and, noting more greatly she resembled his stepmother since last he had seen her, silently beseeched the Lord that only her looks be passed to her by that departed lady. "Having left Wulfen in the hands of our uncle, Stern is my destination. Had not something come to notice that required investigation, I would be there now."

"I am glad!" Fira exclaimed, then frowned. "What came to notice?"

He considered revealing Séverine. However, certain it was best to deal with her distant from those to whom she would appeal, which would quicken his anger and further blacken him in the eyes of his siblings, he said, "Worry not, I have all in hand."

Urging his mount toward the three on the bank, Fira following, he saw the trespasser flick her eyes to the horses as if calculating the chance of reaching hers before being set upon.

"I shall introduce you, Wulfrith," Ondine misinterpreted his interest. "Séverine de Barra is the new companion Grandmother engaged."

De Barra. He had assumed if she truly was the boy's cousin, she shared his surname. Either here proof she had lied, else kinship with Mace was not by way of the male De Chansons.

Attempting no smile for how false it would appear, he halted his mount and set his hands atop the saddle's pommel. "Séverine," he acknowledged without revealing this was no new acquaintance. "Or is it *Lady* Séverine?"

When a swallow convulsed her throat, a glance at Warin confirmed he felt the woman's discomfort, and the concern in his eyes became warning when they swept to Hector.

She raised her chin. "Lady Séverine."

"Of France and longest of Calais," Warin said.

Lest what jerked his insides appear on the outside, Hector stiffened. Here another thing not known of her and of greater note than her surname. Of course, just because once Calais had been her home did not mean she was present during the siege. Though it had remained in King Edward's possession these five years, some of the ousted French had returned and others of France now made their homes inside those walls, providing goods and services to the English.

It was Fira who further enlightened her eldest brother. "Séverine tells she was among those who withstood our king's siege, Wulfrith."

Keeping his gaze on one who likely furthered her deceit to gain sympathy, he said, "Does she?"

The woman who had played a boy fairly well but was now unmistakably feminine with hair about her shoulders and a gown embracing modest curves, set her chin high. "She does,

Baron Wulfrith, and is aware you and your brother were outside our walls during those long, cruel months."

Remembering the townsfolk who yielded when their king's promised relief was withdrawn—all emaciated, including children—he said gruffly, "So we were."

She turned to Warin. "As told, I did not mean to impose. Since I have duties that need tending, I leave you now." She stepped past and moments later so hastily gained the saddle her hitched skirts revealed shapely calves.

As she urged her mount into the trees, Fira said, "Must you be so ill-humored, Hector? Now poor Séverine thinks you do not like her."

She thinks right, he silently conceded, *and better she will know it once I get her alone.*

"Of course Wulfrith does not like her," Warin eschewed his brother's given name as if all here were not family. "That is not imagined."

Baiting, and some of the worm impaled on his hook done in defense of the woman Warin believed worthy of such. But there was value in his cool reception and taunting, giving Hector the excuse to depart without rousing suspicion that could cause those here to follow and make more difficult what was best done before the infiltrator returned to the castle.

"As neither did I intend to interrupt your gathering, I shall see you at Stern," Hector said and looked to Ondine. "The sooner to return the bird to its natural domain, continue."

Providing they remained long enough to allow him to send away the woman and boy, later he could explain what he had done.

Upon emerging from the wood, he saw Séverine de Barra, hair flying out behind her, urged her horse to its fullest stride. Despite its faulty gait, it made good progress in distancing its rider.

To reach the woman before she was in sight of Stern and ensure none bore witness to a confrontation that could set tongues wagging, Hector spurred his mount to greater speed.

When he was close to overtaking her, he commanded, "Halt!"

She whipped her head around, and he saw her distress before she turned forward and bent low.

"So be it," he snarled and, anticipating she would veer away, kept pace when she did so.

Though her evasion kept them out of sight of Stern, the sudden alteration of course caused her mount to lurch. Aware of the danger that presented, especially to a woman lacking the support of weighty muscles and strong bones, he came alongside and reached to pluck her from the saddle. However, she looked around and veered as if to return to the wood—and once more was nearly undone by that precarious gait.

As further pursuit could result in injury or worse, he cursed her recklessness, came about, and reined in.

She continued toward the wood, and though he thought she might return to his siblings to reveal her deception in the hope of gaining their aid, a look across her shoulder made her slow. Then she turned. Face bright, shoulders moved by quick breaths, she stared.

He stared back. And saw the moment she yielded to the inevitable—his displeasure, judgment, and solution to the problem of she who trespassed one too many times.

CHAPTER 10

Feeling bruised as if she had lost the saddle and landed hard, feeling suffocated as if the baron had slammed an arm around her and compressed her lungs, Séverine let her shoulders slump and dropped her lids.

"Father mine," she whispered, "if You will not stand my side, I have no one to aid in fulfilling the promise made Sir Amaury. Give me words that will move this man to do what is right, and let no others pass my lips that provide more reason to refuse his kin. Amen." She opened her eyes.

Sunlight coursing the silver of his hair, he remained unmoving, doubtless certain that just as she could not get past him to Mace, he could intercept her before she returned to his siblings.

Steeling herself for his triumphant smile with the reminder, *You will temper your words as pleases the Lord,* she urged her mount forward.

However, his mouth remained flat, even when she halted so near their horses were almost nose to nose.

She swallowed and, seeing a corner of his mouth jerk,

knew he heard the bob of her throat. And approved. Though again she told herself to speak well, her tongue slung resentment. "Here your *prey of a different sort*, Baron Wulfrith."

His eyebrows rose. "Does one not wish to be brought to ground, they ought not play on the huntsman's path."

Of that she was guilty, though she would not name it play. Setting her hands atop her saddle's pommel, hopeful a show of nonchalance would calm a heart squandering its beats, she said, "For love of another, I do what I must."

He glanced at her hands, and she hated their quaking was seen. "You are persistent, Lady Séverine of...Calais."

Scorn there, but she had proof of her occupancy during the siege, and she would provide it though the kindness of five years past was unlikely to be shown again. "Though you think it a ploy—that I was not present when you and your brother aided in besieging my home—I was there, as was my cousin who was nearly as emaciated as I. The day—"

"Mace is also at Stern, aye?"

"He labors in the kitchen."

"The work of a commoner though you claim he is not only noble but royal?" His lids narrowed. "If so, how is it possible the boy who rebuked you for not better representing him is well with this?"

"He also does what he must."

"Admirable. Unfortunately, you have set him to laboring in the wrong kitchen. But this day that will be rectified since I do not abide deceit and find it more distasteful loosed among those under my protection."

Séverine urged her horse alongside and dared turn a hand around his arm. More aware of the flesh and blood beneath his sleeve than that felt when his brother aided in her dismount, she met his gaze. "Cast me out but, pray, not your kin."

She glimpsed softening about his eyes, but only that. "As

told, the decision to admit one born of France is not mine." He curved his fingers over hers, loosed her hand and set it on her saddle's pommel. "Put your cousin to work in the royal kitchen. If that opens a door to an audience with King Edward and he consents, I will make a place for the boy."

"Baron—"

"There will be rain this eve." He turned his horse aside. "The sooner you depart, the sooner you gain shelter for the night."

"Knave!"

Ignoring the insult, he set his horse to a canter.

Séverine set hers to a gallop. Though she expected him to turn her aside, he did not. Once she was beyond him, she came around and, now the one barring the way, commanded, "Hold!"

He drew rein. "We are done, Lady."

"Not until I give something long due you."

"That would be an apology. But if you think it will move me to yield, you waste your breath."

"No apology. Gratitude."

His lids narrowed.

"Five years gone, I neglected to thank the knight who made a way for me out of Calais." She had only to pause a moment before realization recast the stone of his face. "As you did not look beyond the figure of one come down out of the rafters, hardly did I look beyond your height and breadth. The only thing of note, though not much since I was unaware you were young, was silvered hair—and a scar atop your hand. Thus, not until I came to Wulfen did I know you were my savior. I thought your voice familiar, but I was certain of it when you told me to take my treasures and go. Just as done at the forge."

A muscle in his jaw convulsed.

"The treasure for which I returned home was in the cask

brought to Wulfen—Mace's past and future entrusted to me by his sire who was lost when he and others did not return from a foray that was to provide for the starving."

Once more, she urged her horse near. "I *am* given to deception, but it is to make good my promise to Sir Amaury to secure his son's future." Tears pricking, she blinked. "Whereas what I seek is all to Mace, it asks little of one who surely has his king's ear. If it is true Edward's consent is required, I beseech you to do what I believe not possible for me, and I will leave Mace in your keeping and return to my country."

"Despite the care you profess for your cousin, you would leave him entirely to me, Lady? Would not remain near to ensure his well-being? Would cross the channel without a backward glance?"

It contradicted. If not for pursuers more dangerous than this man, she would not consider it, but to keep Mace safe lest association with her imperil him—and to preserve her life— she must.

Hopeful she moved him closer to providing what her cousin needed in this pitiless world, she said, "Having done what my uncle asked of me and trusting Mace is safe with his relations, no longer will I be needed. Hence, I will go."

"Leaving my sister without a companion."

Surprised it was a consideration, she said, "As your grandmother forced me on her, I am certain another can serve better."

"I will not argue that."

"Then you will do this? Will prove as honorable this day as on that day long past?"

"Honor has naught to do with it, Lady. It has all to do with protocol. Thus, as I have no time to fight this battle for you, gain the king's consent."

Séverine felt as if stabbed in the back—that just as she

turned toward hope, he slid in a blade. "You know how impossible it could be for me to—"

"Enough! I did you a very good turn that day at Calais. Be grateful and trouble me no more."

When he turned aside and spurred his horse, she nearly gave chase, but at the speed he traveled she would be unable to overtake him. And even if she could, for what? As feared, revelation of the compassion previously shown her strengthened his argument against giving further aid.

Yielding to anger, she shouted. "You are without heart! Unworthy of the Wulfrith name!"

Hector heard her pronouncement above the rushing air, but resisted being offended since that was reserved for false accusations. Though much he cared for his family, beyond them his heart mostly kept blood moving through his veins. Thus, just as he had no time to fight Séverine de Barra's battle, he had none for the fanciful side of what beat in his chest. And little incentive since, though nearly all his family had forgiven him, it seemed ever he was out of favor with the Lord.

As he ascended the rise upon which he would catch sight of the jewel made of Stern Castle in the years since his ancestors raised its first walls to lay claim to Saxon lands, he was struck by impulse. After twice refusing to look around, he did.

Though only to himself would he admit his yielding had anything to do with her hand on his arm, as he had looked into a face that was only pretty—and slightly less for a scar at her eye and one atop her cheekbone—the desire consigned to his depths had rattled its chains as if to test its moorings. And that it did again as he stared at the lady who was where he had left her.

She was a pitiful sight with her head bowed, and more he felt for her plight knowing he had contributed to the losses of her cousin and her—and that she was the one coaxed out of the rafters when this heart was less single-minded despite betrayal by the wife whose annulment caused many to speculate over his ability to father children.

Closing his eyes, he recalled his next wife who would have proven the second a liar had she of gentle nature not passed shortly after discovering she was with child. Then there was the fourth who might also have proven the lie false had death not taken her.

Certain it could not be clearer he was not meant to father the next generation of Wulfriths, Hector raised his lids and saw Séverine de Barra slowly moved his direction.

Not my decision, he reminded himself, though she did not err in believing he held sway over King Edward.

"Some," he rasped, the chance of it being enough to see one of French blood admitted to Wulfen slight since he had descended so far out of favor he had nearly fallen from it.

If only he had resisted his king who insisted the Baron of Wulfen take a fourth wife. If only he had not alleviated that lady's boredom over removal from court and her inattentive husband by gifting her a spirited horse.

"Lord," he rasped, then forcing that tragedy from his thoughts, crested the hill. There was his home, though it had not truly been that since the pestilence entered its walls. If not for three riders approaching from the opposite direction, he would have lingered over Stern's beauty, but one of the men was of note for his black tunic belted with a scarlet sash.

Wulfenshire's sheriff had business with the Wulfriths.

ALL CONSPIRED to make this the worst day since the last she had believed that. And so it would be if what she overheard between the horse master and his assistant had all to do with Mace and her.

"Fugitives, ye say?" the younger man exclaimed.

"Aye, 'tis what the sheriff and the two with him told Baron Wulfrith—a woman and boy come from France."

Though Séverine's first thought was to make for the kitchen, retrieve Mace, and depart Stern, she set her back against the stable's wall where she had halted in leading her horse around the side.

"Ye thinkin' the same as me, Master? Mayhap it be Lady Ondine's companion and the new kitchen lad?"

"It occurs, but the oily one accompanying the sheriff told the woman put a dagger in an Englishman's gut."

The oily one...

Séverine turned that over. Might he be one of the two who sought to steal from her cousin?

"Though the French are treacherous, sticking and slashing from behind, running and hiding," said the master of horses, "Lady Ondine's new companion..." As Séverine gulped down bile, he sighed. "Albeit fallen on hard times, she is a lady. And she has been considerate and respectful. Nay, I do not see she could do that."

But Baron Wulfrith might see it, and if he was as heartless as believed, he would hand her over without allowing her to defend herself.

Her horse nickered—and might have been heard by the two outside the stable had not the younger said, "Ye are right, Master. Lady Séverine would not do that."

Not intentionally, but still blood on my hands, she thought and, remembering the crimson, shivered.

"While I tend the baron's mount, see to the others, lad—just water and oats since they depart soon to continue their search."

Footsteps and hooves sounding over packed dirt as the horses were led into the building, Séverine eased the stiff from her muscles, letting them conform to rough-hewn planks.

She must devise a plan, and since Mace would not be pouring drink for the visitors, his duties remaining exclusive to the preparation of meals, she had some time. So how was she to slip past those in the hall without coming to notice?

"The backstairs," she whispered. Though certain she was not to know of the passage, several nights ago a fitful Ondine had risen and, after approaching the screen and peering around it as if to ensure her companion slept, moved the direction of her standing mirror. A slight creak of hinges had been heard and again in reverse, followed by the thump of a door settling in its frame.

Séverine had remained unmoving a quarter hour, then came the sound of the lady's return. The next day when Ondine took her owl to the wood, she had located the concealed door behind the mirror and slipped down stairs converging with those of other chambers. When she had eased open a door at the bottom, she had found herself in an alcove built into a corridor that led to the kitchen.

This day, she would return to the donjon by way of the garden and, after warning Mace, use the hidden stairs to retrieve the cask. Then she and her cousin would make do with the one horse and...

Her thoughts trailed off to explore another. Though it made her ache, since she was responsible for putting a blade in the Englishman and her cousin's safety was more precarious for having only one mount to evade pursuers, it seemed the best option.

She straightened, led her horse to the back of the stable, and tethered it to await her return. "Soon you will be rid of me, Baron," she whispered. "Though not entirely."

CHAPTER 11

The woman who stuck a man and stole his horse fit the description of Séverine de Barra. The young boy accompanying her fit the description of Mace.

Both were French and recently come across the narrow sea.

Injury was dealt with a dagger set with a gem, possibly the same Mace had worn that resembled those awarded to young men knighted at Wulfen.

And the one who sought to gain training for her cousin was desperate to return to France though she would have to entrust the boy to strangers.

All aligned, and yet Hector continued to steeple fingers against his chin as he looked from Wulfenshire's sheriff in the chair opposite to the two on the bench between them who had gulped down their first pour of ale and begun a second.

Glad he had cut short the greetings of his grandmother and Dangereuse and ordered all from the hall save his squire, he looked nearer on the Dover deputy who had presented a document attesting to his position and charging him with capturing the fugitives for return to that port town.

His garments were fine beneath the dust and sweat of days in the saddle and nights on the ground, but it was illusion. Eyes in a large head reflected only a prick of light amid dark brown, smiles were so tight it was as if to conceal the canines of a rabid dog, often he dug thumb and forefinger into nostrils under cover of rubbing his nose, and there was some strain and plodding about his speech to cover having risen higher than birth and experiences had prepared him.

Now as he tipped his tankard to gain the last trickle of ale, a scar was seen arcing from the back of his jaw to his collarbone. A moment later, he raised a forearm but quickly suppressed the habit of dragging it across his mouth. Not so the witness to the crime.

Of middle years, he who claimed to be a business acquaintance of the victim and whose skin was as oily as his hair was not as finely garbed. But he did belch behind his lips, so he made some effort.

As coarse behavior was often given free rein during war campaigns and in the absence of women, Hector was fairly accustomed to such from men of common and noble birth and not easily offended. But he was observant, aware how one presented in public was a good place to begin taking measure of character, second only to catching him—or her—unawares.

"That the crime, Baron Wulfrith," said the sheriff who gripped a pale pewter tankard that contrasted with the black of his tunic and red sash. "Though I think it unlikely the fugitives fled this far north, as Deputy Le Creuseur heard of a young woman and boy traveling toward Wulfenshire, one of their horses brown and of faltering gait, I agreed to accompany them across the shire to ensure a good reception."

"Wise, Sir Percival," Hector said. "Since the Great Mortality, our villagers and townsfolk are less accepting of outsiders—the same as most places."

Le Creuseur cleared his throat. "Well, now you have the tale in full, have you heard of those we seek?"

He did not have the tale in full. However, were he to show greater interest, the man whose scrutiny was closely felt might have his answer before one was due—*were* one due.

Recasting his expression to appear he considered the matter, Hector drew his hand from the wolfhound beside his chair, retrieved his tankard from the small table, and glanced at Squire Gwayn who held a pitcher where he stood with his back to the hearth.

More would be required of the young man before he earned his spurs and girded a sword worthy of a Wulfen-trained knight, but his slight nod told he needed no confirmation those who had trespassed at Wulfen were the fugitives.

As Hector drank, he questioned his hesitation to hand over the lady. He had cause to send a man-at-arms to intercept her when she returned and deliver her to the hall so sooner justice was done, and yet...

It took more effort to read the fairer sex, but he was a good judge of character. The lady was a deceiver, and he would not be surprised if desperation made a thief of her, but he had no sense of her being one to gut a man who only sought to prevent her stealing his horse. Then there was the deputy and his witness. Were one of Stern's women servants accused of committing such a crime, Hector would not permit these men to deliver her to judge and jury.

"Well, Baron?" the deputy prompted.

When the gut growls it is so—or not so—give ear, Hector recalled a lesson his sire impressed on him.

It now telling him this was not the way to rid himself of the lady, he set his tankard on the table and looked to the sheriff, then Le Creuseur whose surname meant *digger* as seemed appropriate.

Grudgingly becoming the lady's savior as at Calais when he ensured she not fall into the hands of those who would have taken her as a spoil of war, he said, "Regrets, but your time is wasted. No tale has been carried to me of any fitting your description." And that was true.

The deputy smiled tautly, thrust his tankard toward Squire Gwayn.

Hector felt the young man's struggle to hide how greatly he was offended, but he was worthy of his training, efficiently refilling the tankards of both men seated on the bench.

Knowing Séverine could not indefinitely postpone facing the Wulfrith ladies and would soon blunder in, Hector called Gwayn to his side and said low, "The lawmen depart soon. See their mounts delivered to the inner bailey so they have no cause to linger—and ensure she stays clear of them."

When the doors closed behind him moments later, the sheriff sat forward. "As we have just enough daylight to reach Abingdale where my escort ends, we shall trouble you no more, Baron."

"Hold!" the deputy proved useful in that moment. "Still there is Wulfen Castle."

Hector narrowed his eyes. "Still there is *not*."

Though his tone caused the wolfhound to rumble as if to add threat to its master's words, Le Creuseur pressed, "Well, I would like to question those there."

"Like all you like, you will not disrupt the training of those whose waking hours are so devoted to proving worthy of their king they have little contact with the outside world. Too, since recently I departed Wulfen, I can attest neither have your fugitives been sighted in that area." Certes, he would not reveal it was this hour he had arrived at Stern since the man might push to question the castle folk here.

"But Baron—"

"Enjoy my hospitality to the bottom of your tankard, then I must tend to the business of my demesne."

The tiny light in the man's eyes departed, and a sneer he could not entirely suppress revealed chipped and discolored teeth.

Neither did the witness who crossed to the table where Gwayn had set the pitcher look pleased. "Great my thirst and good this ale, my lord." He glanced at Hector, then with an unsteady hand, sloppily refilled the tankard.

Ill-mannered, but acceptable since it provided Squire Gwayn more time to do as bid. Gesturing for the wolfhound to stay, Hector rose. "A word, Sir Percival."

A crack in the sheriff's sober expression revealing he believed he knew what was behind the request, he accompanied Hector to the sideboard where the weaponry of questionable visitors were surrendered. His own sword and dagger remaining girded over the scarlet sash, the castellan of Castle Soaring upon the Barony of Abingdale—and a distant relation for an ancestor wedding the twelfth-century Beatrix Wulfrith—said, "What has Martin done?"

It was rare Hector involved the parents or guardians of those fostered, even when offenses were great since it was his and his trainers' responsibility to make worthy warriors of those accepted at Wulfen despite the flaws each presented. Indeed, intervention was almost exclusive to behavior that made expulsion a strong consideration.

Fortunately, though the young man whose ascension from page to squire had been delayed a year due to a penchant for pranks, he was not the reason Hector wished to speak.

"Despite continuing to test the patience of all, your nephew makes good progress. Hence, I but wish to gauge your interest in a match between my brother, Rémy, and your niece."

Though hesitation was expected, it was hard not to take offense when, drawing a hand down his stubbled jaw, Percival grimaced. "You know the great advantage of strengthening our ties with your family, but as you would wish to think long on matching your youngest sister with Martin, this I must consider well ere answering."

He was right that Hector would be ill-disposed to acquiring a prankster for a brother-in-law. Still, that he did not wish his niece wed to one with Rémy's affliction though one day the penniless young woman might become lady of this barony...

"I do not personally object to the match," Percival sought to salve emotion Hector should have masked better. "Though just as I know Rémy is given to anger during his struggles, I know he is of good credit to his family. Mostly my concern is for his compatibility with my niece who..." He shifted his jaw. "Surely you recall what happened years past?"

"They were children, Percival. I assume just as Rémy has matured, so has your niece."

Annoyance over neglect of his title of office flickered in the man's eyes, but only that. Just as Hector had not wished to serve as sheriff years ago and cast it off when he persuaded King Edward it hindered his training of warriors, neither had Percival wanted to enforce the law upon Wulfenshire. But when a vassal was called to serve in that capacity, it was difficult to refuse.

"Children, aye," Percival said. "However, my niece is just as headstrong. Too, though I sanction no suitors since I can provide only a small dowry, the young nobleman fostering with me has drawn her eye and she has drawn his." He forced a smile. "Still, if you will be patient, I will consider a match with the House of Wulfrith."

"Though I wish to be done with securing a marriage contract, I can wait a time," Hector said and did not add what might be known if not merely suspected, which was his options were limited since it was difficult to hide what afflicted Rémy and the superstitious believed it a sign of evil—though not as great an evil as what had caused some to spurn Hector's stepmother which had bypassed the three children made with her Wulfrith husband.

Thus far, reminded the inner voice that sought to render him grateful for what Rémy did suffer as opposed to what he did not.

"Know I am honored, as my niece shall be regardless of the answer given," the sheriff said, then called, "If we are to outrun the rain, we must depart."

Shortly, they were astride horses whose delivery to the donjon had caused Percival to look questioningly at their host. Hector had nodded at gathering clouds that told they were unlikely to reach their destination dampened only by perspiration, then turned his attention to his squire.

Now as his visitors rode out, he listened as Gwayn revealed what had required investigation after those of the stable told Lady Séverine had yet to appear and the smithy's apprentice who had overheard reported witnessing her return. Sentries at the gatehouse had confirmed it, then revealed she had departed again a short while later. Alone.

MACE DE CHANSON was not to be found in the kitchen nor garden. Though it appeared he had fled the same as his cousin, none witnessed his departure and one of two horses said to have been stolen remained in its stall.

Only little Willa had anything of note to report—the lady had taken Mace to the garden as done fairly often, and shortly after his return to the kitchen, he slipped away.

Doubtless, he had departed Stern among those who came and went to fulfill orders that kept the castle supplied with produce and necessities, then joined his cousin beyond the walls.

With rain beginning to fall sooner than expected, just as their pursuers would be wet through in the absence of shelter, so would the prey.

Arms crossed over his chest where he leaned against the high table, Hector considered his family he had gathered so the tale be told only once. His grandmother and widowed sister, Dangereuse, had not been pleased to await the return of the three gone to the wood before learning the reason for the sheriff's visit, but it was known now, Hector having begun with his first encounter with Séverine at Calais and ended with his last on the return to Stern.

Disbelief, dismay, disappointment, and displeasure—the latter ranging from annoyance to anger—had shone from all but Warin who stood before a lower table.

Concern had made an appearance as well. Whether it was because those who had infiltrated Stern were liked and what was told of them rejected or Mace was believed kin, Hector could not know. But Fira's concern was less unexpected than what was glimpsed on the visage of Ondine who, rejoining the others in the hall after delivering her owl abovestairs, had done so absent the veil worn in the wood. As ever, that which marred her uncommon beauty pushed deeper the blade of regret.

Lady Héloise was the first to speak, and what the keeper of *The Book of Wulfrith* said did not surprise despite her being offended by the deception. "I wish to look nearer on the boy's claim. Ere he and the lady are taken by the law, you will deliver them to me, Hector."

"Surely not!" Dangereuse exclaimed as Hector considered

something he should have sooner. "It is ill enough that woman misled us and is a thief, but having put a blade in a man, she ought not be allowed back inside our walls."

Before Héloise could respond, the feet Fira had drawn onto the bench to view her brother from atop her knees dropped to the floor. "I do not believe Séverine guilty of what those men tell. She is not like that." She shot her gaze to Ondine. "Is she?"

"I would not have believed her capable of gutting a man," her sister said, "but can one truly know what goes behind another's face?"

Fira turned to her grandmother. "Surely you do not think Lady Séverine could do that."

"My dear, I am not well enough acquainted with her to say, just as neither are you. My greatest concern is for the boy who bears the surname taken by those he claims as ancestors—Maël and Mercia de Chanson. If he is a relation, protection is the least owed him." She shifted her regard to Hector. "I would examine the writings and treasures that may reveal more of *Tale of the Lost D'Argent*. Should those two be taken from Wulfenshire, the cask will disappear with them."

Ondine caught her breath. "If Séverine brought it here, she would have stored it beneath her bed, and it would still be there since upon her return she would have been unable to venture beyond the kitchen without being seen by Hector and our visitors."

"Unless she used the wall passage," Fira said.

"Nay, she knows naught of that."

"Go look," Héloise said.

With Fira on her heels, Ondine departed.

"Do you think the charges against the lady could be fabricated, Hector?" his grandmother asked what he had been turning over since berating himself for not sooner considering it. "That someone learned of the cask and accusation is a means of gaining it?"

Despite her great age, her mind remained sharp. "Possible," he said and was discomfited by how much he wanted it to be true of the woman coaxed out of the rafters.

"Even so," Dangereuse said, "until confirmed the lady did not bleed a man, I would not have her back amongst us."

Hector understood. The most confident of his sisters and given to risks few women took, Dangereuse did not fear for her well-being. Motherhood and fierce love of her son, Sebastian, had put a cautious edge on her, and as the child was the only one of the next generation of Wulfriths, she had greater reason to ensure his safety.

"What think you, Warin?" Héloise prompted.

"My acquaintance with the lady being exceedingly brief, I cannot be certain of the truth nor lie of her. But her and the boy's tale is compelling and more tragic for both being at Calais."

"True, but it is possible those who pursue them speak false, aye?"

"Many are those who sacrifice others to advance themselves," Warin said and did not need to move his regard to his brother to push that thorn deep. Nor could Hector begrudge him.

Lord, the priest tells You have forgiven me, he sent heavenward, *and all my family save Warin pardon me. Why is that not enough to feel forgiven? Will I be an old man before the sin is even halfway remitted? And if the sun does come out again, how am I to be thankful for being of so many years I have too few breaths remaining to bask in the light?*

"Possible or nay," Héloise said, "I would have Hector and you find Mace and Séverine."

Whereas Warin stiffened and Dangereuse grunted, Hector

nearly laughed. So devoted was his grandmother to the Wulfriths' history, she wished the fugitives to answer questions to determine if their answers were worthy of ink and parchment. But as ever, she was efficient, squeezing as much as possible out of one task to fuel another—in this case, healing the rift between her grandsons.

Hector wanted that as well, but knowing it best not to push the disaffected, he said, "Warin's journey home was long. While he settles, Squire Gwayn and I—"

"Hector!" Fira cried down the stairs. "Make haste!"

Fairly certain her summons had naught to do with the cask since easily it could be conveyed to the hall, Hector pushed off the table. Booted strides that echoed his evidencing Warin counted himself summoned as well, Hector began ascending the stairs.

"Hector!"

He looked around. Seeing his grandmother had risen and leaned on her cane, he said, "Remain with Dangereuse. Soon you will know what goes."

Then he took the stairs two at a time, as did Warin—a reminder of when they were small boys and the younger had patterned his movements, gestures, and words after the older one's. That had altered when Hector departed Stern to begin training at Wulfen.

It was then Warin had begun making his own way as their sire expected. By the time he began his training, though he continued to esteem Hector and sought to excel as greatly, not all his footsteps had fit well inside the ones gone before, and some hardly fit at all. Still, great the brothers' likeness from the early years and fairly similar in later years—until wrong turns taken, the pestilence, and great losses.

Reaching the second floor and seeing Fira beckon from

outside Ondine's chamber, Hector turned his mind to resolving current problems so they not also number among his regrets.

He did not know what to expect when he entered the room, but he had been certain to find Ondine in the midst of whatever caused him to be summoned. Instead, opposite the direction toward which Fira waved him, she stood with her back to him at the unshuttered window, the veil that had been down around her shoulders once more covering her face as if strangers were here.

"Ondine?" he and Warin said in unison.

She gave a sharp shake of the head.

"See here!" Fira said shrilly, which was no fit for the studious one. Then she slipped behind the screen partitioning the companion's sleeping area from the rest of the chamber.

When Hector came around it, sitting on the small bed was one most unexpected.

CHAPTER 12

He was so frightened he wished more he was shamed, bright in the face surely better than tears in the eyes.

Having no choice but to trust Séverine's scheme to keep him from those searching for the woman believed responsible for the death of an Englishman, great the trespass of using the hidden passage to occupy a lady's chamber. But to have then offended that lady...

Though his cousin had warned Ondine was scarred, Mace had been agitated, and so suddenly she came around the screen that when she cried out at the sight of him, he had done the same and thrown his hands up before him. Had he not earlier moved the large ring from palm to thumb, that which Séverine told was of much interest to Fira would have gone flying.

He wished he had given the ring to the youngest Wulfrith when she appeared as her older sister whirled away, but he had frozen. Though quick to clap a hand over her own mouth, more greatly he had been unsettled when Fira patted his shoulder, assured him he had naught to fear, and told she would return with Baron Wulfrith.

Now here that warrior was, having followed his sister around the screen, and more intimidating than at Wulfen—all because of what Séverine had done and Mace was too powerless to do otherwise.

With the return of anger often felt since it was determined to seek his training with kin, once more Mace directed it at his cousin for being unable to make happen what must. He knew it was wrong, that she loved him and did all she could, but it was not enough. Rather than laboring in a kitchen, he should be learning the swing of a sword and thrust of a dagger. He should be tilting at the quintain, wrestling, and hunting. He should be studying strategies and—

"Boy, if I must tell you again to drop it, I will not," the ominous one growled.

Following his gaze, Mace startled at the discovery though he had believed it only consideration to draw his dagger as those boots neared the screen, he had done it. A blade projected from the fist gripping an intricately embossed hilt, its point near Fira whose lids were wide and mouth gaped.

Sweeping his gaze back to her brother, Mace quaked over fury in those eyes that brought to mind when last he had faced such displeasure, causing the skin of his back to burn in remembrance of each slap of the strap he was required to count aloud to avoid doubling his punishment.

Neither had Séverine been able to aid him despite attempts to intervene which saw her backhanded against a wall, and a slap of the strap intended for him to catch her across the face. Though she sacrificed her safety to ensure his, her devotion was of little benefit in matters of great import. Thus, both knew until he was man enough to defend himself, he needed the protection of a warrior. And now there was no chance this one would provide that.

Despising impulse that rendered him equally at fault for the failure of Séverine's plan, disgusted he quaked, he slumped as Baron Wulfrith lunged and wrenched his sister back.

Mace heard the clatter of the dagger he released, next gulping sobs not even the lashes he had been made to count had loosed. Then his knees were bumped and hands turned around his upper arms. He braced for a beating, but it was not the baron who took hold of him.

"Have mercy!" Fira beseeched, having slipped free of her brother. "He is only a boy and very frightened. He would not have harmed me."

Unable to make sense of the baron's response nor that of Lady Ondine and another man who sounded near, Mace opened flooded eyes and saw a hand sweep up the dagger Séverine had instructed him to keep concealed so he had something to give threat were it necessary.

This day it was not, and knowing fear had moved him to foolishness just as pride had done in Dover, both times causing him to lose a dagger, more forcefully sobs moved his body.

"Is that not so, Mace?" entreated Fira who ducked her head to peer into his face. "You would not have hurt me."

"Come away," her brother ordered. "I shall deal with him."

Untucking his chin to plead with her not to leave him with the wrathful man, Mace saw movement to the right, then the young woman was drawn back.

"Non!" Certain he had so shamed himself he could not make it worse, he grasped Fira's gown. And greater his excuse to hold to this unexpected defender when the ring on his thumb glinted gold and red.

Hoping the youngest sister responded as Séverine believed

she would, he said, "The bishop's ring, Lady Fira! I am to show it to you."

She who was prettier up close despite an abundance of freckles, startled. "You have it?"

He released her skirt and raised that hand.

She gasped, reached, and was yanked away. "Let me go!"

Her brother did so only when she was behind him and gripped by one of good resemblance to the baron though that man had pale hair. From excited chatter in the kitchen over the return of one long gone, Mace knew this was the second brother. And just behind Sir Warin was the scarred sister who now wore a face veil.

A moment later, sight of the three was blocked by the eldest, and Mace saw his dagger was beneath the man's belt alongside a sheathed one whose gem-studded hilt attested to it being a Wulfrith dagger—styled after the D'Argent one Mace had lost to him.

As the baron stepped nearer, Mace snatched back his hand and, fighting the longing to lower a damp face whose eyes stung and nose ran, tipped back his head.

"You have much to explain, Mace de Chanson, but all I require now is the whereabouts of your cousin who is charged with a terrible crime I am told you witnessed—perhaps participated in."

In the little time they had, Séverine had informed him of the lawmen come to Stern and instructed him to answer with as few words as possible.

"I do not believe Séverine capable of that," Fira said.

"Quiet, else Warin will take you from here," her brother rebuked.

She went silent, surely averse to being deprived of hearing firsthand what Mace revealed.

"Speak, boy."

He moistened his lips. "Séverine is gone."

"Where?"

He sniffed hard. "She returns to France."

The baron's jaw shifted. "Is my discovery of her deception the only reason she departed, or does she know the law came for her?"

Averting his gaze, he repeated, "She returns to France."

His persecutor's deep breath sounded. "I am to believe with the law seeking you as well, she left you with strangers?"

This anger directed at one it was due, Mace said, "She left me with *kin*. Like it or not, by way of the D'Argents where your family began the same as mine, the Wulfriths are that to me." *Too many words and ill-spoken,* he knew, but more followed. "And training is owed me!"

Hector stared at the boy with whom he had nearly dealt violently when he saw the blade so near his sister a split-second thrust would have put it in her belly.

Fortunately, his ability to quickly assess a situation, experience with frightened—sometimes violent—boys, and instinct had not failed him despite the exceedingly personal trespass. Thus, once the dagger was down, briefly Hector had allowed Fira to soothe the boy, providing her brother time to cool so he not further intimidate Mace and render him unreachable.

"Regardless of whether you are a relation, the only thing possibly owed you is my protection, and I do not doubt it is that to which your cousin aspired."

Seeing Mace's chin crumple, unable to suppress the desire to save him the humiliation of further collapse beneath tears, Hector dropped to his haunches and set a hand on that small shoulder. "Tell me where Séverine has gone."

He shook his head, then words broke through his resolve. "I vow she did not mean to kill him. She but tried to protect me and take back what was stolen."

Amid the boy's revelation, Hector realized how much more certain he had been Séverine had not stabbed a man than that she had. Fortunately, as reported by the deputy and his witness, the boy was ill-informed about the extent of her crime. Thus, if the injury dealt was unintentional and in defense of her cousin, she might escape the harshest punishment—*were* she overtaken by one with integrity like the Sheriff of Wulfenshire whose escort neared its end.

"She only wanted to retrieve my dagger," Mace continued. "It was his fault—*their* fault. And we had to take his horse to get away."

Hector frowned. "I was told your cousin stole *two* horses."

"Non. We bought the first at the stable where I was set upon—and were cheated. Though the horse looked a good one, we were not told something was wrong with one of its legs, which makes the ride uncomfortable."

And renders it easily identifiable, Hector thought. Just as it was fortunate for the lady that those come searching for her had not entered the stable where they might have seen the stolen horse, so it was they were unaware the purchased one had a peculiar gait since the lawman and his witness had only reported it was brown. Were Séverine wise, she would rid herself of it as should have been done sooner.

"I vow, that man and his friend were the thieves," Mace said. "If only I had not—" He squeezed his eyes closed.

Hector jostled him. "Tell me."

"Would I had not done what I did, but no matter how I wish and pray, it changes naught."

"What did you do?"

He lowered his gaze to the weapon beneath Hector's belt that one so young should not possess. "Séverine told me not to, but it is mine, and since we came to England to make a warrior of me, it was my right to wear it." He looked up. "While she arranged for the horse, I removed the dagger from the cask and put it in my boot. Had I not, those two would not have seen it and possibly the cask. When one tried to take it from me, I warned I was of Wulfrith blood, but he would not leave me be."

Then for this the deputy had ventured far north and been determined to enter Wulfen, Hector thought.

Mace gulped. "I should have told Séverine I had spoken of your family, but I did not lest she determine it was not safe to come here, and I was certain once you knew I was kin we would be given sanctuary." Another sob. "I am afeared for her."

Reminding himself of the boy's age and certain his contrition was genuine, Hector said, "I do not believe the lady has abandoned you nor plans to depart England soon, and I am certain you know it as well. So tell where she has gone, and I will do all I can to ensure a good defense for her."

Suspicion leapt across his face, but Hector had what he hoped a cure for it. "'Tis true this day the Sheriff of Wulfenshire escorted a deputy of Dover and his witness to Stern, just as it is true I did not reveal your cousin and you. What is not true is Lady Séverine is charged with murder."

The boy gasped. "He is not dead?"

"He lives and is expected to recover."

"Then…?"

So much hope in that one word. "Better Lady Séverine's chances—"

"Even though she is French?"

Hector could not lie. "As you know, just as your countrymen are distrustful of the English, the English are of the French. Now tell where I can find her."

He averted his gaze. "As told, she goes home to France."

Knowing he must approach the truth from a different angle and certain if he delved the trunk under the bed what likely had been there was gone, Hector said, "Then she left you with the cask you brought to Wulfen, confident you could safeguard its treasures regardless of whether I grant you protection?"

He shook his head. "She took it with her to France."

A lie he must have been instructed to tell. After all Séverine had done to deliver him to England, defend him when he was set upon, and try to place him at Wulfen, just as it was not believable she would depart before being fairly certain he was well-cared for, it was not believable she would deny him a legacy that assured his future even in the absence of Wulfen training.

Had Hector to guess, she had removed the cask in the hope if the Wulfriths believed him abandoned, he would gain their protection. Too, surely she had not kept those treasures safe all these years to place all her trust in the Wulfriths by leaving them here. Hence, once assured as much as possible Mace was in better hands, she would return the cask to him and attempt to cross back to her country—and the longer she delayed, the greater the possibility of escape since crimes came and went and those most recent stayed uppermost in the minds of all.

Looking across his shoulder, Hector saw Ondine's face remained covered, Warin's brow grooved, and Fira had a lean to her body that made it appear she might tip over.

Aware of the latter's quest to find the ring mentioned in *The Book of Wulfrith* that caused her to search the waterways between Stern and Wulfen these two years, he motioned her forward.

"Do you still wish to show the ring to Fira, Mace?"

The boy looked to her. "I do, but you have to give it back."

"My word I give." She held out a hand.

He drew the ring from his thumb. "I am to show you the parchment too."

"Parchment?"

He placed the gold ring with its red gem in her palm. "Séverine says my sire told what is written on it refers to the behest of a Dane, and your ancestor honored it by bringing the ring to France and delivering it to Maël de Chanson many years after William the Conqueror made England his own."

"1097!" Fira exclaimed as he pulled the small parchment from the purse on his belt. "The year Wulfriths and D'Argents gathered in Normandy for the passing of our common ancestor, Lady Robine D'Argent. Though *Tale of the Lost D'Argent* in *The Book of Wulfrith* records it was a Dane who stole the ring from King William's brother when he aided in rescuing the Saxon lady Sir Maël loved, it also tells he cast it in a stream between here and Wulfen lest its discovery lead to those who freed her." She sighed. "Your ancestor was chivalrous, Mace. For love he relinquished his family name and took that of De Chanson to honor his mother, wed Lady Mercia, and erase both from the memories of those who wished to forever imprison her."

Though the details she cited caused the boy to go still, moments later he shrugged. At his age and with all things warrior on his mind, talk of love held no appeal.

When he extended the patch of parchment, Hector took it and read, "Received from the Dane by way of G.W., the Year of Our Lord, 1097." It was a good fit, just as Séverine must have realized when she learned of Fira's fixation on the ring. Though briefly Hector considered Mace's cousin had made it fit to further her deception, the parchment was very old and ink faded and blurring, likely due to heat and humidity over the centuries.

"Hector, the letter *O* encircles the gem's base!" Fira exclaimed.

Was she only seeing what she wished? "As the ruby is

round, it would not be unusual were the base etched thus," he said.

"No mere etching this, the flourishes so intricate it is certainly an *O*—for Odo. Look!"

He reached—as did Mace in a failed attempt to keep his treasure out of Hector's grasp.

"You cannot take that from me as well!" the boy cried.

"As I would only look near upon it, it will be returned to you."

As if Mace had a choice, he nodded.

Fira did not exaggerate. What had been cut into the gold base was so intentional it had to be a mark of ownership by one whose name began the same as *Odo*. And Hector was more convinced it was the bishop's ring after examining a ruby that was the largest and finest he had seen, its facets perfectly cut. Despite Séverine's plan being devised in haste, this alongside all else shown him surely proved the boy a relation.

"You are right, Fira," he said.

"Give it back," Mace snapped, and when Hector raised his eyebrows, amended, "Pray, give it back."

It was dropped in his palm, and he closed his fingers over it.

"You will show that to my grandmother," Hector said, "reveal to her what your cousin told when you came to Wulfen, and list the cask's contents."

Though there was uncertainty about Mace, he said, "I can do that."

"Can you also trust Lady Héloise to keep the ring safe?" When the boy started to protest, Hector said, "It does not present the danger of a blade, but it is dangerous. Recall what happened when those men saw the dagger and took it from you. Not only is the ring worth more, but so small a thing is easily misplaced or lost." As the boy considered that, Hector added, "You will be allowed to remain with us until—"

"You will train me at Wulfen?"

"Naught has changed. Just as still you are French, still you cannot be admitted to Wulfen without the king's permission."

"Then what am I to do?"

"Seek the patience of one beyond your years, which will bring you one step closer to gaining what you seek. Fortunately, there are plenty of lessons learned while serving in a kitchen."

Offense flew across the boy's face. "I am to remain a servant though it is proven I am family and of noblest blood?"

Also in need of patience, Hector breathed it in. "It is no different from what would be required of you were you permitted to train at Wulfen."

"But Wulfen is for training warriors, not servants."

"Wulfen is for the making of men worthy of defending God, country, and family. Thus, here the first of what will be many lessons should you enter Wulfen Castle again. Ere one who ascends high can be worthy of that height, he must do humble things to better lead those on the rungs below." As Mace pondered that, Hector straightened. "Come."

"Where?"

"To the hall. There you will answer my grandmother's questions with much respect."

"Aye," the boy said as he stood.

"Aye, *my lord,*" Hector reminded.

"Aye, my lord."

As Hector turned, Fira slipped past to stand the boy's side, which she did all the way to the great hall where the oldest Wulfrith could not conceal surprise over the one left behind.

Rain had fallen heavily, though not before Séverine witnessed the departure of the three come to Stern to meet with Baron Wulfrith who must now believe her a murderess. "So be it, just have pity on the boy," she rasped.

Shivering beneath a wet mantle that was among the few items retrieved from the trunk, she slid down the tree whose canopy of leaves took the sting out of rain trying to slash at her.

Though her horse whinnied as if to assure her she was not alone in her misery, she felt isolated.

Of which you ought to be grateful, she told herself. *It could have been much worse.*

Had she not overheard the exchange outside the stables, she would be in the custody of those who departed Stern over an hour past. Had Mace been discovered ahead of their departure, he might have been taken, though Séverine was fairly certain the Wulfriths would not have allowed it—especially when presented with the ring. Since that family required further proof of Mace's kinship, hopefully that would serve, gaining him their protection. And greater the likelihood were it believed he was abandoned.

"And what of you, Séverine?" she whispered, though it was only to hear her voice so she feel less alone. In accord with assurances given Mace, she knew what came next.

As done often in France when they moved from one home to another, after being ejected from Wulfen they had found a place to hide the cask to prevent it being stolen and allow for easy retrieval when it was time to leave.

Since she had believed it safe to bring her cousin's treasures to Stern, that hiding place near the town of Ravvenborough had been held in reserve. But now she would make use of it so Mace's inheritance would not be lost should anything happen to her or she escaped to France. If he saw her never again, he would know where to find the cask. Though it hurt they might be parted forever, God willing it would be because he was safe with the Wulfriths and no longer required her protection that had sometimes failed him.

Recalling her greatest failure, she touched the small ridge above her eyebrow, then a longer one angling back from her cheek. She had been fortunate not to lose an eye and Mace unfortunate her interference worsened his punishment.

Tilting her hooded head back, she entreated, "Father mine, let Mace be home at long last. And have you grace to spare, help me find my way forward." She nearly sobbed. "I am glad to have served as Your hands and feet, but I am tired."

Moments later, the clatter of chains sounded. Peering through the trees between her and Stern, she watched two riders emerge from beneath the portcullis and spur away.

The day was too wet and grey and those departing too distant to identify them, but great the feeling one was Baron Wulfrith—and he endured foul weather to search for her.

Fearful he would take the road toward Ravvenborough, which could mean Mace had revealed her destination, she held her breath. When they went a different direction, relief folded her over.

She had time to conceal the cask, take the horse distant to lead her pursuers astray, then once more don the disguise of a young man since the lawmen sought a woman—unless the baron had told she had entered Wulfen and how it was done. Even so, as she believed one of the riders who departed Stern ahead of the rain had been the companion of the knave who stole from Mace, as a woman she would be more easily recognized should they meet again.

Séverine pressed upright. Soon she would be thoroughly

soaked, which might prove the death of her, but she could waste no time seeking shelter were she to keep her word to Sir Amaury.

Chapter 13

Ravvenborough
Barony of Wulfen

As expected, work was not difficult to secure. As hoped, it was mostly indiscriminate, so great the need for laborers whose predecessors had succumbed to the pestilence.

Not only had Séverine in the guise of a young man been offered good wages to work the fields of one of Baron Wulfrith's tenants, but when she sought lodging at the stables, it was provided without cost in exchange for cleaning the stalls.

For nearly a sennight, she had labored from dawn until after dusk. Though fatigued, the abundance of work allowed her to keep to herself—and save coins to fund her return to France so it would not be necessary to take money from the cask which her labors across the sea had increased to ensure against sale of the treasures.

Pressing cramped hands atop her thighs, slowly she

removed the bend from her back and raised her head to peer across stalks of ripening grain whose fertile soil the weeds sought to claim for themselves.

Funny, she thought, *these prickly fiends are not much different from warriors of one country trying to take the lands of others.* Of course, perhaps the weeds merely sought to take back what was first theirs.

She bit her lip. Though at Calais she had hated the English for making war on her country, she had been informed enough to know their king's actions were in response to her king's offenses that caused Edward to set his mind on taking back ancestral lands Philip had seized. Perhaps more importantly, England's king had determined if there must be war, he would take it to France rather than allow his enemy to deliver it to his shores—far better the suffering of innocent French than innocent English. She had loathed that but understood. And wished King Philip had been of the same mind.

Straightening, she pressed back her shoulders and stretched her head side to side. Two other workers clearing weeds did the same, while the backs of the rest remained curled.

She was not unaccustomed to work, but this was the hardest undertaken—and more so for giving her body inadequate rest between tending crops and cleaning stalls.

As she started to return to her task, she heard what most would believe birdsong. Those shrill notes so familiar she knew them formed by lips, she searched out the boy and saw he stood on the strip of mown land between this field and the next. Having captured her attention, he raised a hand and ducked into the crop behind.

Her heart doubled its beat. Mace was to come only were he in danger or ejected from Stern, and since she had been as certain as possible the Wulfriths would not forsake him, something must have come between him and that family's protection.

Counseling calm, she closed the half-filled sack whose weeds would be burned, then confident the cap concealing her hair yet did so, swung the sack onto her back and hoped the other workers paid her no heed.

Being new to their ranks, her wages were less, but the young man she played was expected to reduce the workload in proportion to his size and strength.

If any noticed she was relatively unburdened as she made her way to the rock-lined pit to empty a sack that must be filled many more times this day, none called her to account.

After adding to what would become a hill before being set afire, she traversed the cleared ground between the fields. Upon glimpsing the russet of the tunic sewn for her cousin and confirming she was not watched, she bent and entered the field that had yet to be cleared of weeds.

Moments later, she dropped the sack and fell to her knees before the boy who smiled so brightly she thought this might be a dream. Then her arms were around him.

"I am so glad to see you," she choked. "Pray, tell all is well—that you but do as you ought not."

He drew back and pushed from her brow damp strands escaping her cap. Certain it was safest she cut her hair to hide the woman of her as must have been done by the lady who fooled a Wulfrith two hundred years past, before entering Ravvenborough she had drawn her hair over her shoulder to saw a blade through it. But vanity had made her pause.

Curling tresses her only real beauty, she had concealed her hair beneath a cap and kept her chin down. When escaping hair sought to betray her the second day here, she had threaded sections together and secured them close to her scalp. Then to ensure trespassing fingers and wind not pluck off the cap, she had stitched its inner lining to her hair at the front and sides. However, the strands had become so fouled by oil, dust, and dirt, soon she must unthread all and find a secluded stretch of stream in which to bathe.

When Mace continued to withhold reassurance, she repeated, "Pray, tell you but do as you ought not."

"I do as I *ought*," he said, "and would have done sooner had I been able to depart Stern unseen."

She frowned. "Are you certain none followed?"

"Oui. I was cautious, listening well and watching all sides of me."

Because he believed that did not make it so, but he was here now, and it did her heart good to see him in fine spirits. "I cannot be gone much longer ere I am missed," she said, "just as neither can you, so tell the Wulfriths do right by you and what brings you here."

He stepped back. "The ring worked." He told what he had learned of it as recorded in *The Book of Wulfrith* and ended on a sigh. "Not only have I gained Baron Wulfrith's protection, but he and others of his family believe what I told happened in Dover. And just as he did not reveal to the lawmen I was at Stern, neither did he tell you had been there."

As prayed. "Now he knows you are kin, he will train you?"

Resentment streaked his face. "Though he and his family accept I am a relation, still I serve in the kitchen."

"What say you?"

"The baron tells those worthy of rising high must first do humble things as is the same for all admitted to Wulfen."

She could not know that, having believed training at the renowned fortress was exclusive to the art of war. "But he *has* agreed to train you?"

"Non. As told, that requires his king's permission."

Not what she wished to hear, but it was something. "Then he has sent a missive to King Edward?"

"He considers it, but until he determines what to do, I may remain at Stern."

Again, not what she wanted to hear.

He stepped nearer. "Baron Wulfrith does not believe you abandoned me nor deprived me of my inheritance."

Recalling the riders who departed the castle amid falling rain an hour after the lawmen, she asked, "He searches for me?"

"He does not say, but several times he has ridden out with his brother, and always I hope he brings you back." He drew his lower lip between his teeth. "You should return. For that, I came to tell you it is safe."

She almost laughed. "Even were the Wulfriths to take pity on me for being your cousin, still I am accused of—"

"The man did not die!"

"What?"

"And since he lives, Baron Wulfrith says he will ensure you a good defense."

For a moment, she hoped the same as Mace, but a good defense against the reduced charge of *attempted* murder did not mean she would be absolved. "I thank you for trying to aid me, but I believe it best I stay this course—remaining near until you have what we seek, then taking passage to France."

Seeing tears brighten his eyes, she set a hand on his shoulder. "It is no longer this poor excuse for a mother you require. Your sire knew the day would come when it was not a woman's skirts you ought hold to but those things that make a warrior. Thus, as he provided for a future now within your grasp, further association with me will impede your journey." She forced a smile. "God willing, you will take your next step soon, and I will go home."

Not that France had felt home since Calais was besieged and the country stricken with pestilence that brought out the worst in many, but she would be safest there and might make some small thing of a life once expected to be larger.

Barely a score of years, and yet this must be how one twice as old feels, she thought. *But I do not—will not—resent the charge given me.*

She moved her hand from Mace's shoulder to his cheek. "In the hiding place we chose, you will find your treasures, the sale of some ensuring once you are knighted you will be well armed with a fine destrier beneath you. You remember the great oak, oui?" Concerned by his hesitation, she prompted, "To the west of Lillefarne Abbey near—"

"Peter! Where are ye?"

She caught her breath. Her absence noted and fearing she would be discovered with Mace, she kissed his brow. "Thinking only on your future, be of good speed in returning to Stern ere *you* are missed—and dare not come again unless absolutely necessary."

Then she snatched up the sack, bent low, and did not look back as she traded one field for the other.

When the foreman called again, she showed herself above the stalks and reported these weeds rooted deeper than most—and silently added, *Just like the English who took Calais and continue to hold that jewel beside the sea.*

Chapter 14

Stern Castle

After a cursory search for the lady who discomfited more than she ought—just as she should not steal to mind so often—and confirmation the deputy and his witness departed Wulfenshire empty-handed, Hector had let the matter of Séverine de Barra lie. For the time being.

Unfortunately, the *time being* had not lasted long enough for him to make sufficient progress with Warin that would allow him to return to Wulfen to relieve Sir Owen and others of duties heaped on them.

Four days past, Lady Héloïse had sent Esta to collect Mace so he could expand on events told her for inclusion in *The Book of Wulfrith*. As it had been hours before the next meal and the young servants were allowed to rest, it was not unusual for them to be absent the kitchen. What was unusual was the boy could not be found inside the walls though none saw him depart. However, his return hours later was noted when he tried to slip into the outer bailey by staying near a hay wagon.

Hector having been fairly certain he had either gone in search of his cousin or met with her as could have been arranged before she fled, he had ordered that none confront the boy, allowing him to believe himself a master of stealth.

That event had once more wedged Lady Séverine between Hector and matters from which he should not be distracted. Now this...

He stared at the name signed to the missive Dangereuse had passed to him upon his return from a hunt with Warin who had surely been tempted to alter his plan to put venison on the table when Hector told he would join him.

Though there had been opportunities for the brothers to speak before taking a deer to ground, either Warin had not responded or moved talk distant from where Hector ushered it.

"What has Sir Percival to say?" asked the woman of silvered dark hair who sat well the lord's high seat due to confidence and good height. Indeed, so well it was as if that place of authority was not merely on loan during her brother's long absences.

Content to let her hold court of sorts though their grandmother believed Hector's place was there during his visits, he settled more solidly into his chair and extended the missive.

Dangereuse ignored it. "Of Lady Séverine, aye?"

Since the wax seal had not been broken, she could not have read it. As clever as ever, she had deduced that since correspondence with their relation on the neighboring barony was rare, this had all to do with Percival the sheriff.

Sliding the missive beneath his belt, he said, "Her horse was found south of the Wulfenshire border, but Percival tells Deputy Le Creuseur believes it an attempt to lead him opposite her hiding place."

She set aside her quill and pushed back the ledger whose figures she checked though the family's steward was above reproach. Her oversight annoyed the man, but she took seriously the role assumed upon returning to Stern following her husband's death, which had allowed their grandmother to further indulge her passion for the history of the Wulfriths.

"How does the knave come by that belief?" Dangereuse asked almost indignantly. Though she had little to say about the two who deceitfully gained access to their family, Hector knew she was not unsympathetic to Mace's cousin. How could she be considering what had made her a young widow and traumatized her son whose behavior could preclude him from Wulfrith training if he continued down the path his mother was slow to correct though in most things there was little soft about her?

"Wulfrith?" she prompted, as usual eschewing his given name in the presence of those other than family though no servants were near.

"There is a witness. As the one found in possession of the horse is a beggar with no means of rightly owning it, he came to notice. When questioned, he confessed to trespassing on the monastery's orchard to satisfy his hunger and saw a young blond woman astride. He vowed she abandoned the horse and ran opposite."

"Toward Wulfenshire?"

"That is what the deputy believes, that though the boy was not present, it was Lady Séverine and she is somewhere on our lands."

"You believe it as well."

"I do, and since the deputy has returned to our shire, I must locate her to better protect the boy." *Only for that,* he told himself and jutted his chin at where Mace stood alongside their grandmother's chair.

He who had given the bishop's ring into the safekeeping of Héloïse watched as Fira, spectacles perched on her nose, punched holes into the edge of a parchment for insertion in *The Book of Wulfrith*. The new page inked by the matriarch after interviewing Sir Maël's young descendant and questioning Hector who had read two of the cask's aged documents was incomplete, but it pleased her to further *Tale of the Lost D'Argent*. Now greater her hope for recovery of the cask and Séverine de Barra who could provide further insight.

"You will write to King Edward?" Dangereuse asked.

"I will, and I think it likely since Mace is our relation and young enough to make him a loyal defender of the English, Edward will agree to his training—unless it is seen as a favor he is not ready to extend me."

His sister set a hand over his. "As most would attest, among Edward's strengths that set him apart from his sire, who nearly ruined our country, is his ability to forgive—though wisely he does not *forget* the offenses of those who threaten his reign." She raised her eyebrows. "That your supposed trespass was not. Send the missive, and once it catches up to wherever he is, I believe his answer will have naught to do with what was lost through accident."

Hector pushed back his chair. "I will tell the boy I have decided to write to the king on his behalf and he shall accompany me to Wulfen to await an answer."

"I would not do that, Wulfrith. As hope dashed can wound worse than hope in waiting, best he remain at Stern and learn the missive was sent once the answer is given."

"I might agree had I not a covert motive."

Hardly did her frown form than it dissolved. "You believe if Mace is told he goes to Wulfen, he will steal away to alert Séverine."

"I do. If she is to be found, far better I do the finding than the Dover deputy." He rose and, as he crossed to his grandmother, felt the regard of Warin who applied a whetstone to his sword.

A necessary task, Hector knew, just as he knew his brother was more given to performing it when emotions ran high, the meeting of whetstone and iron a balm to his roiling.

Though finally Warin had returned home, and there had been hope it was a step toward reconciliation that would allow the brothers to train warriors together, either he had decided he was not ready or it had never been a consideration, this merely a visit to others of the family. If the latter, surely that would warrant a stop at Wulfen where Rémy remained in training.

"It is finished!" Fira proclaimed and, as Hector halted on the opposite side of the table, lifted the parchment from atop the template and turned it toward her grandmother. "Perfectly punched!"

"Well done, my dear." Héloise set a hand on one of two sections of the book parted from its leather thongs and looked to Mace. "Would you like to insert the page and use those nimble fingers to aid with the rebinding?" At his hesitation, she said, "Afterward, I will read to you all that is known of your tale."

"May I read it myself?"

She gave a little laugh. "When you have learned your letters and know how they are joined to form words, that will be possible."

"Already I know, my lady. I cannot read fast like Séverine, but I understand most writing."

Doubt raised thin eyebrows. "Truly, you read?"

"Aye, my cousin taught me, as is fitting for one of noble *and* royal blood."

"Why did you not say?" Fira exclaimed, and Hector saw she had plucked off spectacles no longer required for close work.

"I would have had you asked," Mace said.

After glancing sidelong at Hector, the old woman tapped the book's cover. "Read this."

She tested Mace. Since all referred to the ever-growing tome as *The Book of Wulfrith*, she must expect him to fit those words to the ones embossed in leather.

He stepped nearer. "Written in French, it is easy." He put a finger beneath the letter of the first word and, moving it, read, *"Les Wulfriths."* He set his finger to the second line. *"D'abord. Entre. À la fin."* Satisfaction in his smile, he translated, "The Wulfriths. First. In between. In the end." He shifted his regard to Hector. "These words are known to me. Just as this is the Wulfriths' maxim, it is the De Chansons'. Just as your family took it from our D'Argent ancestors, so did mine."

There was challenge in that last. And the timing could not be better.

"For this and that you have become something of a ward," Hector said, "I have decided to write to King Edward. Standing as witness to your kinship and good character, I shall propose one born of France be trained into a defender of England."

The boy's jaw lowered, and emotion not seen since he was discovered in Ondine's chamber wet his eyes. "Truly?"

Feeling the gaze of all, most intently that of Warin who ceased working the whetstone, Hector said, "Though the king may not grant permission, it saves you the difficulty—if not impossibility—of gaining an audience with him."

His shoulders rose as if a weight was removed from them. "Much gratitude, my lord. How long do you think ere my king answers?"

My king...

That already he claimed Edward as his sovereign bespoke confidence that with the Wulfrith's aid he would gain what he desired. Of course, he would not be so certain if he knew the once highly-favored Baron of Wulfen was less so.

Catching movement out of the corner of his eye, knowing Warin approached for having read more into this than met the ear, once more Hector questioned how greatly his brother was affected by Lady Séverine.

Warin loved long and well, as told by how deeply he felt the loss of his wife and his extended absence from England, and from the little Hector had witnessed of the interaction between him and Mace's cousin at the stream, there had been attraction not unlike when Warin met his betrothed.

Returning Mace to focus, Hector said, "Though it is possible we will receive King Edward's response within a fortnight, it could take months." As disappointment sagged Mace's smile, Hector delivered what could move him to behave rashly. "Since you are not done serving in a kitchen to learn the lessons thereof, I believe you should continue at Wulfen."

Eyes wide, he bobbed his chin. "Aye, my lord. Best to await the king's answer at Wulfen. Do we go there this day?"

"Two days hence."

As Hector pondered how long before Mace determined he must inform his cousin of his departure, Fira groaned. "So you leave us again."

He looked to the freckled sister he believed one of those rare women whose loveliness required full maturation—unlike Dangereuse who had come into her beauty by the age of ten and Ondine who was born into it. "As is my duty, Fira, and I am hopeful Warin will accompany me." Seeing his brother's mouth tighten, Hector added, "Even if only to visit Rémy whose training precludes him from journeying to Stern at this time."

"It is a good thing you go, Warin," Héloise said. "I cannot personally attest to the work done there these two years since I am not bold enough to don a cap and steal inside"—she winked at Mace who shot his gaze to her—"but considering how much coin has been spent repairing walls and replacing wooden outbuildings with stone ones, you should see for yourself your family's continuing commitment to keep England safe."

As Warin held his tongue, Hector mused how expensive the work of late, but did not regret the cost of reopening the underground tunnel from castle to wood. Built during the conquest of England and rerouted once, it had served its purpose well. Unfortunately, it was collapsed one hundred fifty years past when the least worthy of England's rulers, King John, succeeded Richard the Lionheart.

Responsible for the loss of many of his family's French holdings and having unjustly, spitefully, and cruelly subjugated his subjects, John had sought to control his rebellious barons by taking hostage those dear to them—the worthiest of sons fostered at Wulfen. Sacrifice of the tunnel had removed the vulnerability that could have prevented the Wulfriths from withstanding the king's siege were its exit in the wood discovered. And it had been discovered—blessedly, too late.

Though many lives were lost defending Wulfen and Stern, both fortresses had held until the barons sent reinforcements and a precarious peace was made with the vengeful John. Had that ignoble king not died shortly thereafter, once more he would have come against Wulfen to try to raze it to the ground.

"You are right, Grandmother," Warin said tautly.

"Of course I am. Now, Mace, as you are the cause of the unbinding of *The Book of Wulfrith,* give assistance in setting the new page and lacing all back together, then we shall have our reading."

From how open the boy's face remained, he was not yet struck by the need to alert his cousin to this day's events.

Hoping when it occurred he would act on it, Hector moved toward the dais to address this day's correspondence and other baronial matters set aside to deal with the sheriff's missive.

Upon becoming aware of being followed, he turned.

He expected Warin to rebuke him for making it difficult to reject a visit to Wulfen, but his brother said, "As you are not given to cruelty—offering hope in such abundance it hurts more when trampled—I suspect the missive received this day moved you to allow the boy to enter Wulfen ahead of receiving permission for his training."

"You are correct." Lowering his voice further, Hector revealed the missive's contents.

"You believe Mace will lead us to her," Warin concluded.

Though he had joined in their earlier search for the lady, seeing an opportunity to exploit his willingness to converse, Hector said, "Us?"

Annoyance grooved Warin's brow. "You know I will give aid."

"But only in this?"

His brother stared.

Sensing he was about to turn away, Hector spoke what further thought would have kept from his tongue, "Because attraction to the lady moves you to champion her?" When resentful silence deepened, Hector posed the question long in waiting, "If not to take your place at Wulfen, for what did you come home?"

As Warin's nostrils flared, Hector glanced at where Fira and Mace worked on the book. Though oblivious to what went here, Héloise was not.

"Though I have unfinished business in Calais, I did return so I might begin taking my place here—to put us back together as much as possible, Wulfrith," Warin finally spoke. "But it is as difficult as I prayed it would not be." With that, he departed.

Hector watched until the great doors closed, then returned to the high table. Ignoring the gaze of Dangereuse who likely knew what had passed between those with whom she shared both father and mother, silently he beseeched the Lord that Warin's admission was some small progress toward a good beginning rather than the beginning of the end.

By way of Cook, little Willa sounded the alarm, making Hector reproach himself for becoming immersed in a dispute between castellans despite Dangereuse's assurance she could resolve it.

If Cook's niece was right, Mace had wasted no time seeking to alert Lady Séverine to his pending departure and was clever enough to do so when the watch over him eased—at afternoon's end when he should be busy with supper preparations.

Instead, he had pleaded illness and Cook had instructed him to nap in the store room. If not for Willa, he might not have been discovered missing, having departed and returned in all the hours before the castle folk bedded down.

Now, dropping to his haunches before the little girl who radiated guilt, chin tucked where she sat on a stool, Hector said, "I thank you for reporting Mace's absence, Willa. As you are his friend, that is no easy thing, but you do right since he could be in danger. I shall depart soon to bring him back, so if you know anything that might aid, I would be grateful."

Peeking from beneath her lashes, she said, "Ravvenborough."

Though previously Hector and Warin had searched the nearby town that in three hundred years had grown from a modest village to the barony's largest settlement, there were so many places to hide in and around it he was not overly surprised the lady could be there.

"That is helpful, Willa. Would you tell how you know it is his destination?"

She looked to the woman over Hector's shoulder, with apology said, "I followed him, Aunt."

"Surely not this day," Hector said.

"Four—mayhap five—days ago."

She spoke of the first time the boy slipped away and was allowed to believe his absence unnoticed. "You followed him all the way to Ravvenborough?"

At her hesitation, her aunt said firmly, "Continue, Willa."

"Aye, and since mostly he ran, I was very tired."

"What did you see?"

She dragged her teeth across her lower lip. "I do not want to get him in trouble, nor Lady Séverine."

Then Mace *had* met with her. "I wish only to help them, Willa. Where did they meet?"

"In the fields. At first I thought it a man Mace called over, but though I could not see well from where I hid, I think it was Lady Séverine wearing tunic and chausses, her pretty hair under a cap."

Once more in the guise of a boy. "Do you know which field?"

"Nay, he went to five or ten before he found her. And once I lost him and..." Her lips quivered. "I was so scared because I did not know how to get home."

"What happened after they met in the field?"

"She went back to work and Mace to Stern." A smile arose. "He never saw me."

"You are certain?"

"If he had, he would have been angry." She made a face. "He does not like when I follow him."

He patted her hands. "You have been helpful. I believe we will bring both back safely."

"Both?" she said, surely like many speculating on what caused the lady to depart without warning.

"I think that best, but we must take into account what Lady Séverine wishes."

Within reason, he silently added and stood. As he advanced on Gwayn, he said, "Find my brother and tell we ride in a quarter hour."

CHAPTER 15

Ravvenborough

Birdsong. Again.

"Ah, non," Séverine whispered.

Hating Mace once more defied her, hoping that was what he did for what it could mean otherwise, she continued down the road toward the town among others following a day's work in the fields.

Shortly, she gasped and stepped to the side. "Accursed pebbles," she muttered loud enough to be heard. By the time she had shaken from her shoe those barely felt, the other workers were well ahead.

Once they went from sight, she hastened across tall grass toward trees from which the birdsong sounded.

When Mace showed himself, his smile was so broad her heart leapt in anticipation of good tidings. Thus, as they hugged in the cover of trees over which dusk cast shadows, she said, "It is true you are to train at Wulfen?"

He stiffened, but when he drew back, much of his smile

remained. "Baron Wulfrith is to seek King Edward's permission, but as he takes me to Wulfen two days hence, he must know his request will be honored."

Though disappointed, Séverine thought this a great stride toward that distant door. "I believe you are right." Then thinking to when he was deemed a man in full, she said, "It is dangerous for you to be here, but as there is no guarantee we will meet again since I depart for France once I am certain your place at Wulfen is secure, we should use this opportunity to better mark in your memory the location of your treasures for when it is time to collect them."

"I recall where we decided to hide the cask," he said, but even had she not sensed uncertainty again, still they would go. He had only seven years behind him, and though she hoped to see him again, much could happen between boy and knighthood.

"Of course you remember, but as I know it is what your sire would wish and it is not much out of your way in returning to Stern, let us go there."

He shrugged, then as if to prove her misgivings were warranted, began moving through the trees in a northeasterly direction.

She drew alongside. "From here we go a bit south and east."

"I know that."

She did not argue. Engaging what remained of this day's strength that would have been spent on cleaning stalls, she increased the pace, certain the sooner this was done, the less likely his absence would be noted.

That haste going hand in hand with optimism and twilight proved their undoing.

"I think that the boy!" someone shouted as Séverine and

Mace crossed a corridor of grass between the lesser wood and the greater wood embracing Lillefarne Abbey.

"Run!" Séverine cried and, seizing Mace's arm, glimpsed the silhouettes of two spurring toward them.

With the last of the sun's light casting itself across the riders' shoulders and over the fugitives, Séverine and her cousin sought to return to the lesser wood that would sooner offer the cover of shadows, trees, and foliage.

It was not soon enough. Barely had they made it inside the tree line than a rider shot past and so suddenly came around his horse reared.

She wrenched Mace back, causing both to drop to their backsides. It saved them from hooves, but caged them between the riders.

As Séverine scrambled to get Mace behind her, digging palms and heels into moist earth, one of their pursuers laughed. "I think this the woman though she makes herself look a man."

There was too little light to identify him by sight, but she placed his voice. Here the oily companion of the one who set himself at Mace in Dover and moved to participate in the attack only after the dagger drew blood.

"Then we have both fugitives," said the rider behind.

When she looked around, she saw the one who must be the port deputy sat loose in the saddle. "The patience and persistence of a hunter, ever the prey's downfall," he said. "Now we have only to name these animals brought to ground." He swept his sword from its scabbard, sidled nearer, and with the sharp point an arm's length from Séverine, said, "On your feet. This deputy who will soon be sheriff wishes a formal introduction."

That he did not know their names confirmed the Wulfriths had held them close, but it was of no comfort. The only comfort was the likelihood a keen intellect was not paired with patience and perseverance since had he thought to check the manifest of the ship that docked that day, he would have discovered the names of the French woman and boy traveling alone.

"Now!" the deputy commanded.

Easing to the side, Séverine got her feet under her.

As Mace remained unmoving, and for how sorrowful his face amid fear, she knew even if later he turned anger upon her, he blamed himself for this just as he had the stable attack.

Keeping the sword in her line of sight, she reached down and touched his arm. "Pray, love, stand beside me."

He set a hand in hers and mostly supported his own weight as she drew him up.

"I am Deputy Le Creuseur," the man said. "Now your names."

She raised her chin. "Lady Séverine de Barra."

"Mace de Chanson, son of Chevalier Amaury de Chanson," her cousin said.

Séverine did not know whether to be alarmed by his defiant tone that would offend, or pleased he did not curl his emotions in on themselves. For as frightened as he was, courageously he sought not to show it.

"Were you English, I would not believe you a lady," the deputy said. "But as all know the French are rustic, one might even say *uncivilized*—'tis believable your countrymen afford you that title."

Lord, Séverine silently appealed, *as feared, already I am condemned and likely Mace. Aid us.*

"You have the one you seek," she said. "Release the boy, and I will go with you peaceably."

He laughed. "Peacefully or nay, you go, as will your accomplice."

"He had naught to do with what happened!"

"Well, that is not what this witness tells." Le Creuseur nodded at the other man. "But on occasion I am reasonable, so it is possible a bargain can be struck."

"Tell me!"

"In due time." He motioned her forward. "You shall ride with me and the boy with Rutger."

"Where?"

"Well, as Ravvenborough is the direction from which you came, we shall start there."

"Start what?"

"You are in no position to ask questions," he said and looked to Mace. "Give Rutger trouble, and what this Frenchwoman did to an Englishman will be done her." He lowered the tip of his sword toward her abdomen.

"Do as he says," Séverine prompted.

After her cousin was on the fore of the man's saddle and a search revealed he was weaponless—Mace likely having surrendered the D'Argent dagger to Baron Wulfrith—the deputy said, "Now you will yield all weapons, Lady. And be warned if I find you have not surrendered all, the boy will suffer with you."

Though she would not risk endangering her cousin by attempting to use her concealed knife now, she had hoped to retain it for whatever opportunity might later present. Feeling nearer the hangman's noose, she raised the left leg of her filthy chausses, removed the knife fixed to her calf, and extended it.

"As that thing's only value is being out of the hands of one who sought to murder my countryman, toss it," the deputy said.

She cast it aside and stepped forward.

"I am to believe that your only weapon?" he scorned.

"I have no other."

"Well, for the boy's sake, I hope you speak true." He slid his sword in its scabbard and reached to her. "Step your foot atop mine."

When he closed fingers over her hand, a shiver went through her, and not because his skin was cold and moist. There was cruelty in that hand, the only surprise that she had not expected to feel the darkness all the way through.

Lord, she sent heavenward, *this gift of fear given all who heed its icy claws tells he awaits an excuse to exact punishment ahead of my end. Pray, help me deprive him of that excuse.*

When she set her ragged leather boot atop his in the stirrup, he yanked her up and landed her between his thighs.

She should have been prepared for the arm slammed around her waist. Mostly she was. She should have been prepared for how invasive the hand searching her. Mostly she was not. She had known those fingers would venture places only a husband should go, but she did not expect him to be so rough and thorough.

If not for Mace, she would have struggled as done the one time another trespassed on her—albeit not to the extent of this man.

Sliding fingers from her boot, he chuckled, then trailed them from her calf to her hip and curled them into the flesh there. "Though aided by loose clothing and being slight enough of breasts to pass as a boy, you are female. And more so you will appear if, as I suspect, you could not bear to cut your hair."

Séverine reached to hold the cap to her head—not to keep hair from tumbling forth but avoid the pain of bound tresses unable to come free—but he slammed his forearm against her hand, causing her to cry out, and when the cap resisted, demanded, "What is this?" Then he wrenched.

"Leave her be!" Mace shouted. "Miscreant!"

As whatever else he spat was muffled by the hand clapped

over his mouth, Séverine ground her teeth against further protest. She did not know what gave first, strands torn from her scalp or the thread, only that it hurt so much she nearly wept.

As unwashed hair fell about her shoulders, he flung the cap away. "Well, you are a clever one, Lady. Certes, you do not cover this mess to hide its beauty."

Not in its current state, she thought and was glad it was nothing to admire lest it tempt him to further exploration.

Winding a swath around a hand, he dragged her head to the side. "But you have potential." His hot breath in her ear made her stomach turn. "Well, we shall see."

As it struck her how often he prefaced what he spoke with the word *well,* as if needed to launch what came after, he released her hair.

Seeing the other man remove his hand from Mace's mouth, Séverine longed to offer her cousin a smile of assurance, but even if he could see it in the dim, he would not believe it.

"To Ravvenborough!" Le Creuseur said and spurred forward.

JAILED. And so law abiding were the town's citizens, only one of four cells was in use—by the two thrust into it this night.

Just as there was some comfort in Séverine and Mace occupying the same cell, there was some in not being out of reach of the family who had granted her cousin protection. However, as there was no way to get word to the Wulfriths, the latter seemed of no use.

The deputy, who obviously possessed greater authority than the town's jailer, had sent away the man before removing the sacks placed over the heads of the prisoners in advance of entering the town. That same authority he had first exercised over the gatehouse keeper when the one who closed up the town for the night had told he must look upon the concealed faces and was refused.

At first Séverine had thought the secrecy was to prevent any from alerting the Wulfriths the fugitives were captured lest it was suspected the family had aided them and would interfere, but were that so, Le Creuseur would have taken his captives from the barony.

Now, leaning forward on the stool he straddled to consider the two on the other side of the bars, he said, "Well, Lady, let us begin with where you have concealed yourselves since your arrival upon Wulfenshire."

Did he suspect they were aided by the Wulfriths? If so, had he the power to bring the law down upon that family for thwarting his efforts?

Beseeching the Lord's forgiveness in advance of speaking falsehoods that seemed the only means of protecting her cousin and keeping undue punishment from the Wulfriths, she whispered, "Remain here and speak naught."

She crossed the cell lit by a lantern in a wall niche behind the deputy and gripped the iron rails. "As we only just arrived upon this shire, we sheltered in the wood out of which you saw us depart."

"A lie! How do I know? Rutger tells when his friend confronted the boy over attempting to steal his horse, that one boasted of kinship with the Wulfriths."

Séverine's heart sank, not because Rutger lied in telling the confrontation was over an attempt to steal a horse rather than their attempt to steal the dagger, but because of Mace's lie of omission in not confessing he had alerted his assailant to his relation with that family. Impatient to gain entrance to

Wulfen, he had known she would not venture here while there was a chance the shire would be searched for them.

Le Creuseur dug thumb and forefinger in his nose, flicked his fingers, then clapped his hands between his knees. "As I am not unsympathetic to the ill-fated, I will let that lie pass—but only one. Now where in Ravvenborough did you shelter?"

Knowing without her aid he could discover that were he to make inquiries or display his captives, exposing her as one who had presented as a man, it became more obvious he wished to conceal exactly what went here. Just as this was beyond preventing the Wulfriths from learning of their capture, this was more than bringing to justice the one responsible for injuring an Englishman.

Let not that more *be the cask,* she thought, though nearly certain of it.

Mace had assured her only the dagger had been seen, but whether that was a lie or he was mistaken, likely the deputy believed wherever they had lodged was where a treasure would be found. For this the two men entered the town ahead of its gate being barred for the night and would have none of the inhabitants know their purpose lest the treasure was compromised.

Affecting confusion, Séverine said, "Since I am in the power of a lawman entrusted with ensuring those accused of crimes receive fair trials, of what consequence where I have been that I no longer am?"

He arched an eyebrow. "*I* am the one asking questions, not—"

"Where is the cask?" Rutger pounced.

Further Séverine's heart sank. It would be hard enough keeping Mace out of the eye of this storm, but the treasures as well? Neither of these men required good intellect to know threat of harm to the boy could yield its location providing she cared more for him than herself.

Thinking it ironic had Rutger exercised control when he sighted Mace, allowing the two to continue onward, they would have been led to the cask, she said, "I would ask what you want with that old box, but as it is long gone, it matters not."

"Gone?" the deputy said sharply.

"Liar!" Rutger snarled.

That she was. "Though mostly it contained items of sentimental value, we kept coins there. However, their number was so depleted that when the box was lost while fording a river, we did not try to retrieve it lest we drown."

"I saw silver in it—a large expanse," Rutger said.

Knowing he had glimpsed the psalter of such value it might be priceless, she scoffed, "A *rustic* would think it that, but it was pewter—the backing of a hand mirror that lost its looking glass years ago."

The deputy narrowed his eyes. "Your lodgings?"

Séverine weighed the truth against the lie. Were she to maintain ever they were on the run, at the worst he would turn violent, at the least present her and Mace to the people of Ravvenborough to expedite the search. If the latter, not only would it be revealed the woman disguised as a man worked the fields and cleaned stalls, but none had seen the boy. Hence, when the cask was not found in the stable, intense interrogation would follow and Mace, whose whereabouts were unaccounted for, would not be spared.

The truth, she decided, though it would only give the Lord more time to decide whether to intercede.

"In exchange for cleaning stalls at night after my work in the fields, I was given a pallet at the stable near the Burly Bear Inn."

The deputy smiled. "Well see, you made that harder than it had to be—unless you lie again." He set his head to the side. "Do you?"

"Ask the owner where his new stable hand sleeps, and he will tell you the loft." Knowing he would also reveal Mace had not been with her, she continued, "There you will find my pack beneath my pallet. But, alas, no cask."

That last was added in anticipation that, like many, he believed the opposite of what was repeatedly denied and would conduct a thorough search, the most time consuming of which would be the hay bales.

Once her claim of the cask's absence was proven, he would be furious, but in the meantime, Mace could rest while she turned over every rock of their predicament, one of which might hide the answer to ensuring his safety.

When Le Creuseur stood and took the single stride to the cell, Séverine jumped back. However, with the speed of a striking snake, he thrust a hand into the cell, captured her wrist, and yanked her forward.

Ache in her chest that slammed against bars.

Pain in her head that connected with iron.

Foul in her nostrils that his breath swept.

A cry in her ears that Mace protested.

Throwing her free hand up behind her, she croaked, "Stay back!"

"Aye, you are safe there, boy, for I have no key to this cell," the deputy mocked.

Rutger laughed, and as he shook that rattling bundle, the one holding her to the bars snarled, "You must know if I do not find what I seek, you and the boy will pay for wasting my time."

Pain bounding from one side of her skull to the other, she forced open blurred eyes. "Just as I know this eve you will not find a cask that is at the bottom of a river, I know there is naught I can do to change that."

He bared his teeth. "For your sake, best that another lie." He thrust her back, and as she staggered to remain upright, both men strode from the room.

With Mace snuffling behind, Séverine strained to make sense of the hushed voices. She could not. All she knew was there was anger about them.

Shortly, both departed the jail, likely neither trusting the other to share what they hoped to find.

Grateful to be out from under their watch though there was no possibility of escape, Séverine touched her throbbing head as she crossed to Mace. Unsurprised by the swelling, she dropped to her knees before him.

Chin down, shoulders up around his ears, he choked, "I hate them, but more I hate me. I try to do good, but always it comes out bad!"

She wanted to protest, but it was obvious what had put them in this position—his determination to wear the dagger that exposed the cask and his boast of kinship with the Wulfriths that brought the lawmen far north. Thus, all she could do was put an arm around him, tell him she loved him, and pray as he wept himself to sleep.

CHAPTER 16

Less than an hour. That was all Séverine was given to make a way for Mace out of the mess for which she was more responsible since she was not a child.

Having heard through the grate set high in the wall the voices of the two returning to the jail, she eased her cousin onto his side to face the wall and drew over him the thin blanket that had been folded upon the cot.

Though it was too much to believe he was so exhausted he would sleep through whatever happened, still she hoped—and to that end stood center of the cell when the door in the outer room creaked open.

As she waited for Le Creuseur and Rutger to appear, once more she considered the two things that might keep Mace out of harm's way, the second of which was her greatest hope. If she must resort to it, she would fail Sir Amaury in leaving her cousin's future less secure, but better that than Mace's fate prove the same as hers.

"As told, the cask was lost," she said when their persecutors appeared.

The deputy swept a hand toward the other man, indicating he should proceed no farther, but Rutger did. Halting before the bars alongside the lawman, he demanded, "Where is it?"

She raised her chin. "I do not wonder about your character, it being obvious. What I question is your hearing—and lack of respect for Deputy le Creuseur." She looked to the one of greater danger. "Now it is established I spoke true, ere you take me to Dover I would have you send word to Baron Wulfrith that his ward who was sent on an errand to Ravvenborough has been detained."

He knew of Mace's claim to kinship with that family, but she expected some surprise over her confirmation and much surprise over the extent of her cousin's relationship. Mace was not truly a ward, but the protection afforded him and responsibility taken to gain King Edward's permission to train him was nearly the same.

Though her intent was to make the lawman more cautious in dealing with her cousin, scornfully he said, "This your answer to the foolishly uncooperative stable owner who revealed you lodged there alone?" A chuckle rolled from his throat. "Either Baron Wulfrith spoke false when he claimed he knew naught of the fugitives, else the boy gained employment in his household and its lord is unaware he harbors a criminal's accomplice."

"Mace de Chanson is his ward!"

"Holes in your tale!" He jutted his chin at Mace. "A Wulfrith ward—a mere boy—charged with an errand requiring him to travel the demesne unsupervised?" He stepped nearer the bars. "Even were I wrong, since none know we have him, we can do with him what is required to recover the cask."

Fear raking her, she said, "I say again, it was lost in the river. And were it found, naught of value would be gained."

"There I may be wrong as well, but only a fool possessing the means of testing the verity of a malefactor's claims would not do so. Too, great my need for what the cask holds—"

"Your share of it!" Rutger corrected.

The deputy inclined his head, then ordered, "Open the cell."

Séverine lurched back, but there was nowhere to run, only Mace to protect from whatever punishment was believed would yield what they sought.

As the key scraped the lock's innards, she accepted her cousin's future must be rendered less secure and exclaimed, "I will tell where the cask is—will take you to it."

"You will not!" Mace shouted as the door swung inward. "It belongs to me."

No sinking of the heart this time, but sharp pain. At seven years of age, more greatly he feared losing his treasures than the possibility of not living long enough to make use of them. Despite how they had survived since Calais and his regret for the mistakes made since arriving in England, still he was not well versed in consequences, nor did he grasp how frail the thread of life.

With the men advancing on her where she stood between them and her cousin, she looked behind at Mace as he dropped his feet to the floor. "Be still," she entreated. "We do what we must to—"

A hand gripped her shoulder and snatched her aside.

"Non!" she screamed as Rutger lunged at her cousin. Struggling against the deputy, she swept fingers toward his face and scratched his cheek.

Naming her something foul, he propelled her against the bars between this cell and the next. Her back landed against iron, and as she opened her mouth to drag in breath, past his shoulder she saw her cousin evade his pursuer.

"Release me!" she cried and tried to thrust a knee between the deputy's legs. The press of his body too close, she could only watch as Mace was caught by the back of his tunic and wrenched off his feet.

"Do not do this!" she cried above the boy's shout of rage. "I have said I will take you—"

Le Creuseur gripped her jaw, digging fingers and nails into flesh. "So you will after given a taste of the consequences of further deception. But fear not. Though Rutger believes hobbling the place to start"—at her gasp, he smiled—"I prefer small increments that leave an informant with just enough hope to keep apathy from rendering him or her useless. So... which hand does the boy prefer? Right or left?"

Another gasp.

Another smile.

"Since most favor the right, we shall begin with the left as a show of goodwill."

"Non!" she shrieked as Rutger dropped her cousin onto his back.

The shouting and writhing boy was straddled, his torso and right arm clamped between calves. Then his left wrist was pinned alongside his head and a knife appeared in the man's other hand.

Séverine pleaded and, failing that, sank her teeth into the soft flesh between the deputy's finger and thumb.

He punched her ear, causing tearing pain to render her as helpless as Mace in preventing the barbarous thing being done him. Non, more helpless—and blessedly so she saw when a bellow moved her wavering gaze past the deputy's shoulder to Rutger who fell to the side and collapsed.

As evidenced by where he clutched himself, what she had failed to do to Le Creuseur, Mace had done to the false witness.

Then her cousin was on his feet. And moving the wrong direction.

"Run!" she cried as the deputy thrust her to the side.

Head reeling, she lost her balance. As her shoulder hit the floor, her little savior slammed into the deputy's legs as if it were possible to topple him. It must have been like running into a wall, for he rebounded and would have fallen onto his back had not the miscreant caught his tunic and flung him across the cell.

As his arms and legs flailed like those of a disjointed puppet, Séverine screamed, and when Mace landed near the bars, she cried his name and struggled onto hands and knees to get upright. Hardly were her feet under her than her arm was seized, then she was down again and sliding across packed dirt that scraped cheek and jaw.

"French whore!" Le Creuseur spat.

Lifting her head, seeing Mace remained unmoving three feet distant, she called to him and pressed palms to the dirt. She got no further, the booted foot that slammed into her ribs dropping her. Then something landed center of her spine.

Amid wavering consciousness, she realized it was his knee when his head came alongside hers. "Just as you are about to learn a most painful lesson, so will the boy once Rutger can stand again."

She should have been terribly frightened when he wrenched at her tunic, but nearly all fear was reserved for her cousin whose head seemed at a peculiar angle.

"Mace!" she croaked and tried to dig fingers into the earth to drag herself out from under her assailant. "Mace!"

The deputy forced her head down, grinding into the dirt the ear he had punched. "Be still!" he shouted so near that all other sounds were muted.

Struggling to remain conscious and keep Mace in sight,

uncaring what happened to her out of sight, she continued to call his name—more than anything needing to see movement. But there was no evidence of the slightest breath.

THE BOY'S name screamed over and over felt a rope about his neck.

Hector, Warin, and their squires had pushed their mounts harder after encountering the jailer half a league from the town walls, that man having departed to alert the baron of the usurpation of his authority to detain and oversee the care of those who disturbed the peace. However, Séverine's cries portended if aid did not come too late, then late enough that already ill was done her and the boy.

After correcting his course to avoid trampling townspeople come out of their homes in response to the din, Hector dragged on the reins and was out of the saddle with his sword unsheathed before his mount's hooves stilled.

Warin was equally efficient, his shoulder brushing his brother's as he dropped back to yield the doorway.

What they saw upon entering the room at the rear made both bellow above the cries of the pinned lady who futilely reached to the crumpled boy—until her assailant pushed up and brought his sword to hand.

"Rutger!" the deputy warned the one limping toward Mace. The man's pain evident, Hector guessed what Séverine had failed to do to Le Creuseur she had first done to the witness, whether before or after what had befallen her cousin.

For naught? That question cut through him as he swung against steel that deflected his blow. Was Mace badly injured? Perhaps dead? Was Séverine severely injured? Ravaged? Might death averted later claim her?

Anger seeking to color all red, preventing him from seeing even the grey needed for heart and body to emerge as whole as possible from a bloodletting, silently he recited the lesson dealt by his sire and uncle, *Allow not wrath to command your actions nor words. As is your calling before God and man, protect those weaker of body and mind. Be worthy of your name!*

Grounding his feet for his next swing in close confines, Hector saw Rutger snatch up the boy as if to make a shield of him.

Warin swung, slicing the man's back and causing him to cry out.

Hector arced his blade up, averting the deputy's attempt to sever his sword arm.

Mace was released to the ground and a spasming Rutger went to his knees.

Hector brought his sword down and sank its edge into Le Creuseur's thigh.

The miscreant howled and lurched.

The sobbing Séverine crawled toward her cousin.

The deputy slashed as he fell backward—and caught Hector in the neck and across the collarbone.

More stung by lowering his guard than the opening of flesh that could be the end of him were it the blood of the great vein moistening his skin, Hector was flashed with remembrance of Sir Owen standing over him.

How many times must I say it? he had barked as he pulled his nephew to sitting and thrust at him the sword sent soaring. *Ever be aware of what goes all sides of you, but when life is at stake, deal first with the most immediate threat.*

It was what Hector expected of those he trained, and this day had done—until he had not. In the time it took to look nearer on the lady than necessary, he was cut. Hence, the lament of old—given the chance, women turn men from their purpose.

He growled, brought a boot down on the deputy's blade-wielding arm, tore the sword from the man's hand and dagger from his belt, and tossed both outside the cell in the path of the squires coming behind their lords.

Straightening, he swept his sword to the man's chest and, struggling against the longing to thrust it deep, clapped his other hand to his bloodied neck. Of greater interest than the wrath and pain on Le Creuseur's face were scored lines on one side—fingernails, the weapons of a nearly defenseless woman.

"I have him, Lady!" Warin called.

Assuring himself his tunic would be soaked were he in danger of bleeding out, Hector looked around and saw his brother land a kick to Rutger who reached for the boy, then sweep up Mace and stride to the cell door. Though surely the impulse had been to aid the woman first, Warin had correctly assessed the situation.

But now another. With knife in hand, Rutger began dragging his injured body across the space separating him from the lady.

Though she had risen to her forearms, as if no more was required of her with her cousin out of harm's way, her head hung, mess of hair curtaining her face.

"Attend, Séverine!" Hector shouted and, bringing his sword around, commanded the two entering the cell behind Warin's exit, "Secure the deputy!" Then he lunged toward the woman slowly lifting her head.

He did not know Rutger's exact intent, only that the man with little hope of surviving the injury soaking the back of his tunic was more likely to spend his last breaths on vengeance than seek salvation for the afterlife. Hence, when that rusted blade was within range of Séverine, Hector severed it from the arm that drew back to deal a blow.

Had the injury done the man by Warin not ensured his passing, that done by Hector did.

Amid the shouts of Le Creuseur being secured by the squires, Rutger rolled to his back. Gulping air, he gripped his wrist with his remaining hand.

Before the pooling crimson could mark Séverine more than the flecks had done, Hector loosed his sword and scooped her from the floor.

He had known she, once more clothed as a man, was slight of figure and anticipated her injuries would be more felt when she was lifted, but he had not expected how little effort was needed to get her quaking body aloft nor that whatever was done her would set her to weeping. Of greater surprise was how much was required to keep hold of her when she began struggling as he carried her from the cell.

As if her pain was naught compared to fear, she thrust her hands against his chest. "Let me down!"

Tightening his hold on her, becoming more aware of moisture on his neck and the likelihood of greater bleeding, Hector halted before the cell door. "He is safe," he spoke what might not be true, Warin having removed the boy who could prove beyond unconscious.

"Providing he lives!" the deputy snarled. "Does he, I shall ensure the accomplice of one who sought to murder an Englishman hangs as well."

"Gag him!" Hector commanded the squires as the lady fought harder amid gasping sobs.

Though Hector knew much of what wrenched at her was emotion, in those sounds of misery was physical pain. Lest she worsen her injuries, he said loudly, "I do as you ask, Séverine. Be still and I will put you down."

When her struggles eased, he lowered her but did not release her, certain she would not stand on her own for long.

He was wrong in that she could not stand at all. With a muffled cry, she turned into him and gripped his tunic. When she raised her face, shifting hair revealed abrasions and the flushed skin of a jaw cut with crescents. Just as she had marked the deputy with her fingernails, he had marked her. And there would be bruising.

"Mace's neck," she whispered, tears traveling her face. "It looked twisted."

Not to him, but he had not been as near. Hoping she had seen wrong, and he would not be responsible for the loss of another innocent life, he said, "Warin has him. Be assured, he will be well tended."

"Then he is...?"

"He but needs rest." Were that a lie, it was warranted in her fragile state.

She sighed and her lids lowered, but as he started to lift her again her brown eyes sprang wide. "I am so grateful you came for him. It would have been very bad had you not."

Emotion tightening his throat, he said, "The boy is kin."

"Oui." She leaned more of her weight against him. "Also of D'Argent blood."

Once more, something in him moving toward her that had moved toward no woman in a long time, he said, "Lady, I must take you from this place."

She nodded again, and he glimpsed another injury. Tempted to beat the deputy senseless for her swollen ear, Hector started to return her to his arms.

"You bleed!" she cried.

The fingers she set on his neck were so light, they should have felt only a winged pest—all surface, no depth—but again, the forbidden in him moved toward her. Resenting it, he said sharply, "Warriors bleed, Lady."

Her gaze flickered. "I did not mean to make trouble for you. I just had to..." She shifted her regard to where still he felt her touch, then slid fingers through his whiskers. "Our savior then and now, though you were not so bearded in...Calais." Her lids fluttered, forehead dropped to his chest, and before what little that kept her upright ceased to do so, she rasped, "I thank you."

This time when he swung her up, she did not weep with discomfort nor pain. But it would be waiting for her on the other side of unconsciousness.

"Bring him!" he ordered the squires.

Then hating it was not possible to make the return journey this eve for the necessity of Séverine and her cousin being tended by the town's healer, dealing with Le Creuseur and the demise of his witness, sending word to Percival, and arranging for a cart to deliver the injured to Stern, he carried the lady from the jail.

CHAPTER 17

Barony of Wulfen

Light. Not candlelight. Not lantern light. Sunlight. And what flashed gold against her lids was wonderful—until a deep breath of grass- and heather-scented air caused pain to pierce her chest and receding consciousness to blot out the brilliance.

"Stay," she whispered and, trying to raise her lids, became aware of movement beneath her. Identifying the roll and jostle of wagon wheels, she turned her attention to sounds beyond those of birds passing overhead and bustling insects. There were horses ahead and not only those drawing the wagon, and one—perhaps two—alongside.

Gold once more penetrating her lids, cautiously she drew her next breath lest the discomfort of expanding lungs drag her back to the black. Then she forced her eyes open and, peering into the sun, snapped her head to the side. More pained by the ear onto which she rolled than the glare, she would have turned her head opposite if not for what she saw.

He was there, guiding his horse alongside the wagon in which she lay under a blanket behind the driver's bench. Eyes on her, gaze so intent she felt a curiosity in need of thorough study, she lowered her lids and turned her head away. So great was the relief of relieving pressure on that ear, she began moving toward sleep, but some of what had happened in a place of bars returned to her.

Again she looked around, this time not so far as to put weight on that ear, and saw a white bandage encircled his neck and was stained with dried blood.

It was then she recalled what came before he lifted her in his arms and drew her against his chest, and that was followed by swiftly appearing and disappearing memories—or were they hallucinations?—of her cousin seated beside her on a mattress, hand gripping hers, lips forming words.

Pained by a sharp breath, she entreated, "Mace! Tell me... " Her voice muffled one side of her, she filled her lungs to increase her volume and nearly whimpered over the effort. "Pray, tell he is well."

"He is well, Lady."

Did he lie? Had a grave been dug for the one thrown across the cell whose head had seemed at an unnatural angle?

"Show me!" she demanded, but her mouth and throat were so dry, even she was not certain of her words. Struggling onto her elbows to search for Mace, she sobbed when pain whipped around her chest and back.

"Warin!" Baron Wulfrith shouted, and as Séverine fell back to rustling straw, drew his horse near the wagon, stood in the stirrups, and dismounted. When the weight of what was poured into tall boots made the planks creak and he lowered to his knees beside her, she could barely breathe.

As he took something from his belt, further movement to the right drew her regard, and she saw the young man who had admitted Mace and her to Wulfen. Holding the reins of his lord's horse that must have been passed to him, Squire Gwayn urged the beast to drop back with his own mount.

"Be at ease," the baron said. "My brother has taken charge of the boy and delivers him hither."

In advance of proof Mace was well, she longed to thank this man who had coldly sent her cousin and her from Wulfen, to kiss his hands, and speak whatever promises were required to see her cousin trained—even if never again she saw the one she had raised. Of course, that last was probably a given.

Séverine did not know where the deputy was. What she knew was the prejudiced law of England was not done with her. Eventually, she would stand trial and pay a high price for defending a child set upon by an Englishman.

"You are dry, Lady. I will raise you, and you will drink slowly."

Across a tongue that felt wrapped in wool, she said, "Please."

As he slid an arm under her, more vividly she recalled when the one whose Christian name she did not know had held her following his miraculous appearance in the cell. Safety in those strong arms as she wept. Comfort against a solid chest. The longing to stay there forever—until struck by the need to get to Mace.

Now as he raised her, pain once more streaked her side, and she jerked.

Peering into her face, he said gruffly, "Fractured ribs, one of several ills done you. It will be weeks ere you can move well and gain a full breath without discomfort."

As she stared into green eyes shafted with grey, her memories sharpened further. "He kicked me."

Carrying a wineskin to her mouth, so greatly a muscle at his jaw moved that the thick of his beard could not conceal it, then his teeth disappeared behind lips pressed tight. Though what she had revealed was nothing over which to smile, she wanted his face that only presented as serious or disapproving to be acquainted with curves beyond his full lower lip and the peaks of the upper.

Not that my own is conversant with smiles these past years, she thought. *And may never be again.*

"Drink, Lady."

She closed her lips around the spout and, raising her gaze, found her face reflected in his eyes. It was a fearful thing to delve the yearning for him to see himself in hers, so she did not, but she kept her eyes fixed on his throughout each swallow. And wondered at his given name.

"That is enough." He withdrew the skin.

As he eased her down, sidelong she saw Sir Warin bring his mount alongside. She turned toward him. Painfully aware of that ear, she looked from the handsome man lacking his brother's dark, silvered hair to the small figure before him about which there seemed no movement.

"Mace? What is he—?"

"He sleeps again," Hector said.

She shot her gaze to his. "Again?"

"Look nearer."

She did. Head back, mouth open, Mace's shoulders rose gently.

Returning her regard to the baron, she asked, "Truly, he is well?"

"Not entirely."

She had feared that, but the threat to burgeoning hope made her demand, "What say you?"

His eyebrows pinched, and she thought he was too offended to answer, but he said, "Upon regaining consciousness after Warin brought him out of the jail, he told his head hurt and he was stiff in the neck but seemed otherwise unaffected—indeed, insisted on sitting with you for a time."

Then no hallucination that. Mace *had* sought to comfort her. "But?" she prompted.

"Ravvenborough's healer determined the blow he sustained was forceful enough to warrant close observation and ordered rest with frequent awakenings. Though twice in the night he vomited, not since. Hence, the worst may be past."

Reliving more of what had happened, she said, "When he tried to defend me and that miscreant flung him across the cell, I feared his neck broken."

The baron hesitated over something, said, "The boy is strong. Mayhap the D'Argent of him, hmm?"

There was so much assurance in those words, she nearly wept. "The De Chanson made of a D'Argent," she said. "I know for me this is only reprieve, but tell me Mace is safe from Le Creuseur and that other man."

"Rutger is dead. Warin having set that stage, I dropped the curtains over it."

It was wrong to be relieved a man had lost his life, but it was one less person to harm her cousin. "The deputy?"

"He remains in Ravvenborough so the injury I dealt him is tended and he can be thoroughly questioned by Wulfenshire's sheriff whom I summoned last eve."

"What of when the sheriff discovers I was taken from there?"

"Having arrived this morn and begun his investigation with testimony from me, Warin, our squires, Mace, and the jailer, he is satisfied you will be at Stern where he can question you once you are recovered."

Stern. Wherever she was taken afterward—likely Dover—at least she could heal and regain her strength near Mace and among those of honor. Even if they took the precaution of locking her away, it would not be as bad as a jail.

Tears spilled. "I thank you, Baron," she said and wished she knew his given name as she did that of another owed gratitude. Looking to his brother, she rasped, "And you, Sir Warin."

He smiled slightly, inclined his head, and urged his horse ahead.

When Séverine turned back to the baron, he said, "Your ear pains and sound is muffled that side."

Swallow dry, she nodded, then raised a hand and fingered her lower face. Scratches and cuts dealt by the deputy's nails were there and bruising for how tender those places.

"He was hurting me, so I bit him and he punched my ear. He threw me to the floor and kicked me, then put a knee to my back and..." Though fairly certain of what had not followed, she ceased prying at that memory. "I do not recall much afterward."

Again the muscle moved beneath his beard. "I ordered the healer to fully examine you to ensure the sheriff was aware of all that transpired that should not when one is in the custody of a lawman."

Heat moved up her neck.

"It is believed you were not violated, Lady."

"I did not think it, though had you not come..."

"Your ear is quite swollen," he shifted the conversation to what was speakable. "Last eve and this morn, the healer drained a large blood blister to relieve pressure. May I look?"

Thinking how strange it was he tended her and wishing such attention did not draw her to him, she nodded.

When he hooked fingers around the back of her jaw and turned her face toward him so that ear was up and her eyes on lower thighs whose muscles were encased in dark blue cloth, she shivered.

She had not realized a bandage covered her ear until he removed what passed up over her crown, down beneath her chin, and up again. As he dropped it, she glimpsed upon it blood stains like that on the cloth binding his neck.

"How were you cut?" she asked as he leaned in to examine her ear.

"Carelessness. The wages of not heeding a lesson taught me."

"What lesson?"

"Against allowing a woman to turn me from my purpose."

As silently she rued what she had done, he probed tender flesh. "More blood gathers, Lady. Though less than before, if it is not drained, permanent damage to your ear's appearance and hearing is more likely."

She did not believe he sought permission but said, "Then I would have you lance it."

What looked approval flashed in his eyes, and he called, "Driver, halt!"

When the wagon stilled, she turned her head to present her ear and saw him draw the jeweled dagger.

Heart beating faster, struck by the longing to hold to him, she dug her fingers into her palms. But as he moved the blade toward her ear and his other hand followed, she snatched up his fingers.

He tensed. "There will be pain, Lady, but it should not be great since the skin is stretched very thin. Indeed, releasing the pressure may cause relief to be felt more than any sting."

She did not think he spoke false, but though she told herself to release him, her fingers tightened.

"To ensure you remain still and the blade goes only as deep as needed, I require both hands," he said brusquely.

She lifted her chin. Seeing disapproval in his eyes, she

commanded herself to loose him, instead heard herself say with desperation, "What is your name?"

His brow furrowed. "I require both hands, Séverine."

Telling herself it mattered not he knew her Christian name as she did not know his, she nodded. And held on.

He muttered something, twisted his fingers up into hers, and drew them to just above his knee. "Hold there."

Still she resisted doing as commanded, though for a different reason. The meeting of hands could lead to intimate things, but her palm on his lower thigh seemed already an intimate thing for one who did not know his—

"Hector," he rumbled, the shadow he cast over her deepening as he leaned so near she saw the lines in his lips. "I am Hector. Now hold to me."

"Hector," she said and liked that his name was nearly all breath. "Of the Trojan War."

His mouth curved. "Hector of Troy slain by Achilles."

"Slain, but that city's most valorous warrior." Remembering more, she added, "One of The Nine Worthies."

"What those of France call *Les Neuf Preux*," he revealed he was aware his namesake was among the historical and scriptural princes esteemed for personifying the ideals of chivalry, others being King Arthur and Charlemagne. "Now hold to me, Séverine." Drawing back, he pressed his hand over hers.

Though she could not get her fingers around that muscular expanse, she dug into it, then felt a sting that became a burn, next moisture and the release of pressure.

"You are with me?" he asked as he dried her ear with a cloth.

Keeping her eyes closed, she said, "I am with you." She liked the sound of that though the meaning this bumping heart assigned to it was different from what was meant.

Realizing how quickly she had moved from dislike of him

to this, silently she prayed, *I am thinking and feeling wrong, Father mine. Quickly heal this injured body that renders mind and emotions vulnerable. Soon I shall be gone from Wulfenshire, and it will be hard enough abandoning the part of me that is one with Mace without leaving behind a part that cannot be one with Hector Wulfrith. Do I, what remains of me will be so very lonely.*

"Séverine?" When she opened her eyes, he said, "Good," as if fearing she had lost consciousness. "Now as my leg has served its purpose, return its use to me and I shall bandage your ear to keep pressure on it and reduce swelling. Then I will give you more drink and you will rest."

She snatched back her hand, causing her elbow to jostle fractured ribs. Seeking to conceal her discomfort, she asked, "How long ere we reach Stern?"

As he began applying a clean bandage likely the healer had given him for the journey, he said, "Since we make slow progress, it will be hours."

She was to blame, and though moved to apologize, she sensed he wanted only to distance himself and anything that delayed that was unwelcome.

Once more anchoring her against his chest, he said, "Drink."

She told herself to keep her eyes averted, not to seek her reflection in his so he might be reflected in hers, but when he tipped the wineskin, she saw herself. And thought it a good thing after all. Her reflection was not distinct, but had she any hope of him finding her pleasing to the eye, she would have saved herself the disappointment.

The mess of Séverine de Barra was suited to the guise of a young man of labor.

Chapter 18

Stern Castle

She had thought to never again see this chamber. She had *never* thought to find herself in this bed. As far from a jail cell as possible. As near a privileged lady as she was not.

Had she suspected this a dream, the deep breath straining healing ribs would have dissuaded her. Drawing slower, shallow breaths, she sent her gaze all around, lighting on the garderobe's door, an unshuttered window through which dusk's light shone, the screen concealing the companion's bed, the hearth, and the clothes cupboard.

She was alone. Grateful to have time to herself before once more facing a Wulfrith—likely several—and assured Mace was safe, she groped backward for what came after the one who had tended her in the wagon yielded the name of *Hector*.

There was naught between that and her arrival at Stern, and the latter was indistinct—except for the arms lifting her from the wagon, the pillow made of a muscular chest, and the scent of a man unaccustomed to idleness—a mix of perspiration, salt, and something she did not know that might be him alone.

She backed up her thoughts. Salt had no scent. Then—?

It had not been in her nostrils. With her face turned to his chest, drawn breaths had put the salt of him on her tongue. Though it disturbed how much he affected her, she could not deny his masculinity comforted—and the thrum of his voice, albeit clipped amid those belonging to his sisters.

Vaguely recalling his ascent of the stairs and being lowered to the mattress, she wondered how much Ondine had protested having a fugitive in her chamber as well as her bed. And why had her brother so greatly trespassed for the sake of one for whom he had little care?

"It matters not," she whispered. "Just be grateful for this reprieve." That she would do, holding close what time was given her to heal and prepare for what lay ahead.

Séverine raised a hand from beneath the blanket and touched her bandaged ear. It was tender, but she felt no blister in need of draining. However, she had other pressing needs.

Easing her head to the right, she saw pitcher and cup were on the bedside table, hopefully the latter filled to make it easier to answer one need. As for this other need, since relieving herself required crossing to the door that was visible unlike its neighbor that accessed the wall passage, much discomfort ahead.

Though she knew it best to visit the garderobe before quenching her thirst, once she elevated herself, the cup was too tempting. It was half full, and the wine infused with herbs so quenching, she drank all of it.

When she returned the cup to the table, dusk was slinking out the window. Unless someone brought light within, soon she would be in the dark.

Moving slowly, she lowered her feet to the floor. As expected, much discomfort. As feared, pain in making her way forward, largely due to how quickly she moved as the need to relieve herself became more pressing.

When she exited that place of privacy, she did so in anticipation none would witness she wore only her tunic. It had hurt to get the chausses down, but that had not compared to getting them up. Thus, she had let them drop despite what would be thought of her when they were found on the floor.

Closing the door, she considered the darkening chamber, then started forward. She meant to return to the bed directly, but as she passed the standing mirror behind which that other door was concealed, she was tempted to look upon what Hector had seen.

Do not, she told herself. And turned in front of the looking glass. Even lengthening shadows could not hide how right she was about the mess of her. And she shuddered knowing how kind this dim reflection compared to what earlier filled the eyes of the one who had once more saved her.

But there was marked improvement about one thing. Bared legs previously concealed beneath shapeless chausses were of credit to the woman of her. Fine calves. Well-turned ankles. Nicely-shaped feet.

Returning to the face around which the bandage was wound, she grimaced. Even at the end of the siege, she had not been this distant from pretty. Although no longer gaunt, her face was dirty, abraded, cut, and bruised. A bath like the cooling one enjoyed when Ondine finished with hers would not remedy this, though it would benefit hair that had never been so fouled.

Disgusted, she forgot the frailty of her beaten body and swung away, causing her head to lighten and pain to turn around her chest. Had that not been enough to drop her to hands and knees, her gasp ensured it.

Jolted by the impact, she whimpered, then determinedly brought the floor into focus and commanded, *You will not be found down here. You will get yourself to bed, and no one will know hopeless vanity put you here.*

Counting each breath to keep her mind from drifting and to distract her from her aches, she rose. And once more was beset by the sensation of spinning.

As she gripped the mirror, the door behind opened and light swept in.

So vexed was she at being found like this, she almost cursed. Were it Hector, she might yield to that ungodliness, but likely it was the kindly Esta who might no longer be kindly to the deceitful Séverine.

"Lady!" barked one who ought not be here. "Your machinations nearly render my patience speechless." Boots sounded and veered toward the bed where she heard the scrape of metal on wood that told he set the lamp on the table.

She wanted to protest the ill believed of her, but she was learning the imprudence of moving ahead of much thought. Since she was caught out of bed and there was no hiding she wore only a tunic, she would let her grudging savior come to her.

HECTOR STRODE to the lady who sought the wall passage, which she must now realize was impossible for the necessity of holding to the mirror to remain on bare feet beneath bare legs he declined to look near upon. It was inappropriate enough he entered here knowing she was alone, but that she was out from under the covers and barely clothed...

However, when he saw her white-knuckled hold on the mirror, he set aside thoughts of what was inappropriate and took hold of her arm. "Fool woman! Determination is admirable in the absence of foolishness. In its presence, it is pathetic desperation."

She lifted a very pale face. "I fell," she whispered.

And furthered her injuries? "Almighty! In such a state did you truly believe you could depart Stern unseen and on foot?"

Her eyes widened. "That is what you think? Garbed in naught but a tunic I sought to escape?"

Did she not? Considering his experiences with her thus far, it seemed a fit, especially since previously she had made covert use of the wall passage. But if she spoke true, for what was she so near the concealed door when she could not possibly wish to stand before a mirror?

"The garderobe," he muttered.

Face coloring, she said, "Much needed."

He berated himself for assumption that impeded an accurate assessment of the situation, then said, "I apologize for not coming sooner. Though Fira who kept watch over you this last hour alerted me you began to stir and I instructed her to join the others at meal, I was waylaid."

By that accursed owl, he thought. Despite Ondine's dedication to returning it to flight, would the creature disappoint her? Would it never vacate their home?

If not for tolerance of seemingly frivolous impulses that were due her more than Dangereuse and Fira, Skyward the screecher would recuperate elsewhere and never again must this warrior retrieve *the poor thing* whose attempt to fly from the upper room had stranded it on a ledge.

Unfortunately, women were not the only ones capable of turning a man from his purpose. Guilt was as accomplished, and when it went hand in hand with a sister whose life had been devastated by his actions—

"You wish to speak with me further?" asked the woman who also stirred guilt for what befell her and the boy that would not have had he dealt with them differently at Wulfen. Despite all presented to support Mace's claim to kinship, as Hector had been exceedingly occupied, impatience had afforded them little more time than other claimants. And that *little more* was due to curiosity over the missives shown him and those things that had remained concealed.

Many times since Mace confided the reason for the attack on him and the lady and that the cask was sought by the deputy, Hector had questioned if initially he would have been more receptive to appealing to King Edward on the boy's behalf had Séverine not been deceitful. Always the answer was the same—very possible.

As a result of the annulment of his second marriage, he had become sensitive to the deception of women. Even his third wife, of whom he had been fond for her great innocence, had not escaped prejudice that caused him to closely examine her words and actions. Séverine's error had been impersonating a man to enter Wulfen. Hector's error was in taking it too personally.

"Will you aid in returning me to bed?" she rasped. "My legs are unsteady."

And he was inconsiderate, the strain on her evidenced by how much of her he supported.

As he leaned in to lift her, hastily she added, "I need only your bracing and direction."

Because she was averse to being so close? Or thought him averse? Certes, he was, though not for the reason likely believed by one who, though she gave him little reason to be attracted to her, once more caused restrained desire to test its moorings. More strange, it was not all desire.

Lord, I do not wish to be acquainted with such feelings again, he silently beseeched. *I know my mind, and You could not make more clear Yours toward me and plans for the continuation of the Wulfrith line. Pray, do not scatter more rocks on my path. It would be an ill thing to grow more weary of life than already I do.*

"Please, Hector," Séverine hissed, his given name causing his heart to kick his breastbone.

Hold to your purpose! he silently demanded of the shamed warrior, then put his other arm around her shoulder and turned her toward the bed.

It was not slow-going, Séverine moving her legs in time with his and providing little proof of discomfort though it must be felt. Were she one training toward knighthood, words of praise would be due her.

He eased her around. When she lowered to the mattress, the hem of her tunic rose to reveal knees above shapely legs above dainty feet—and brought to mind when the yielding of his Christian name in the wagon caused her to grip his lower thigh. Both his hands had been needed to drain her ear, but his solution had been a poor one.

Wishing what she stirred in him was all due to the long absence of intimacy with a woman, he swept his eyes to hers and saw questioning there.

"I thank you," she said and momentarily considered his bandaged neck. "Why am I in Lady Ondine's bed? She cannot be pleased—"

"It was my sister's suggestion."

She blinked. "Why?"

"Isolated as she is, Ondine is loyal to the few friends she has."

"But I am not that to her. I am—*was*—a maid. And companion in name only."

Though uncertain of his reasoning for what next he spoke, he said, "Then become more to her. Prove yourself worthy of her good regard. No matter how shallow hers may be, I assure you it is genuine."

She tipped her head back further, swayed. "Forgive me, Baron, but I am confused."

Telling himself it was good she used his title again, he said, "Lie back."

She shifted around and eased her legs onto the mattress. Once she settled into the pillows and he turned the covers over her, she said, "I do not understand how I can be well regarded by your sister."

Recalling his grandmother and siblings gathered in the hall before the meal, he settled into his heels. "I can make no promise of what the outcome will be when you stand before your accusers—and that you must do for a chance at a life worth living—but as our family is persuaded what you did was in defense of Mace, your cause has become ours."

She gasped so loudly it must have hurt. Then tears brimming, she smiled.

Discomfited by a show of teeth he had not expected to be so straight and bright, he continued, "That is what I wished to speak to you about, though there is another thing of import."

As with one whose experiences have taught her there is a cost for kindness, wariness smote her smile. "Oui?"

Regretting he could not prove her wrong in this instance, he said, "I speak of the bishop's ring your cousin gave into my grandmother's keeping."

The soft fleeing her eyes, she said sharply, "And?"

Annoyance flared. After all, Mace had told she had yielded to the deputy's demands, agreeing to reveal the cask's location.

Not the same, he told himself. Having been assured she was among friends, now she feared they were of the grasping sort. And he could not deny his grandmother was eager to delve the contents.

"We must retrieve what you brought to Wulfen."

"That is the price for our cause becoming yours?"

"Hear me, Séverine—"

"Hear *me,* Hector. We will pay it since we are without choice just as when Le Creuseur sought to gain the cask. But do not think me so fool to believe our cause is yours when conditions must be met that deprive my cousin of an inheritance I have done all to protect since the day—"

Her outpouring ceased, and when her lids dropped, he guessed she recalled the aid given her at Calais that allowed her to keep hold of precious things that would have become spoils of war—just as could have been her fate.

She raised her lids. "If Mace will not show you the place we chose in advance lest the cask must be hidden—and he may not since he is determined to keep what belongs to him—I will take you. Just give me your word he will be trained into a warrior, even if you cannot gain your king's consent for it to be done at Wulfen." She swallowed. "And if you can aid in my defense against wrongful charges, I would be grateful. God willing, I shall be judged innocent and return to France. If not, the end is the same—you are rid of me."

Hector had listened. Now he was done listening. "If you have finished trampling my family's honor, it is time *you* listen to what will more likely gain King Edward's permission than the missive earlier sent him. Indeed, if played well it may extricate you from punishment without standing trial."

Interest flickered in her eyes, and across a cracked voice, she said, "I listen."

Hector lifted the pitcher and poured drink, then with brief

contact between their fingers, yielded the cup. As she drank, he lowered into the chair last occupied by Fira.

Settling the cup against her chest as if to make a shield of it, Séverine said, "I am ready to hear what you would tell."

Hector leaned back, the length of the legs stretched out before him requiring his booted feet and calves extend their reach beneath the bed. "This day, you and your cousin have been the subject of discussion between my brother and me and others of our family. It is decided once you have given a full accounting of what happened in Dover and Ravvenborough and the cask is inventoried, a missive will be composed to our king."

"Another one?"

"Aye, and of greater interest. Edward will learn the guardian of the kin who seeks training is the same who stands accused of attempted murder and theft and whatever other charges the deputy brings for Ravvenborough—and for which Warin and I will be held accountable for the death of his witness. Your defense and ours will be presented, and to ensure the king takes a personal interest, he will be informed of Mace's inheritance. I believe he will be interested in the Godwine brooch and the missive of Countess Gytha, both of which evidence your cousin is descended from King Harold from whom Edward's ancestor took England."

"And much interest in the bishop's ring."

He inclined his head. "If none offer temptation enough for Edward to give ear, it is possible other items, of which Mace is reluctant to speak, may." He raised his eyebrows, indicating this was the place to reveal what else was in the cask, but she averted her gaze.

When finally she looked back, only a glimmer of wariness remained. "Forgive me for disparaging you and your family. Our journey has been long with danger lurking around every other corner. Lacking a protector, it is hard to be a woman and a child in this world."

Struck by the thought of becoming that not only to Mace but this courageous woman, he said, "Understood, Lady. Now what think you of the plan?"

"Though it could rob my cousin of his inheritance should your king take possession of the contents, if it gains Mace training at Wulfen, better his chances in this world without his treasures than with them and lacking the ability to defend himself."

"You think right. However, if Edward does wish to add those items to his collection, I am certain Mace will be compensated."

"For the ring as well? I ask because, from what I know of the tale, it is believed stolen from William the Conqueror's brother, Bishop Odo, when Mace's ancestor freed the woman he loved from that man. Hence, without compensation your king may claim what he considers a family heirloom."

"It is possible, but if nothing else, your willingness to relinquish it may dispose him to intercede for your cousin and you."

She sighed. "It seems we have no choice." Before he could move her to reveal what else the cask contained, she said with a slur he guessed the result of herbed wine, "Unless Mace wishes to see me, I would like to sleep."

"As he remains at rest in Warin's chamber, the morrow will be soon enough."

She startled. "He has been given your brother's chamber?"

"Nay. A pallet was laid for him there to ensure quiet between awakenings."

"But he improves?"

"Though tired, he is otherwise well."

She sank deeper into the pillows. "I thank you."

"Thank my brother who is the one who made room for him."

"When next I see him," she murmured, "as I shall thank your sister for making room for me here."

He raised his eyebrows and, more lightly than intended, said, "You see, not all Wulfriths are heartless."

Her blink measured, she looked to his bandaged neck. "You make it sound as though I should be wary of some of your family." Her mouth curved, transforming her ravaged face into one nearly pretty. "Though once I believed *you* heartless, no longer. So, which Wulfriths *are* without heart, Hector?"

Wishing she would not use his given name, certain soon the medicated drink would render her senseless, he drew in his legs, stood, and took the cup loosely pressed to her chest. "Once I have looked at your ear, I will leave you to your rest."

Her lids dropped.

Hoping were it necessary to drain the blister she would sleep through the discomfort, Hector set the cup on the table and moved the lantern to the edge to cast more light on her face. Then he turned her cheek into the pillow and lifted the bandage. The ear remained swollen and livid, but no further blood pooled beneath the surface. Pleased it did not require another lancing, he refit the bandage.

"Which of the Wulfriths ought I be wary of?" she breathed.

He stilled and, peering into nearly vacant eyes, guessed she would remember little upon awakening. "I believe most would agree, including my family, best you remain wary of me."

"But just as you are Mace's savior, you are mine." Her lashes fluttered. "So valorous, Hector of Les Neuf Preux."

He would have ignored medicine-induced adoration had she not set a hand on his jaw. Though her palm was barely felt through his whiskers, he was very aware of her fingers on his cheek and thumb at the corner of his mouth. Fighting the temptation to look closely at her lips, he said, "I am glad to have been of aid, but reverence is more due God who made all align and me His instrument."

"You are right." Again she looked to his neck, this time her hand followed. When she touched the bandage, he was further disturbed in a way he did not wish to be. "Only of flesh and blood," she said.

Only. It was a word that did not sit well with this warrior, nor what sounded disappointment. But what next she spoke hardly compared. "For it, the mighty Hector Wulfrith fell victim to another's blade."

He told himself her thoughts were muddled and she did not mean to offend, but his dignity had been scraped raw over Le Creuseur nearly ending his life. More deeply feeling what would take time to heal, he growled, "Even saviors have the right to bleed."

"They do." It was more mouthed than spoken. "I am grateful you deemed me...deserving." Then her lids closed and the hand at his neck dropped to the mattress.

He should have withdrawn, but he lingered over one who looked a trampled daisy but would surely straighten the bent stem of her when night gave unto day.

Yielding to impulse, he touched the injuries done her face and traced the curve of lips that should not tempt.

"Lord," he rasped and, as he straightened, was struck that this scrap of understated femininity named him a savior when Mace would have been lost to death or poverty if not for her. Such character was what he sought in those trained at Wulfen. A pity Séverine de Barra had not been born a man.

Or was it? questioned the man drawn to her. Before he could remind himself he was not destined to grow old with anyone firm at his side, the door opened and Ondine entered on feet that had too little liking for the floor to give much warning of her approach.

Though Hector did not care to be caught standing over the sleeping Séverine, he knew were he to withdraw immediately, his sister would make more of what he did here. And so he held.

"I did not expect to find you within," she said and softly closed the door.

"As you are aware, there were matters I needed to discuss with the lady, and I did so ere Cook's herbed wine took hold."

Her veil down around her shoulders as he wished ever it would be—and believed it could be were she unshakeable enough to ignore what others thought—Ondine crossed to his side. "Only now she returns to sleep?"

Only now being relative, he said, "She does."

She considered the woman who had served as her maid, and when she raised her chin, the face he believed beautiful despite its flaws dealt his heart another tear. "I was so frantic over Skyward, I neglected to thank you for retrieving him."

When he inclined his head, she murmured, "Of late, many birds with broken wings come to Stern."

"We do seem to draw them."

She sighed. "Do you truly believe you can save her, Hector?"

This man *only* of flesh and blood? he wondered, then drew his sister to the door. "I did not say I could save her. What I believe is she has a good chance of being absolved of the crime if we proceed as planned."

"Warin believes the same, and I wonder if he may prove more determined than you to see the lady acquitted since he is attracted to her."

Muscles once more straining against bones one side, skin the other, Hector said, "He has barely met her."

"Aye, but the last time I saw him warm quickly to one with whom he was initially cool was his betrothed."

And so devoted had Warin been to the lady he wed, still the loss of her was felt, Hector reflected on what had put a wall between brothers who had been close. Now here someone else who could build the wall higher.

No sooner did he think that than he rebuked himself. Despite attraction, he had no claim on Séverine and would not seek one—and more resolved he would be if his sister did see more of Warin than he had.

Did she? Before Hector had shown himself at the stream, he had noted his brother showed interest in the lady, bestowing smiles that might have been half-hearted flirtation, but that was all. However, had Hector witnessed his initial, indifferent reaction to the lady, perhaps he would have drawn the same conclusion as Ondine.

It does not concern me, he told himself before being struck by something that made him rethink that.

Were his brother partial to Séverine and she was acquitted and receptive to his attentions, a union with the lady could reestablish Warin's ties to Wulfenshire—providing she wished to remain in England. Had she no cause to flee, would she not stay near Mace?

"What are you thinking, Hector?"

"That I would give Warin good cause to stay and finally take his place here." *And be my heir,* he silently added as he looked to the one beneath the covers he would never have considered for the mother of a future Baron of Wulfen. "She may be the good cause we require. Though there is reason enough to rouse King Edward to her side, there might be further reason of benefit to our family."

"A replacement wife," Ondine breathed.

Her choice of words pricked, but it was truth. He doubted

Séverine could be to Warin what his first wife had been, but if in some measure she replaced the one whose loss Hector was responsible for...

"Albeit a wife of scandalous proportions," Ondine noted. "However, it would not be the first time a Wulfrith refused to allow society to dictate the reach of his—or her—heart."

Indeed not, he concurred. She, Rémy, and Fira were proof of that, the three born of their sire's second marriage to a woman deemed entirely inappropriate. And the love not given Hector's mother had been gifted his stepmother.

Not that their sire's first wife would have minded much, her own love nearly exclusive to God who was denied her undivided attention when she was plucked from the convent so her sire could make good on her betrothal to the Baron of Wulfen though she wished to take holy vows.

"Not the first time," Hector agreed and, recalling the tale of his ancestor who wed the first lady who dared enter Wulfen in the guise of a male, wondered if that history was ripe to repeat itself.

It had been an act of desperation to save Annyn Bretanne from the cruel one promised her hand in marriage by King Henry II. Though Garr Wulfrith had come to feel for the deceiver, he had taken a chance on feeling more by putting a ring on her finger in defiance of his sovereign.

As Séverine de Barra's fate could prove worse than being forced to wed one likely to abuse her, Hector entertained providing the same protection—rather, the protection of Warin whom he wished to succeed him. But that would require pressing his brother to do something that could leave him twice widowed if the lady did not escape punishment for her offense. Then not only would Hector be responsible for the loss of another of Warin's wives, but set his brother on his own path of wedding and wedding again.

Ondine mewled with amusement. "Our brother knows not our plans for him, but—"

"Not plans," Hector said. "Consideration only. I will not put thoughts in his head he would otherwise not allow there. With Lady Séverine's cooperation, we proceed as planned, and if his attraction becomes something more, he alone determines the extent."

A mischievous smile dissolving, her eyes moistened. "It is more than three years, Hector. Though once bitter me, determined to blame anyone other than myself, was well with you punishing yourself like those misguided flagellants who believed the cure for the pestilence was scourging their bodies, you must know I no longer feel that way."

He did, though little of it was spoken these two years since the bare civility to which she subjected him eased. What he did not know was why she had any reason to avoid blaming herself. Since she was the first of their family struck down by the pestilence, did she feel responsible for those who fared far worse? She could not have known death had entered her and breathed itself into loved ones and retainers as she flitted among them until symptoms appeared that caused her to be removed to the hunting lodge just as done his squire—and one by one others.

The guilt of survivors, he named it that with which he was most familiar, then set a hand on her shoulder. "I am glad to be forgiven as much as possible, but I know the blame lies with me alone. Hence, there is no comfort in you or others sharing it."

She averted her gaze.

"What is it, Ondine?"

"A day too long," she muttered, then quipped, "And little prospect of good sleep in a bed not my own."

It was more than that, but when she raised the drawbridge

and dropped the portcullis on her true feelings, not even a well-planned siege could lower one and raise the other. Which was not unlike Dangereuse.

"I will leave you," he said and, at the door, looked around. "Should I send Esta to sit with Lady Séverine so your rest is uninterrupted?"

"Nay. If she requires anything in the night, I will see to it."

"Then good eve." He closed the door and, traversing the corridor, wondered again how his sister was able to move with so little disturbance of even the air. It was as if she had left the realm of the living long ago and some small part of what she had been lingered.

If not for all her scars, more he might be given to such fanciful thought, but Ondine Wulfrith was quite real, quite sad, and quite lonely.

"God help her," he rasped. "And God help me help Séverine de Barra."

Even if it means her becoming my sister-in-law, which I do not want, he silently added. And refused to think on what he did want since it had no bearing on the life to which he was committed—and God surely ordained.

CHAPTER 19

Séverine wanted to believe the kindnesses shown her since awakening to find Lady Ondine bedside were genuine. But it was safer—and less hurtful—to doubt, especially when something was sought from her.

Following last eve's exchange with Hector, which shamed for remembrances of touching his face and neck and naming him her savior, she wanted to trust him. However, the light of day, less discomfort, and thoughts no longer fogged by herbs made her question everything as was her duty to Mace.

Now as Esta helped her from the tub, Séverine looked to Ondine who ordered the bath for her former maid when she insisted on dressing to receive Mace so he not guess the extent of her injuries. Sitting before an open window outside which rain gently fell, the lady bent her head to a psalter.

Too much kindness shown you, experience told Séverine, tempting her to scathingly assure both women that as long as Mace's future with the Wulfriths was secure, they need waste no time nor effort on one who had agreed to give the cask into their keeping.

"I see the lady again," Esta said as she plucked a towel from a nearby chair, voice muffled for being spoken on that side of Séverine from which the bandage had been removed. "Once your ribs are not so tender and you can be laced into a gown of good cloth and proper fit, even more the noblewoman you will look."

That nearly slipped past Séverine as she stepped into the towel's embrace. Wincing over shifting ribs, she said, "You do not speak of my gowns. Even were they not with the cask, they would be considered of poor fit and cloth."

A snap of the psalter sounded, next a creak of the chair. "Hence," Lady Ondine said as she stood, "we shall go abovestairs and delve long unused garments to secure a gown that can be freshened and altered for you if needed." She halted before Séverine. "Until then, you may wear one of mine."

"Nay, my lady," Esta said. "You are taller and fuller of breasts. One of Lady Fira's gowns will fit better."

Annoyance skipped across Ondine's brow. "As my sister is set on fording dirt, mud, and water, hers are plain so she waste no moment on changing clothes."

"I am well with plain," Séverine said.

"I am not. As you are solely my companion rather than maid now, plain will not do. Too, when you stand before your accusers, they must see a gently born lady."

Séverine gripped the towel closer. "This is the day I stand before them?"

"Of course not. You have much healing to do. It is only that one should start as close as possible to where they wish to end up."

There was sense in that, and though Séverine suspected there was something more to it, she said, "Then do with me as you will to sooner reunite me with Mace."

It took an hour to put Séverine together for how careful

they were to avoid paining her ribs and ear. And the results were admirable. After her hair was toweled, it had been combed and brushed until further removal of moisture restored its golden color. Next, the upper waves were parted on one side to provide a curtain for her disfigured ear and her lower curls picked apart to add fullness to hair skimming the middle of her back. Then a flesh-colored ointment was patted over her face to lessen the appearance of scrapes and bruises.

Though Ondine's light green gown had to be closely laced to accommodate smaller breasts and a wide belt fit low, beneath which excess length was tucked, never had she looked more a lady.

"Easier to catch a man's eye now," Ondine said where she had stepped behind Séverine after drawing her before the mirror.

Surprised by those words, it was her eye Séverine sought to catch in the mirror, but the woman's gaze was on the gown loaned her companion. "I thank Esta and you for setting me aright, my lady. Now if you would send for Mace—"

"Nay, as you are up out of bed and your cousin belowstairs, that is our destination." Before Séverine could protest, Ondine turned to Esta and said, "With rain upon us, likely my brother is in the hall. Fetch him so he may carry the lady down."

Séverine gasped. "I would not disturb Baron Wulfrith."

"As 'tis Warin I speak of, you will not."

Less disconcerting, but still bothersome. "Provided I move slowly, I need impose on none."

"As Warin would be pleased to aid you, it would be no imposition."

Suspecting Ondine had given some consideration to this, Séverine said firmly, "It is kind to offer on his behalf, but I prefer to go slow."

Ondine gave what seemed an indifferent shrug, and when they departed the chamber, led the way.

There was discomfort traversing the corridor and descending the stairs, but Séverine found relief in holding her breath between sips of air.

Before they reached the hall, voices were heard, not only of Hector's siblings and grandmother but him.

Beat not so fast, she silently commanded her heart. *You wear yourself out for naught.*

The Wulfriths were not seated before the immense fireplace. As she and the two women came off the stairs, drawing their regard, Hector and Warin rose from an upholstered bench in a large chamber beyond the dais.

Though Séverine had noted great carved panels behind the high table, she had not known they articulated open. Doubtless, it was the castle's original solar, centuries past separated from the hall by ceiling to floor curtains that mostly offered visual privacy to the lord and his wife.

In France, when renovation of aged castles allowed for relocation of the lord's bedchamber abovestairs for greater privacy, many solars were converted into communal space to enlarge halls where lords conducted business and gathered family and retainers for meals.

It followed the same was done in England, though the Wulfriths had made theirs a place for private gatherings, likely because their existing hall was of considerable size. That was as Séverine concluded until she ascended the dais and saw what had appeared the back wall was a screen far larger than the one enclosing her bed in Ondine's chamber.

Were sleeping accommodations here? This yet the lord's solar where the baron slept while in residence and would one day make a family with a lady suitable for continuing the Wulfrith line?

Heart squeeze not so hard, she warned again as she crossed the threshold. *You have no right to regret what is not yours to regret.*

"You look better than expected, Lady Séverine," said Lady Héloïse who remained seated beside Dangereuse, a wolfhound at their feet, then gestured to the chair Ondine was to take in the absence of Fira who likely searched for other rumored treasures now the bishop's ring was believed recovered. "Sit beside me."

Séverine looked to the brothers standing to the left and hesitated over what might have been glimpsed on Hector's face and was seen on Warin's—something like the admiration shone on her by the smithy's son well before she yielded a kiss.

As Ondine moved toward her brothers, Séverine halted before the imperious old woman. "My lady, I know there are things you wish to discuss, but first I would see my cousin."

"He is in the kitchen," Dangereuse said.

Séverine landed her gaze on one of glossy black hair liberally streaked with silver. "But he took a blow to the head. He should not be working."

"He is not," Warin said.

She looked to him and saw the brothers had lowered to the bench with Ondine between them. Despite the latter's unveiled countenance, she looked a bird of beautiful plumage sharing a ledge with two uncommonly handsome gargoyles.

"Having become bored with our talk, Mace told he wished to visit with little Willa," Warin continued. "Fira accompanied him."

Bored, indeed, if he sought the company of she who annoyed.

"Sit, Lady," Héloïse said and patted the chair.

Séverine was cautious in lowering, but when the belt rode up and rubbed her ribs, she caught her breath.

"Appearances deceive," the old lady said as Esta moved to stand over her mistress's shoulder. "You suffer."

"I am well enough, my lady."

"Then while we await your cousin's return, tell what happened in Dover."

No surprise. What surprised was Séverine was not better prepared to relate what had entered every pore of her memory that day. Because she had ceased to perseverate on it, she guessed. There had been so much to occupy her since arriving in Wulfenshire that though memories rushed her now, the words to describe them were so muddled it was difficult to distinguish the beginning from the middle from the end.

"Lady?" Hector prompted, and she startled to find him before her, a goblet extended. At her hesitation, his mouth curved slightly as if he recalled what she had spoken under the influence of herbs that eased more than her pain. "Not medicated. Only unwatered wine."

Feeling watched all sides, she accepted it and was so distracted by his gaze she did not avoid his fingers.

One should not have to consider that, it being but the innocence of hands in passing, but this man affected her in ways that made little sense—until she was struck by what should have been obvious sooner. This was infatuation, which was surely natural to feel for one who had saved her from things that ought to be unthinkable—and more natural for how handsome he was. And unattainable.

Hoping he had neither seen nor felt her shiver, she said, "I thank you," and raised the goblet.

He straightened, then as if he had felt her response, crossed to the relatively small fireplace, added more logs, and provoked the flames to burn brighter.

"So observant, my grandson," Héloise murmured, voice barely heard for being spoken on the side of Séverine's injured ear. "And considerate though Wulfrith's responsibilities are of such weight he has no time for himself."

Séverine lowered the goblet. "I appreciate his kindness."

The old woman adjusted grey braids coursing her chest. "Mace has shared what happened following your arrival in England, assuring us it was an accident that led to the man's injury. However, either some things he does not recall or he withholds—perhaps one as much as the other since he is young and quickly becomes defensive when pressed for details."

Wondering how much he had been pressed and wishing she had been present, Séverine said, "Of course he does not like speaking of those events."

Were the lady offended, it did not show though Dangereuse gave a grunt of disapproval.

"I am sorry for what you and Mace suffered at the hands of my countrymen," Lady Héloise said, "but if we are to aid, we must know what he did not tell."

Only then did Séverine wonder at the old woman leading the inquiry, though not long. Like Hector, she was commanding and sharp of mind, but being a woman as well, thereby deemed less threatening and more sympathetic, she might expedite the gathering of information.

Determined to trust the Wulfriths as much as possible, Séverine said, "The day that turned ugly was beautiful when we came ashore at Dover." She moved her gaze to Dangereuse, next Warin and Ondine, last Hector who leaned against the stonework.

Wishing his eyes on her did not matter the most, she continued, "Having learned to be observant and vigilant after the siege of Calais deprived us of our home, I noticed two men astride who paid much attention to disembarking passengers —though not in the way of those come to greet travelers. My cousin and I fell to their regard, but a woman of middle years and her grown daughter held their attention. I feared for them, but more I feared for Mace and me. When the men went the same direction as the women, we hastened to the dockside stables the ship's captain told would be the place to purchase a horse for our northward journey."

She replenished her breath. "Since Mace was tired and slow to adjust to trading water for land, I settled him near the stable doors and within sight. After much time spent choosing what I believed a horse of good age and health, I saw it saddled. However, as I led it forward, I noticed its stride was a bit uneven. Hoping it was but a stone, I checked its hooves. And let down my guard." She swallowed. "I do not know all would have been well had Mace not taken a D'Argent dagger from the cask, but had those who stealthily followed us rather than the two women doubted they chose their victims well, that valuable weapon assured them their efforts would be well rewarded."

She moistened her lips. "When I heard Mace cry out, I looked and saw one of the men attempting to wrest something from him while the other watched from astride his horse outside the stable. I ran, and when I yanked back my cousin, he dropped something. Seeing it was the dagger they struggled over, I thrust him behind and sought to retrieve it, but his assailant reached it first. I know I should have taken Mace and gone, but all I could think was the thief meant to deprive him of his inheritance and would try to take the rest had he seen the cask. Thus, I set myself at him and got my hand around his on the hilt. As his friend shouted encouragement, he wrenched back, and I stumbled against him." Remembering warm moisture on her hands, fingers beneath hers loosening, a shout paining her ears, she closed her eyes. And startled when fingers closed over hers.

"When you are ready," Lady Heloise said.

Once more Séverine looked to the others. Settling her gaze on Hector, she asked, "These things Mace told you?"

"Mostly."

"Did he...?" She trailed off.

He raised his eyebrows. "What, Lady?"

"If he told you he was holding the dagger when it bled the man, it is guilt speaking for him having exposed the cask."

"He did not claim that."

"Good." She drew another breath her ribs protested. "I recovered my balance and jumped back, and what I saw was so horrible, I nearly retched. The blade was in Mace's assailant."

Hector strode to her, and she realized he had taken control of the interrogation. "Horrible and yet you fled only after pulling the blade from him?" At her gasp, he dropped to his haunches. "Such things will be put to you by those who shall determine your fate and will believe you guilty for being so unfeeling. How will you answer, Lady?"

"With the truth."

"The truth being that so great was your need to recover the dagger, you forgot how horrified you were and drew out the blade."

"That is not the truth!"

"It is as told me by Deputy Le Creuseur and his witness. What is your truth?"

Feeling shoved into a corner, she said, "I wanted to pull it free, but I could not bring myself to do it. As his companion dismounted, I snatched up Mace and our possessions. When that one—the deputy's witness—came for me, I swung the packs, and that which held the cask staggered him long enough for us to get astride. As we exited the stable, I grabbed the reins of one of their horses to better ensure our escape. It is true I am responsible for that man's injury in part, but impulsive theft is my greatest crime."

He narrowed his lids. "In my possession is the D'Argent dagger Mace had on his person when you fled Stern. Thus, you cannot have left it in his assailant."

She blinked. "I can have and did since my cousin has two daggers, one that belonged to Hugh D'Argent, the other to his son, Maël—the lost D'Argent."

He searched her face. "Mace did not speak of a second dagger."

"Of course he would not. He does not trust easily."

"Have you proof of two? Has anyone seen both?"

She glowered. "I dared allow none to know of the cask and its contents."

"Then you cannot prove there was a second."

Ribs aching more for her tension, she said, "No proof." But remembrance made her catch her breath.

"Lady?"

"The cask holds two scabbards, both worked with the same initials found on the daggers' blades—*HD* and *MD.*"

Hector frowned. "Since no scabbard was in Mace's possession, I assumed it lacked one."

"They are in the cask."

"Why there rather than protecting the blades?"

"Long ere his inheritance was entrusted to me, they suffered deterioration from exposure to moisture. What stitches remain barely hold."

"You seem to have an answer for everything."

Offended, she snapped, "Is that not usual when one speaks in truth?"

"And when one is accomplished at deceit."

She sprang out of the chair. Ignoring protesting ribs, she

said, "When you possess the cask you so desire, you will see I speak in truth!"

Body brushing hers as he regained his height, he said, "Calm thyself!" and turned a hand around her arm. "As told, I put to you things requiring answers, regardless of whether you go to trial or the king intercedes."

Trying to remain as aware of their audience as she was of him, she sought to gain control of herself by taking the long way to his eyes—moving her gaze up his neck, chin, mouth, and nose.

It was of no aid, and possibly of detriment, making her more aware of him in places they touched. And those they did not.

Alarmed by the longing to lean into him and once more feel his chest against her cheek and hear his heart, she snatched hold of defensiveness like a drowning woman taking the first rope within reach though it came from below rather than above.

Pushing to her toes, she set her face nearer his. "It sounds more than that, as if because desperation caused me to deceive you and your family, it renders me capable of a brutal attack when it was only defense and an attempt to prevent theft that ended in great misfortune."

His nostrils dilated. "Hear me, Lady."

Wanting *him* to hear her, she leaned in. "Were I not French and did not my pursuers believe great reward would be had in overtaking me, they might not have given chase though injury was done Mace's attacker—"

"Lady Séverine!" When he set her back against the seat's edge, she realized how near she had been for how distant she now felt. "You rile yourself for naught. As told, we stand your side, which we would not do if we thought you guilty."

It was hard to hold his gaze, especially for how much she

was drawn to his mouth whose breath fanned her brow and swept down her nose toward her lips.

"Just as trust is difficult for Mace, I know it is for you," he continued. "Thus, all I can do is assure you my family's intentions are honorable."

Fatigue sweeping Séverine, she sank a little. "I wish to believe you."

"Then we will get there, Lady." He firmed his hold. "I apologize for pressing hard. Despite appearances, I know you are far from recovered."

She moistened her lips. There was little thought behind it, and yet it seemed purposeful when his gaze lowered to them.

Séverine did not know why she took hold of his tunic. She had given him cause to steady her, but her legs were not buckling.

"If you are to remain here with us," he said with less warmth, "best you sit."

Us... Having forgotten Hector and she were not alone, grateful he provided her an excuse to take hold of him, she nodded and began to lower.

"Not what Ondine was thinking, is it, Grandmother?" Dangereuse murmured.

Before Séverine could ponder that, a wonderfully familiar voice called to her. Looking as if naught had happened to him in the jail, Mace appeared behind Hector and was followed by Fira.

Holding her gaze to him as the youngest Wulfrith veered toward her siblings on the bench, she said, "I am much recovered, Baron. I can stand on my own."

He released her, and when he stepped aside, the small feet of the boy who aspired to become a warrior halted in the space formerly occupied by the sizable feet of a renowned warrior.

Though Séverine sensed Mace wished to fling his arms

around her as done when he was very little, whether moved by rare joy or frequent uncertainty, he did not. Either he told himself he was too old or he had been warned against jolting her.

He considered her, expression wavering when he paused on her lower face whose injuries could not be entirely hidden—unlike the ear concealed by curls which caused her to tilt her other ear forward to compensate for the muffled side.

"I did not know you were so pretty, Séverine, nor that you could look so much a lady."

Was it good those were the first things of which he spoke? It must be, and were she able to hug him, she would.

"For this, you could not fool Baron Wulfrith into believing you a man." His mouth curved. "From the beginning he knew—"

"Not the beginning, boy," Hector admonished. "But soon enough to minimize the damage your cousin did."

Mace turned wide eyes upon him. "Aye, my lord."

"Know you the lesson in this, Mace?"

He shook his head.

"I believe you do, but here the words you are to put to memory. Unless asked of you and you have cause to trust the one who asks, do not speak for others."

"I will remember, my lord."

"You will," he said and strode to the bench where his siblings—save Dangereuse—gathered.

Mace looked back at her and pulled a comical face that surprised. It would offend Hector, but it delighted Séverine who knew how rarely he was moved to lightness of heart.

He will flourish at Wulfen, she thought. *When the matter of me is resolved one way or the other, all will fall into place.* And that meant the cask must be retrieved and as many of its contents as possible given into the keeping of the Wulfriths for when he was old enough to do with them as he wished.

"Mace, we must—"

"I was worried for you," he said in a rush.

More grateful for what Ondine and Esta had done to ensure a semblance of good health, she said, "As you see, I am much improved."

He was slow to answer, and it bothered that at seven years he was accustomed to searching a face to verify the truth of words, but it was survival and would serve him well throughout life. "Oui, but they might have killed you, and all because I led them to you."

"You could not have known that. But what *I* know is that in seeking to protect me, you were brave."

"Not brave enough."

"Not *big* enough. One day you shall be and, like Baron Wulfrith and his brother, will aid those who cannot protect themselves." Seeing doubt in his eyes shift toward determination, she said, "Now tell, how does your head fare?"

"It is sore when I touch it." He looked to the left. "But easily remedied when I do as Sir Warin tells."

Following his gaze, she skipped over the eldest Wulfrith where he stood beside Fira, and paused on Ondine who had veiled her face as if the scars were so frightful Mace must be spared. Heart aching for the young woman, lastly Séverine considered the second brother. "What does Sir Warin say you ought do?"

He laughed. "Not touch it."

"Good advice." She reached to him, and he set his hands in hers. "As I am assured your knighthood training will be overseen by the Wulfriths, and I trust them—"

"You do?" he interrupted, then as if they were not watched, said with urgency, "I want to, and I do some, but..."

She squeezed his hands. "I think we are right to have faith in the Wulfriths. They are your greatest hope."

"Mine, but what about yours?"

Her throat constricted. He loved her, but the helplessness of youth that caused him to think foremost of how he was affected sometimes made her feel little more than protector and provider. "Baron Wulfrith believes some of the items in the cask will bring the King of England to your side, possibly even mine."

He bit his lip. "You want me to show him where it is hidden."

Father mine, she sent heavenward, *do not let the Wulfriths fail him.* "I do."

Emotions waxed and waned across his face, then he looked to Hector. "I will show you."

Pleased he would have what was needed from the boy, Hector said, "Cloudless skies or pelting rain, we go on the morrow."

"Oui—er, aye—my lord."

"You appear well enough to aid Cook in the kitchen. Are you?"

Séverine caught her breath. "But he is—"

"Lady, allow the one whose training toward knighthood begins with serving as a page to answer for himself."

Mace's expression moving toward offense veered away. Hector's words a reminder of that to which he aspired and would be privileged to attain under the Wulfriths, he stood taller. "I am much recovered."

"Then hie to the kitchen."

When he was gone, Séverine turned to Héloise. "I am tired. With your leave, I will return abovestairs."

"We are enlightened enough for one day," the old woman said. "Esta will accompany you."

"As shall I." Ondine rose and lowered the veil Hector had been glad she had not worn when first she entered the hall. Though it was surely for Warin's benefit she had covered her face at the stream, not so when she joined the family here in the private gathering place that had been the lord's solar centuries past, a portion of which had been transformed into a sleeping chamber last year when it became difficult for Héloise to negotiate the stairs.

As the three women descended the dais, Hector noted Séverine moved more slowly.

Fighting the impulse to assist her, he watched as she crossed the hall and, once more between Esta and Ondine, began her ascent. Further she slowed, then slapped a hand to the wall.

Hector started forward, but Warin was on his feet and moving past, and it was his name Ondine called to give aid.

Better him than me, Hector told himself as his brother pounded across the hall.

Though Séverine protested, soon she was in his arms.

Better his than mine, Hector firmed his conviction that had faltered even when he pushed hard for her full accounting of Dover. Though no beauty, she had nearly looked one following Esta and Ondine's ministrations, and he had told himself it was for that he was mostly moved, but it was not.

He was not indifferent to the lure of women fine of face and body, but ever such attraction was secondary to what was in the eyes and reflected in words. For such, he had chosen his third wife and might have come to feel deeply for that innocent had he not lost her so soon.

He ground his teeth. Since the arrival of the pestilence across Wulfenshire that, though quick to depart, devastated his family and people, guilt continued to fall in folds about him. Though less weighty than once it had been, it became more so when he visited Stern.

Aye, if Séverine is to have the chance of a good life, better with Warin—or another—than me, he reiterated, then feeling the need to be astride, descended the dais.

"Hector, we must speak," said his all-seeing grandmother.

Not wanting to be seen more than already he was, he did not falter.

"Is it to be a run in the rain?" Dangereuse asked, though she needed no answer since she herself enjoyed riding when the heavens opened, providing what fell was not chill.

"May I join you?" Fira called.

"Stay!" he barked, longing for peace within that was hard to attain at Stern. Neither was it easily had at Wulfen, but there he had fewer reminders and distractions aplenty. There he filled his emptiness by training England's future protectors and subjecting his own body to rigorous routines. True, each day he had to be filled anew, but better that than be filled with the things of Stern that bubbled and roiled. Things that now included Séverine.

When the porter swung open the door, Hector stepped into softly falling rain. "Rain harder," he rumbled and made for the stable.

CHAPTER 20

She slipped out of his hold as easily as he had slipped her into it, causing her to miss the strength and feel of his arms—though not as she missed his brother's. And when Warin straightened from the bed, she wished when Hector looked upon her thus, that smile was known to his mouth.

Though attracted to this knight who might be more handsome than his brother were one partial to flaxen hair, what Séverine felt was of less depth. And it was not because she had known one longer than the other.

Hector Wulfrith is far from known, an inner voice reminded as his brother continued to look upon her with...

Was it expectation? Not only had he done her a good service, but she picked her gaze over him. And now in his eyes was what seemed admiration that did not fit feelings she had for another.

Fearing her scrutiny was believed flirtation, with less warmth than deserved she said, "I am thankful for your aid."

His smile wavered. "Is there anything else you require?"

"I—"

"Stay, Brother!" Ondine drew a chair near. "While Esta and I straighten the chamber, keep the lady occupied."

Her tone and urgency told something was afoot, but Séverine's mind was too frayed to delve it and her body too desirous of sleep. Thus, when Sir Warin started to lower, with a sharp edge of desperation she said, "I do not need occupying."

Ondine stilled and the knight looked to his sister.

"Forgive me, but I wish to rest," Séverine said.

Now he was the one lacking warmth. "Then I shall leave you to it."

"Though the day is hardly begun, it has been long for the lady," his sister said with apology. "Once she has slept, I am sure you will enjoy conversing one with the other."

Sir Warin inclined his head and departed.

Ondine drifted down into the chair and set her head to the side, causing silken black hair to bend into the elegant curve of neck and shoulder. "Having envisioned that in a different light and confident I left no shadow unturned, I am disappointed."

Though Séverine longed to burrow into the pillows, she shifted to sitting. "How have I disappointed, my lady?"

Ondine glanced at Esta who put order to the chamber disarrayed by efforts to make Séverine presentable. "You ought know Wulfrith is determined not to wed again. Hence, Warin will become his heir—*if* he remains. If not, our youngest brother, Rémy, who trains at Wulfen will be his heir."

Feeling as if caught doing something very wrong, Séverine said, "Of what concern mine whether your brother weds again?"

"Of greater concern than I thought, but I am fairly observant, and this is what I observed—Wulfrith makes your mouth go dry, skin warm, heart beat fast."

"My lady!"

"Regrets, Séverine, but such feeling is wasted on one some cruelly name *Pale Rider*."

"Pale rider?"

As if Ondine regretted speaking it, she did not answer but continued, "If you are going to set yourself at one of my brothers—"

"I set myself at neither!"

The lady's smile was sympathetic. "Best look to Warin. He is attracted to you, and were that encouraged... Well, it is all possibility."

Now sense made of when Séverine forgot she and Hector had an audience and Dangereuse commented to Lady Héloise her sister erred. The two were aware Ondine entertained matching Séverine with her brother—but not the brother to whom her companion was attracted.

"It sounds you want me for a sister-in-law, and that is not possible, my lady."

"Because you are trouble? I am trouble and would be more were my circumstances not..." She breathed deep. "Because you are French? The Wulfriths are not French all sides of them, but there are plenty amid the English—the same as most nobles descended from the conquerors. Because your circumstances are so reduced you took the work of a commoner to provide for your cousin? That makes you strong—a survivor—which is much valued by our family."

Séverine stared.

"Now sense made?" the lady prompted.

"Some, but..."

"Ask and I shall answer as best I can."

Though more was known of Séverine than she wished and it seemed a waste to become better acquainted with impossible things, she said, "I do not know how it happened, but I feel for your eldest brother. Is the reason he will not wed again, even to gain an heir of his body, because his first marriage was bad?"

Ondine's mouth flattened. "Nay, it was acceptable. The second marriage was bad—very bad. Then the third...tragic." Eyes going distant, she touched the largest scar on her neck. "And the fourth marriage—"

"He wed four times?" Séverine exclaimed.

Ondine blinked. "Shocking for one so young, and more so since it would be five had not his first betrothed passed ere they wed."

Then all had died? Or had some marriages been dissolved as was possible for powerful nobles adept at courting the pope? "I am sorry, Lady Ondine. How did he lose so many?"

"All but one gone to God, and that one—a cruel, self-centered creature—attained an annulment under false pretenses. I am ashamed to admit I gloated when it was learned that on the day she was to wed her lover, the one who cuckolded my brother disappeared. But there was no gloating when she spread terrible rumors about Wulfrith, certain he had murdered his rival. Blessedly, they were dispelled when her lover appeared at court." She sighed. "And here more gloating for which much I have beseeched the Lord's forgiveness. That knave petitioned the king for the hand of another—a very young heiress. As is fitting, he was refused and Wulfrith's second wife was wed to a man thrice her age."

Ondine settled back. "I tell more than you must know, but now you can have no doubt that Wulfrith is beyond any woman's reach. Even our king knows better than to match him again."

"He tried?"

"Aye, and despite resistance, succeeded. One of Queen Philippa's ladies, of whom Edward was fond, was Wulfrith's fourth and last wife. Since in one way or another he has lost every woman with whom he was to grow a family, he has accepted God does not wish him to continue the Wulfrith line."

"Do you believe it?"

"The evidence is compelling," Ondine murmured, then jerked her shoulders. "My brother has made dire mistakes, but as he is not alone in doing so and they were not of evil bent..." She looked to her knit hands. "Nay, I do not hold the Almighty would deprive his wives of their lives when He could simply render infertile one He did not wish to father future generations."

Wondering at the mistakes made by the man for whom she hurt, Séverine eased down the pillows. "I regret your brother is so burdened."

"More burdened than you can know, but if you remain and draw close to Warin, he will enlighten you."

Not Hector? Séverine nearly asked, but Ondine made clear the woman to whom she yielded her bed had drawn as near as possible to her eldest brother.

"Now I shall aid Esta in setting the chamber aright," the lady said and stood. She started to turn away, hesitated, looked back. "As Wulfrith's responsibilities are too many for one man, Warin is needed at Wulfen at least until Rémy is knighted and comes alongside our eldest brother. Thus, in the hope of giving Warin greater cause to remain, I ask you to consider the attentions of one who is drawn to you as I have only seen him drawn to the wife he lost long ago."

More family history scattered with casualties. "How many times has *he* wed?"

"Only once, but unlike Wulfrith, I believe he will marry again. So think on him."

As the two women moved about the chamber, Séverine tried to move her thoughts to Warin, but they went Hector's direction though there was nothing there for her. Of course, neither did she believe there was anything for her with his brother. Despite the attraction Warin felt, it could not be of a strength that held a man to a place he did not wish to be.

But why do you not want to be here with your brother, doing the work of training up England's greatest defenders, Sir Knight? she questioned once...twice...then slept.

CHAPTER 21

The clouds were kind in holding their rain. Hoping they would continue until those who retrieved the cask returned, Séverine looked from Ondine who had gone to her owl upon entering the room, to Fira who carried an extra lantern in one hand and a blanket under an arm.

She had known this place was large, but as its true depth was revealed by the brisk young lady, she amended her assessment. It was enormous, and it would have to be for how much was stored here. Since the items were draped or wrapped in canvas and the majority of good size, most had to be furniture.

"Where did all this come from?" Séverine asked as they moved toward a corner.

"'Tis the accumulation of three hundred years of Wulfriths," Fira said, "including pieces from Wulfen Castle that belonged to the Saxon family ere the Norman blood of the D'Argents mixed with theirs. Grandmother has entrusted me to verify the inventory begun a century past, add detailed descriptions, order repair when necessary, and ensure all is done to preserve these pieces of our past."

Holding a hand to ribs Stern's physician had examined upon his return from pilgrimage this morn, the light pressure providing some relief, Séverine said, "It looks quite the task."

"'Tis, and I could not be happier!" Fira halted before canvas-wrapped trunks placed end to end. "Well, a little. Though I like Skyward, I count the days until he flies. It is good of him to dispose of vermin who steal within and he keeps much of his mess to the box, but when he does not... And the feathers!" Expelled breath lifting hair off her brow, she hooked the lantern on the wall. "My sister is considerate in cleaning up after him, but as I am to be keeper of *The Book of Wulfrith* and tale-giver after our grandmother, my standards are higher."

Séverine smiled. As yet, she had no cause to like Dangereuse, was beginning to like Ondine, but had liked Fira from the beginning. There was something wondrous about her —as if she were a sprite grown too large to wander a wood of blades of grass and wild flowers.

"This is the trunk." Fira spread the blanket atop a nearby one and loosened a rope that bound canvas close to rectangular planes. "Though others hold gowns of less age and more current style, I believe one or more here will fit you well."

"How old are these? Séverine asked.

"One to two hundred years."

Séverine's sharp breath made her grateful she stabilized her ribs. "That is quite old."

Fira dropped the rope and turned back the canvas. "And you are thinking I am about to offer a moldering gown whose seams will tear through."

She was.

"Fear not. Just as I know what I am about, so did my grandmother and the keepers come before." She pulled the trunk's pin from its clasp. "Granted, items have been irreparably damaged by things unforeseen—an attack one hundred fifty years past by the foul King John whose siege engines damaged the walls of what was then the uppermost room, and a storm seventy-five years ago that tore off half the roof—but much protection afforded our heirlooms. Come see."

As Séverine stepped alongside, from the opposite side of the room sounded a cry that brought her and Fira around. "Very good, my fine fellow!"

The wings of the owl on Lady Ondine's gloved hand were fully extended, but then the bird wobbled and drew them in.

With a groan, Fira turned back and raised the lid.

It was not stale, mustiness, nor rot that wafted from what was encased in linen. Among lavender and other fine scents was one of such rarity Séverine wondered if it truly was cedar, shavings of which filled tiny purses she had placed between the garments of one of the ladies she served in France.

Fira, who might grow somewhat taller than Séverine, looked up. "I know I ought not boast, but if I am not naturally gifted at this, I am an exceptional pupil."

Struck by the thought, *I could love her as a sister,* Séverine wondered if the young lady was of Ondine's mind to make that possible by way of Warin, both so desperate for him to remain upon Wulfenshire more they would expose their family to one in dire straits.

Fira parted linen to reveal a gown of rich brown samite. "This she wore past her middle years after multiple pregnancies put weight on her. Not much weight, mind, but enough this gown will not fit as well as those of her younger years."

Séverine drew nearer. "Of whom do you speak?"

"Did I not say?"

If she had, Séverine had missed it, whether because her thoughts drifted or it was spoken on that side that would not recover its sharp hearing until the swelling resolved—if then. "If so, I did not catch it."

"I speak of Lady Annyn who wed Garr Wulfrith two hundred years ago."

A tale with which Séverine had become more acquainted since Hector told of the first to disguise herself as a man to enter Wulfen Castle. Though she had not been present for all of Lady Héloise's nightly readings, she had learned enough of Lady Annyn to admire her.

"This trunk holds her finest gowns and those belonging to her daughters, daughters-in-law, and granddaughters," Fira continued. "As I know them well, having aired and cleaned and replaced some stitching, I am certain one of Lady Annyn's gowns will fit best. Too, since she was not one for elaborate dress, the style is not as bygone as some."

She looked up, and lantern light danced in eyes of a brighter green than her brother's. "I am delighted at the irony that just as you are of a similar size, you disguised the woman of you to enter Wulfen, though..." She grinned. "...you must admit she was more accomplished at that deception."

Séverine nearly laughed. "I bow to her."

"I am taking Skyward to the wood," Ondine called. "I think this the day."

When the door closed, Fira said, "Let us hope." Then she lifted out the first gown, revealing a sheet of linen between it and the next, and carefully laid it atop the blanket on the other trunk. "If not for the fur collar, I would suggest this scarlet dyed with kermes—quite rare at the time." She peeled back another sheet to reveal a simple gown of fine linen. It was set aside as well, and the next of cream-colored wool. "Now this..." She touched the silver gown's lightly embroidered bodice. "What think you?"

"It is lovely, but I would fear damaging something so treasured."

"I doubt that would happen. But if so, more history for the garment that I could record." Pitching her voice higher to affect doing so, Fira said, "This spot on the sleeve of a gown first worn by Lady Annyn who disguised herself as a man, next worn by Lady Séverine who also disguised herself as a man..." She chuckled. "Mistakes and flaws are what make people and things most interesting, do you not think?" She drew out the gown, gave it a shake, and held it against Séverine. "As thought, a good fit."

Séverine would have agreed had she not glimpsed the color of what was beneath the next sheet. "What of the purple?"

Fira hesitated, then the silver gown joined the others. With greater care, she removed the rich purple interwoven with gold thread. "It was worn only once and required much cleaning and mending to restore it since what befell it was not corrected until twenty years ago when my grandmother determined to ensure its preservation."

Séverine lowered the hand she reached to the low-waisted gown whose back was longer to trail after its wearer. "What befell it?"

"You can touch it, Séverine. The threads having not weakened from years of wear, it is the least fragile of Lady Annyn's gowns."

Lightly, Séverine ran fingers over the embroidery at neck and the wrists of sleeves that fell open to halfway down the skirt.

"As you recall from a reading of the *Book of Wulfrith*," Fira said, "when Duke Henry arrived at Stern, he discovered the lady he promised to another had become Garr Wulfrith's wife."

"And the duke was accompanied by her former betrothed," Séverine said.

"Aye, an ancestor of our good neighbor, the Baron of Abingdale."

Séverine nodded. "At that time a bad neighbor, one who tried to murder Lady Annyn."

"I knew you were engaged in the tale!" Fira exclaimed. "Well, this is the gown completed in haste after Lady Annyn's wedding night so better she present to he who would become king. Later, when the one to whom she had been betrothed attempted to hang her, so wildly she fought that the gown was dirtied and its skirt and hem torn." She clicked her tongue. "As much as it was her husband who saved her, her struggles saved her, keeping her alive long enough for him to reach her—similar to what happened to you in Ravvenborough when my brothers came to your aid."

Uncomfortable with the parallel, Séverine said, "For that, she could not bring herself to wear it again."

"And yet she did not discard it." Fira put her head to the side. "We cannot know, but I wonder if it served as a reminder of how precarious our world, how strong we must be to survive it, and how precious those who aid in our defense."

Séverine smiled. "You are beyond your years."

"I quite agree." Fira returned the gown to the trunk and pulled spectacles from her bodice. "See here the repairs made." She pointed out seamed places cleverly disguised by embroidery one would not know was stitched nearly two centuries later.

"Much work your grandmother did," Séverine mused.

Fira peered over her spectacles. "Do you like this gown best?"

Was it being offered? "I do, it being of a color similar to the violets my aunt grew in her garden at Calais."

"Though purple is beautiful," Fira said, "I like it for the colors from which it is formed. To me, it symbolizes the union of Wulfriths and D'Argents, their colors red and blue respectively. This gown will fit you well."

"But now I know its history, I would not think to wear it, Lady Fira."

"I believe you should, though I will have to obtain my grandmother's permission."

Permission that would not be granted, Séverine was certain.

Fira dropped the spectacles down her bodice. "I will ask her now."

"But—"

"Lest she say nay, remain here and decide on another." Fira hastened to the door.

Séverine did not have to look nearer on the gowns to know she would choose the silver when Lady Héloise refused the purple—should that be allowed. She was drawn to the color, and its sleeves were close-fitting to which she was accustomed. Elongated ones were lovely, but unlike in years long gone, few noblewomen indulged for how impractical they were.

Over the next quarter hour, she peeked under draped canvases and, surprised at the simplicity of the items, guessed those wrapped and roped were the finest pieces. Though tempted to unbind them, she returned to the purple gown and examined the embroidery concealing evidence of a life nearly lost to the evil that trespassed at Stern. On the outside, one would not know of rips in fine silk. That could only be discovered by looking closely at the backside.

When Séverine became aware voices in the inner bailey had taken a turn that indicated increased activity, it was too late to get to the window to see if it was caused by the return of the Wulfrith brothers and Mace. A moment later, the great doors closed behind those she prayed were not guests lest they were here for her.

They would not have been admitted, she assured herself, but it was hard to calm breaths that made her more firmly hold her ribs.

"Mace and you are safe," she told herself. "Hector has made it so, and his family stands your side as once they stood Lady Annyn's." But were these Wulfriths as honorable as those?

She bowed her head. "Lord, I have no husband to aid me, only the kindness of strangers You place in my path. I..." She trailed off. What else could she say not already said many times? So many times that once more she wondered if her belief in the Almighty was warranted.

She shook her head and, reminding herself of all that had gone wrong that could have gone far worse, whispered, "As ever, I ask first You make all right for Mace, then as much as possible for me. Amen."

"Séverine?"

She turned so quickly she stumbled back against the trunk. Relieved she did not jolt her ribs, she stared at the man advancing on her and berated herself for not catching the protest of cranky planks. "I did not hear you enter!"

Two more strides brought him within reach. "You were much at prayer."

Warmed by embarrassment as if caught doing something she ought not—and perhaps she had since it was nearly all pleading rather than praise—she released the trunk. "You retrieved the cask?"

He nodded, and she saw his neck was no longer bandaged, exposing seamed flesh tracked with stitches. "It is good your instructions were clear, Lady, since—"

"You could have died!" She stepped forward and raised a hand. "I did not know it was this bad."

He drew his head back, but in keeping his feet firm to the floor, it did not occur she encroached until she touched warm flesh beneath what would become a scar by which to remember this troublesome French woman.

As she dropped her hand, he said stiffly, "The injury Le Creuseur dealt me is not as bad as it appears."

"It could have been. To save me..." She frowned. "Why did you?"

His eyes lowered but so quickly returned to hers, she could not be certain they looked upon her mouth. "You needed saving and, just as at Calais, I am at least partly responsible for that."

Why does that not satisfy? she wondered. *And why do I continue to stand near though I know the answer and hopelessness of this?*

She took a step back. "I regret the trouble caused you and your family."

"As do I."

Painful, but truthful. The only good thing she had done was insert Mace in their lives and, hopefully, one day they would view it that way.

Having not seen his hand rise, she startled when it settled on her jaw, caught her breath when his fingers slid to the back of her neck, trembled when he tilted up her face. "And you are not done causing trouble, are you?" he said across a low growl.

This was wrong. But for as long as the moment lasted when it seemed he wanted to kiss her, she wanted to pretend it was right. "Forgive me, Hector, but it is true." She stepped nearer. "I am not done."

His eyes told he rethought this, and she knew she ought to since it could never be more than a kiss and this was not the brother Ondine believed might be moved to something more than attraction, but she hooked a hand over his shoulder and set the other on his chest. "I want this, Hector." If he did as well, he would have to come down from that great height.

He was still so long she was certain he would set her back, but he lowered his head, spoke her name against her lips, and closed his mouth over hers.

CHAPTER 22

There was so much hunger in their kiss, Séverine could not have said who sought the greatest portion of the other though she was far from experienced and even further from the experience of a man wed four times.

Gripping Hector's shoulder tight with one hand, his tunic with the other, she gave and took as he gave and took, breathed in him as he breathed in her, and marveled over senses spinning one direction then the other.

Hence, it was good she had aches to remind her of boundaries not to be crossed. And for as gentle as his hands were on her neck and hip, neither did he forget her fragile state. At least, she wanted to believe that was what kept him in control where the rest of their bodies were concerned.

Then his mouth abandoned what it had claimed, and he eased her to her heels.

She thought he would set her back, but when he merely removed his hands, she dropped her forehead to his collarbone and, feeling his heart slam beneath her knuckles, told herself, *This is only attraction. It will pass.*

"Just as you should not speak my Christian name, you should not want this," he said.

Keeping her head down, she whispered, "But I did, and I do."

"I am no good for any woman, Séverine," *he* used her Christian name. "And you are no good for me."

She splayed her hand against his breastbone. "Then why does your heart beat so?"

Breath expanded his chest. "You are desirable."

"That is all?"

"Whatever your path, it cannot merge with mine again. Not like this."

She raised her head. For how high his chin, as if he dared not lower it again, she had to draw back. "As I am aware some call you *Pale Rider,* do you think it would doom me?"

His lids narrowed.

"Though Ondine gave little detail, she told of your lost wives and said if I am to set myself at one of her brothers it must be Warin."

He stepped back, causing her hand to fall from him. "It is true the Wulfrith line will not continue with me. God has made that very clear."

She frowned. "He has told you so?"

"He has shown me so."

"Has he? Often since Calais, I believed terrible happenings to be signs from God that I ventured the wrong direction since he did not provide clear answers to prayers. Had I not given my word to Mace's sire, his son would not be here now, safe and future assured." She swallowed. "What if you but misinterpret events simply because your answers to prayers are not the same as God's?"

Hector was relieved the wondrous scent of Séverine's hair was now so faint he might have missed it had he not recently breathed her in. He did not want to be angry with her for questioning his conclusion about one great loss after another, but since it was better than once more falling under the power of one he was moved to kiss—and not only to satisfy desire—he said more firmly, "Whatever your path, this will not happen again."

And that it had happened made him hope Warin was not on her path since what transpired here would have to be told and his brother could view it as an attempt to deprive him of another wife. Were it possible still Warin wanted Séverine, he would have to take her far from Wulfen or the strain between brothers would become intolerable.

More ruin I make of things, he sent heavenward. *When I should think of others, I think of myself—what I want in the moment.*

"Hector?"

Ignoring her persistence in being familiar, he said, "There is a reason I came abovestairs rather than Fira."

Her eyes widened. "Is Mace—?"

"He is well. In the charge of Warin, he directed us near where you hid the cask. Had you not been specific as seemed to elude him, far longer it would have taken to retrieve it and your pack."

"*Seemed* to elude?" She shook her head. "As I had cause to believe Mace could not recall which tree, it was there we ventured before we were intercepted by the deputy and his witness. Thus, I do not believe he meant to thwart you."

He considered that. "Still, though he wants to trust us and does in some measure, what I believed bent in him when you came to Wulfen is more so after what happened in Ravvenborough—so much there may be splintering."

Her gaze wavered. "Meaning?"

"As told, Mace will be trained at Stern if not Wulfen, and

just as much will be required of him, much will be asked of the knight assigned to him who will be most accountable for that training. Hence, one of estimable repute, firm discipline, and empathy is needed to move from boy to man one who has suffered much, and I believe that is Warin who begins to establish a bond with him. But that is only possible if my brother remains on Wulfen."

Understanding lighting her eyes, she touched her lips. Flushed amid bruises, cuts, and abrasions, they evidenced the passion of their kiss. "Your sister thinks I could give him cause to stay, and if he is what Mace needs..." A sound of distress escaped. "Were she right, I have ruined all."

He started to assure her she was merely an accomplice, but there was something amid her words he could not overlook. "You are saying more for Mace than yourself you would bind yourself to my brother?"

"My cousin could be my son more only had I birthed him. It is not just blood, not just a promise made his sire. I love him, and no good portion of my heart will truly be my own again until he is firmly on the path his sire desired. Thus, were I cleared of charges and your brother wanted to make a match, I could have been happy with him though he is not the one I..." She shrugged. "You know me to be deceitful, but in this, I cannot further Mace's cause."

He needed no convincing. What was best for all was she be found innocent, Mace enter Wulfen, she return to France, and the line of Wulfriths continue through the second or third brother. "We are of the same mind then. Now the reason I came abovestairs. Shortly after our departure from the wood of Lillefarne Abbey, we encountered Sheriff D'Arci and his squire en route to Stern."

A strident breath made her press a hand to her ribs. "Then I shall be—?"

"You will not be taken into custody. He but wishes to question you about Ravvenborough."

"I did not know it would be so soon."

"I had hoped you would have more time to recover, but it is best he obtain your testimony while events are clear. What you must know is that when he asked whence we came and for what Mace accompanied us, it occurred were I forthcoming, our unexpected meeting could benefit you."

She caught her breath. "You told you retrieved the cask!"

"And showed it to him, though not its contents."

Her hands clenched.

"Of all who may be against you, he is not one, Lady. A distant relation and neighbor, Percival D'Arci is honorable. Thus, I believe if he is present for the opening of the cask and accounting of its items, he will see the sheriff and his witness had much cause to twist the truth of what happened in Dover, and the two scabbards within will testify to the character of a lady who left behind a valuable dagger, which it is unlikely one capable of intentionally gutting a man would do."

She took a step forward. "But Mace's treasures will become evidence and taken into custody."

Once more catching the scent of her hair, he would have stepped back would it not evidence how greatly she affected him. "Nay. Though I trust Sir Percival, he will have to trust me the same as you that *I* will keep them for Mace."

"Just because you can keep them out of the hands of the sheriff does not mean you can prevent more powerful hands from seizing them."

It was true but, in the end, irrelevant. "The cask is your greatest defense, Séverine—the cause of the attack on Mace in Dover that required you to come to his aid, and the reason you were beaten in Ravvenborough. Hence, we make use of it, and since it is in the safekeeping of this Wulfrith, far less chance Mace will be deprived of his inheritance."

Grudgingly, she nodded. "When must I appear before the sheriff?"

"Now."

"What?"

"The contents of the cask will be inventoried in his presence, then he will question you."

As fear glanced across her face, he quickly assessed her. "A bit of straightening is needed, but that is all. As your words shall be truthful, you have no need for practice."

Pressing teeth into her lower lip, she looked to the trunks behind. "What of Lady Annyn's gowns? Your sister went to speak with your grandmother about them."

"A matter to be resolved later."

Her shoulders rose with breath. "It was kind of Fira to offer, but I am not surprised she met resistance."

Séverine guessed right. His grandmother had agreed to support this woman and her cousin, but was not as enthusiastic as Fira, Héloise's years of experience warning against drawing near others until they proved themselves—and well.

"Be at ease, Lady. You have champions enough here and have only to set a few things aright ere meeting the sheriff."

Or nearly so, he silently amended. Still her mouth evidenced his had been there.

"Return to your chamber and refresh yourself—and do not cover the injuries Le Creuseur dealt your face."

"How long have I?"

"A quarter hour, which ought to be enough for Ondine to be collected from the wood so she may also bear witness." He stepped aside.

Purposeful steps evidencing she took care with her ribs, she crossed the room. At the doorway, she looked around.

"There are things about my cousin you must know to better understand him and smooth the splinters. I will tell you and your brother, but not in Mace's presence."

"That is best."

She glanced down her front. "Should I change into one of my own gowns?"

"Nay, even had I not sent your pack of garments to the laundress for cleaning, more you look the lady in this gown."

She turned and departed.

Standing before the mirror minutes later, Séverine saw what Hector had seen. Amid healing injuries he said she should not cover, she had fairly full and naturally red lips, but more so now. And though her hair had not been mussed, the gown had gone askew and a portion of the excess skirt tucked beneath the belt had escaped.

After dealing with the latter, she stepped nearer her reflection and looked more closely at her mouth. Had he felt their kiss as deeply as she? Had he wanted it to last as long as she? Had he wished to feel the beat of her heart as she had his?

"Father mine, I know not what I do, and I think neither does he," she said. "Pray, make obvious Your plan for us."

Séverine crossed to the table where she completed her ablutions. After patting a damp towel over face and neck, still her lips remembered Hector's, but unable to make herself more presentable, she went to the hall.

Servants bustled there, freshening the rushes and straightening furniture, but no one was before the hearth nor at the high table. And the panels of the private gathering room were closed.

"I am to escort you," said Sir Warin who came at her from the same direction as had Fira the night the two women became acquainted. This Wulfrith's smile flushed her with guilt she had no real cause to feel. She had done things with

Hector she should not have, but she had not betrayed his brother.

"Escort me where?"

He nodded at the paneled room. "We meet there again, though more privately."

Then the other family members were inside. And the sheriff. Searching for something to hold them here awhile longer, she recalled what was due him. "I am remiss in expressing gratitude for the special attention shown Mace."

Further his smile warmed. "I see much good in the boy—even now."

"Even now?"

"I believe he nears a line that, if crossed, could make it exceedingly difficult to return him to the side he must stand to be worthy of knighthood training."

She hated such talk, and more so it was in accord with Hector's conclusion, but the balm of it was knowing Mace remained this side of that line and, God willing, was now less likely to cross over.

"They await us," Hector's brother said.

A fluttering in her breast, she tugged forward hair the side of her damaged ear to ensure the ugliness was covered.

"You look lovely," he said and offered an arm.

"I thank you, Sir Warin." No surprise defined muscle was beneath her fingers. No surprise contact made her heart beat only a little faster. That which dwelt in her breast was set on Hector.

He led her forward, and when he drew her to the left of the dais and down a corridor that accessed the steward's office, she noted other doors there, and the nearest opened into the family's private gathering place.

Inside, all was rearranged. Around a large table placed center of the room and set with a pitcher and goblets were the

Wulfriths, and now the one at the head pushed back his chair and stood.

Warmed by remembrance of their kiss, she considered those present who were not his family—to Hector's left, Mace seated between Lady Héloise, an empty chair, and Fira, to his right the steward before whom sat the cask and writing instruments. Standing before the fireplace was he who must be the sheriff and possibly his squire, the former wearing a black tunic belted with a scarlet sash.

Though Séverine noted no great resemblance between the Wulfrith males and this distant cousin of brown hair and blue eyes, she questioned if all those possessing even a small amount of Wulfrith blood were gifted with attractive countenances and good builds.

"Lady Séverine," Hector called her gaze to his.

Hoping the heat moving up her chest did not reach her face, she said, "Lord Wulfrith."

He gestured at the hearth. "This is Sheriff D'Arci and his squire, both of whom will witness the cask's contents before you are questioned about Ravvenborough."

Grateful he had prepared her and certain Mace was as well, she nodded at the lawman and looked to her cousin. Though she glimpsed anxiety, he did not appear frightened nor angry.

"Warin," Hector said and his brother guided her into the chair between Mace and Fira.

Beneath cover of the table, Mace took hold of her hand as he watched Warin circle the table and seat himself between his brother and the steward.

When Hector returned to his seat, Séverine looked to the latter who peered over spectacles of greater size than Fira's, then Dangereuse. If not for the little boy asleep in his mother's arms, likely the lady would have presented as cool as usual, but ever there was warmth about her when Sebastian was near, even when he behaved as it was muttered did not befit a Wulfrith.

Beside Dangereuse was Ondine whose owl must have been returned to the upper room while Séverine worried over her appearance. Once more the lady was veiled, glittering eyes visible above the dense weave of flowers worked into gossamer cloth.

"The purple suits you best," Fira whispered. "I have yet to gain permission, but I shall."

Séverine managed a smile, reached to the goblet before her.

As she sipped, Hector passed two wrapped items to the steward. "Here the dagger and ring Lady Séverine removed from the cask and left with Mace when she fled Stern. They are to be included in the inventory and returned to the cask."

The man unwrapped the ring and read aloud the accompanying piece of parchment, "Received from the Dane by way of G.W., the Year of Our Lord, 1097." Next, he examined the ring, inked his quill, and wrote a description on parchment. The same was done with Hugh D'Argent's dagger, the man commenting that the greatest difference between it and a Wulfrith dagger was a blue rather than red gem. Then he drew the cask near.

"Sheriff," Hector said, and Percival D'Arci and his squire came to stand behind the steward.

As the lid was raised, Séverine saw Lady Héloise sit forward.

The two scrolls presented to Hector at Wulfen Castle were lifted out and each silently read by the steward who recorded what he believed relevant.

"I am anxious to read them," Fira rasped, "and I am sure grandmother's feet tap out impatience."

Returning the goblet to the table, Séverine glanced at the young lady whose gaze was fixed on the aged missives.

Next came the Godwine brooch whose letter *G* was intersected by a sword. After the steward read what Sir Amaury inked, he muttered, "Excellent workmanship. So advanced, I question if it is truly three hundred years old."

"It *is*," Mace said forcefully. "*G* for Godwine the earl who sired my ancestor, Lady Mercia, before he was crowned King of England." Amid deepening silence, he looked to Séverine. "I speak true!"

"You do." Though she longed to set her eyes upon Hector, she shifted to Sheriff D'Arci and found herself watched.

He judges me, she thought. Attempting to keep the shiver beneath her skin, she reminded herself Hector had told this man was not against her. He sought what could be known of the truth so it be presented when she was given over to those who would determine her fate. Were she the ignorant wife of either of those who had attacked Mace and her, she would want this man to take his duties seriously.

After the steward recorded the brooch's details, he lifted out the silver-bound psalter whose cover was set with a large opal. "Magnificent," he breathed, and it was some moments before he set it aside to read Sir Amaury's words. He looked up. "Origin uncertain, but I concur that which came into the hands of Lady Mercia by questionable means is over three hundred years old and likely commissioned by Saxon royalty. Though I thought the ring valuable, this..." He turned back the cover and carefully looked through the first illuminated pages.

"Oh my," Fira whispered and leaned forward to peer at her grandmother who was so still it appeared she held her breath.

Once more the steward put quill to parchment. Then from the cask he took the bundled leather scabbards of little value except to prove there had been two daggers and one lost when she could not bring herself to pull it from Mace's assailant.

Affording them little examination, he said, "If these are salvageable, the cost of repair could easily exceed their value."

"*Monetary* value," Hector said, and more Séverine's heart set itself at him. "What did Sir Amaury tell?"

The steward picked up the parchment. "Here the dagger and scabbard of Hugh D'Argent who died at Hastings fighting for his liege. Here the dagger and scabbard of his son, Maël D'Argent, who became Maël de Chanson to wed Lady Mercia, daughter of King Harold who lost his kingdom to William of Normandy." He looked to the baron. "There is only the dagger of Hugh D'Argent, and it cannot be known if either of these scabbards was made for it."

"It can be known," Séverine said. "Look close and you will see just as the blades bear initials, so too the leather."

Moments later, he nodded. "This one shows *HD*, the other *MD*."

"Suggesting the dagger of Maël D'Argent could have been left in the boy's assailant," Sir Percival said.

"Not *suggesting*," Mace said. "It is obvious it was left in him."

The sheriff looked to him. "Not obvious, but even were it, what is obvious is not always truth."

Mace pulled his hand from Séverine's. "It *is* truth."

The man stepped into the space between the steward's and Sir Warin's chairs. "I am not saying I do not believe you and your lady cousin. I am saying there is room for others not to believe."

"Then they are stupid or prejudiced because we are French!"

"Mace!" Séverine tried to retrieve his hand, but he dropped his feet between his chair and that of Lady Héloise who raised her eyebrows.

When he started across the chamber, Séverine began to rise, but Hector called, "Attend, Mace de Chanson!"

That would not stop him. Or so she thought. As she struggled to remain seated, her cousin came around. Eyes bright, he said, "Baron Wulfrith?"

"You did not ask for nor were you granted permission to leave."

"I want to go to the kitchen."

"For?"

"I..." His gaze shifted, and Séverine thought it was Sir Warin who fell beneath his regard.

"Look at me, Mace," Hector commanded.

He complied. "My Lord, I do not want to be here anymore. May I go to the kitchen?"

Hector inclined his head. "Permission granted providing you give the word of one worthy of his lineage that there you can be found should I have further need of you."

"You have my word, though..."

"Though?"

"The garden is part of the kitchen?"

"Parts of it. Hence, you may go there, but no farther."

When Mace closed the door behind him, Séverine breathed out relief.

"Methinks he will seek little Willa," Fira said.

Séverine looked around. "What say you?"

"Since learning she is the reason Wulfrith and Warin were able to reach you in Ravvenborough ere greater damage was done, less easily your cousin is annoyed by her."

In answer to Séverine's unspoken question, Hector said, "Unbeknownst to Mace, Willa followed him when first he visited you in the fields of Ravvenborough. What she told us when your cousin went missing again saved us much time."

Were the little girl here, Séverine would hug her.

"Continue," Hector instructed the steward.

When the man drew out the last item, Séverine was more grateful for Mace's departure. This scroll was sealed with wax. Mace knew of it, but just as she had not trespassed on what was written there, neither had he though now he could read well enough to make sense of it.

When the steward thumbed the wax seal, Séverine snapped, "Do not open it!" As all eyes turned to her, she said, "Written by Sir Amaury to his son, it is for Mace's eyes first and not until he moves from the training of a page to that of a squire. I beseech you—honor a dead man's wishes as Mace and I have done these years."

"Leave it be," Hector commanded.

The steward returned it to the cask and added one last line to the parchment. "The inventory is complete, my lord."

"Then while Sheriff D'Arci speaks with Lady Séverine, you will make three copies, one for each of them and one to be included in the missive I send King Edward. Then all here this day shall put their names to the copies and the original will be kept at Stern."

Inclining his head, the steward reached to return the items to the cask.

"I will do it!" Fira rose and started around the table.

"You are well with this, Lady Séverine?" Hector asked.

Though she glimpsed nothing about him to encourage her opposite the belief even if she stood on the shoulders of one of great height she could not reach him, she was struck by something more than attraction. She did not merely move toward love, she looked from this side of it to that.

Do not cross there, she told herself. *Just as he does not wish it, neither should you.*

"Lady Séverine," he prompted, and she saw Fira hovered

alongside Sir Percival's squire whose tanned face had gone ruddy.

Wondering if it was due to awareness of that young lady, Séverine said, "I am well with it, and if Lady Fira and Lady Héloise would like to look nearer upon their kin's inheritance, I trust them to handle it with care."

Fira gave a chirp of excitement and reverently filled the cask as the steward gathered his implements.

Knowing soon she would be alone with the sheriff whose gaze was felt nearly as much as Hector's, Séverine reminded herself he was not against her—a dozen times before the steward and ladies withdrew.

"Lady Séverine," Sir Percival said, settling in the chair Hector yielded, "as you know, I am here to take your testimony which my squire shall record." He nodded at the young man who now sat where the steward had and was removing writing instruments from a pack. "Would you have the baron or his brother remain for the questioning?"

This she had not dared hope for. "Oui, Baron Wulfrith," she said, then something on the air making her aware of his brother, added, "and Sir Warin." Fairly certain it was offense radiating from him and sensing it was not directed at her, more certain she was when he flicked his gaze to his older brother.

Though she doubted she would ever know the story wedged between them, she wanted no part in adding unwarranted jealousy to it.

"Both may remain," the sheriff said, "but they stand distant and out of your line of sight."

Lest she seek to be guided by those sympathetic to her cause, she guessed, as was possible with nods, shakes of the head, and hand gestures.

"You agree to stay for the questioning, Baron Wulfrith? Sir Warin?"

"Agreed," both men said and moved to the hearth that would require her to peer across her shoulder to look at them.

"Squire?" Sir Percival said.

The young man poked his quill in ink. "I am ready, my lord."

"Then we begin. Not with Ravvenborough. With Dover."

CHAPTER 23

The knight was nearly as confrontational as he was thorough, causing Hector's hands to fold into fists, but considering what had happened during Percival's first months in serving as an officer of the Crown, he could not be faulted. Doubtless, his conscience remained burdened by the tragedy he might have prevented had he been more thorough in his investigation, striven to remain neutral, and not been distracted.

Now as he sat back, flexing shoulders that caused his black tunic to strain its seams while his squire recorded what Séverine had twice answered, the last time with anger sharper than when first she was pressed, he said, "Nearly done, my lady."

When his squire lifted the quill and nodded at his lord, Percival raised the pitcher. "More wine?"

Though Hector wanted to rebuke him for attempting to loosen her tongue with drink this past hour and a half, he knew it would be grounds to send him from the room. Thus, he could only hope Séverine would decline a third fill and, if she did not, skittering thoughts would not contradict earlier statements.

"Non, Sheriff." She set the goblet out of his reach should he pour regardless of her wishes as done the last time she hesitated over his offer. "It makes me slow and heavy-eyed, and as it will not change what happened at Dover and Ravvenborough, all you will have to show for it is frustration for how long it takes me to answer."

Was that a smile tempting the man's lips? Proof of chagrin if not amusement?

Percival glanced at Hector and Warin, and whether the latter glowered the same as the former, the sheriff's only response was an arched eyebrow. Returning to Séverine, he said, "You have responded well to my questions. Have you anything to add or ask of me?"

"Mace will not have to answer for any of this, will he? He is only seven and..." Her swallow reached Hector, and not for the first time during the interrogation, he felt a pang at his center. "As told, he thinks to claim he was the one struggling over the dagger when his assailant was injured, but I vow it was me, and I but tried to retrieve what belonged to my cousin."

Percival clasped his hands atop the table. "I cannot know what the authorities will require to resolve this matter, and much depends on whether the gutted man continues to recover and how well received his version of events absent the witness slain by Baron Wulfrith. Too, as told, the deputy has departed Ravvenborough. Having failed to secure you who are now under the Wulfriths' protection, he has little choice but to seek the aid of his sheriff who may appeal to the king."

He looked to his squire and raised a hand, indicating what next he spoke should not be recorded. "I find your tale convincing, and more so for having looked near on the injuries you and your cousin suffered whilst jailed."

She caught her breath.

"All part of the investigation, my lady, with care taken to preserve your modesty while you were insensible. Though it was enough to see what was done your face and ear, your broken ribs attest to unwarranted violence in the presence of men of good strength. Unfortunately, since those prejudiced against the French may disregard that, even if my earlier questioning of Mace suffices, I believe it would be to your advantage were he to stand with you."

"Non! Given a choice, I would not have him further traumatized lest he is pushed to a place from which it will be hard to retrieve him and..." She lowered her chin, braced a hand on the table.

Percival surprised in placing a hand atop hers. "Lady?"

Her head came up, and Hector expected her to snatch free, but she entreated, "He is my only purpose. If I fail him, for what did God preserve my life?"

Lines worked across Percival's brow, then he said, "If you are lost to the boy and he goes through life believing he could have saved you, ever he could be lost to himself, unraveling what you believe your purpose."

She pulled her hand from under his. "Non, whatever comes of me, I trust the training he receives from the Wulfriths will ensure he finds his way through this fallen world with honor and valor."

Percival settled back. "At this point, 'tis out of our hands. Should it come into yours, I advise you revisit what I have said."

She said naught, though the clench of her jaw told she would not revisit it.

"Worthy," Warin murmured, and the admiration in that one word furthered Hector's regret he had kissed the lady. Ondine was right, Warin was drawn to Séverine. Should he decide to pursue her, what had happened this day between the one he could not forgive and the lady who had trials ahead could end all hope of reconciling the brothers.

"I would like to rest awhile," Séverine said and stood.

Percival pushed back his chair and gained his own feet. "Ere I depart Stern, I must obtain your signature on the inventory, its copies, and your statement."

"I shall be in Lady Ondine's chamber."

Hector told himself he was glad Warin moved to escort her abovestairs, but it bothered, and more when his brother drew alongside and she set a hand on his arm.

When the two departed and Percival had sent his squire to the steward's quarters with instructions to copy Séverine's testimony, he strode to the hearth. "I sense great unrest," he said.

Though once Hector had counted himself fairly well known by this relation whose training overlapped his, that was before the French campaign and pestilence. However, the eyes and tone of Percival indicated he at least glimpsed something beyond the barriers raised since.

"As I believe her and the boy," Hector said, "I am concerned for what is ahead of her."

After scrutinizing Hector as thoroughly as he was scrutinized, Percival said, "I also believe the lady and her cousin wronged and agree it best to bypass Dover authorities. Compose your missive to the king, confident a copy of my report will strengthen it as much as possible for one who may be deemed biased for our kinship."

Hector reached and briefly they clasped arms. "As I know it is required you be only the side of gathering information and securing the accused so justice is done, I am grateful for the assurances offered and advice given the lady."

"Yet neither do you believe, given the choice, she will be

moved from keeping the boy distant from the proceedings," Percival said.

"She has yet to reveal the reason his back is scarred, but methinks it evidence enough her concern is warranted."

"At least that atrocity cannot be laid on the English," Percival muttered.

Hector shook his head. "Not so. Edward's great triumphs at Crécy and Calais that gave our countrymen a firmer foothold in France mean there is a good chance it *was* an Englishman who taught Mace a lesson in cruelty."

"Were that true, it is hard to believe Lady Séverine would bring the boy to England, especially at so vulnerable an age."

Hector considered that. "Well thought, Sheriff. You are a credit to the profession forced on you."

"I am learning." It was said with meaning. "Too late for some, soon enough for others. As surely you know, I look forward to the day I shed this office."

"Understood. You will pass the night here?"

Percival sighed. "Would I could, but many the affairs of Castle Soaring I have set aside. As I am remiss in my duties to Baron Lavonne, once the parchments are copied and signed, I depart."

Another thing Hector understood well—in his case, the obligations of a lord of a sizable demesne *and* the responsibility of training England's defenders. "I shall be in my chamber composing the missive to the king. Send for me when it is time to set my name to the documents."

"Hector?"

It pleased he eschewed formal address. "Percival?"

"I am sorry the ground between Warin and you remains hard, but encouraged it no longer seems strewn with glass."

Easily done again if Séverine comes between us, Hector thought. "I am glad someone is encouraged."

Percival raised his eyebrows. "He has come home—a good beginning."

"But in the absence of something to hold him here, only that."

"Or someone," Percival said, "and I guess already you are thinking that."

Hector narrowed his eyes on one who had always been perceptive but not to the extent to which he alluded. Either this further evidenced he learned well what was required of a sheriff or was aware of Ondine's belief attraction to Séverine could prompt Warin to take his place here—*if* the lady was acquitted.

As if following Hector's thoughts, Percival said, "Much depends on the outcome of your missive to King Edward."

Another beginning. But if it opened the way for Séverine and Warin, all was dependent on whether that way stayed open once the latter learned of this day's kiss. And it was nearly unbelievable honesty would yield anything good other than that confession over revelation lessened anger and a sense of betrayal.

Percival's set a hand on Hector's shoulder. "Just as I do not believe the pestilence was sent by God, I do not believe one man—let alone thousands—could have held it back. It struck everywhere. If it did not get in one crack, it found another, entering the abodes of commoners, nobles, even those of the Church. And God let it run its course, answering few prayers for healing and paying little heed to doorposts marked with lamb's blood in the belief evil would pass over as in the Bible. Hence, had the pestilence not come to Stern when it did, it would have come another day, just as done at Wulfen though you did all to keep it out."

Hector had heard this from his grandmother, uncle, Dangereuse, and others. But ever he came back to the obvious though Warin said what was obvious did not make it truth. Had the Great Mortality struck a different day and by way of another's vanity and ignorance, those it claimed shortly after his return from the king's games at Merton might have been passed over.

Might have, Stern's aged priest had said during Hector's confession to one who neared his own death despite being an irreproachable representative of God and every effort made to cast out that merciless sickness. *Still, they could have succumbed, my son. And if not them, others precious to you would have been lost.*

Sound reasoning, but still Hector struggled to absolve himself even if God had—and Ondine whose blessed survival would ever serve as a reminder should he need one.

"I thank you and encourage you to be as understanding of your mistakes as you are of mine," he said, knowing Percival carried his own guilt though it could not be as great as Hector's. "Now to compose the missive."

SHE HAD NOT RESTED. For weathering questions better than expected despite anger, Séverine was so afflicted with hope she was unable to remain still.

As Hector had told, the sheriff was not against her and might even be for her. God willing, his support, that of the Wulfrith family, and proof of Mace's lineage would cause his king to intervene and deal fairly with her. Thus, while pacing Ondine's chamber, her greatest worries had been keeping Mace from further proceedings and his treasures out of grasping hands.

Now, the documents signed by all, including her cousin who wrote his name large and bold on the inventory and its copies as if in warning, the sheriff had departed after declining the evening meal.

Though Séverine had been tempted to eat abovestairs, she had seated herself beside Esta. And how glad she had been when Mace was among those ladling sauce.

Garbed in the new tunic that was long enough to mostly conceal chausses that must be replaced, he comported himself well—head up, shoulders back, and so precise it appeared he lost no drip. She had not wanted sauce, but had nodded and received a slight smile with her pour.

At meal's end, she would have returned to the chamber had she not wished to ask after the cask. Thus, when Fira waved her to the hearth, she complied.

As others gathered, Séverine leaned toward the young lady seated beside her, but before she could speak, Fira said, "Much gratitude for allowing us to examine the heirlooms. Be assured we were careful."

"I am glad they were of interest. Where is the cask now?"

"In the keeping of Wulfrith. With your permission, my grandmother would have me copy the missive of Countess Gytha to Lady Mercia and that of the ailing Sir Maël to his wife so both may be included in our family's history exactly as written."

"Of course."

"Oh, this is all very exciting! I adore mysteries, and all the more when solved—though not in their entirety. Some luster must remain, hmm?"

Before Séverine could respond, Lady Héloise called her granddaughter to her side. Whatever passed between them, it sent Fira to the kitchen. When she reappeared, Mace accompanied her.

Smile genuine, he lowered to the other side of Séverine and said in her good ear, "I am to hear again *Tale of the Lost D'Argent*

—how Sir Maël came to love Lady Mercia and sacrificed all to escape his king's wrath."

She longed to hug him, but it was enough that when she set a hand over his, he turned his palm up into hers.

He was not the only male present. Sebastian was perched on Dangereuse's knees and, shortly, Hector and Warin crossed to the fireplace. Immediately, the boy who had been unusually quiet throughout the meal sprang away from his mother and tugged at his uncle's chausses. Hector lowered to his haunches, listened, then hooked an arm around his nephew and straightened.

Something about the warrior holding the little boy made Séverine's heart ache. He should be a father by now and looking forward to the day he began training his son in the ways of the Wulfriths.

Lady Héloïse cleared her throat, and Séverine saw she had opened the book. "Much you have added to *Tale of the Lost D'Argent,* Mace," she said, "and though now you are acquainted with it, I thought in the company of Lady Séverine more you would enjoy a reading of Sir Maël and Lady Mercia."

"I would, my lady."

She looked to Séverine. "The accounting having long passed mouth to mouth and its ending held close to protect Mace's ancestors while they lived, what the tenacious Sir Elias de Morville put to parchment is a puzzle missing pieces, quite a few of which we now possess and aspire to fit in their proper places." The old woman lowered her chin. "*Tale of the Lost D'Argent. Part One.*"

There it began, first told in poetry the listener gently unriddled, followed by composition should one wish to unriddle more. So transfixed was Séverine by verse made of the life of the only child of Hugh D'Argent, she did not realize how many parts made up the known of Maël D'Argent until Lady Héloïse paused to sip wine. "Now for part four, in which we learn of Bishop Odo's attempt to destroy Lady Mercia whose ability to draw rebels to her side threatened his brother's reign. Ought I continue or save it for another night, Mace?"

Since he was fully awake, it had to be teasing, which Séverine would have thought beyond the old woman.

"Pray, continue, my lady."

She sent her gaze amongst her audience, most of whom had to be acquainted with the tale, and did as beseeched.

"Now tell I tale of bishop well,
whose kin renown stole England's crown.

Of pomp and sly and falsity,
Odo, too, of Normandy.

Garbed in robes, hands bejeweled,
lust for power, God ne'er fooled.

Now come Maël of face sword-slain,
now draw near, Ingvar the Dane.

Free Mercia of lock and key,
take proof of blood, take bishop's ring.

From Stern to Wulfen and stream betwixt,
cast the stolen lest love eclipsed.

Ye of full heart, claim mother's name,
and Saxon bride sought not in vain.

Across the narrow sea now wing,
though lost to us—hark!—yon sparrows sing."

Lady Héloise looked up, her face so aglow it was no reach to see the beauty she had been. "Entrancing, is it not?"

As her eyes were on Séverine, it was she who answered. "Aye, my lady, quite."

Next she read the composition expanding on the events. This being the final part of that tale until Fira and she included what was learned since Séverine and Mace's arrival at Stern, it ended with Sir Maël and Lady Mercia departing England for parts unknown—though Sir Elias added a note that his research had uncovered the possibility they made a life in Flanders distant from King William and his brother, Odo.

Lady Héloise closed the book, returned her gaze to Séverine. "I know God worked in this old woman when you came seeking employment. Several times the flesh of me nearly ended our interview, as I thought there was something false about you. But that which is not flesh was moved to make room for you and the boy. And see, a blessing to you and yours and me and mine, the sanctuary given allowing our family to fill some of its holes."

Emotion constricted Séverine's throat. The Wulfriths were Mace's kin, and yet it almost felt she belonged among them.

"You are still trouble, Lady Séverine," the matriarch said, "and only the Lord can see how this mess will be untangled, but take comfort in knowing light found amid dark is far more precious—and can affect greater change in one's life for the better." She smiled, looked around, and when her lips took a turn toward sorrow, Séverine followed her gaze to Hector and the little boy asleep on his shoulder. Did she also think he ought to be a father and want that for him though he told the Wulfrith line would continue through another?

"As we are all tired," Lady Héloise said, "let us seek our rest, praising this day and lifting up the next in prayer."

When Séverine and Mace rose, Fira said, "Can you imagine

what verses Sir Elias would have composed had he known what came after?"

"I begin to," Séverine said.

"If only he yet lived," Fira bemoaned. "I shall have to share with you the beautiful words he wrote for the woman he loved. Though his works are much circulated as you know, this one his family held close though they shared it with ours for his great friendship with the Wulfriths."

Séverine did *not* know, though his name sounded familiar. "Did he gain the woman he loved?"

"No easy thing, but he found the light amid darkness of which my grandmother speaks, and there is no doubt she whom he wed was more precious to him."

"I look forward to you sharing it," Séverine said, then as they and others moved toward the stairs with the veiled Ondine in the lead, said, "Still you have a pallet in Sir Warin's chamber, Mace?"

"Oui. He has been kind. Hopefully, he will aid in my training."

Alongside Séverine's hope Hector's brother would take his place at Wulfen was that hope.

But let it not be because of me, she thought, recalling Warin's gaze upon her mouth when he escorted her to Ondine's chamber after the questioning. As unbelievable as it was both brothers were attracted to her, it seemed so, and it was wrong to let happen between her and Warin what had happened with Hector. Hence, she had quickly thanked him and slipped into the chamber.

"I also hope Sir Warin will aid in your training alongside Baron Wulfrith," she said.

He nodded and lengthened his stride to overtake the former.

Once more Séverine became aware of Hector coming

behind with Dangereuse whose son he conveyed to his sister's chamber. The two spoke so low that even were half her hearing not impaired, she did not think she could have made sense of their words. However, something he said must have angered his sister, for she raised her voice.

"He is not ready. What happened…what he saw—"

"Enough, Dangereuse. We will speak of it later."

"Whether or not I like it."

"Enough!"

"Aye, *my lord*. Later."

Doubtless, their disagreement was over her son, though as yet none had confided the reason he was shielded despite bouts of unruliness. Whatever it was, it seemed Hector was not content for the coddling to continue.

When they reached the second floor, he said, "Lady Séverine, I must speak with you."

She stepped to the side. "Baron?"

He looked from Dangereuse who continued past to the boy on his shoulder. "Await me outside Ondine's chamber. It will require only a few minutes."

"Of course."

When he returned to the corridor, they were the only ones not behind closed doors. "Earlier, I neglected to ask after your ear," he said.

She reached to ensure it was covered, but he brushed her hand aside and hooked back her hair. "The swelling decreases. Your hearing?"

She sipped breath. "Still muffled that side."

Moving his gaze to hers, he drew back.

"What is it you wish to speak of, Baron?" she asked tautly.

"The missive to the king is completed."

"Oh. That was quick."

"As it should be the sooner to reach my sovereign ahead of

whatever the deputy intends. Too, it is best received as close as possible to your statement and the inventory Sheriff D'Arci will send."

"I thank you for telling me."

"There is more. I depart for Wulfen on the morrow."

Hoping her startle masked disappointment, she said, "The morrow?"

"As Warin wishes to reunite with our youngest brother, he will accompany me along with your cousin."

"Then Mace's training commences?"

"Absent the king's approval, not officially, but we shall begin shaping him into a knight."

She smiled. "He will be happy to enter Wulfen."

"And safer there. Since the whims of a king might not go our way, Stern is more vulnerable."

Our way... That would please more were those whims not so forbidding.

"Wulfen Castle is not inviolable," he continued, "but as close as possible in England. I do not anticipate your cousin will be taken from Stern, but it is even less likely at Wulfen."

Great her relief, though *she* might be taken from here.

"As there are things we must know about Mace, you will meet with Warin and me in our family's gathering chamber after the breaking of fast."

It would hurt to speak of those revelations—and would reveal more of her—but it was time. "I shall join you and your brother there."

"Until then, my lady."

Minutes later, despite Ondine's insistence her companion continue to use the postered bed, Séverine went behind the screen. Here her place and, should she be acquitted, perhaps it would become permanent—providing she could bear Hector's visits, infrequent though said to be.

CHAPTER 24

Séverine was grateful it was an audience of two—and for the absence of formality. The large table where she had been interrogated was returned to the wall and three chairs placed around a small table on which sat a pitcher and cups.

Having this day donned one of her own laundered gowns, she took another sip of mead, then folded her hands in her lap.

"I am ready." She looked between the brothers. "After Calais, it was necessary to take Mace from one of my relations to another since we were unable to remain long with any, whether because of the need to stay ahead of the pestilence or withdrawal of the little welcome extended us."

Hector frowned. "Not only poorly received but set out?"

She had hoped she would not have to elaborate, but as he made time for it despite the desire to depart Stern within the hour, she said, "When I was orphaned, the only one who would take me in was my mother's sister, the wife of Sir Amaury. My parents having broken betrothals to others so they might wed, their families disowned them. Thus, though some compassion was shown Mace and me, it was no great difficulty to turn us out when earning my keep conflicted with the need to care for my little cousin."

Warin sat forward. "What of Sir Amaury's family?"

Since honesty could reflect poorly on Mace, more she wished they did not have to venture there. "Many the branches across the continent, but the few with whom he was best acquainted are outside France."

"His immediate family?" Hector trampled evasion.

"What I tell must not reach your king since it could cast Mace in a light that, though not his own, might see him banished from England."

She had their interest—and agreement when both nodded.

"Sir Amaury understood what it was to be estranged from family. A younger son who had to make his own way in the world, after earning his spurs he yielded to the temptation of gaining wealth by depriving others of theirs."

Disapproval fit their faces, and there would be more. "He was called Fléau de l'Anglais."

There it was—darkening eyes, tightening lips.

"Scourge of the English," Warin translated.

"A pirate," Hector said. "The rumor he had silvered black hair that could be of the D'Argent line was truth."

"Oui. He justified what he did as acceptable since he took from English merchants, but when his family learned he had turned to piracy, they would have naught to do with him."

"And Calais was the perfect base," Hector said. "Doubtless, he was encouraged by your king long ere mine brought war to France."

Fearing this might turn them against Mace, she said, "Years before the siege, he accepted he did wrong and wed my aunt and settled down to life as a merchant. Though esteemed by many who thought piracy was warranted against the

English, it was not easy for him to transform his reputation into one of integrity."

Hector grunted. "I imagine not."

Judgment there, but she understood, having been disappointed to learn of Sir Amaury's past. But having known him only as a good husband, father, uncle, and citizen, it had not been difficult to give grace when he asked it after dispelling the belief the rumors she heard were born of jealousy.

"As King Edward surely knows of *Fléau de l'Anglais*," Warin said, "you are right not to wish him to learn of this."

She nodded. "If all is not ruined by what happened in Dover, it could devastate."

"Now the obvious question," Hector said.

"How did the cask come into the hands of a son not only second in line but out of favor?" she said.

"Did he steal it from his family?"

"Non, what Sir Amaury told—and I believe—is it was his inheritance. Since ever he revered the heirlooms and tales attached to them unlike his older brother who had little regard for the past, his sire gave it to him upon his attainment of knighthood in the belief the line come from him would best preserve that heritage."

"Unaware it could have been a line of pirates," Hector said.

She sat forward. "And was not! Dare not tell me you have not done things of great regret."

The muscles in his face jumped. "I would not dare. Would I, Warin?"

Seeing that one's jaw work as if he struggled to hold all of him in one place, she wondered, *What have I done?*

"The lady is right," Warin said. "Who among us of an age of accountability has not done things that burn holes in our conscience? Difficult though it is to accept, grace is owed those who make an effort to right wrongs where possible." He jutted his chin. "Continue, Lady Séverine."

She cleared her throat. "For Sir Amaury's failing, it was of great import his son receive the best training to become a man and warrior."

"Understandable," Warin said. "Now tell what ills your cousin suffered."

She clenched hands to which Hector's gaze lowered. "Wherever we went, mostly he was treated well beyond being more of an outsider than I. Once he attained the age of five, those with whom I found work set him to menial tasks, believing he should also earn his keep. Thus, it became more difficult to keep a close watch on him—and more necessary since other children could be unkind as well as adults who thought nothing of smacking a little one who did not move quickly enough."

She moistened her lips. "We counted ourselves blessed when, after leaving the employ of a lady whose husband's offer of coin for my virtue I declined, we found a home upon the Barony of Valeur."

She did not need to see their exchange of glances to know they recognized the name. "At Castle D'Argent, Mace was accepted as kin, and I became companion to the eldest sister. But the blessing was short-lived, it there Mace suffered abuse I was powerless to stop."

Hector sat forward. "You say the family whose blood flows through his veins and ours did him injury?"

"Not them, but those who have taken control of the D'Argent heir who is two years older than Mace."

His brow grooved. "We are unaware of this, having little contact with the D'Argents since our incompetent King John lost his family's Duchy of Normandy and other French lands over a century past, forcing that family to answer first to those the King of France set over them."

"They are a fine family still, but the losses suffered in fighting for King Philip at Crécy and then the pestilence render them vulnerable."

"The heir's sire is dead?"

"Oui, and an uncle, and another uncle wrongfully imprisoned."

"For what?"

"I never learned, only that it is an attempt for those in control of the heir to make the barony their own, and all the easier if they persuade one of his sisters to wed. Fortunately, one is too young, and the other whom I served refuses, certain her little brother will meet an ill end if she speak vows."

"A wicked place this world," Warin muttered.

Séverine looked to Hector, and more than seeing he turned all this over, felt it.

"If 'tis possible to aid that family, this is not the time," he said. "Tell us what led to the abuse of Mace and the one responsible."

When twice she opened and closed her mouth without result, he said, "First drink."

So different from when I brought Mace to Wulfen, she thought as she carried the cup to her lips. *Far from unfeeling.*

For how much Hector wanted to depart Stern, he was surprised by the depth of his patience. And from another questioning look cast at him, Warin noted it as well. Perhaps more than anyone, once he had known nearly all sides of his older brother, and now it felt he picked at threads between Hector and Séverine that should be easily cut.

Pray, let him not want her, Hector entreated again. *I would not add to the gravest of mistakes.*

Séverine returned the cup to the table and said, "The animal is Louis fitz Géré."

"Fitz Géré!" Warin exclaimed. "I know the name from grandmother's readings."

As did Hector, Mace's abuser likely a descendant of the eleventh-century malefactor defeated by Godfroi D'Argent. Three hundred years later, it seemed that family had not corrected its ungodliness and, quite possibly, sought vengeance against the D'Argents.

"He is determined to wed the eldest sister, but of equal import is keeping control of her little brother until he can dispose of him in a way none are able to prove his involvement." She swallowed. "The D'Argent heir, hoping to take refuge with a neighboring baron he believed would secure him an audience with the king and allow him to report Fitz Géré's abuse of wardship, enlisted Mace to aid in his escape. When they were overtaken distant from the castle, the heir was locked in his chamber and my cousin sentenced to a thrashing."

Hector's hands ached for the grip of his fingers. And he did not have to look to Warin to know it was the same for him.

Tears in her voice, she continued, "When the pleadings of my mistress were ignored, I tried to stop it, but Fitz Géré's men held me back. I screamed as Mace refused to do, freed myself and got between the belt and my cousin." She touched the small scars previously noted near one eye. "The leather caught me across the face, and I fell. Then I was forced to watch as punishment was given in full—and then some. Blessedly, Mace retained his tunic, so only if you look closely at his back will you see evidence of the lashing. Far more evidence is found in his distrust, quick anger, and determination to defend himself and me even when it is not possible." She looked to

Warin. "He likes and admires you. Do you remain upon the barony, I beseech you to aid with his training."

When he did not respond, she continued, "I did not wish to leave the D'Argent lady I served, but we had no choice. It had become dangerous for Mace, and Fitz Géré set us out."

"Where next did you journey?" Hector asked.

"Deciding it was time to honor Sir Amaury's wishes that Mace train at Wulfen, we moved west. I took work wherever I could, adding to our savings to ensure we had enough funds to buy passage across the channel, a horse to deliver us here, and keep us in food and lodging so no treasures must be sold. As feared, it was nearly as dangerous to pass over lands held by the French as those controlled by the English, but we made it to the coast and across the sea—never guessing greater danger lay this side of it." She smiled sorrowfully. "Now you know all about us that is of any import."

"A picture lacking only a frame," Hector said.

"A frame?"

"That which we hope will result from what was gathered on the day past once it is presented to the king—acquittal of the charges and approval of Mace's training. It is owed you, and we will do all in our power to secure it."

Eyes brimming, she jerked her chin.

Suppressing the longing to go to her, Hector stood. "We appreciate your honesty. Now it is time to take Mace to Wulfen. Since it is best he remain there until all is resolved, I am sure you wish to see him away."

"I do," she said, and when Warin came to her, took his arm.

Noting they looked good together, Hector thought a match might still be possible. It would require lies of omission from the two who had shared a kiss, but—

Nay, even were he not greatly moved by her, even were

there no chance of being found out, he could not—would not—betray his brother.

When they departed with their squires and Mace who shared Warin's saddle, Hector did not allow himself to look back at those before the portcullis, but his brother did. And likely it was for Séverine he did so.

CHAPTER 25

A fortnight. Still no word from King Edward that would give her hope nor cause for despair, and only one missive from Wulfen. Written by Warin, it assured her Mace fared well and expressed hope she continued to heal and was at peace. Though she had wished Hector's name affixed to it, the words comforted.

She did heal, her swollen ear resolved and hearing mostly restored. Though it was unlikely her ribs would fully mend for a month or more, full breaths were possible with only mild discomfort that reminded her to move cautiously lest what gains were made must be made again.

Now as Séverine set aside a second tunic fashioned for Mace after sewing two pairs of chausses she would send to Wulfen when next a messenger came, her eye was caught by what seemed predatory movement near the dais—a small and ineffectual predator.

Following a nap Sebastian had made known he did not wish to take, Dangereuse's son had come belowstairs with seemingly none the wiser.

None but me, she thought after confirming Fira and Lady Héloise continued to delve the journal of a thirteenth century lady newly wed to the second of three Wulfrith sons.

Of the Jewish faith, the marriage had been made to protect her family and her from persecution. That was all, and yet love had followed—and twelve children, all surviving to adulthood.

Slipping beneath the high table, Sebastian moved toward the skirts of his mother who worked quill and ink over the accounting. However, something halted him five feet from his destination, and Séverine realized he had sensed her gaze when he turned his upon her.

Smiling, he put a finger to his lips. As he had never gifted her such, all Séverine could think to do was touch her own lips and nod.

He continued forward, threw his arms around his mother's legs, and laughed at her cry of surprise. His expression of joy was as unexpected as the lady's response. Dangereuse dropped her quill and, face lit with delight, plucked her son from beneath the table.

Séverine was not the only one enthralled, all others pausing in their labors—Lady Héloise, Fira, Esta, and servants.

"What is this mischief, Bastian?" his mother revealed his pet name as she settled him on her lap.

He splayed a hand. "Five days I not make you cry."

She startled, then with what sounded false gaiety said, "Of course you have not, my love." She pushed back her chair.

As she rose and shifted him to her hip, the boy said, "Uncle say five days and he give me wooden sword."

It was the most Séverine had heard him speak, revising the suspicion he was incapable of complete sentences.

"Did Wulfrith? Well, that we shall see."

Her tone of disapproval did not escape him, and from his

jutting lower lip, a tantrum stirred, but when she said something low, he drew in his lip. "I will try, Mama."

Curiosity further roused, Séverine longed to ask after the little boy who was quite handsome when his face was not twisted with frustration or anger, but just as Dangereuse's tale must come to her, so too her son's. Meaning unless her future was here as seemed unlikely, these things she would never know.

An hour later, what was told by the knight who had ridden hard on the castle and crossed the hall with long-reaching strides made the likelihood of Stern becoming Séverine's home barely possible.

Quickly she was shed of her gown, then cloaked, mounted, and a pack containing her possessions tied to her saddle. Struggling against tears over leaving behind those who accompanied her to the outer bailey and fear of what lay ahead, she followed the one who had come for her and was followed by that one's squire to ensure they reach their destination unimpeded.

Wulfen Castle

Coursed with perspiration, tunic and chausses forming a second skin the same as Rémy's garments, Hector completed a swing that sent his brother's pole axe spinning toward the fence at which Mace, Warin, and others watched their practice. Then he took a step back from his panting opponent and jutted his chin at the five glimpsed moments earlier. "There!"

Two of the riders were of the patrol—squires soon to be knighted. The other three had been intercepted, whether due to trespass or this their rightful destination.

"'Tis Sheriff D'Arci!" Warin identified the warrior just as Hector concluded the same and that the other whose chain mail caught light was Percival's squire. As for the hooded figure, though chausses and boots were visible beneath a mantle, likely here was one come to Wulfen once more in the guise of a man—this time for a very different reason.

He looked to those in the training yards outside the outer walls whose practice had been suspended to observe Hector and Warin at arms. The victor of that contest had been matched with Rémy who had surprised in besting fellow squires.

Since his skill with bow and arrow greatly outweighed his facility with other weapons, here proof these past weeks of training under Warin was a better match than the knight to whom he was assigned. Just as Warin was able to shoulder past Mace's defenses, so too their youngest brother's. Unfortunately, though Hector made progress in convincing Warin his place was here, the lady could undo all.

"Return to practice!" he barked, and as those given into his charge obeyed, he turned to Rémy. "Well done, Squire. Mastery is nigh."

His brother inclined his head, and though often what sufficed in place of words was all to be expected of him, he said, "I am pleased Warin is home. He will stay, will he not?" So smoothly spoken, it was as if practiced.

"Be assured I will do all I can to convince him his place is here. Now as he and I must meet our visitors, 'tis a good time to give Mace his first lesson in fletching."

Rémy looked to the approaching riders. "Is it his lady cousin?" he asked, her tale and the boy's having been shared with him.

"Aye, and it is an ill thing Sheriff D'Arci brings her."

"You think the D-Do-?" Rémy cleared his throat, more

slowly said, "You think the Dover authorities reached Edward ahead of your messenger and the sheriff's?"

"Let us hope that is what this is, rather than the king's judgment following presentation of evidence both sides."

Rémy nodded and crossed to the fence.

Though Mace was reluctant to depart, having likely recognized the sheriff and suspecting the hooded one was Séverine, he went with Rémy to the carpenter's shop in the outer bailey, a portion of which was dedicated to producing arrows.

When the three riders and their escort reined in, Hector and Warin greeted them amid shouts and clanging steel both sides.

"Regrets, Baron Wulfrith," Percival said as Séverine lifted her chin and the sparkle of shadowed eyes was seen. "Unfortunately, what is not permitted inside Wulfen must be let in until you determine how to proceed."

Tensing at being affected by that sparkle despite the passage of a fortnight and so much to occupy him he was fortunate to gain four hours sleep each night, Hector glanced at Warin and was panged by annoyance at not knowing what would bother more—finding himself watched as he certainly was or had it been the lady his brother fixed on?

Doubtless, he sensed something between Hector and Séverine. As concluded before, were Warin seriously drawn to the lady, there would have to be disclosure though it could prevent him from returning to the fold. And more imperative than Hector having another besides Owen to help maintain and strengthen the family's reputation was that this brother remain for Rémy, Mace, and others who must overcome challenges faced by few of their peers.

Were one who wielded weapons to be so afflicted, far better Warin's firm, steadying hand than a frustrated one.

"Remain mounted all the way to the donjon and go directly

to the solar, Sheriff," Hector said. "We will join you once the patrol is strengthened and others set out for Stern to increase their numbers."

Percival gave a one-sided smile. "When I told Lady Dangereuse you would send men to her, she said of course you would, and I should remind you that those sent be receptive to a woman's command."

A mistake made once and not again. For the disrespect shown her by two squires nearing knighthood, lessons on answering to the fairer sex had been expanded to better prepare warriors defending a land much altered by the pestilence whose macabre dance had left many demesnes in the hands of women.

"Certes, they will be receptive."

When Hector, Warin, and Owen entered the solar a short while later, all of Séverine was seen where she stood beside the table at which much of Wulfen's tedious business was conducted between the great postered bed and stone hearth.

As known and now clearly visible absent her mantle, she wore tunic and chausses, but he did not see a man and believed he would not again even were her hair beneath a cap.

She was more lovely than remembered, and he thought it due to high color and hair escaping her braid, the golden strands prettily disarrayed all about a face no longer evidencing Le Creuseur's beating.

Though Hector was rarely self-conscious about his appearance, he wished there had been time to set himself aright. But he was not the only one capable of offending a lady's senses, neither brother nor uncle wasting time better spent unfolding the situation to examine its wrinkles and creases.

Pleased with the efficiency of Squire Gwayn who had seen the table laid with filled goblets and individual servings of viands, Hector said, "Refresh yourselves."

As he seated himself at the head, Warin pulled out the chair to the right of his brother, and Hector saw Séverine press a hand to her ribs as she went into it. Hopefully, the ride had been only uncomfortable, it being an ill thing to twice heal an injury. As Warin claimed the chair on her other side, Percival and Owen lowered into those opposite.

Once thirst and hunger were satisfied, Hector said, "When you are ready, Sheriff."

"Percival," the knight corrected. "This day I am here more in the capacity of friend than lawman."

"Understood. And appreciated."

"Last eve, I received a missive from our relation, Sir Achard Roche, who has resumed his duties to King Edward now his brother is recovered from a near mortal sickness. He told of a complaint against my office that reached the king whilst traveling his realm, and that it was submitted by the Sheriff of Dover." He nodded. "A thorn in my side, but of little consequence compared to what his deputy gained from Edward. Though Achard knew not the specifics, he told the king granted the sheriff's deputy permission to enter any place upon Wulfenshire—be it castle, hovel, or workshop—to find and arrest a French lady who attempted to murder an Englishman. Additionally, lest he encounter resistance, Le Creuseur was given a contingent."

Hector glanced at Séverine and, for how still her face, was certain already she knew this. "Surely they may not enter Wulfen Castle," he said, it hard to believe the king would allow so great a trespass.

"Not told, and Achard may not have known to ask since he seems unaware of your family's involvement in the matter. But he learned the one injured in the Dover stable is a knight, which the deputy did not reveal to us, possibly because it is less believable a man of the sword fell victim to a woman—and a slight one." His gaze flicked to Séverine from whose eyes shone interest as if she had not been told this.

"And here the last thing of note," Percival said. "Hours after Le Creuseur gained from the king what he sought, the messenger I sent with Lady Séverine's testimony overtook the royal entourage."

Did mine as well? Hector wondered.

"By then Edward had determined to spend what remained of his time away from court in hunting and jousting. Thus, all who wished an audience were to follow him to London. Though Achard does not know what my messenger is to deliver, he guessed correctly it has to do with the complaint against me. To ensure all is known before judgment is passed on Lady Séverine, I determined to deliver her here so you may decide how to proceed."

Hector mulled that, then fairly certain of the answer he would gain, asked, "What would you do were you me?"

Percival looked to Séverine. "As I think you cannot run without endangering your cousin, the Wulfriths, and my family, I believe what is begun must be finished as planned, Lady."

He did know Hector's mind. What Sir Maël had done with Lady Mercia could not be done with Séverine. As recorded by Sir Elias, that had been love of the full of the heart. Attraction here, but neither Hector nor Warin felt so greatly for this lady. And as Percival said, it would endanger others should she disappear after being entrusted to the Wulfriths, especially since both parties were sympathetic to her cause.

"What say you, Sir Owen?" Hector asked.

This Wulfrith also of silvered dark hair unlike his much older brother who sired Hector, ceased rubbing his jaw. "From what you have told and now this, I agree with Percival."

"Warin?"

He nodded.

"Lady Séverine?"

Lashes fluttering at being consulted, she was slow to answer. "Though I am in agreement and grateful for the aid given my cousin and me, what if the deputy is permitted to search Wulfen Castle as well?"

"He will not enter here. Even if I must defy my king, I will not have the families of those in training question the safety of walls that previously withstood an attack from Edward's miserable ancestor, King John. Too, my actions will be justified since it will be made clear to the deputy and king's men they have no cause to breech these walls nor those of Stern."

"Your plan?" Percival asked.

"It forms, and much hinges on Le Creuseur remaining confident we are unaware of his arrival." Hector looked to his uncle. "To further ensure the defenses of Stern where he is sure to go first, I shall send you there."

Discomfort was visible about Owen's mouth. He had avoided the family home since well before the pestilence, and though he had not revealed the reason he preferred not to enter the place of his childhood, Hector suspected it had much to do with a woman.

"Continue," Owen prompted.

"When Le Creuseur arrives, from atop the walls you will represent the Baron of Wulfrith in denying him and his men entrance, informing them Lady Séverine has been moved to Wulfen Castle for disruption of Stern's household."

"What say you?" Warin protested.

"Neither do I like it," said Hector, "but I think it best protects those of Stern and renders Le Creuseur's forces less formidable since he will leave some men behind should an attempt be made to steal her away when he rides on Wulfen."

"Well thought," Warin said, "but what of when you do not let them in to search for the lady?"

More thoroughly, Hector examined all sides of that, cast out one possibility, decided on another. "It will not be necessary for them to enter. At nightfall, I will show her to them from atop the walls."

Séverine gasped.

"They will be told since night is upon us, the matter must await the new day. Just as at Stern, they will suspect an attempt to take her elsewhere." He smiled. "And we will not disappoint."

Seeing in the eyes of his fellow warriors they worked through this, likely forming plans similar to his own, he said, "This is what I propose and would take counsel from all."

CHAPTER 26

Nightfall.

As expected, those sent by the king had gone first to Stern and left a half dozen in the wood when Sir Owen told the prisoner had been moved to the great fortress—this reported by two of Wulfen's knights set to watch at a distance.

Thus far, all went to plan. Would the rest? Séverine wondered as she bent toward Mace who, earlier permitted to dine with her in Hector's curtained solar, had further brightened when presented with new garments.

Though he was not fully acquainted with the plan, he knew enough to seem certain of its success. And that was a balm to she who would not have him burdened by worry for her.

"My sire's family will protect my mother's family," he said, his confident expression visible in the light of numerous torches set about the walls. "I trust them. You do as well, oui?"

"I believe they will aid me as much as possible." She kissed his cheek, straightened, looked past Warin who would return him to the hall, and nodded at the gatehouse where Hector awaited her. "I must go."

"To sooner return," he sought reassurance.

Unable to make that promise, she said, "I am anxious for that and will miss you more than I have these past weeks." She swallowed. "I know you shall continue to make your sire proud."

"Were he alive," Mace said as never before done, though he had stopped suggesting it was possible Amaury de Chanson lived. It seemed now he had others to fill the role of a father, he could let go of impossible hope. It both gladdened and saddened Séverine. Though surely it was best to cast off broken ties, there was something wondrous in the hope of a child.

"I love you," she said then stepped past Warin. Raising skirts she would not long wear, she began ascending to the gatehouse roof, pausing only when Mace called, "I love you!"

This is not farewell, she told herself as she continued forward. *And if it is, I will not have him remember my tears by torchlight. They are for me to pray through.*

Upon reaching the roof, she looked across her shoulder and was glad Warin and Mace had started for the inner bailey.

"Come, Lady," Hector called where he stood with his back to the battlements.

The light of flames chasing silver through the black of his hair made her heart beat harder—and her rue these feelings were not merely desire.

Hearing restless horses outside the walls and the voices of those kept waiting a half hour for an answer to the king's decree that custody of the criminal be passed to the Dover deputy, Séverine stepped to Hector with whom she had spoken little since her arrival. "I am ready."

He set a hand on her jaw, studied her face. Then lips parting amid a beard trimmed closer than before, he said, "You look afeared. That is good for those come to our walls, but be assured all aligns."

"I thank you," she whispered and hated her teeth began chattering. Though the night was cool, and more so for not wearing a mantle so her gown would be seen, it was not that cool.

When he lowered his head, she nearly stopped breathing, but no great intimacy this—unless she pressed her mouth to his in sight of those manning the walls. "I know you to be of admirable courage, Séverine. Do not cease now."

"Admirable courage," she murmured. "Spoken by the Baron of Wulfen, I dare not disappoint."

He withdrew his hand. "When I call you forward, show yourself to confirm your identity and let it be seen you are attired as a lady. Whatever is spoken to you, your response will be of a duration only enough to reveal your accent as further proof you are the one sought."

Already she was counseled in that which was to ensure the deputy did not return to Stern and would later aid in leading him astray. "I am prepared, Hector."

Whatever glanced across his face, she thought it due to her use of his Christian name, then he stepped to the embrasure overlooking the drawbridge.

"Deputy Le Creuseur! The lady is here. You may approach to look nearer upon her."

Glancing around the walls, Séverine confirmed what was seen from below. Every other embrasure was filled, whether with a knight or one in training. Though bows were not drawn, their upper portions would be visible amid an abundance of torchlight.

Since the king's men were present, it was no great threat to Wulfen's visitors, but a fine line was walked since quickly it could turn serious with Hector's command that would see arrows nocked and strings drawn.

"Send her out!" shouted one whose voice returned her to the jail cell—and imaginings of what else Mace and she would have suffered had Hector and Warin not arrived.

"As told, with strictures in place to ensure the sons of greatest promise to our realm are not imperiled ere they are fully a danger to their enemies," Hector called, "that is not possible with night upon Wulfen."

"'Twas not night when we arrived!"

"Many my duties to God, king, and country. I am certain our sovereign would agree what comes after..." He exaggerated a shrug. "...comes after."

After a long moment, the deputy said, "Well then, the morrow. Now prove that French whore is here."

Remembering when he had her face to the ground, Séverine crammed fingers into her palms.

"As no such woman is at Wulfen, it appears you have wasted my time and that of the king's men," Hector said.

The one below cursed, said, "Show me Lady Séverine!" When Hector remained unmoving, he amended, "I wish to see the lady, Baron Wulfrith."

Hector motioned her forward as done that day at Calais when he opened a way for her to reach the gates unmolested.

Let not courage desert me, she beseeched the Lord as she stepped to the side of the embrasure. *I would disappoint neither You nor him.*

Though she needed no further reminding of how she was to present, she wished Hector would repeat his instructions to allow her to delay looking upon the vile one.

"It goes to plan," he said low, then sidestepped.

Glad to share the embrasure with him, she leaned forward to ensure the gown was seen and looked first to the king's knights who sat their mounts with impatience, this a menial task for those with appetites for sword and shield. Next she moved her regard to the deputy mounted at the place where the end of the drawbridge seated itself when lowered—and ground her teeth.

As if Hector knew the depth of her fear, he settled a hand on the small of her back.

"Well, she does look a lady now!" Le Creuseur trumpeted. "Actually quite pretty, which makes me question if it was disruption of Stern's household that caused her to be removed to a place exclusive to the darker sex. Mayhap she who thinks naught of gutting a man makes the mighty Baron Wulfrith—or should I say *Pale Rider?*—a good bedmate."

The pressure on Séverine's back increasing, she knew Hector was not as unmoved as he might appear. "You dishonor the lady who is of no such bent," he said. "And were she, it would not be possible since she is barely able to walk, having yet to recover from the beating you, a man of the law, gave her and her seven-year-old cousin."

"Greatly you misinterpret what you happened upon, Baron. The two having turned vicious, they were dealt with in accordance with the law."

"I know of no law in our civilized country that permits violation of a jailed woman," Hector said.

Torchlight jumped across the deputy's flushed face. "I did not violate her!"

"Nay, but when my brother and I arrived, it was obvious that was your intent."

"You but seek to justify doing me injury and slaying my

witness." The man smiled. "Well, you and your brother shall answer for that."

"We but await the king's summons."

"Which you will receive, albeit at a different time and place than the French woman who shall be tried in Dover."

Greater Séverine's fear. In Hector's solar, it was concluded the deputy but sought the king's aid to get her out of the hands of the Wulfriths and surely hoped between that and her trial he would discover the cask's whereabouts. But it was hope in vain since Mace's treasures were in Hector's care, and that would make this man more vengeful.

"Well, *Lady,* what say you?" the deputy asked.

More than she had been directed to speak. "That I am the one wronged at Dover by Englishmen and again at Ravvenborough, one of those knaves a deputy of low repute."

As Hector's hand traversed her back to her side, Le Creuseur bared his teeth. "When you are handed up on the morrow, more thoroughly we shall discuss this."

Yielding to Hector's urging, she moved to his back.

"We are done," he called down.

"Be warned," the deputy shouted, "we will keep watch throughout the night lest you think to steal her away."

Hector turned to Séverine. "You did well. Now we rest as they shall not."

Shortly, she learned her own rest was to be had in the donjon's tower room where she had prepared for this meeting. Accessed by a wall passage up from the solar, Sir Owen had delivered her there and revealed its purpose was for a Wulfrith wife to discreetly spend time with her husband when he was unable to visit Stern.

This time, the one who preceded her up the stairs was Hector, who likely had been visited here by each of his wives.

When he opened the door and motioned her inside, she

wanted to say, *Stay. Speak to me of things you speak to no other. Reveal your burdens as I have revealed mine. Mayhap I can help as you have helped me.*

But though once more she was to occupy this lovely chamber, she was not his wife and would never be. Turning to where he stood in the doorway, she said, "'Til the hour ere dawn."

"'Til the hour, Lady." He closed the door.

Aching for what she wanted more than anything she had wanted for herself, she listened to his every footfall. When the turning of steps stole what remained of them, she changed back into tunic and chausses and went beneath the bedclothes one would not need this time of year had they another to hold to in the night.

THE HOUR ERE dawn would soon be past, but as Hector assured, all went to plan.

The diversion was sprung, causing half a dozen of those camped outside Wulfen to set after three northbound riders who came near to slipping past, one of whom was to be seen wearing a gown. Doubtless, an unhappy squire.

Once it was confirmed the remainder of Le Creuseur's men had broken camp to follow the others, moving opposite the direction they should go to prevent the lady and her escort from reaching London, traversal of a wondrous underground passage was completed.

When Séverine emerged in the wood behind Hector and ahead of Warin, there was little time to appreciate the concealed outlet that had to be one of several since she had seen other iron-gated corridors branching off the one taken by torchlight. As revealed by the dark orange glow of a sun aspiring to return to the sky, here were others of her escort, including Percival D'Arci.

None spoke as Hector secured packs to his saddle, one of which held the cask. Nor did Warin speak as he led Séverine to her horse and assisted her astride, careful to avoid ribs she had firmly bound in the hope of withstanding the speed required to stay ahead of the deputy and king's men should they too soon turn back.

Providing the bait made of the three first to depart stayed within sight but out of reach, drawing their pursuers farther north before taking cover to change garments and go separate ways, a day's lead could be gained—more if, unaware of being duped, they continued north.

Unlikely. What *was* likely, was they would go to London to report the Wulfriths' defiance. God willing, by then an audience would be had with King Edward that would bring him to her side.

Séverine smiled her gratitude at Warin, then watched him mount alongside his brother.

Though she knew Hector would have preferred leaving Wulfen in Warin's charge, it was necessary he accompany them since not only was he present for the events in Ravvenborough but must answer for the witness's death. Thus, until Sir Owen was comfortable with Stern's defenders resuming complete charge of that castle's protection, Hector's uncle would remain there while the second of Wulfen's senior knights kept this fortress for its baron.

"Lady, out of necessity we ride hard," Hector said. "If it becomes too much, alert me and we will slow as much as possible."

No utterance of protest, Séverine de Barra, she told herself. *Not when far greater harm may be done you or these men should you be overtaken. Stay courageous.*

"I shall alert you."

Though still too dim to see his face clearly, she sensed doubt, but he inclined his head.

Moments later, warriors who numbered nine, including three squires, began the journey south to save a lady of no true relation to the Wulfriths.

CHAPTER 27

She began to think they would sleep in their saddles, trusting the horses to find their way to London—and perhaps with her aid since so great her discomfort she feared she would find no rest outside of unconsciousness.

At last, beneath a moon bright sky, Hector called, "Make camp!"

They turned into the trees they had ridden alongside for hours lest they encounter riders who might inform the deputy of the path his prey took. And they would have encountered them had not the scouting squires provided enough warning for all to go to the wood until the way was clear again.

It took Hector and his men a quarter hour to search the area and determine the best place to pass the night, then all dismounted—except Séverine who struggled to keep a face over her aches as Warin approached.

"You must hurt even more," he referenced the last time they paused to water the horses and she groaned when he lifted her down. "Tell how best to aid you, my lady."

"Stand near, and I shall come to you." She got one leg over, turned, set hands on his shoulders, and told him to grip her high beneath the arms.

The slow slide down his body was uncomfortable, but of greater discomfort was the breathlessness between them, though hers was of regret for what she feared stole his.

Drawing her hands from his shoulders, she said, "I thank you. Now I require privacy." Not only to relieve herself, but to undo what she had done in the hope it would make the ride more tolerable.

Releasing her, Warin nodded over his shoulder. "Yon boulders will provide good cover and are well within the perimeter around which Wulfrith sets a patrol."

Though somewhat distant, the great stones hedged by sparse trees were opposite the direction the men had gone to tend their bodily needs and would ensure privacy. Thus, with purposeful steps, Séverine crossed to them as her escort began encamping.

Upon gaining their backside, desperate impatience made her press a hand to the nearest moss-covered boulder to brace herself for the pain of a full breath. When it resisted going as deep as craved, she assured herself she would have breaths aplenty once she removed the binding that had held her together throughout the ride and maintained posture conducive to healing.

Though she longed to cast off her tunic, she jerked one arm from its sleeve, whimpered, and more carefully withdrew the other. Hands free to work beneath the garment, she hitched up the hem to shed light on the binding cloth and began picking at the knot—and picking and picking.

"God help me," she rasped and dug into what had tightened during the ride, straining and bending nails whose hurt was tolerable compared to shifting ribs and the need to breathe well. Still it resisted.

Her next whimper becoming a muffled cry, she shoved her back against the boulder, casting more light on the knot. As she clawed at it, she told herself panic was of greater hindrance than help, but—

She wrenched at the material both sides, but it would not be torn. Of course it would not!

Sobs escaping, harder she pressed her back against the boulder, curled fingers beneath the binding's lower edge, and tried to make room for a deep breath. Just one...

Blessedly, through the mist of what some might think madness, she was struck by a ridiculously simple solution. Unable to silence her misery, she leaned to the side and thrust a hand down her boot. Out came her meat dagger. Off came its scabbard.

Now to still shaking hands to cut the knot without slicing herself.

HECTOR HALTED, listened to sounds so faint beneath the voices of those making camp it took some moments to determine their direction. Suppressing the impulse to sound the hue and cry lest whoever sought to quiet Séverine acted rashly, Hector drew his sword and stretched his legs opposite where he had set a knight of the first watch.

There being a slippery balance between speed and stealth, he beseeched the Lord to aid him in reaching Séverine before she was irretrievable.

When the low-burning campfire came into sight, the sound of her struggle was of so little volume it was nearly buried beneath her escorts' voices.

Certain it came from the boulders where she must have sought privacy, silently he cursed himself for his certainty the area was clear of two- and four-legged predators. Hoping he had not erred in believing they were well out of Le Creuseur's reach and whoever trespassed was more foolish than dangerous, Hector approached at an angle that allowed him to see what moonlight revealed without revealing himself. So unexpected was the sight, he halted.

Shoulders moved by grunts and soft cries, Séverine stood alone against a boulder, tunic raised up her waist and hands working beneath it. She struggled, but not against someone—against a binding cloth she sought to cut away with a blade coursed by moonlight.

"Almighty!" he growled. Glad fear for her safety had kept him from alerting others, he returned his sword to its scabbard and abandoned stealth.

When she did not react in any way to indicate she was aware he was near and the blade flashed again, he rasped, "Séverine!"

Her head came up and splayed hands lost hold of the blade. "Help me. I can...hardly breathe."

He halted to the side to keep her in moonlight, drew his dagger, and cut the knot. Then as the cloth continued to bind for being wound several times, he returned his dagger to his belt and commanded, "Keep your tunic out of the way."

As if she trusted none more, she raised it beneath her breasts, making no maidenly protest as his fingers brushed her abdomen and waist as ought to be exclusive to lovers.

When the binding fell, she sank against the boulder, and he was struck by the longing to follow her there and feel upon his face the breath restored to her. Thankfully, he had the control to step back—and the wit to distract his body by summoning words of rebuke.

Keeping his voice low to delay the moment others sought assurance she was well, he said, "Do you not know the harm that can be done in binding cracked ribs? It can delay healing or cause them to mend wrong—worse, lead to sickness of the chest for lack of full breaths."

"At Stern, the physician told it was unnecessary, but..." She replenished her breath. "...as I found relief in holding to my ribs, I thought constant pressure would aid during the ride."

"You should have consulted Wulfen's physician or me. As you did not lose consciousness and take a fall that could have broken your neck, you must be in God's favor."

Her mouth convulsed toward a smile. "Let it be so. To survive England, much favor I require."

"You will survive it. Now return your arms to your sleeves."

After more breaths ending on sighs of relief, she did so, but the first arm was more easily sheathed than the second.

Hector caught up the sleeve and raised it to allow her hand to find the opening. When it slid inside, he should have retreated, but realizing she no longer drew the breaths craved, returned his gaze to hers. And saw desire there that caused his own to strain its chains and further loosen its moorings.

Before he could step back, she placed a hand on his jaw. "Do I survive England, it will be because of the Lord's grace and you."

Further reason to retreat, and he thought he could have were this base desire only—and had she not pushed off the boulder, moved one hand to the back of his neck and the other to his shoulder.

"Lady!" he warned. And nearly laughed at himself since he had only to walk away.

"Because of you," she said.

"We will not do this again," he spoke across the shadow deepening between them. "Warin—"

"Is a good man, but could I have any, it would be you."

"I am not to be had," he said, strain in his voice for feet refusing to retreat and hands unwilling to set her back.

"Not to be had, as may prove my own fate," she murmured and offered her mouth.

With a groan, Hector lowered his head.

Her response beyond sweet, he did not heed the voice reminding him she was too tender to lay hands upon. However, he heeded the tread of boots ceasing an advance that should have been heard sooner.

Fingers thrust into her hair, he lifted his head and looked to the left. Had he suspected an enemy, he would have pulled back and brought his sword to hand, but he knew who stood fifteen feet distant. As the damage was done and it would be worse to behave guiltily, he met his brother's gaze and said, "Warin is here, Séverine."

She tensed, but as if also realizing a hasty withdrawal would exaggerate their indiscretion, lowered her hands and stepped back.

Hector saw emotions convulse his brother's moonlit face, then Warin looked to Séverine and said, "Lady."

"Sir Warin."

Silence fell as if none knew what came next.

Hector knew—providing his brother did not stalk away. Though this was not how he wished Séverine to learn of the loss of Warin's wife, if that was what it took to air out three years of dark, damp, and mold, he would bear it over once more being given his brother's back.

Warin warred a while longer, then strode to within a fist's reach of his brother. "You told you would not wed again, that you would have me for your heir."

Focusing on him to ensure Séverine did not affect his response, Hector said, "I shall not take another wife, and it *is* my wish our line continue through you."

"If that is so, for what do you kiss Lady Séverine? Why were your hands all over her?"

Is that all he had seen—Hector kissing her, not her kissing him? Hector's hands upon her, not hers upon him?

"Were she a harlot, I would understand, but she is not," Warin said. "Though..."

Offended by what that single word suggested of Séverine, Hector said sharply, "Though?"

"This is not the first time you are intimate, is it?"

Hector drew a slow breath. "We have kissed before, but the lady's virtue is intact."

Briefly, Warin closed his eyes. "I suspected there was something more between you, hoped I was wrong." He looked to Séverine. "You must know I begin to feel for you." He nodded. "Not yet enough to be lasting, so I am glad I sought to ensure your well-being. If an end must be made of a thing, best done sooner than later, do you not agree?"

Hurting for him and hating she built higher the wall between the brothers, Séverine said, "Oui."

Warin looked to Hector. "At least it is not the affections of another wife of which I am deprived. That would be unforgivable."

From his bitterness and the trebling of Hector's tension, much was lodged between those words, and she understood what it was. Warin blamed his brother for the loss of his wife, and it seemed Hector accepted responsibility. But what had he done? From how it was worded—

"Apologies for the intrusion," Warin said and moments later went from sight.

"God's teeth," Hector rasped and turned opposite the camp.

Séverine followed and jumped in front of him. Though it jolted ribs more sore than since long before she departed

Wulfen, she held close her pain and said, "What happened? What your brother spoke suggests..." She shook her head. "I would not believe that of you."

His jaw worked. "I do not think he meant it to sound that way, and though I am grateful you do not believe I fit that frame, it does not change that I deprived him of a much loved wife."

"How?"

"Hubris," he clipped, then nodded over his shoulder. "See to your needs have you not already and gain your rest. For how hard this day, the morrow will be harder, though I shall have your saddle padded with blankets. Should that not suffice, one of my knights will take you up before him so you need only attend to stabilizing yourself."

It was best she not ride with him, Séverine told herself. She believed Warin had no great feeling for her though he had moved that direction, but after what he had witnessed, it would be insensitive for Hector and her to share a saddle.

When he started to step around her, she caught his arm. "At least tell me this—is the wife lost to Warin among the reasons some call you *Pale Rider?*"

He jerked as if to shake her off, then growled, "Very well, let us slay all hope you have for me so we may fix our attention on ensuring you not suffer the same as those to whom I was wed—a fate my sister-in-law shared though my hubris was her end rather than God wanting another to continue the Wulfrith line."

When he looked to her hand on him, she removed it and pressed it to her ribs.

"Still you hurt," he said.

"Some, but better this than feeling as if my lungs collapse. Now tell what Ondine began in speaking of your lost wives."

"So none question what goes here, let us move within sight of the others."

She was glad he considered that and, after retrieving her knife, followed him to where they could be seen by those at the fire who satisfied thirst and hunger—among them Warin though he stood apart.

"It began with my first betrothed whom I hardly knew," Hector said. "Shortly ere we were to wed, an accident took her life. These things happen, and I did not see it as warning."

"I am sorry."

"Another wife was found for me. I did not love her, but we were content with each other. She and our son"—further his voice deepened—"died during childbirth. These things happen, and so neither did I see it as warning and once more yielded the search for a wife to my grandmother and sire. I did not love the one with whom next I spoke vows, and she gave me no cause. However, she proved more unhappy with me than I with her."

"As your sister told."

"Which she should not have," he growled, and she thought he would tell no more, but he said, "Unbeknownst to me, the lady was besotted with another whom she would have wed had her family not preferred a Wulfrith. While I served Edward in France, I was delivered word she sought an annulment on grounds of lack of consummation."

Séverine caught her breath.

"Aye, she told I was incapable."

"But your first wife was lost in childbirth."

"She explained that away by submitting either I was no longer capable, else another fathered the babe and for that God took the lives of mother and child."

Séverine was shocked by the cruelty. "But surely you had relations with your second wife."

"Surely, but during my absence from England she visited her family and gained the cooperation of their physician in confirming she remained a maiden."

"You knew this when you aided me at Calais?"

"I did, but though tempted to cast anger and bitterness at all women, it went against reason since those of the fairer sex with whom I am longest acquainted are mostly righteous and generous of heart. Too, after what some of my countrymen did to the women of Caen, I could not leave you to such a fate."

"Again, I thank you."

"The physician's testimony and my wife's having satisfied the Church, an annulment was awarded, resulting in sly asides against my first wife and me." He ground his teeth. "It is good I could not get home. I would have contested the annulment and might still be bound to her—that is, providing God did not take drastic measures to ensure mutual animosity was not bridged and a child made."

Séverine longed to protest God would do such, but she feared he would close up.

He glanced at those before the fire. "I was soured on marriage, but it being necessary the Wulfrith heir wed, I determined to choose my next wife and, upon returning to England, made a match. Unlike my first wives, she was no beauty, but she was intelligent, absent affectation, and so tall and sturdy her prospects narrowed each time she gained another year's growth." He smiled slightly. "She was nearly my own height."

Beginning to feel the cool of the night, Séverine crossed her arms over her chest and, cupping her ribs, found more relief in deep breaths.

"Though set on making an heir with her, it was not only for that I visited Stern often as not done with my other wives. I became attached to her, and when she told she was with child..." Briefly, he closed his eyes. "Now here the hubris of which you should beware. Not only did that sin lead to the death of Warin's wife but mine, our unborn child, my sire, and nearly Ondine."

She blinked. "What say you?"

"For vainglory, I went where my wife beseeched me not to go and brought home something besides gifts—the pestilence I was unaware had entered my squire."

In answer to her disbelief, he nodded. "Not only did he and members of my family succumb though I isolated them, but some of the castle folk. Albeit happening all across England, I took the loss of another wife as a warning against wedding—and punishment for pride that ignored the wishes of others and the danger into which I ventured."

She frowned. "Where did you venture?"

"What matters is others paid a price that was mine to pay." He looked to the camp again. "I seek forgiveness, but fail to make a good case for it." He went silent, then said, "Though I was determined not to wed again for giving many cause to name me *Pale Rider,* I did."

"Why if you did not wish it and how did your fourth wife die?"

"The match was the king's doing. I resisted, but the lady expressed an interest in me and Edward wished her wed away from court, the rumor being she was too tempting for one who sought to remain true to Philippa. I yielded, and ere long greater my regret. Never before was a Stern household so disrupted. Bored and restless, she stirred trouble with the garrison, servants, and my sisters—and once rode without escort to Wulfen to complain to her inattentive husband. Detesting the monotony of Stern, she demanded we spend time at court and, when seduction did not move me, told even the riding was bad. Thinking to provide a distraction for one much accomplished in the saddle, I sent word to the horse master she was to be gifted with whichever mare she chose. I knew it would be spirited but did not believe it would surpass her skills. Shortly thereafter, she took a fall from which she did not rise, angering the king for my failure to ensure her well-being. I have been out of favor with him since."

"Oh, Hector."

"A betrothed and four wives lost in seven years, only one surviving by way of annulment," he said. "There the *Pale Rider* of me. There further proof my great commission is altered such that I keep Wulfen in highest standing until it passes to one not born to me."

Though she could see how he would think that and might herself in his circumstances, she said, "I do not believe the Lord would ensure against you siring children by taking up your wives—nor making mockery of vows with false annulment of your second marriage."

He drew breath. "Believe as you will and find your rest. Good eve."

This time Séverine let him go, but it was hours before she slept, and only after he and others of his watch were relieved and he went beneath a blanket on the opposite side of the fire. And turned his back to her.

CHAPTER 28

London, England

Two and a half days of avoiding riders, villages and towns. One and a half days of Hector distancing himself from Séverine and Warin distancing himself from both. Throughout, the others feigning ignorance.

Now London. Even on its outskirts, it had teemed with more people than Séverine had seen in one place. She had been unnerved by Dover, firstly due to the desperation of finding a way through unfamiliar streets, but it was naught compared to this. And the more deeply they penetrated London, further Dover shrank.

"There Westminster," the sheriff said near Séverine's ear.

This was the only day since departing Wulfen that she had shared a saddle, Hector insisting she enter the city in the charge of a lawman lest Le Creuseur or one under his command had reached London first with tidings of Baron Wulfrith's defiance of the king and authorities sought to detain the lady—if not the entire party.

Thus far, from the city's gate through its crowded innards to the road bordering the River Thames, they had progressed toward the palace unhindered. But that was no guarantee barriers would not be raised before gaining an audience with Edward.

Had Séverine not kept her head down beneath her hood, focusing on the buildings and people all sides, it would not have been necessary for the sheriff to point out the place they would enter providing the king responded to Hector's dispatch as believed he would—especially since it would be accompanied by a piece of Mace's inheritance her cousin accepted could be lost to him.

Taking in the collection of buildings around the bend in the expansive river, Séverine gasped. When they had passed the Tower of London also built on the bank of the Thames, she had thought it imposing, but Westminster with its palace and the great abbey pointing the way to heaven seemed more so.

"It is grand, Sir Percival."

"And will be grander yet," he said wryly. "Edward spares no expense on it and Windsor Castle."

"Why should he when he has only to raise taxes to pay for his excesses?" Hector said as he drew alongside. As he had brought up the rear since entering the city, Warin leading the way with the squires and knights between, she had not looked on him for over an hour.

Hoping for a smile in return, she curved her mouth and said, "In France it is told often his royal purse is as light as it is heavy."

He did not smile, but risen eyebrows lightened his face. "It is so. Though in many things our king is to be admired, too much of the people's coin is spent waging war and reflecting his grandeur."

"Is that not true of all monarchs?"

"'Tis, though it seems ours is determined to surpass every one." He looked to the sheriff. "I shall send my squire ahead to secure lodging and stabling at the Fair Minster."

"The same inn I would choose," the man said.

Hector returned to Séverine. "Soon you will be out of the saddle."

Of comfort to body, but also mind. Though she dreaded meeting his king and what might come of it, there was good in it drawing her nearer the end of this ordeal.

Hector waved Gwayn forward, delivered his instructions, and as the young man urged his mount past the others, dropped back again.

Unfortunately, the nearer they drew to Westminster, the less wondrous it became as anticipation of being inside the walls shifted nearer that event. But though it could be days before an audience was granted despite the inducement Hector would provide his king, she hoped for the morrow.

Upon their arrival at the Fair Minster that was so near the palace the remaining distance could be walked with ease, Squire Gwayn proved efficient in doing his lord's bidding. Rooms had been secured for all, and stable lads took charge of mounts in need of water, grooming, and rest.

After the sheriff aided in Séverine's dismount, he retrieved her pack and his and led her into the inn that enjoyed a brisk trade in drinks and viands as evidenced by the clamor and few vacant tables.

The others awaited them near the stairs, and it was Hector she settled on where he stood with a pack over an arm—the one that held the cask containing Mace's treasures except for Sir Amaury's missive that had been left at Wulfen to ensure his son was the first to read his words.

Shortly, Hector drew the sheriff aside and she was passed into the care of Warin. It was the nearest she had been to him since confrontation over the kiss, and though she longed to speak with him, this was not the place. However, when Percival returned and passed her pack to Warin with a key, it seemed all would align.

"After you have escorted the lady abovestairs and set a watch over her, join us in the back room." He jerked his head toward a corridor to the left of the bar.

Warin motioned for knights to follow him, but as they started up the stairs, Percival said, "Hold, Lady!" Then he opened his pack and drew out a bundle wrapped in cloth. "This is from Lady Fira."

Séverine faltered in reaching for what had to have been given him before he took her from Stern, and was fairly certain of what it was. Perhaps without permission, Hector's sister had done as intended.

"I thank you," Séverine said and felt a thrill when it came into her hands.

It was fanciful to draw courage from strands made to travel over and under others stretched on a loom then come down off that frame to be cut and sewn into something that fit a woman's curves, but it strengthened her spine.

Lord, let me prove worthy, she beseeched as they ascended the stairs.

Down one corridor they went, then another also accessed by rear stairs. Upon entering the room Warin told was bounded on the right by one he would share with the sheriff and their squires and on the left by one Hector would occupy with his men, he passed her pack to her. As she set it and Fira's gift on a table, he turned away.

"May I speak with you privately, Sir Warin?"

He looked around. "Lady?"

"I would discuss that night."

"Not necessary."

"I believe it is."

Grudgingly, he instructed the knights to settle in their room. When that door closed, he stepped inside, leaving her door open as was proper.

"First, know I am honored you had some interest in me and that I find you attractive," Séverine said.

He stared.

"But..." Realizing direct comparison to his brother was a poor way to preface the rest, she said, "You cannot know this, but I initiated the kiss, and I think you did not see well what you happened upon."

He remained unmoving.

She filled her lungs. "More my hands were on your brother than his were on me, and I do not believe it was because he did not want what I wanted, especially after what he told of the wives lost to him and the pestilence he brought to Stern that took another of his wives with yours."

He ground his teeth loud enough to be heard.

"You must know he thinks God is against him. You must know he repents of hubris he believes took the lives of many at Stern though just as that great evil crawled down every road in France it crawled down every road in England. Perhaps what you do not know is he resisted allowing anything to come of what he feels for me because he is convinced he should not father Wulfen's next heir and believed you had some interest in me."

So many emotions worked his face she braved herself for an angry rejoinder, but he lowered his chin and gripped the back of his neck.

"Sir Warin?"

"Though I thought myself ready, I should not have come home. Not yet. I am aware had Wulfrith..." He trailed off, met her gaze. "Had Hector not brought the Great Mortality to Stern, it would have come."

She felt a pang over him speaking his brother's Christian name as if the kiss he witnessed made family of her.

"But would it have taken my wife...sire...sister-in-law...her unborn child?" he continued. "Would it have ravaged Ondine?" He dropped his arm to his side. "Mayhap it would have chosen others. Mayhap it would have taken the same and more. Mayhap it would have passed over, claiming none, farfetched though that is." He shook his head. "These things I think in the night when, upon awakening with no body curled into mine, sleep refuses to come again."

"You loved your wife very much."

He nodded. "I did not believe I could love again like that but...I thought to try."

Séverine set a hand on his arm. "I am sorry for your losses and the unraveling of ties with your brother."

He breathed deep. "In the presence of God, I thought I had mostly forgiven him as called to do, but in Hector's presence and the absence of my wife, I falter. Now I am beset with a sense of betrayal that has naught to do with a desire to be my brother's heir."

He spoke of his attraction to her. "I did not think it did, Sir Warin."

He seemed to go inside himself and, when he emerged, stood a bit taller. "There are things I must set aside to make things right with my brother and take my place upon Wulfen. I shall, but in *my* time."

"I am glad. Will you remain upon Wulfenshire?"

"Since distancing myself did not sufficiently resolve my losses, it seems best I deal with them there."

"Your family will be pleased."

"I seek that end, and do you pray for me as I do you, mayhap I shall reach it."

She smiled. "I do pray for you and am grateful for your beseechings on my behalf."

He dipped his chin. "I shall set a watch outside your chamber and order drink and viands for you and your guard." He turned. "Bolt the door."

She did so, and though she longed to lie on a bed that was so well-clothed likely it was not infested as more expected at an inn than not, she went to her knees and prayed for the Wulfrith brothers.

Achard. His unannounced appearance in the doorway of the back room had told much though not all.

The king was aware England's renowned trainer of knights had come to London and learned his destination since no attempt was made to hide his progress. Either a soldier at the gate had deemed Hector's arrival to be of import and sent word, or a watch had been kept for the defiant Baron of Wulfen as a result of the deputy or one of his men reaching the king first.

Blessedly, it was the former, but what Achard told beyond that was unwelcome.

It was not the morrow Lady Séverine and her escort would appear before the king. It was this waning day. And as thought possible—and hoped since Edward had provided Le Creuseur men to arrest her—it was confirmed Hector's and Percival's accounts of Ravvenborough had been delayed in reaching Edward during his travels. Received after the Sheriff of Dover presented the law's side of those events, Achard was certain the king was not as set against the lady as when all he knew of the matter was what was first reported.

Having come to the Crown as little more than a youth, Edward's struggles to retain the privileges of kingship when his mother's lover sought to make a puppet of him had rendered him observant, cautious, and distrustful of those in authority who had abused their power and influence to aid Roger Mortimer in usurping Edward's rights, and among them had been men of the law.

Hence, as a different account of what transpired in the jail had been presented, the king would not kick the matter into a corner for others to clean up. And Hector was fairly certain even in the absence of curiosity over the French lady's cousin, Edward would have made room in his schedule to lend her an ear.

Though no longer necessary to request an audience and include the bishop's ring as inducement, the sleep promised Séverine would be denied her. She, Hector, Warin, and Percival were to present in The Painted Chamber of the Palace of Westminster when the church bells marked the fourth hour past noon—less than an hour hence.

"My lord," the knights outside her room acknowledged as Hector strode the corridor, the pack containing the cask draped over a shoulder.

He halted. "The squires prepare the horses. Though the king provides an escort, you shall accompany us to the palace. Await me at the stables."

When they departed, he checked Séverine's door. Pleased it was locked, he rapped. "It is Wulfrith. Open."

Thinking he roused her from sleep, he settled into his heels. However, barely a moment passed before the lock turned and door opened.

From the fair, tousled hair curtaining one eye and skewed

tunic baring a shoulder, either she had slept light or tossed about. "Hector?"

As gravel lined her voice and a squint hid the brown of her eyes, he concluded she had slept lightly and interruption had come at a time after her mind accepted it was no nap it was gifted but restorative sleep. Beyond naturally occurring incidents, he was acquainted with interrupted sleep the same as all knighted at Wulfen who, to ensure they could defend themselves and others, must learn to compensate for slowness of head resulting from abrupt awakenings.

Once more, silently he cursed Edward for his impatience. Better Séverine had not slept than this. Hoping by the time they entered the magnificent room that served as the king's bedchamber and meeting hall she would rise above her unsteadiness, he said, "We are summoned."

She glanced at the unshuttered window through which blue sky yet shone. "I did not sleep away a day, did I?"

"You did not. Ere I could request an audience, the king was informed of our arrival and sent men to deliver us to the palace."

Seeing alarm, he said, "Be of still heart. The commander of our escort is my relation, Sir Achard, who believes Edward is receptive to the accounts belatedly received from Sheriff D'Arci and me. We have the audience we sought, and it was not necessary to part with the ring."

She blinked, and though clearly she remained incapacitated, more of her was present. Eyes shifting to the pack, she said, "Not *yet* necessary."

"I am aware. Now ready yourself to stand before the King of England."

As if feeling cool air on her bared shoulder, she straightened the tunic, causing hair to shift and reveal the damaged ear whose appearance was much improved. "How long have I?"

"A quarter hour."

"That is not enough!" She swung away, stumbled, and might have dropped had Hector not gripped her arm. Firming her feet, she looked to his hand on her and said, "I have wanted to ask how you came by that scar."

"Gained in service to Prince Edward at the battle of Crécy, the victory of which allowed his sire to move against Calais."

She looked to the ridge on his neck. "Did you save his life as likely you saved mine in that jail?"

"I do not know I saved the life of the king's heir, only that I aided in preserving it. Thus, for as angry as Edward was over the death of my fourth wife, he is grateful to me beyond providing England with worthy defenders."

And has yet to reward me, Hector mused, though not bitterly since twice Edward had tried to give what once was coveted—and been twice refused.

He released Séverine. "I shall await you in the corridor."

As he closed the door, he caught the scent of his body. It was not potent but could displease the king, especially since the garments from which it wafted were not fresh. Edward was familiar with the odors and dishevelment of those who warred, hunted, and indulged in other outdoor pursuits, but in courtly settings he valued cleanliness and neatness.

It was the same for those trained at Wulfen, though desirable beyond the formal. As much as possible, warriors were to temper the body's scents lest they find themselves in circumstances requiring stealth. However, better those summoned alongside Séverine were not entirely presentable than keep the king waiting.

A quarter hour later, the door opened on a sight only half expected. Percival had revealed Fira had asked him to deliver a gown to Séverine, but Hector had not considered it would be so fine, albeit of a style far from current. Of greater surprise, its gold-threaded purple evidenced this was the one glimpsed when he sought Séverine in the upper room while his sister attempted to gain their grandmother's permission for her to wear what had belonged to Lady Annyn.

Also unexpected was how Séverine presented beyond the gown fitting well. Despite the pall of lingering fatigue, she was comely with hair curving about her face and curtaining her to her waist. It was acceptable since she was a maiden, but as most her age wore braids to appear restrained, mature, or elegant, the king would not expect the lady of France to present thus.

However, there could be gain in her merely ordering her hair. Though it roused in Hector a vision of her head on a pillow with golden strands cast across it, outside of inappropriate imaginings she appeared fresh, innocent, and incapable of harming any.

"Hector?" She moved aside the arm over which hung her mantle, looked down the gown. "You are well with this?"

Too well, he thought. "Why would I not be? 'Tis a good fit and you look the lady as you ought when you stand before the king in The Painted Chamber."

She frowned. "You are aware this belonged to Lady Annyn?"

"I thought so, though the nearest I have looked on it was years gone when my grandmother set to preserving it."

She nipped her lower lip. "I cannot believe Lady Héloise agreed I should wear it."

"It is possible Fira defied her, but I am glad you make use of it."

Relief lightening her mouth, she turned. "If you would snug the laces and make a bow of them, I would be grateful."

At his hesitation over imaginings of further loosening them, she said, "I tried, but strained my ribs."

Having assisted one wife or another with the same, he was capable, but what had been mostly a simple task with those ladies seemed complicated with this one. He tightened them, tugged at the crossings to better distribute the tension and, feeling her shudder, quickly bowed the ends.

She came around. "I thank you."

A kiss hovered between them, and he might have set his mouth on hers had he not realized this one had less to do with desire than the others. It being more imperative he not yield, he said, "Our escort awaits," and took her mantle and set it on her shoulders.

She had also felt the kiss between them. He was certain of it then and in the silence that followed as he guided her down the corridor. When they began their descent of the stairs, as if to relieve the tension, she said, "Why is it called The Painted Chamber?"

Then she had not heard of the magnificent room that was the envy of other rulers whether they laid eyes on it or it was viewed through the eyes of others who praised it.

"You will see, Séverine, but do not allow it to distract you as some have done to their peril. Fix your eyes on the king."

CHAPTER 29

Palace of Westminster

S he *had* seen. And knew why it was named The Painted Chamber though she had not lingered over the walls of the lengthy room into which she was led. That which she had longest looked upon was what the door had opened onto.

At the near end stood an immense canopied and postered bed that sat inside the frame of another canopy whose posts were dark green patterned with gold stars, and to those floor-to-ceiling posts were tied burgundy curtains surely drawn at night to tame the draught let in by a wall of arched, elaborately-paned windows.

At the far end, past knights both sides and vibrant murals depicting biblical scenes accompanied by explanatory texts, King Edward had awaited Séverine and her escort upon a skirted dais whose cloth replicated the starred green posts.

Though beautifully clothed, cradling a gold goblet, and sitting erect on his throne—no slide in his seat, bow to his back, slump of his shoulders—the handsome man nearing his fortieth year looked comfortable and, strangely, unpretentious. And she realized he had appeared the same when those of Calais trudged past him and his queen.

This son of an inept English king and French princess was confident of his place in the world, though that place had been far from secure when his sire was forced to abdicate to his heir. At the age of four and ten, the third Edward had been under his mother's control and she under the control of her husband's greatest enemy who was also her lover. Four years it had taken him to cast off those chains, and when it was done none could dispute he was different from the second Edward.

Sir Achard of strangely mismatched eyes, to whom Séverine was briefly introduced before departing the inn, had led the way down the chamber, during which she noted the knights within acknowledged him with nods as if in assurance they had done as bid in his absence. Now, a flick of the fingers granting Sir Achard permission to ascend the dais, he bent and spoke something in his sovereign's ear.

Eyes shifting between Percival, Hector, Séverine, and Warin who stood before him, Edward motioned his man aside. As the knight settled to the left, the king looked to Hector. "We began to think you might never again show yourself at court, Baron Wulfrith, that you found our company lacking," he said in a voice of good depth and volume. "Now here you are with a fugitive of more interest than expected."

He reached to the table beside him, tapped one of two documents among other items that had escaped Séverine's notice—further evidence of too little rest. "Enlightening this account of your French kin's guardian who is accused of attempted murder and theft at Dover and now an attack on Deputy Le Creuseur that ended in his witness's death." He raised an eyebrow. "As confirmed in your missive, a collective effort between you and your brother."

"It was I who dealt the killing blow, Your Majesty. As told, it was warranted in defense of an unconscious boy and beaten lady."

The king moved his gaze lower. "The injury Le Creuseur dealt you came near the great vein."

"Certes, I did not honor my training."

A nod. "We are pleased you make no excuses, Wulfrith. And concerned that one who is to think first of providing our realm with worthy warriors was moved from his purpose by what we are fairly certain was a woman."

I am responsible, Séverine thought and, seeing his eyes shift, expected them to settle on her. But they skipped to Warin.

Upon their return to Hector, he said, "Having met the Dover deputy and now satisfied with Sheriff D'Arci's documentation of what happened in the jail that supports your account—despite possible bias toward kin—we have determined to close the matter of Ravvenborough, rendering the death of the witness and injury to Le Creuseur defensible."

Feeling tension decrease both sides of her, Séverine also eased, though not for long.

This time the king's gaze did not skip her. He scrutinized her face, then looked down her. "A most royal color," he murmured and fit eyes to hers. "Being slight of figure and no more than a score aged, you are not what we expected of one said to have gutted an Englishman. Are we as expected, Lady Séverine?"

"I..." She cleared her throat. "Having survived the siege of Calais with my cousin, I saw you there. Hence, you are mostly as expected."

"You were among those we pardoned."

"We were, much gratitude to the six who were ready to die for their fellow citizens."

His lids narrowed. "Much gratitude to them alone?"

Her first mistake. "I am grateful to you as well, Lord King."

He took a drink from his goblet. "Acknowledge it or not, the third King Edward has a higher regard for the lives of others than does Philip who called himself King of France and now his son, John."

She wished she could argue that, but never would she forget the joyous relief of finally seeing her king and his forces arrive at Calais—then depart without attempting to lift the siege beyond showing themselves as if that alone would scatter the English. As for John who inherited France's throne two years ago, she knew too little of the man to compare him to England's king.

"You know it to be so, Lady," Edward said. "As for those six, they were courageous and honorable. For that and our wife's pleadings, we spared them." He set the goblet on the table. "Let none dispute we are fair, at times to a fault—albeit not to a fault in the eyes of God who shows England's king favor, hmm?"

"Much evidence of that, Your Majesty."

"We are pleased you agree. Now tell, are you recovered from your injuries?"

Was it asked to determine if she was well enough to stand trial? She touched her ribs, lifted her hand, and hooked hair behind the ear that still bore some evidence of the fist dealt it. "Not fully, though I am much improved."

"Then the Wulfriths have treated you well."

"They have, and been kind to my cousin who was delivered to England to train with his kin."

"And there all your troubles began, eh?"

Deciding to be truthful, she said, "Our troubles began at

Calais. Not only did my cousin lose a sire and I an uncle, but we were deprived of our home. Hence, great our labors to secure shelter, feed and clothe ourselves, and save coin so I could keep the word given Sir Amaury his Wulfrith kin would train his son into a warrior."

"Which as you know, requires my consent since the boy is of France."

"*Was* of France," she corrected and, feeling Hector's disquiet, regretted what sounded disrespect.

Edward's gaze darkened. "That is to be seen—*if* we wish to see it."

"Of course."

He settled back and once more looked between the four. When next he spoke, it gave her hope—even if only for Mace. "We are of a mind to allow a case to be made for your cousin."

Before she could express gratitude, Hector said, "Your Majesty, now Ravvenborough is resolved, might we speak of the Sheriff of Dover's charges against this lady?"

The king snorted. "Since much depends of the verity of her claims in the name of Mace de Chanson, which may prove useful in revealing her character, that would be getting ahead of ourselves."

Séverine believed there was some truth in that, though likely the greater truth was impatience to examine the contents of the cask that Hector's missive had referenced to ensure Edward took a personal interest in her case.

"We assume you brought the treasures, Wulfrith."

Hector drew the pack from his shoulder. "The inheritance of Mace de Chanson is here, my liege."

"First we would see the ring."

As Hector drew out the cask, Edward said to Séverine, "We tasked clerks with searching the royal archives for mention of a ring of high office stolen from King William's brother, Odo."

"Was a record found?"

"It was and, to our delight, included a description, doubtless in the hope the ring could be retrieved and lead to the thief who may have been your cousin's ancestor."

Ingvar was of no relation to Mace, unlike Sir Maël to whom the Dane had seen the ring delivered.

"Though it came into the hands of my cousin's ancestor," she said as Hector raised the lid, "it was not by way of thievery."

The king grunted. "Were that possible to know, you would not admit it lest it reflect poorly on your cousin." He waved a hand. "Sir Achard, bring the cask to us."

Alarm shot through Séverine. Though it was agreed he would be shown all but the most precious item that was removed to ensure Mace looked first upon it, it was feared he would be less likely to return the items were all yielded at once rather than presented and returned to the cask ahead of revelation of the next.

Though she sensed Hector's silent warning as the king's man advanced, she said, "It is with much trust my cousin's inheritance was brought—"

Edward snapped forward. "You do not trust us?"

As Sir Achard moved past her, she folded her hands at her waist. "Your Majesty, I—"

"Our king," a beautifully accented voice called, and a buxom woman emerged from an arched entrance to the left. Beyond the recessed door, a glimpse was had of what must be the queen's chamber since here was the same woman who appeared to look upon Séverine during the exodus of Calais.

As Philippa hitched up blue skirts to ascend the dais, her eyes glanced over Séverine.

"Our queen," her husband said and, expression softening, extended a hand.

As Sir Achard halted on the other side of Edward, Philippa crossed to the king and set fingers in a broad palm that appeared as weapon-calloused as Hector's.

Drawing her alongside the seat of state, further the king eased when she whispered something in his ear, then he gave what sounded a rumble of agreement.

The queen straightened, and when Sir Achard offered the cask to the king, Edward said, "May we, Lady Séverine?"

That surprised, as did the longing to smile over the power exercised by a wife well beyond the blush of youth and of lost figure from the many children gifted her husband. Though Séverine regretted Hector's fourth wife had died after being sent from court to slay temptation that could have divided the royal couple, she was glad that lady had not spoiled the affection between these two.

As the queen settled a hand on her husband's shoulder, Séverine said, "I entrust all my cousin has in the world to the king he shall loyally serve should he be permitted to become a defender of England."

Smiling slightly, he set the cask on his lap, raised the lid, and considered what could be seen of its contents, not all of which were wrapped.

The first item he removed was the smallest. "The bishop's ring," he said and examined the wide gold band and faceted ruby. Then turning it top to bottom, he surveyed its inner planes. "O for Odo," he proclaimed and looked to Séverine. "Beyond worthy of a bishop, and that it matches the description proves this was stolen from King William's half brother by Mace de Chanson's kin."

"If it is the same ring," Séverine said, "you will see it was not stolen by that chevalier do you read the small parchment that accompanies it."

"It is there, lord husband." Philippa pointed at the cloth on his lap.

He retrieved the note likely unnoticed for its size and the magnificence of what had perched on it. "Received from the Dane by way of G.W.," he read aloud, "the Year of Our Lord, 1097." His eyes shot to Hector. "This speaks of Guarin Wulfrith, once of the D'Argents?"

"That is fair certain, my liege."

"And the Dane?"

"From our family's written accounts—"

The Book of Wulfrith," Edward said with what sounded admiration. "That which you have yet to lend us."

Not something he wished to do, Séverine sensed, it being precious to his family.

Hector inclined his head. "The Dane is thought to be a warrior who aided Maël D'Argent in freeing Lady Mercia, daughter of King Harold, from Bishop Odo who would have imprisoned her for life to ensure she birthed none capable of rallying the Saxons to reclaim England's throne."

"Lady Mercia," Edward fit the name in his mouth.

"Better you will understand what came of her and why if you read the folded scroll first," Hector said.

Edward removed them and, in the prescribed order, he and his wife learned of Lady Mercia by way of King's Harold's mother, Countess Gytha, and Mercia's beloved husband, Maël D'Argent.

"A wondrous tale," Queen Philippa said. "Granted, many holes the intrusive would wish filled, but enough substance with which a talented bard could enthrall his audience."

"Agreed," the king said and set the scrolls beside the ring on the table. Next he examined the Godwine brooch, closely examined the psalter, frowned over the scabbards, and mused over the dagger of Hugh D'Argent, "So like a Wulfrith dagger." He looked to Hector. "You are aware our family possesses the first struck by Guarin Wulfrith for award to one he was to knight?"

"You speak of Prince Richard," Hector said, "beloved second son of King William who might have inherited England's crown had he not died before the ceremony."

"Tragic," Edward pronounced, then said, "Why two scabbards and only one dagger?"

"May I answer that?" Séverine said.

"You may."

"You were told it was with cold intention I gutted the man who assaulted my cousin at Dover and pulled the dagger from his body. But it was an accident that saw him stuck, and I was so horrified I left behind the dagger belonging to Maël D'Argent, which is identical to that which belonged to his sire, Sir Hugh." She flicked her gaze to it. "Identical but for initials scratched into the blade."

Edward examined the dagger again, nodded. "So someone—the assailant or deputy who Baron Wulfrith tells pursued you to gain these treasures—possesses the second dagger whose absence may prove of greater worth in supporting the charge of attempted murder leveled against you."

Realizing she breathed easier since the queen's appearance, Séverine said, "That is what I believe."

He began returning the items to the cask, giving her hope all that belonged to Mace would be restored, but when he passed the cask to Sir Achard, one item remained on the table.

She knew what it meant and, though disappointed, was not surprised when he retrieved it and said, "As clearly this was stolen from the brother of William the Conqueror, without prick of conscience or compensation, we could take it."

She moistened her lips, and as Hector accepted the cask

from Sir Achard, said, "Aye, Your Majesty, but I pray you do not."

He glanced at his wife. "We will have it, Lady, without prick of conscience but *with* compensation. Whatever its value in gold and jewel, twice that we shall render since it is worth more than its materials."

Séverine inclined her head. "I think that fair."

"But not enough, hmm?"

"I am content as, I believe, my cousin shall be, but I pray you grant permission for Mace to be trained at Wulfen."

"As we are satisfied he is kin—and possibly of royal blood, though our ancestor refused to acknowledge King Harold held that title before him—permission is granted."

Séverine feared she would cry. All was resolving, and possibly the charges against her.

"And one other form of compensation we shall afford your cousin from which you will benefit, Lady. So as not to make mockery of the trust our people place in us to ensure justice is done, the charges of attempted murder and theft stand."

Knees weakening, anger rising both sides of her, distantly aware of hands gripping her, Séverine stared at the king as she struggled to make sense of how she was to benefit from that.

"However, it is not the Dover authorities who will see your fate decided. That we shall do in London to ensure a fair trial and sentence should you be found guilty. Hence, to the Tower of London you go."

CHAPTER 30

Tower of London

Soft confinement.
 Compassionate confinement.
 Dignified confinement.
All these King Edward had named it, though still it was imprisonment. But more daunting—no matter what form imprisonment took—was separation from those of Wulfenshire. Especially Hector.

After Sir Achard was instructed to assemble a royal escort and Séverine was dismissed, Hector had been granted a private audience with his king. Though she had not known all he wished to discuss, she had been certain of his support of her request that Mace not appear at her trial to which the king had given no answer.

While waiting for Hector to rejoin them at the stables beneath a sky gone to dusk and in the path of a breeze carrying the muddied scent of the River Thames, Sheriff D'Arci had sought to distract her with assurances Edward spoke true regarding her confinement.

The Tower of London was another royal residence, he confirmed what she believed of the great fortress, but unlike when it was raised by William the Conqueror, many of its residents were noble prisoners. And those housed in the great donjon known as the White Tower or one of many smaller towers built into the inner wall were well enough regarded to be treated more as guests than transgressors.

Thus, though she would be confined, it would not be in a barred underground cell but a chamber over which a guard was set. Providing she caused no stir, she could venture to other areas inside the walls.

When Hector had rejoined them at the stable following his meeting with the king, his was an impassive face. Certain it masked grim emotions, her churning had turned to roiling. Unfortunately, there was no ease of it during the ride that delivered them to the first of many gatehouses.

Though the White Tower was prominent from outside the Tower of London, Séverine was unprepared for its size where it stood center of the inner ward whose great wall boasted smaller towers, the one facing the rear of the donjon that which would be her prison.

Foreboding swelling, more she was grateful Hector had accompanied her unlike the rest of her escort who had not been permitted to progress beyond the Fair Minster Inn.

Now, having lifted her out of the saddle, he said, "I will see you settled in the chamber prepared for you." He turned her toward the round tower built in the bend between two walls. "Fear not. Though I prefer you remain with me, the constable knows what his king requires of him and will keep you safe."

She looked up to ask if he would visit, but he jutted his chin. "That is him."

Having stepped through the doorway of the wall tower

into the torchlit ward, he presented as a relatively young man of decent stature and build—and much confidence with legs spread and hands clasped behind his back as if little warning was needed to sweep his sword from his belt.

"He is Baron Darcy of the same name as Sir Percival but of different spelling," Hector said as he led her forward. "If they are kin, it may go too far back to confirm. Have you any concerns, address them to him, including the need to send word to me."

"Will you visit?"

His only answer was, "The king has not forbidden it." Then he said, "Later I will send Squire Gwayn with your pack. Anything else you require will be provided by the constable's staff. Do not be concerned by the guard outside your door. He is there to serve you, ensure you venture only as far as permitted, and keep others awaiting the king's judgment from encroaching on your privacy without invitation."

"It sounds very civilized."

"The same as all men, Edward has his faults, and likely there are as many things he does not like about me as I do not like about him, but he is a better king than England has had in a long time. And I am not the only one who believes much of that is due to Philippa of Hainault."

"Never have I heard ill spoken of his queen."

"If you did, likely it would be brewed of jealousy or an attempt to strike Edward from behind. Since the day they wed young and were pawns of his mother and her lover, she has not faltered in standing his side."

"You think it a marriage of love?"

He glanced at her. "My grandmother says she is as much the other half of him as he is hers."

"As God intended."

"And too few achieve, to which I stand as testament," he said.

She longed to speak on that and learn what his private discussion with his liege had yielded, but they neared the constable.

"Well come, Baron Wulfrith," the man said, then lowered his gaze to the latest addition to The Tower. "And you, Lady Séverine."

She dipped. "Baron Darcy."

"You are informed," he said, then pivoted and led the way into the tower whose spacious circular ground floor was furnished with a table, padded chairs, a sideboard, and a bench before a brazier. Not the guard's station expected.

"Your apartment is on the upper floor," he said as he led them to spiraling steps lit by lanterns in nooks. "As it comprises the entire floor, it is of good size and includes a small chapel if you are of a faith that inclines you to commune with the Lord."

"I am," she said, trying not to be offended by the implication her faith was lacking, possibly because she was French.

"Then you will be comfortable."

When they reached the first landing with a short corridor into which was set a single door, she saw beside it a man-at-arms whose presence evidenced she was not the only prisoner here.

Wondering whom he kept watch over, beneath Hector's guiding hand she continued upward.

"As I was not instructed to provide a woman servant," the constable said over his shoulder, "hopefully you are well with seeing to your own needs."

"I am more than capable. After all, this lady is of France."

She expected Hector to warn against provoking the man,

but he did not react in any way to indicate she overstepped. And did the constable chuckle?

"This is Lady Séverine, Jonesy," he said when they stepped off the stairs and halted before the sentry outside her apartment. "Do your duty, staying close and affording all respect."

"Aye, my lord." The middle-aged man nodded at Hector and settled his gaze on his charge. "My lady, I serve."

"Much gratitude, Jonesy."

"Refreshments shall be delivered shortly, Baron Wulfrith," the constable said. "I leave you to settle the lady."

When he turned away, the man-at-arms opened the door. As Séverine stepped into the chamber that would be hers for a sennight...fortnight...perhaps longer, he said, "I should keep the door wide, my lady?"

As was proper, though he made room for the alternative and likely only because of Hector's good reputation. She looked around. "As there are matters I would discuss with Baron Wulfrith, I wish it closed."

"Do you require anything, I am here," he said and did as bid.

Turning back, Séverine took in the circular room with its unshuttered windows through which she could easily pass had she a rope to lower herself and the hope of besting all who stood between her and escape. It was well furnished the same as the ground floor, but more beautifully as if for a lady.

The bed was in possession of plump pillows and a thick coverlet, at its foot a paneled trunk that could serve as a bench, before a lit brazier two upholstered armchairs with a table, between windows another table on which sat basin, pitcher, towels, and a covered basket she guessed held items believed essential to her stay. And to her right was a doorway, its curtains drawn back to reveal the chapel built into a portion of the inner wall. Even it was made ready, the altar with its large cross and a kneeler clearly visible amid candlelight.

Séverine turned to where Hector stood before the door. "I feel a royal prisoner."

"Certes, this chamber has held those of highest nobility," he said, "which would not have been afforded you had Edward believed it was with intention an Englishman was stuck."

"That does not mean I will be acquitted."

"There is a good chance."

She swallowed. "Without Mace's testimony beyond the written, oui?"

"The king is mostly in agreement."

"Mostly?" Her voice pitched high. "Then he might be summoned?"

"Unlikely since Queen Philippa agreed what Sir Percival recorded should suffice as well as his impression your cousin spoke in truth, but Edward did not give his word."

Then naught else could be done. "I thank you for adding your voice to mine. Is that all you discussed?"

Something glanced across his eyes. "There were things to be said regarding Wulfen's past and future."

"Still he is angered over your fourth wife's death?"

"If he is, less so in the presence of his queen who attended our meeting."

Hoping he would not erect a wall against her, Séverine asked, "What of Wulfen's past and future?"

"Unlike Philippa, Edward agrees it is possible God would not have me continue our family's line—that perhaps I should yield my place to Warin and…"

"And?"

"You have heard of King Edward's Order of the Garter?"

She raised her eyebrows. "Even those of France fallen low have heard of that senior order of knighthood, just as now we are acquainted with the Order of the Star that King John formed a year following his sire's passing."

"To rival our king's order."

"Competition in all things," she said. "You are a member of your king's order?"

"I was to have been, but—"

A knock sounded and Hector stepped to the side. "Enter!"

Jonesy ushered in one bearing a tray on which sat viands, two cups, and a pitcher. The young man gave Hector a respectful nod, placed his burden on the table between the armchairs, and departed.

As I ought, Hector thought, but he had decided to tell Séverine the rest of what she did not know of the great commission to which he had nearly laid ruin. Thus, more easily she could resolve what she felt for him and set her heart and mind on what could mean the difference between freedom and unjust punishment.

When Jonesy closed the door, Hector nodded at the ladened tray. "It appears I am to take meal with you."

"Would you?" Her question was all hope, and he knew it was not only of continuing their conversation but keeping company with him a while longer.

He took her arm and seated her before the brazier, poured wine, and settled in the other chair.

While they picked over viands, he ordered his thoughts. And did not think he could be more prepared to finish what he had begun when she set aside her cup and said, "Will you tell more of what you discussed with King Edward? What he believes should come of you with regard to his order?"

"Aye, but best to start with this scar gained at Crécy." He raised that hand.

"You said it was dealt while preserving the prince's life."

"It was, and so grateful was the king he promised a reward to the future Baron of Wulfen."

"That was?"

"He did not name it, but all knew he planned to form an order of knighthood numbering twenty-six, including him and his eldest son, its members appointed at his discretion in recognition of exceptional contribution to king, country, and people." The flames brightening her hair and casting golden light across her face, he looked to the brazier's deep iron bowl held aloft by four curving legs whose three-pronged feet resembled fleur-de-lis. "That was what I hoped for—rather, coveted, and when finally it was within reach..."

Recalling arrival of the invitation at Wulfen that was no guarantee of inclusion in the order but portended well, he returned his regard to Séverine. "I was invited to attend the games Edward was to hold at Merton in January of 1349. It was rumored there he would determine who would be inducted into his order and much depended on attendance and performance."

"You went?"

"As I should not have."

From flits of the eyes, he could see she tried to fit the pieces with those earlier provided when he told hubris was responsible for the lives taken and ruined at Stern.

Deciding to fit them for her to sooner be done with the telling, he said, "The Great Mortality that was so long in coming to England most believed it would not, arrived, and all knew it, including the king. He had lost a daughter and son and deaths were on the rise, but he refused to be intimidated, keeping plans and making new ones."

Séverine wide-eyed, Hector dry-mouthed, he poured more wine and wet his tongue. "Though the pestilence was creeping around the edges of Wulfenshire and slipping through cracks—seeking a window, seeking a door—since the losses were relatively minor, I ignored my conscience and good sense. Despite my pregnant wife's beseechings that I not attend the games and warnings from my sire, I went to Merton. After proving worthy of serious consideration for the order, I returned triumphant, unaware I opened wide a window into Stern by way of my squire."

Feeling the beat of his heart, remembering the young man's suffering that had been the beginning of far more, Hector took a long drink. "I cannot know if the sickness entered him in Merton or between there and home, for he seemed hale until the morn after we arrived at Stern, but he and others would not have died had I not yielded to hubris."

Her brown eyes glistened. "Perhaps not that day, but—"

"Do not make excuses for me! Aye, the pestilence cast everywhere, but its great spread upon Stern began with me." He set aside the cup and chose a thick slice of bread to soak up wine beginning to burn his belly. Not that he overly imbibed, having learned well a lesson taught him as a youth.

Hear me, Hector? his sire had demanded, in his hand a pitcher Hector and a friend had emptied several times in as few hours. *Excess drink and ill-found pleasure are not cures for what ails one's emotions. They are bandages that take with them a layer of soul when wrenched off upon the return of good sense—if it returns.*

Amid much heaving and shame, he *had* heard his sire. But this was not excess drink in which he now indulged. This was drink-soaked guilt. He fed it more bread.

"Will you tell what came after?" Séverine asked.

Hector started to remind her already he had revealed the losses suffered by his family and people, but realized she wanted more. Though tempted to depart, he was not ready to put the unscalable walls of the Tower of London between them.

"I moved my squire to our family's vacant hunting lodge between Stern and Wulfen. When I was not tending him, much time was spent beseeching the Lord that no others battle death there—that if any were to be taken it be me. But not long ere that young man breathed his last, a place was made for Ondine."

He lowered his lids, but still he saw his beautiful sister—at the beginning of the sickness and at the end that had not been her end though she was so ravaged he had been certain she would go the way of his squire.

Opening his eyes upon the brazier, the base of its bowl now glowing, he said, "It entered her as well—and others. Next came my wife and our unborn child, followed the day after by Warin's wife, then our sire and half a dozen retainers." More breath was needed. "Unlike many men of medicine across England who, realizing their efforts would more likely cost their lives than save others, our physician aided me. Just as the pestilence did not take my life, blessedly it did not claim his nor Ondine's. But it took the others—some quickly, some slowly, all cruelly. And Warin..."

Throat tight, what moved in his chest making him feel a boy, Hector reminded himself of his age and all the battles fought and blood shed. But it was of no use.

"Almighty!" he rasped and, hearing a chair creak, knew Séverine came to him as he did not wish. And yet when she sank to her knees alongside his legs and curled a hand over one of his fists, some calm was had.

"Forgive me," he said. "I know better than to tell so much."

"Then what you know is wrong. If there is only one with whom you can speak, God is best, but if there is another of flesh and blood—who has much care for you—that is second best." She squeezed his hand. "I would be that to you, Hector."

How strange it seemed wrong she rank second best though it was the Lord she placed herself behind. How discomfiting this longing to rank her first in other things. Things not meant for him.

"Tell me of your brother, Hector."

"He was en route from Wulfen to Stern when he received word his wife had been moved to the lodge. He went directly there and, when not allowed past the guard set around the perimeter, his anger was heard across the distance."

As if Séverine heard the shouts and curses due Hector, she shuddered.

He shifted his cramping jaw. "My wife and our babe had passed and been removed for burial, and though Warin's wife was close to succumbing, she remained present enough to know her husband was near, weep for his grief, and entreat me to record words I was to deliver him following her death. Though I inked the parchment..." He lowered his gaze to Séverine's hand atop his. "...I was loath to deliver it."

"Why?"

"They were not just words of love but beseeching against allowing her death to come between brothers. Though she put her name to them, I feared Warin, believing her too ill to verify what was dictated, would think it deception to serve my purpose. I vow I wrote exactly as spoken, but it is true she could barely raise her lids to ink her name. After containment of the pestilence following my sire's passing, the physician, Ondine, and I let a fortnight pass ere returning to the living. My guilt was terrible and Warin's raging..." He shook his head. "Finding no opportunity—and making none—I determined to wait on keeping my word to his wife, though his anger could be worse for the delay. And so it was when I delivered the missive weeks later. He drew sword on me."

She gasped.

"Though much blood could have been drawn, there was so little most would think it practice had they not witnessed the ferocity with which he struck and I fended off blows. Hence, of this I am certain—had he bested me, still I would live and without great infirmity the same as he."

"I am sorry, Hector."

Liking her hand on his, he said, "As am I and all my family for what I wrought."

"From your grandmother and sisters I sense no ill toward you."

"For a time it was there, walking arm in arm with grief and, as expected, most broadly cast by Ondine whose beauty is forever marked by what few survive. That first year, while the pestilence sought to gain ground across the shire and numerous measures were taken to prevent its spread, mostly she hid herself away and rarely spoke to any save Rémy when I gave him leave to visit Stern."

"Your youngest brother."

"Aye, he was ten and three when it happened and much affected, especially by the loss of our sire." Though those not well-acquainted with the big youth would have been aware, Hector reflected. The serious Rémy had burrowed deeper into his training and, already of few words, gone mostly silent.

"Ondine and he are close?"

"Indeed." Feeling her soft palm against his hardened one, he tensed, and further when he saw he had turned his hand up into hers. "So now you know the black of me, Séverine."

She slid her thumb down his wrist. "Just as I know the light of you that first shone at Calais."

Longing to raise her hand to his lips, next her lips to his, he reminded himself of where this discussion had begun and what yet dangled. "Three months after Merton, at the height of the disease ravaging England, once more King Edward summoned me. Against the advice of his physicians, he was to hold a tournament at Windsor to formally institute the Order of the Garter. When I declined, another was given my place."

"As you wished."

Though there was no question in her words, he inclined his head. "Edward was displeased but added my name to the list of candidates to replace current members in the event of death. Shortly after wedding my fourth wife at his bidding, a place opened, and again I declined. Though fairly certain my name had been permanently removed—and entirely certain when that wife died—this day I learned still the king seeks to reward me for aiding his son at Crécy."

"By giving you a place in the order."

"Aye, and if I am not to wed again, he believes I should cede my title to Warin within a year and enter Prince Edward's service to better the training of his men."

"What will you do?"

"Regardless of whether I retain my title, I see no reward in joining the order nor serving the prince. However, I have told I will think on it."

Knowing it was time he departed and the longer he stayed the harder it would be to let go of her, he lifted her hand and considered her fingers. "But first to resolve the matter of Séverine de Barra." He drew her up with him. "I will leave you to your rest."

She gripped his fingers. "Come with me to the chapel."

"It grows late."

"And yet the Lord is full awake, and we are in need of prayer." At his hesitation, she entreated, "As I know not when I shall see you again, I am not ready to be parted from you."

This was not fear of what would come of her in his absence. This was fear of being absented from him. Though it would feed her feelings for him, he said, "I will go with you."

The small chapel was spacious, built deep into the upper portion of the inner wall to the left of the tower, its ceiling the underside of the wall walk. Simply furnished, it possessed one kneeler before a candlelit altar draped in white cloth, nooks like those on the winding stairs that held lanterns, and a bench.

Hector handed Séverine onto the kneeler, and as she clasped her hands atop the shelf, crossed to the bench.

He had not wanted this, but it felt right to be here with her, to clasp his hands and lean into prayers as she did hers. When he finished, it felt right to pluck from the air whispers with too little form to make sense of her entreaties. And when she crossed to him, it felt right she lowered beside him.

Light flickering over her, she said, "Will you tell me what you prayed for?"

"My prayers were for you, Séverine."

"As were mine, but also for you—that your relationship with Warin heal and, even if others cannot extend grace for what came of hubris, you let God's forgiveness be enough."

Longing to put his face against her neck and breathe her in, he stood and led her from the chamber.

"Let it be enough," she entreated as he continued to the door.

He turned. Seeing all about her what the wife lost to the pestilence had felt for him, he said, "Do not love me, Séverine."

Her eyes widened, a laugh escaped, and she set a hand between her breasts. "Did you hear that, heart? You are not to love Hector. As he commands, I command."

"Almighty," he growled and, drawing her to him, yielded to a kiss born more of a heart no longer content with merely pushing blood through his body than desire long loosed from its moorings. Ardent, but so brief it could be said to be stolen, he ended it by setting her back. "Until I see you again, Lady."

When he opened the door, Jonesy stood to the side, posture erect, eyes ahead. Since he had to have ideas about what went in the chamber this past hour, to ensure none were confirmed, Hector closed the door. Not that Séverine was in disarray, but her mouth surely evidenced there had been the possibility of becoming so.

As he descended the tower, what he had spoken aloud to her he told himself—*Do not love her, Hector.*

CHAPTER 31

Ravens.

Unlike Ondine's owl, there appeared little to recommend the large birds. With their long beaks and so much black about them it caused something beneath her skin to tiptoe, they seemed harbingers of ill. Thus, she had not expected their presence to become nearly a comfort these ten days.

Unlike her fate languishing with her inside the Tower of London, the birds were known. She did not like the din they made when they gathered in numbers and argued amongst themselves, but she enjoyed watching these sleek, well-fed specimens, especially from the ground peering up—providing she chose her vantage well since they had no care for where they dropped their waste. Even then, often she had to quickly shift when one or more shifted.

Once again settled on the outdoor blanket the constable had provided the day after her arrival, Séverine propped her hands beneath her head. Breathing deeply, pleased her ribs barely noticed, she moved her gaze over the ravens perched amid trees in the park across from the tower in which she spent as little time as possible.

Hers *was* a comfortable prison, especially as she was delivered whatever small item she requested, but she was restless and more so each day without tidings from those she wished to hear from.

Twice she had sent word to the constable asking him to discover if her London escort remained in the city. After a time, he had confirmed it, but that was all, and she sensed that was as forthcoming as could be expected of him regardless of whether he knew more or could learn more.

Of a sudden, four ravens moved from branches to the left to directly above. She gasped, snatched the blanket's edge, rolled to the side, and transitioned from knees to feet.

"I know not why you bother, Lady."

Another gasp, another turn, and there stood a man leaning against a tree of such height and breadth likely it had rooted long before the White Tower was raised.

No more than twenty and ten, the attractive one garbed as a nobleman put his head to the side. "Has no one told you the foolishness of expecting different results following great failure if you do as done before?" He raised his eyebrows. "And then to continue to do so again and again and again… Alas, some might name it madness."

Séverine recognized the voice that was somewhere between English and something else—rather, she was fairly certain it was familiar since previously it was heard through the floor of her chamber and once beyond her door on the stairs below.

She had asked Jonesy about the man with whom she shared the tower, but the only insight offered was words of gratitude she was his charge rather than he who ought to be chained in the cellar of the great white donjon for as much trouble as he caused.

It was then Séverine became aware that just as there were prisoners here treated as guests, a handful of whom she had encountered during her walks, also present were those treated as captives of low regard.

"Surely I have not confounded you," said the one who trespassed on her privacy.

Realizing she held the blanket before her as if to cover a bared body, she lowered it to her side and demanded, "Who are you, and why do you sneak upon me?"

He strolled forward and, at half the distance, halted.

Even more handsome, she thought of high cheekbones, intense blue eyes, and a full mouth. If not for a thick beard at odds with his hair—the former russet and nearly unkempt, the latter lustrous, dark brown, and waving back off his brow to just beneath his jaw—he might be beautiful. But perhaps for that this one of warrior's build did not shave.

"I do not sneak upon you." He set a hand on his chest, gave a slight bow. "Lady Séverine, allow me to introduce—"

"How do you know my name?"

He looked across his shoulder at Jonesy who kept watch where he was seated on the half wall outside the park. However, now the one who stood sentry over the apartment below hers was there as well.

"The night of your arrival, your guard told my guard. My guard told me." The man raised a finger to his lips. "Pray, do not apprise England's king that the one who has yet to fail him has a healthy fondness for my wine." He lowered his hand. "I have not found a way to fully exploit that, but hope makes the days pass more quickly—though to what end, hmm?"

Indeed, she thought and, though wary, knew he presented no threat since neither guard showed concern—at least with a goodly space between them. "You were going to introduce yourself," she said.

Hand to the chest again, he bowed. "I am Sir Sinjin."

A name never before heard though similar to one known. "From the name St. John?"

"Not *from*. Though long adopted by the English as a form of St. John, what few know—or care to know—is first Sinjin was of the Hebrew."

It surprised he mentioned that since those of the Jewish faith were expelled from England by the first King Edward and later from France though, eventually, they were allowed to return to her country. Was it possible he was—?

"Do you not shift again, what narrowly you avoided will make muck of such pretty hair, Lady."

Attuning to the rustling overhead, she hastened forward.

"That was very close," he said as she halted within reach.

Yet more handsome, she thought, *though of little appeal since it is Hector I wish to see and stand near.*

"Your gratitude is welcome," her fellow prisoner teased.

Though annoyed, appreciation *was* due him. But first she gave her blanket a shake and folded it over an arm. "I thank you, Sir Sinjin."

"I am glad to be of aid." He offered an arm. "Walk with me?" At her frown, he said, "You have not yet told why you persist in watching foul birds from a position that invites them to spatter you."

Keeping her hands at her waist, she raised her chin.

"Lady, as 'tis a fortnight since I was permitted outside our tower, all my observations of what goes here have been limited to what is seen from my chamber windows. Pray, show a small kindness in return for mine."

She looked to Jonesy and his companion, saw still neither seemed concerned. "They will be well with it?"

He leaned in. "Weapon to hand or otherwise, I am no danger to women—unless one tries to gut me."

She nearly caught her breath. Was this coincidence? Or had he learned more than her name? Though likely the latter, curiosity and the dull prospect of returning to the solitude of her chamber made her agree. "Though I shall decline your arm, I will walk with you a short while."

"Proper," he said and, as he turned, added, "and perhaps a bit in love."

That he could not have learned from his guard since she held it close and Hector surely did the same, meaning he inferred it from whatever he knew of her arrival here when the one who accompanied her to her chamber remained a considerable time.

She reconsidered walking with him, but here something more interesting than ravens to fill hours that ever defaulted to angst over the judgment to come.

She drew alongside, and once they passed those certain to follow if their charges strayed too far, he said, "Why position yourself to watch dirty birds as if they be gentle stars in the night?"

"The tedium of what King Edward calls *soft* confinement. Not only are the ravens more interesting than thought—and quite intelligent—but there is some fun in outwitting them."

He looked sidelong at her. "That implies they seek to sully you."

"Mmm," she murmured as they angled toward the rear of the great donjon beneath the watch of their guards and patrolling soldiers. "I cannot attest to that, but my suspicions are valid."

They spoke no more until they drew as near the White Tower as was allowed and two of those protecting she knew not what started forward as done each time she ventured close.

"This but one of many boundaries," the knight said as they turned back.

Confirming their personal guards had left the park and maintained a good distance, Séverine asked, "Who resides in the White Tower—or should I ask who is *held* there?"

"The last great noble imprisoned in the donjon was Scotland's King David. That was six years past, and his stay was short."

If that was his answer, did it mean none was held there since? Perhaps only those of less nobility? Or did he not know?

Guessing the latter, she said, "But King David remains Edward's prisoner."

"He does," he drawled with what sounded more than mere comment. "He was moved to Windsor Castle and surely longs for home though he has comfortable quarters and is supplied with servants and permitted regular outings—and visits from his wife."

Queen Joan who was the King of England's sister, Séverine reflected on the shambles made of relations between this country and Scotland, then of the mess of this man's life that made him an enemy of his king. Or *was* Edward his king? "You are English, are you not?"

His hesitation was so slight she could have missed it. "Born in England, my lady."

Wondering if that was confirmation and seeing they neared their guards, she gestured at one of the benches against the wall where the patrol took turns satisfying hunger and thirst. "Shall we sit?"

"It *has* been a long and vigorous walk," he quipped.

When they were seated with distance between them, her

blanket draped over the bench's arm, he said, "This feels nearly the same as attraction, Lady."

She blinked. "What say you?"

"*Nearly* the same. Be assured I am versed enough in this and that to feel the difference."

"Then you know I am not attracted to you."

"Not as many women are."

A laugh escaped her. "That sounds boastful."

"And yet that is fact, which I cannot say I have not enjoyed many a time—though no opportunities have I here."

Before she could ask how long he had been held and if there were other women imprisoned at The Tower, he continued, "Nay, it is not attraction you feel for me. 'Tis curiosity."

"It is, and I do not think you mind. After all, you must be more weary of this place than I."

"Beyond weary."

Thinking now he would tell what transgression put him here, she waited, but he settled against the stone wall, closed his eyes, and turned his face to the sun.

Séverine considered a profile as handsome from the side as the front and, once more marveling at the difference between the color of his hair and beard, crossed her ankles beneath her green and red gown.

"Aye, Lady?" he murmured.

Taking that as invitation, she said, "If I tell my tale of what delivered me here, will you tell yours?"

His smile grew. "Since I know yours, no fair exchange that."

And no great surprise that. "How do you know it?"

He rolled his head toward her, opened lightly-lashed eyes that supported the masculinity of his face rather than its beauty. "A healthy fondness for my wine."

Having confirmed his guard was the source, she said, "As I

have naught to exchange, here I sit wishing I yet challenged the ravens."

"And insulting my good company." He turned his face back to the sun, murmured, "Though more I lean toward your innocence than guilt, I suppose you could tell your side of the tale. That would entertain some."

She nearly smiled, but this was not yet victory. "Then *you* will entertain me?"

He did not answer, and just as she began to think that was answer enough, he turned his face and narrowly opened his eyes. But not upon her. He listened, she realized when she heard what he heard—the arrival of riders who passed through numerous gates to reach the inner ward. And they sounded many.

"Alas, too late to entertain either of us, Lady. At least, not as we care to be diverted." Standing, he took her elbow and drew her up.

She pulled free. "What do you?"

"Considering how many come—and yet astride—this will be the king."

Having believed it was at Westminster she would stand before him again and unprepared, she hoped he was wrong. But he would know better than she.

THE ALTERNATIVE UNACCEPTABLE, this was a good thing. Though Hector resented the pittance of time given him to prepare for the extrication of Séverine, he was grateful that with what remained he could better order his thoughts ahead of entering her chamber and revealing her day of judgment was at hand.

However, as he guided his mount farther into the inner ward behind the king, he saw the time left to him was a lie. He did not need to look nearer on the one standing distant to know it was Séverine, not only for the blond of her hair but rarity of women held at The Tower. But who was—?

"Sir Sinjin," Achard supplied, causing Hector to consider the figure differently, now with an eye to measuring an opponent. "Let out of his gilded cage, he has made good use of his time with one who surely admires a countenance so fine that few believe it capable of concealing great cunning."

What did that mean for Séverine? Hector wondered, disturbed by something beyond jealousy. Though he had never met the knight, he had first heard of him after they narrowly avoided meeting at Calais. And he was aware of the northerner's further exploits that caused King Edward to lock him away when he got his hands on him.

"Forget not his skill at arms," Achard added.

That went without saying, Hector thought as he assessed the man's height and an impressive breadth for one long imprisoned.

But Warin had something to say about it. "As you forget to whom you speak, Sir Achard?"

Progress, Hector thought and, hearing the king's man grunt, silently thanked the Lord that while working with his brother to fill the holes in Séverine's defense, the mortared joints of the barriers between them had loosened. No forgiveness yet—if ever—but at times the lost scent of brotherhood wafted between them, and most strongly when, with Percival's aid, they uncovered the identity of the man Séverine was said to have gutted.

"Dismount!" Edward shouted and, leaving behind the score who accompanied him from Westminster, continued toward the lady and knight under watch of guards.

As the warriors reined in, the lads who had followed from the stables hastened forward to take charge of their mounts.

Though Hector longed to go to Séverine, and not only to prepare her for what was to come once the constable ensured the ground was made ready on the opposite side of the White Tower, he had no choice but to wait on the king who halted his horse before Sir Sinjin and her. It was the same for the others left behind—those Hector's side who supported the lady, those Le Creuseur's side who sought her death, and the king's guard in between lest the two meet and shed blood ere its time.

Whatever Edward said to Séverine, it was brief, then he turned to his less than loyal subject and she began moving toward her prison tower.

"I shall speak with her, Achard," Hector said. "I grant you are well with that."

"Our liege expects it." The king's man glanced at Warin and Percival as they moved to accompany him, added, "You alone, Wulfrith."

Hector needed no aid in apprising Séverine of what transpired these ten days and what to expect this next hour, but it was not good for this man and that woman to be alone when it was imperative the warrior of him firm itself in mind and body.

There being naught for it, he stretched his legs long to reach the tower ahead of her, and she made it easier by slowing the moment her gaze slipped to him.

"There are things we must discuss," he said when she reached the doorway.

Her eyes were moist. "I am so glad you are here."

Then she remained uninformed as to what, exactly, his presence meant. Looking to her guard, he said, "I would make use of the lower room to speak with Lady Séverine."

"I shall wait out here, my lord."

Hector motioned her in ahead of him.

As he closed the door, she came about and said in a rush, "I did not know my heart could be so rebellious."

This was not the direction their conversation should venture, but he said, "Even after spending time with the much-vaunted Sir Sinjin?"

She frowned. "Though he resides in the apartment below mine—"

"Does he?" Disapproval slung the words from him.

She blinked. "Not an hour past, I met him for the first time. But even had this hour been one of many across the days since last I saw you, it would not change what I am not to feel for you. I feel it—more strongly than fear for what King Edward does here."

But that was what they must discuss. He jutted his chin at the table, and when they sat across from each other said, "I know my silence has been worrisome, but until recent I had little to report of efforts to strengthen your defense."

"Of recent?"

"In response to the king's order the knight you are accused of gutting appear, the Sheriff of Dover sent word it was not possible since infection set in and the man battled death."

"Lord!"

He nearly reached to her. "Since the sheriff ignored the request I made through King Edward for the victim's name of which there has been no spoken nor written reference, I thought it suspicious. For that, Warin, Percival, and I rode to Dover where first we learned the witness who claimed to be your assailant's business acquaintance was a thief many times jailed. Of greater import, from the stable owner we learned the name of the knight injured—and to further support your testimony of what went there, obtained his statement attesting to your purchase of one of the two horses."

"I am grateful. Is the name of aid?"

"It is. The sheriff *forgot* to provide it lest he was deemed biased—more, further shamed than he is."

"Shamed?"

"The one with whom you struggled is his nephew, a knight of the ilk we at Wulfen term *chevalier devenu noir—knight gone black*." *And for which Sir Sinjin might also qualify,* he did not say. "He is Colbern Witter, best known to King Edward by way of Sir Achard who reported the knight was responsible for instigating grievous assaults on the women of Caen when our forces took that city before the Battle of Crécy."

Her lashes fluttered. "Tidings of those atrocities reached Calais."

"And were not to be repeated there. For that, Sir Achard and I oversaw the removal of the ill and detainment of strays who defied the order to vacate immediately, whether they sought to harm us or depart with valuables the victors would claim for themselves."

"That is how you happened on me, though you did not detain me."

"Not only did I believe you were of no danger to us, but since I hardly knew those assigned to my command, I did not trust any to hold you. It was foul enough you should be relieved of whatever you carried, beyond the pale you should suffer the same as the women of Caen."

Her mouth curved. "I know you question your honor and worth for not being without sin or fault as is impossible for all men and women, but I do not doubt it."

Again, he wanted to take her hands in his. "Had I to guess, the sheriff did not wish to pursue what happened in the stable and, impelled to do so, chose Le Creuseur to apprehend you. When I revealed to King Edward the identity of Mace's assailant in Dover, certain it would aid you since the man's nature became clear at Caen, he commanded Sir Colbern to appear—even if only his corpse."

Her breath caught. "Did he appear?"

"In the company of the sheriff and deputy and feigning great incapacity."

"Feigning?"

"In Dover, we were able to get near enough to see he is much recovered—and still fond of tavern ale and the women who fill his cup."

"What happened when he appeared before the king?"

"I was not present, so I know only the result of the meeting, Edward having met separately with the plaintiff and his representatives and your representatives."

She swallowed. "The result?"

"Come to the window." She followed, and when they peered at those waiting on the king who yet conversed with Sir Sinjin, he said, "Sir Colbern is to the left between Le Creuseur and the Dover sheriff."

When she tensed further, he knew she had picked out the two with whom she had suffered encounters, one from which she had yet to fully heal. "I recognize the knight, but I do not know I would have had you not told it is him." She looked up. "He was not as clean and groomed then."

"Nor when we saw him in Dover. As ever, one does well not to offend the senses of a judge."

"Hector..." She caught up his hand. "What is to happen this day?"

Lest any look their way, he drew her from the window. "Ever one for great gestures and spectacles, King Edward has decided your innocence or guilt shall be determined by wager of battle." That being the term more commonly used in England, he clarified, "Trial by combat."

Her eyes widened. "The judgment of God, it believed He

gives victory to the one who speaks in truth. But surely I..." She caught her breath. "Who is to stand in my stead?"

"I put myself forth, and the king accepted."

Before her smile of relief enlarged, he said, "It is not Sir Colbern I challenge. As the one gone black feigns incapacity, King Edward provides an approver."

"What is that?"

"He who fights in another's stead for gain rather than in support of one side over the other. Usually it is a prisoner willing to fight for the Crown in exchange for freedom—rather, the possibility of freedom since it requires winning five trials, and even then 'tis no guarantee of release since usually the final trial presents the greatest challenge. Thus, though the approver may best the champion, often his own injuries are his end."

Understanding lit her eyes.

Hector inclined his head. "Not only will this day's fight determine your fate but that of the prisoner who has four times bested the champions of others."

"Then your opponent is very skilled."

"If he is as versed in arms as I am told, he will be a challenge, but I *will* gain your freedom."

"I believe it," she said, but he sensed fear for him. Then as if to cover it, she hastened to ask, "And afterward?"

Loath to tell her what came after freedom, he said, "You do not wish to know with whom I am to cross swords?"

She frowned. "Surely I have not met him."

"You have, albeit quite recently."

She released his hand. "The one who defeated four champions is Sir Sinjin?"

"He is the approver Edward uses to greatly increase the odds of a champion's failure. And for being at the king's disposal, that knight's immediate reward is being kept in great comfort whilst imprisoned and much tolerance when he tests Edward's patience."

Though Hector expected fear for him to become more apparent, it did not, whether because surprise at his opponent's identity distracted or she had great faith in his skill. Glancing at the window, she said, "Only now the king informs Sir Sinjin his fifth trial is nigh?"

"Nay, as word was sent earlier this day, he with whom you visited knew that should he win his freedom, the one with whom he conversed could lose her life."

"Oh," she breathed. "He told he knows my tale by way of his guard and he is more convinced of my innocence than guilt."

"Do not think that will have any bearing on how he fights, Séverine. As I want your freedom, he wants his. As my loss could mean your death, his loss could mean his."

She stepped near. "You will not lose."

Wanting to draw her to him, he kept his arms at his sides. "I will not."

Momentarily, she closed her eyes. "It is wrong Sir Sinjin should be deprived of the chance of freedom, might even die for Sir Colbern."

"I agree, but he chose his path."

She mulled that. "As you are to be his greatest challenge, do you think Edward allowed you to champion me because he leans toward my innocence? Or is this how he guarantees Sir Sinjin never gains his freedom, whether by death at your hands or loss of soft confinement?"

"All I am certain of is the king is more your side for the black of Colbern, the sheriff withholding the miscreant's name, and the lie about the state of the knave's injury. Likely, were the wager of battle not an option, Edward would absolve you of the charges as done me for slaying Colbern's accomplice. Most unfortunate, but if our warrior king can make something big of something small amid the monotony of court, he does."

Tears brightened her eyes. "Then we are but playthings."

"Whether of the King of England or the King of France, we are ruled. But as my parents sought to impress on my siblings and me, and at which I sometimes fail, we answer first to another."

"God."

He nodded, then recalling what was told him upon attaining his twelfth summer and thinking it might comfort, he said, "Do we accept first we are answerable to God, we will not be rendered helpless in the shadows of men who think themselves giants because of the size of the dark they cast. As best we can, we move in the light all sides of those shadows, and when we fail and they cover us, the faith we carry into that dark will aid in extricating us."

"Such words," she exclaimed. "How can you think yourself unworthy?"

Panged, he said, "They are my sire's words." Then catching voices and movement that told those outside proceeded toward the ground prepared by the constable, he looked down her. "Unless you wish to quickly don the gown of Lady Annyn to draw strength from it as Fira believes possible, we must rejoin the others."

She did not hesitate. "As I shall draw strength from you, I am ready."

CHAPTER 32

"Eighty feet square," said Sir Percival into whose care Hector had passed Séverine when Warin declined so he could assist his brother in preparing for battle. "Though the standard size of a judicial list is sixty, when the king is present, often 'tis enlarged since he likes to leave his chair and move about the perimeter to better observe the combatants—and advise."

To ensure the big made of something small entertained, Séverine thought as she sent her gaze around the list in which the contest between Hector and Sir Sinjin would determine her fate.

Wishing she had retrieved her mantle for the chill disregarding the day's warmth, further she was nipped when once more she looked upon those standing to the right of the seated king, his guard, and a priest. There the aged Sheriff of Dover with hands clasped behind his back, Deputy Le Creuseur with bandaged thigh attesting to the injury Hector dealt him, and Sir Colbern with hand pressed to his abdomen to maintain the pretense that afforded him benefit of one to fight for him.

Craven! she silently named the one for whom Sir Sinjin could lose all.

As if heard, the *knight gone black* looked to where she stood on the opposite side of King Edward, bounded by nearly all those who had escorted her to London.

When Colbern glared, she sustained his gaze as done several times since Sir Percival led her to the side of the White Tower where previously she was not permitted to go. As before, Mace's assailant gave a dismissive roll of the eyes and turned his attention to the deputy.

Séverine looked to those near the seated king and the empty chair Sir Percival told was for Philippa who had arrived after Hector and she withdrew from the ward. Wondering where the queen was, Séverine glanced from the constable to Sir Achard whose face was stony as he looked where she had looked.

He who had spoken against the atrocities Sir Colbern committed at Caen had not put them behind him, and from the white of the hand on his hilt, he considered a permanent means of doing so. Then as if feeling her regard, he released the weapon.

"Ah, our queen!" Edward thrust out of the chair.

Séverine followed his regard to Philippa whose every other step caused her grey gown to recast itself as pale purple as she advanced from the direction of the White Tower in the company of two men-at-arms and a young woman.

"And she has taken pity on the scandalous Lady Adelaide," the king said wryly.

Wondering if this the answer to the question put to Sir Sinjin regarding who was held in the great donjon, Séverine considered one of significant height, good figure emphasized by a fitted gown of yellow, and loosely braided hair so blond it was nearly white.

"Who is Lady Adelaide?" she whispered.

"As my king told, scandalous." Sir Percival said, and that was all.

Without acknowledging the lady who positioned herself to the side of the chair into which the king handed his wife, Edward lowered. Then taking the queen's hand, he called, "Show yourself, champion of Lady Séverine de Barra. Show yourself, approver of Sir Colbern Witter."

The chill inside Séverine slipping out, she crossed her arms beneath her breasts and hugged herself as two figures emerged from opposite ends of a stone building far left of the White Tower.

They were easily distinguishable despite being equipped the same—chain mail over tunic and chausses, over chain mail a white surcoat against which blood would contrast starkly, and sword belted one side, dagger the other.

As she looked between the knight of silvered black hair and most impressive build to the knight of red beard and quite impressive build, all went quiet beneath the regard of those on the walls provided a raven's view, those gathered before the judicial list, and the combatants.

"Come forth!" the king called, and nearly all that could be heard was the ring of mail as the warriors strode toward ground raked free of debris, its perimeter marked by flags atop poles excepting the farthest corners. Those were marked by twelve-foot pikes.

Recalling Sir Percival had revealed one could be used only if an opponent lost his sword and it was no easy thing to retrieve before being cut down, she shuddered—next startled when something dropped to her shoulders.

She glanced around at Hector's brother who lowered hands that had gifted her his mantle. "As no better champion could you have than my brother," he said, "your great trial nears its end."

"I thank you, Sir Warin." Looking back, she saw the combatants had entered the list from opposing corners marked by pikes. For a moment—just long enough to mouth the name of the man onto whom her heart had hooked itself—his gaze belonged to her. Then the priest met the two at the center of what was to become a battleground.

Too low to be heard, he spoke to Hector and Sir Sinjin and, it seemed, had much to say ahead of prayer.

"Does he give counsel?" she asked.

"Aye, but not on the rules of engagement which were recounted to each whilst being fit for battle," Warin said. "He warns against using sorcery such as incantations and charmed objects to defeat an opponent."

She swept wide eyes to him.

"'Tis procedure, Lady, and though the king's priest makes more of it than most, be assured his efforts are mostly directed at Sir Sinjin."

"Why?"

"Apparently the northerner spends more time in the company of the Scots than he ought, and though the Wulfriths do not hold that those of Scotland are heathens, many do." He jutted his chin. "Now the priest gains their oaths, after which he will pray for them. Then they fight."

She shivered. "For how long?"

"Until one is dead or greatly disabled or yields by shouting *craven* to acknowledge defeat."

More closely hugging his mantle to her, she whispered, "Craven," which she had applied to Sir Colbern for his contemptible lack of courage. How terribly offensive it must be for a warrior to name himself a coward to preserve life and limb—and more offensive were it one who fought in another's place.

"He who yields thus may lose the privilege of a freeman," Warin said.

"Even when he is but a champion or approver?" she exclaimed.

He smiled reassuringly. "You have only to fear for Sir Sinjin. Were my brother not exceedingly capable, King Edward would not be indebted to him for the aid given his son at Crécy."

His confidence comforted, but she did not think she imagined a crack of disquiet. No matter how slight his questioning of Hector's ability, it frightened, and yet there was good in his concern.

To ensure Sir Percival on her other side did not hear, she angled toward Warin. "Surely all will be well with you and your brother."

His lips flattened.

"The divide between you will close, and you will take your place at Wulfen, will you not?"

"After France, I return to the fold, Lady."

It was the answer she longed for, but his qualifier troubled. "France?"

"As I have business there that needs concluding, I assure you, 'tis no trouble."

Before she could make sense of that, King Edward proclaimed, "To arms!" And of a sudden, there was only that.

Hector stance-ready far right, Sir Sinjin far left.

The drawing of swords.

Great strides propelling warrior toward warrior.

War cries assaulting the ears.

Steel on steel resounding all around.

CHAPTER 33

Formidable. When last had he faced an opponent of such mastery?

As Hector came out of a turn following the meeting of blades high above their heads, he acknowledged that would be Warin after his wife's death when anger and grief caused him to challenge the one at fault—and fight as Hector had known he was capable, though not so capable as to nearly best his older brother. Afterward, Warin had departed for Calais, just as he would do again this day when the contest between champion and approver ended as it must.

Sir Sinjin firmed his feet the same as Hector, then in answer to the sword beckoning him, he whose handsome face was thus far spared unlike other parts bleeding onto his surcoat, bared his teeth and lunged. He feinted left, right, bent, and swung his sword toward the backs of his opponent's knees.

Hector barely saw it coming, the man's eyes giving away little of his intentions unlike many vulnerable to the observant. However, there was enough time to alter his stance and counter with a downward stroke that landed so near the cross-guard of Sir Sinjin's sword it achieved what had eluded Hector this quarter hour of pursuit after pursuit, clash after clash, and cut after cut that caused his own blood to sully his surcoat.

Séverine's freedom nearer now the knight was deprived of the sword that landed distant, leaving him only the dagger he brought to hand, Hector drew his own. Having no desire to play with his prey, the wielding of two blades would sooner end this.

His opponent making no move to engage again, doubtless weighing options he had not expected to weigh, for the first time since before commencement of the contest, Hector glanced at Séverine who gripped the lapels of the mantle Warin had put over her shoulders.

Then as now, he thought they looked well together. Then as now, he wondered if they might find a good fit after all. Then as now, he knew were that to happen it would be best if Warin did not take his place at Wulfen—unless the king was persuaded to change his mind about what was to become of Séverine should her champion prevail. If Edward was so moved, then Hector would cede his inheritance, accept membership in the Order of the Garter, and enter Prince Edward's service. However, whatever was to come would not until defeat of the one who had begun circling his opponent.

Appearance only, Hector determined. What Sir Sinjin wanted—rather, needed—was to position himself for retrieval of his sword or to gain a pike. The former being nearest, Hector must deal with it first.

He lunged, swept his sword forward, and as the knight sprang out of his path, brought its tip up and sliced into the red-bearded chin that would, for a short time, conceal the blood taken from it.

Still, as told by the audience roused to murmurings and gasps, and someone daring to whistle from atop the walls, all knew if the face beneath those thick red hairs had not been marked before it was now.

Continuing past, Hector slowed enough to ensure the accuracy of a kick that propelled his opponent's sword outside the list. That blade now out of play, Sir Sinjin had only his dagger and the hope of a pike. And Hector had gained enough respect for him to know it was to the latter he now turned his efforts.

Perspiring so heavily his tunic passed moisture to chain mail that passed it to his surcoat, Hector came around and swiped an arm across his trickling brow.

As known, Sir Colbern's approver was swift, hand turning around the spear whose shaft was no easy thing to draw from the ground. But once freed, a greater reach he would have than his opponent. Fortunately, not only was the pike an awkward, graceless thing that did not pair well with a dagger, but Hector was well versed in how to avoid and counter the thrusts. Still, that did not mean victory was assured—nor yet desired by the king who, for the first time, left his chair.

Refusing to look near on the one glimpsed running the perimeter toward the pike that would sooner yield if Sir Sinjin relinquished his dagger to add the strength of his right hand to his left, Hector surged forward.

"Both hands, knave!" the king shouted as Hector neared. "Risk all or lose all. *This* to the death."

Which had not been determined until this moment, Hector silently seethed over what he must do to save Séverine from what could be a fate worse than this knight would suffer.

However, Edward's threat did not gain him what he wanted from the one impelled to fight another's battle. The blood of a sliced chin running Sir Sinjin's throat, the man kept his dagger before him and eyes on Hector. Before the sword coming for him was within reach, he sprang to the side.

As Hector corrected his course, a crack sounded. Now

before him was eight feet of splintered pike, its iron head thrusting at him as the king shouted approval.

Blessedly, Hector was swift as well. Otherwise, he would have been bruised in the side or put through had the iron head penetrated his chain mail.

More impressed than he cared to be, further angered the king would find in favor of Séverine only if Sir Sinjin gave his life for a knight gone black, Hector hooked his sword up beneath the pole as his opponent wrenched it back. He did not have adequate space for the force required to cut through the shaft, but enough damage was done that two feet partially parted from the remaining six and angled toward the ground.

"This what happens when you disregard your king, Sinjin," Edward shouted. "Now finish it, Wulfrith—to the death."

As the knight who had only the dagger to defend himself cast aside the pike, the light in his eyes began to dull as if he accepted his end was at hand. Hector did not believe it.

Think what you—Wulfen-trained—would do were you on the other side of pending victory, his uncle had instructed. *One worthy of sword and spurs fights all the way to the grave, even as dirt rains down on him.*

Hence, as Sir Sinjin swept back an arm, Hector leapt to the side and, to ensure that keen edge skimmed no bit of exposed throat, brought his sword up.

Steel struck steel. The dagger flew.

As the audience stirred in anticipation of mortal bloodletting, most loudly Sir Colbern who cursed his approver, only then did Hector realize how quiet it had been.

"Finish it!" the king commanded as if there was no dishonor in slaying an unarmed man.

Hector looked to Séverine who was wide-eyed and trembling, doubtless not only over this great trial ending in her favor, but the life another must give for the life returned to her.

Confirming those surrounding her were alert to mischief from her accusers, Hector strode to the knight who breathed heavily. "There remains one pike, Sir Sinjin," he risked Edward's wrath. "Retrieve it and we shall end this as honorably as—"

"Craven!" a woman cried. Not Séverine. Not the queen. The lady garbed in yellow. "If he will not beg mercy, I shall!"

Sir Sinjin snapped his head around. "That is for me to do, Lady. And I will not!"

Her eyes flashed. "Big silly men and their chest-thumping pride!"

Laughter sounded from the king as he delivered himself to the victor's side. "'Tis rumored we cut out your tongue, Lady Adelaide. Disproven now." He nodded at Sir Sinjin. "The knight is right. Declaring *craven* for another is not how this is done. It is the defeated who decides how he shall be regarded the remainder of his life—or death. And clearly our rebellious northern subject does not wish to have *coward* attached to his name. Hence, secure Lady Séverine's freedom, Wulfrith."

Hector met his gaze. "Just as 'tis not for another to cry *craven,* this is not how Wulfen-trained warriors end a confrontation, Your Majesty."

Displeasure grooved Edward's brow, though not deeply.

"Our lord husband, most magnificent king," the queen called as she rose, "grant us the boon of ending this contest not with death but pardon of the one who fought courageously in service to the Crown."

Hector could not know if this was prearranged, but it was possible. As for Lady Adelaide's side of it, likely she had unwittingly added to the drama of which Edward was fond.

At Calais, Hector had suspected his king was not set on hanging the six who came before him with ropes around their necks. As had become fairly common with offenses Edward believed justified a tyrannical response to serve as warning to others, he could be magnanimous given the proper incentive.

The queen's pleading allowed him to be lenient where he wished without appearing weak outside the bounds of love for his wife. And how the people of England—and some of France—esteemed Philippa for her good heart. She played her husband's games and for it gained grace for those otherwise doomed.

Edward sighed. "For my wife, no dishonor nor death this day, Sir Sinjin. But you do owe us one more contest ere we determine whether you are trustworthy enough to be loosed upon our kingdom or locked away the remainder of your days in less comfortable accommodations." As relief flickered in the knight's eyes, the king waved a hand. "Return to your chamber and see your injuries tended."

The knight drew the back of a hand across his bloodied beard, looked to Hector. "I am not greatly disappointed at losing to you, Baron. Not only do I believe God provided for the innocent party, but it is long since my skill was so tested. Indeed, quite exhilarating this."

"You are a worthier opponent than most, Sir Sinjin. Had you prevailed, little shame my due."

"And not even Wulfen-trained," the knight said with mock wonder. "I warrant I could impart skills to those young men of yours—were I of a mind to better England's prospects." He pivoted and called, "Much gratitude, Queen Philippa! No gratitude, Lady Adelaide. Godspeed, Lady Séverine." With long-reaching strides that belied the toll exacted by their contest, he strode from the list toward the tower shared with Séverine.

"Come, Wulfrith, let us have done with this to sooner see you tended," Edward said as he crossed to those before the list—the discontented one side of the queen, the contented the other. And at the center of the latter was Séverine, Warin's mantle now open upon her, eyes seeking Hector's.

After commanding Sir Colbern and the deputy to silence, the king said, "Here your valorous champion, Lady Séverine."

Shakily, she curtsied. "I thank you for lending one so worthy, King Edward." Another curtsy, this one angled at Hector and assisted by Warin gripping her arm. "Much gratitude for risking your life to save mine."

Wishing he could be alone with her since there were things best told in private now the contest was done, he said, "I am glad to have served you well, my lady."

"Most well," Edward said. "Sir Sinjin being accustomed to winning the day, now he knows the folly of crossing us and our trainer of knights." He leaned toward her. "Truly, we do not enjoy leashing one so diverting and more likable than not, but he persists and persists—a thorn in our saddle from one end of England to the other."

When he pulled back, Séverine returned her regard to Hector, and there glimmered feelings that made his chest tighten for how impossible they were, just as they would be had he failed her.

Nay, that would have been different, he thought. Had he not been victorious and her sentence death, she would not long suffer what she felt for him as she might when she learned what the king intended. And as Edward had other matters to attend to, soon she would know.

"Could we be assured Sir Sinjin would remain in France," the king continued, "it is he we would send back with you, Lady Séverine."

Known sooner than anticipated, Hector acknowledged as confusion sprang onto her face, followed by disbelief, then belief. Still, when she returned her attention to one few would dispute was the most powerful ruler in Christendom, she said, "Send back with me, Your Majesty?"

Edward harrumphed. "Baron Wulfrith did not tell what to expect should you gain your freedom?"

Her throat bobbed. "There was not much time."

"Was there not?" He looked to Hector. "We do not know what to make of what seems more consideration than lack of time, Baron. Or perhaps we do, though we are certain our son would not approve." A reminder he and the prince leaned toward the current Baron of Wulfen yielding his title and strengthening the training of Edward the younger's men.

The king shifted to Séverine. "Your innocence proven, you shall return to your country."

Holding herself together, which was difficult for how great the relief of answered prayers for Hector's safety, her acquittal, and deliverance of Sir Sinjin, Séverine said, "What of my cousin?"

"As already decided, since he is kin to the Wulfriths and of an age his French sympathies can be reshaped, he will train at Wulfen as his sire wished. Hence, now your promise to Amaury de Chanson is kept, guardianship of the boy passes to his English relations."

She was grateful, Mace's protection and training of utmost importance, but to put the narrow sea between him and her seemed cruel. And to never again see Hector...

"We have been generous in our dealings with your cousin as well as personally assuring a fair trial for you, Lady," he prompted.

Forcing past her throat words so thick they hurt, she said, "So you have been."

"And here one more thing for which you ought to be grateful." His hand replacing Warin's on her, he drew her past the queen toward her accuser.

Thankful his grip countered knees gone soft, Séverine shot her gaze to Hector and saw he started to follow, but then he nodded as if to assure her she was safe in the king's company.

Edward halted before the knave of flushed face. More than she disliked being so near the one with whom all this began, she loathed being within reach of the deputy entrusted with ensuring others did not do as he had done to Mace and her.

"Sir Colbern," the king said, "disloyal subject and ravisher of women, now also known for a liar, thief, and one who grievously misleads the law, restitution is owed this lady."

"*She* is the liar! Had Baron Wulfrith been my approver, damages would be due me!"

As if to strike the knight, Edward released Séverine, but he let the man's words pass.

"And the French harlot would hang for what was done me," Sir Colbern said more loudly, this time causing saliva to fleck her—and his sovereign.

Edward's slap, could what was delivered by a broad palm be named something so benign, knocked the man's head to the side and his feet out from under him. That blow would bruise the same as a fist. As for pride... It surely hemorrhaged.

As the sheriff and deputy drew back from the one with whom they had sided, Edward stepped nearer him. "For what you did at Caen despite our orders women and children were not to be harmed, we dealt harshly with you. But not harshly enough. Imagine our disgust when we learned the name of the one who attacked a lady and boy who sought sanctuary in *our* England..." He looked to the sheriff one side, the deputy the other. "This was no oversight but deceit worked on your king who has not the time to dig for pieces we must assume are of little account."

Sir Colbern sat up and dragged a hand across his bloodied nose. "Your Majesty, no deception was intended—"

"It was and would have been unnecessary had you let lie being bested by a woman! But your greed—and yours, Le Creuseur—abused the law. As for you, Sheriff, since long you have kept Dover in good order, we shall assume it was kinship alone that caused you to be a party to injustice. Thus, 'tis enough we deem it time one of younger years and keener mind keep the peace of that port town."

Séverine ached for the older man though he could have quickly ended what was begun in the stable.

"Now, Lady, tell the damages to be paid by Colbern and Le Creuseur," the king said.

"Surely not me!" the deputy squawked. "I—"

"Will no longer represent the law, Le Creuseur. Lady?"

These two had caused much suffering, but if he wished her to demand payment in blood, she could not. Longing for this to be over so she might straighten out emotions pounding at her heart, she said, "It is enough that neither of these men ever again be in a position to harm others."

The king leaned in. "*That* we do for us. Tell what is to be done for you."

She was about to shake her head when she remembered. "I wish returned to my cousin the dagger over which Sir Colbern and I fought."

"That is all you want?"

"That is all."

"It shall be done." He lowered his gaze to Sir Colbern. "Where is the dagger?"

"I do not possess it. After she gutted me, she pulled it from my—"

"Enough! The lady's innocence established, she left it in you as told."

A whimper sounding from the knight, he turned his face to

the sheriff. "Was I not delivered to you in a delirium and bearing no weapon save my own?"

Though his kin was slow to answer, Séverine did not believe he searched his memory. The favor done his relation had cost him his sovereign's good regard and a position in which he surely took pride.

"He speaks true," the sheriff said and pointed at the deputy. "When I was told who bled out in the stable, it was you I sent to handle the matter discreetly. If you did not pull the dagger from Sir Colbern and add it to riches you believe will buy you into high office, I wager you know who did. And retrieved it."

"A wager you would lose," Le Creuseur spat. "I did not—"

"Regardless, you will see it returned to Mace de Chanson," the king spat.

Thoughts shifted across the man's eyes and twitched at their corners, then he said, "I shall begin searching for the culprit immediately."

Edward snorted. "You think we trust you to investigate the dagger's whereabouts ahead of punishment? Either you are exceedingly foolish or believe it of us." He set his head to the side. "Great the incentive of chained men at the mercy of the unchained to conduct investigations without setting foot outside a dank cell. Thus, we have every faith you will locate the dagger. And quickly."

As Le Creuseur sputtered, Edward motioned forward men-at-arms. "See delivered to Newgate Prison Sir Colbern who is *Sir* no more and Deputy Le Creuseur who is *Deputy* no more while we ruminate on what comes after imprisonment—if anything."

"Newgate!" Colbern exclaimed. "That is—"

"Harsh, indeed! And yet kinder than what you intended Lady Séverine." The king turned to a soldier considerably older than the others. "Tell the warden we would have word from these men only if it is of the stolen dagger."

As those exuding fear were herded opposite, the king said, "This the end of it, Lady Séverine."

Hand pressed to her abdomen beneath the mantle, she looked to him and saw he stared after the men whose helplessness reflected their king was as near God as one of flesh could come. But it was illusion. Though this day offered further proof there was much good in England's ruler—and his wife—Séverine was certain his power was out of balance with grace.

When the two bound for a prison unlike the one provided her went from sight, Edward commanded those on the walls and patrolling the ward to return to their duties and moved toward his vacated chair.

Séverine followed, and looking beyond the queen and Lady Adelaide, saw Hector stood before Sir Percival and Warin. Hating his surcoat was marked with blood, she summoned as much voice as she could. "When do I depart for France, Your Majesty?"

He glanced around. "These things are best done without delay. Providing the weather holds, you sail on the morrow."

"The morrow! But surely I may see my cousin ere I depart."

"Were he not so distant," he said curtly.

Tears causing his countenance to blur, she breathed, "Lord," then hoping for the one thing left to her, though were it granted she would hurt more at its end, asked, "Who is to escort me to France?"

"As Baron Wulfrith served as your champion, Sir Warin offered to return you should his brother prevail. Since he has business to conclude in Calais, he shall accompany you."

Hope come to naught. And confirmation Hector had known she was to be expelled from England and not told though there *had* been time. However, she could not be angry.

Watching the contest that could have seen the man she loved—oui, *loved*—terribly injured or slain had been barely tolerable. Had she known of the dark after the light should Hector triumph, she might not have remained standing as long as she had. And now no longer as King Edward veered toward his queen.

So heavily she landed on her knees she had to slap hands to the ground to keep from toppling onto her face.

She thought it the king who, amid expressions of surprise, stepped before her. But as she focused on fouled boots into which chausses were shoved, she heard the ring of chain mail as Hector set a hand on her shoulder and dropped to his haunches.

"Lady Séverine," he said as she pushed back onto her heels.

Though struck by his formality, she did not heed it as she realized she was meant to do a moment after naming him what she should not in the company of others, "Hector!" She did, however, catch back her hand, but just as the familiar use of his given name was heard, the reach was seen.

As she peered into disapproving green-grey eyes set in a face marked by battle, King Edward said, "Why Baron Wulfrith, when did it transpire the Christian name of he who rules Wulfen is no longer reserved for intimates?"

As Hector's nostrils flared, Séverine heard the queen rebuke, "Edward!" verifying her husband played with his liegeman.

"Pray, forgive me," Séverine whispered, hurt over leaving England and never again seeing him trebling at the thought now he regretted revealing his name.

"When?" Edward pressed.

Momentarily, Hector closed his eyes, then asked low, "Do I assist, can you stand?"

"Oui."

He drew her up beside him and turned to the king with his wife who had risen from her seat. "It has not transpired, Your Majesty."

That Séverine did not expect, and from quickly deflected surprise, neither did Edward. "Then, Wulfrith?"

"I am fond of the lady."

This time Edward did not attempt to hide astonishment, just as Séverine could not have had she tried very hard. Though Hector might have submitted his name was unintentionally revealed, and it would be truthful enough since he had given it to gain her trust while tending injuries dealt by the deputy, further he opened himself to entertaining the king.

Now frowning, Edward said, "You were adamant about not wedding again. After the last misfortune of a wife of the Baron of Wulfen, I agreed it was best. That has changed?"

What he insinuated caused Séverine's pained heart to venture a different direction, but Hector did not allow it stray far. "It has not changed. As told, I feel for Lady Séverine, but I will not wed again."

As the king mulled that, Queen Philippa's eyes made themselves felt, and Séverine shifted to her. Smiling, the woman leaned up and her husband lowered his head to receive her words.

When he straightened, he said, "I do not think I need ask if you have feelings for the baron, Lady."

The hand on her tightening, Séverine wondered if a response was expected. If so, what was she to say? Certainly naught that could see Hector more cornered than he was.

"Are you aware of the fate of Baron Wulfrith's four wives?"

"I am, Your Majesty."

"Many, including the baron, suspect it God's means of ensuring another sire the next great line of Wulfriths. You?"

She swallowed. "Since the siege of Calais, I have weakened

and questioned the goodness of God, but if what I have been taught of Him is right—and I believe it is—He would not take the lives of three innocents nor lead one far from innocent to betray her husband."

His eyes narrowed. "Then you would chance wedding such a man?"

Feeling Hector's anger rise, Séverine determined she would be the one to end what seemed a game since she had little to lose. "Your Majesty, you are too busy to ask that of one you expel from England." She pulled her arm from Hector's hold. "With your leave, I shall return to my chamber and prepare for my departure."

After a wait, he said, "Go, Lady, and be ready to take ship come morn."

As she turned away, she saw Jonesy. He had been so absent since her arrival at the list she had forgotten him—as soon he would forget her in turning his attention to one who might not prove as fortunate as she.

As it was unlikely she would see Hector again, it was hard not to look back before she went around the White Tower, and the moment she was out of sight, she regretted she had not. Still, it was for the best, already too much effort expended on undoing the mess of Séverine de Barra.

CHAPTER 34

Church of Saint Mary the Virgin

"We must needs speak, Brother."

One of many come to kneel before the altar to petition God for intercession, Hector had been aware he was far from alone, but he had barely attended to those coming and going despite rendering himself vulnerable as a warrior ought not.

Now at his shoulder where previously a priest had stood praying for him was Warin who had first told he wished to speak when they had reached the inn following the contest.

Hector had only nodded, then gone to his room to shed battle-worn garments and bathe, during which he reflected on Séverine from their first meeting at Calais when he wanted only to save her from depraved men to their final meeting at The Tower when he acknowledged feelings he named *fond* though that did not encompass this. Next had come fits of prayer, as much owing to the distractions of a restless mind as the restlessness of those in nearby rooms and diners below.

Yearning for the peace of a House of God, he had descended the stairs and seen his brother and Percival at meal and, unbeknownst to him, was followed.

When had Warin come inside? How long had he watched? It bothered, but at least he approached only after Hector sat back on his heels when no answer to beseechings was received that could be believed God-inspired rather than self-inspired.

Unfolding his battle-fatigued body, Hector turned and asked low, "Of what must we speak that cannot wait?"

Candlelight skimming flaxen hair, Warin said, "Of things of loss that have waited too long to be put into words and things that cannot wait longer without risk of further loss."

Though Hector was so uncomfortable in body, mind, and heart he did not want to speak of this now, since it could be the only opportunity for resolution of entreaties put before God alongside those for Séverine who would fare better were she loved by another, he said, "Let us speak."

Dusk was moving toward dark when they exited the church and strode to the great river that was as much the heart of England as it was London. Away from the docks, it was not difficult to find privacy—nor trouble had they been unarmed and mistaken for other than warriors. All those encountered, the seemingly benign and obviously malign, went the long way around them.

"There." Hector motioned to a boulder on the rock-strewn bank of the Thames whose rippling water began to reflect the lights of night.

As they lowered, Warin said, "Merely fond, Hector?"

He almost lied. "I have come to feel much for her, but as you know, it can become no more."

"*Do* I know that?"

Hector turned his face to him. "I believe she would have me, but even did the king not return her to France, I could not make a life with her."

"As Edward put to the lady, you dare not chance it?" Warin said.

Hector cleared his throat. "You told we should speak of loss that is long in being addressed. Let us do that."

"Providing we return to Lady Séverine."

In whom he took too much interest—unfortunately, where Hector was concerned. "As I wish to ensure the lady's safety and ability to prosper, we shall speak more of her. But now tell, where do I stand with a beloved brother greatly harmed by my actions? And how, beyond ceding the barony, do I aid in restoring a life to which you wish to awaken each morn?"

Warin shifted his eyes to the river, but not before moisture was glimpsed on their rims. "When I left Wulfen, I wanted you to feel the guilt I believed your due, just as I believed it fitting some named you *Pale Rider*—for that to be penance to your end days for those lost and all who suffered the losses, but..." He breathed deeply. "While serving in Calais, I honored the Wulfrith name and my training. However, when my duties were done for the day, I drank to excess and kept company with men so content in lacking honor as to be proud of it. I will not tell now the mistakes I made, only that good came of them, causing me to look again to my faith. With much prayer and guidance, grief and anger began to recede."

He tipped his face to the blackening sky. "At last, I moved toward acceptance of what many before me accepted of those who spread the pestilence. Had you not brought it home, others would have, and our losses could have been greater. Too, though I refused to look close on your contrition, I knew it was genuine. Grieving your own wife and unborn babe, you risked your life to separate the sick and tend them. I told myself were penance due, that was enough, and once fairly certain I believed it, returned home to test it in anticipation of taking my place alongside you."

"The test failed," Hector said.

Warin looked around. "Better told it was not entirely successful. What we believe of ourselves in one place does not always hold firm in another. Though I longed to embrace you as brother and friend, what seeped through cracks I believed sealed..." Briefly, he closed his eyes. "Lord! It is almost four years since they were lost to us—and nearly Ondine. That ought to be enough time."

As if feeling Hector tense further, he said, "When you cannot avoid Ondine, you indulge her."

Grateful for the breeze coming off the water though there was no sweet about it, Hector said, "Though yet lovely, it is difficult to look upon one who makes these years feel far more, her scars reminders of the suffering my pride caused. And still cause, having changed the course of her life. By now she would be wed and—"

"Or not," Warin said. "Whether from the pestilence come later, another illness, childbirth, or accident, she could be dead. Nay, that to which both of us must turn our attention is what can be done with the present and future that cannot be done with the past. When next I return from France, I believe I will be ready. Will you?"

Forgiveness perfusing these shadowed years, Hector felt what constricted begin to ease—all but the part of him of which Séverine had hold. "I will be ready, and more so once it is for you to provide the Wulfrith heir."

"This where we return to the lady," his brother said.

Hector was jolted over what was in words close on the heels of mention of relinquishing his title. Though Warin was aware of feelings between his brother and the lady, might he be open to—?"

"Nay, Hector. Do you think I refer to the lady being tied to *my* future, that was poorly worded and timed. I *was* drawn to her, but once it became apparent her heart was turned to yours and yours to hers, I determined not to blunder there—not even with your sacrificial blessing. That would only make worse what we seek to heal and deprive the rightful Baron of Wulfen of continuing our line."

Hector jerked. "I should not have to repeat this, but I will not wed again. Thus, you will be baron."

Warin shook his head, the shift of hair on his brow making him appear a youth again. "Though words spoken in anger may have caused you to believe that would satisfy me, only your death would make me don that mantle. Do you wish to cast it off whilst living, you will have to wait until Rémy is of an age to wear it. Until then, Prince Edward must find another to hone his men's training and, in between, perhaps you will cease resisting and persuade our king a courageous lady of France is worthy of being your wife and the mother of your children."

As Hector opened his mouth to correct him, Warin shot up a hand. "The lady did not answer when King Edward asked if she would chance wedding you, but she need not, it already told by her profession of faith. Like her, I believe God did not take the lives of your wives, though I venture it is possible He did not save them because none were the one needed at your side."

Hector stared, warring between wanting to believe the same and fear that acting on such could cause Séverine to pay the highest price.

"What say you?" Warin prompted.

Hector stood. "With regard to the lady, no different than

before. For the grace granted me of which I shall do all to prove worthy, I am thankful beyond words."

He sensed further argument, but Warin gained his feet and said, "Then to France I go on the morrow."

As it sounded he would not make the journey were their king given cause to allow Séverine to remain in England, Hector said, "You told you have matters to conclude in Calais."

"I do, after which I shall join you at Wulfen."

Hector turned back toward the inn, came around. "Though for now we leave be who shall follow me as Baron of Wulfen, I am content having you at my side again."

The white of Warin's smile visible, he said, "You will see me away on the morrow?"

"At a distance. Thus, upon our return to the inn I shall give you coin to ensure the lady a good situation and a letter allowing her to draw funds if needed."

Warin sighed. "I expect no less from one who denies himself what he wants."

"As he should," Hector tempered his retort.

Blessedly, a comfortable silence settled between them as they walked side by side—one nearly as tall, broad, and imposing as the other, one of silvered dark hair, one of light.

CHAPTER 35

Tower of London

To soar so high then fall from the sky, Séverine mused where she stood with her head back as the highest raven plummeted. An instant later, the resemblance between the bird and her ended. Whether it lost sight of its prey or merely played, it returned to the heights.

Séverine lowered her gaze to the hand pressed to her heart, dropped her arm to her side.

What had remained of the day past had been long and much of the night as well, and now the morn. Since it had dawned clear and a breeze evidenced a good wind eager to fill sails, there should be no delay in expelling her from England. Hence, soon Warin would arrive to serve as her escort.

"Very soon," she whispered, having expected him before now since ships departed as early as weather permitted to increase the chance of making the crossing in a single day—something of a rarity due to how suddenly storms descended on the channel even at this time of year.

Though she had no wish to be carried away from Mace and Hector, each minute that passed added to her ache. Hopefully, once England's shores receded she could distract herself with what lay ahead, there being matters of import to decide, foremost how best to make use of her coin, which had doubled when the constable tasked Jonesy with delivering a purse provided by Queen Philippa.

Though the amount would keep Séverine in good comfort for a short time, minimal comfort would stretch it to a year or more.

Knowing it could not be much longer before her escort was let into the inner ward, and almost certain if any accompanied Sir Warin it would not be Hector, Séverine turned. Catching Jonesy's eye, she smiled at one who had told that though he remained at her service he was no longer her guard.

Unaccompanied, she entered the tower's lower chamber where, after vacating what had been a comfortable prison, she had left her pack and mantle, as well as a bundle to be delivered to Hector. And there was Sir Sinjin.

She had not expected to see him again, certain he would remain in his chamber to recover, but he stretched long in a chair near the unlit brazier, his guard standing beside the stairs with a cup in hand that surely held the knight's fine wine.

"My lady." Sir Sinjin uncrossed his ankles and, somewhat stiffly and with cracking that bespoke the abuse Hector had inflicted, rose from the chair. As seen on the day past, his face suffered cuts and scrapes. As not seen then, the most serious was that dealt his chin. Beard having been shaved, the stitches laddering up the line of seamed flesh were visible.

Though Séverine had known his facial hair added years and masculinity to a handsome visage, the transformation was somewhat extreme, and further when he grinned.

"Aye, Lady, the face more closely matches the warrior's body when hung with beard." He shrugged. "As 'tis better to look boyish than sport a stripe of bared flesh on my chin, this we must suffer until I heal well enough to cover the scar with whiskers."

"Forgive me, Sir Sinjin. I knew your beard was good cover, just not how much. I imagine a warrior must think it a curse to be almost beautiful."

He looked to his guard. "I think you would agree the lady is safe with me."

The man nodded, crossed to the door and, leaving it wide, exited.

"I do not consider it a curse, Lady, it being easier to turn the sightly unsightly if concealment is needed than the unsightly sightly."

His observation brought to mind Lady Ondine who, though not unsightly, sought to hide lost beauty behind a veil just as this man tried to conceal found beauty behind a beard.

"I am glad you are content with how God made you," Séverine said, "and that it appears you suffer no lasting ill in fighting for Sir Colbern."

"I do not regret losing his battle. Though had death been my end... Well, I am grateful it was not and hopeful do I fail to devise an escape from the tower, the next one for whom I serve as approver is innocent and my ability to secure that one's freedom will see me at liberty again."

"But still at odds with your sovereign?"

Another shrug, a nod at the table. "You are ready to return home."

Home. She wished that was what she considered France, but she did not with any depth. "I am as ready as can be. Could I stay, I would."

"And not only because of your cousin, hmm?"

She crossed to the table and cinched her pack's straps, then set a hand on the bundled gown she would ask Warin to see returned to his family and felt nestled atop it the missive composed for Mace. "I am surprised Sir Warin has not arrived to deliver us to the dock. Surely we will set sail before noon."

A hand touched her shoulder, and when she swung around, he was much too close. Further he discomfited in crooking a finger beneath her chin.

"Sir!" she protested and hastened to the side lest he try to pin her against the table.

"Though you appear much recovered," he said, "'tis still in your eyes, and one need not draw near to see it."

"What is in my eyes?"

"Just as I am certain you catch some of what goes in my chamber below, I hear some of what goes in yours." At her startle, he nodded. "Your pillow could not entirely muffle so much misery."

Séverine was embarrassed he had heard her tears, outraged over violation of her privacy, and bitterly humored she should think to hold him accountable when he had not been listening at her door. She was the one who trespassed.

Staring at him with eyes that had felt gritty since awakening, she said, "I apologize for disturbing your rest."

"Too great my aches to make much of the hours anyway. Though I believed Baron Wulfrith my match and it proved nearly so, nearly was not enough to best him. A pity he is distant from the age of one with so much silver in his hair." He frowned. "Quite rare that which is the mark of Wulfriths—rather some."

She started to tell him Dangereuse was silvered as well, but he continued, "I have seen it only once before on a young man, and that was in France."

"Likely a D'Argent, the Wulfriths being descended from

that Norman family whose surname acknowledges the silver of them. My cousin, Mace de Chanson, is descended from them as well."

"Then it was probably one of that family." He crossed his arms over his chest. "Once you are returned to France, what then? Have you kin to take you in?"

Mostly comfortable with him again, she settled into her heels. "I do not, but as Sir Warin has business in Calais and once that was my home, it is a possibility I will remain there since a good number of my countrymen have returned despite the English continuing to hold it."

Noting the tightening of his brow, she said, "What, Sir Sinjin?"

"Were you in Calais when it was under siege?"

"I was."

"With your cousin?"

"Oui. I lived with my aunt, and when she died before King Edward besieged Calais, I became Mace's caregiver and ran my uncle's household."

"Was the boy's sire also there during the siege?"

It began to feel interrogation, but she said, "He was but was lost to us when he did not return from a foray to gain supplies." She put her head to the side. "Why so interested?"

"I—"

Voices outside made him straighten from the table and her turn toward the doorway.

It was not Warin but the constable who stepped inside. "You are to come with me, Sir Sinjin."

The knight stood taller. "For what reason?"

"Though your stay here is assured—for now—matters need discussing."

Seeing Sir Sinjin's stance ease, Séverine guessed he had cause to believe his jailer.

"Do I not see you again, Lady," he said, "I wish you Godspeed."

"And you, Sir Sinjin."

Port of London

He had told himself he could watch her go from him, and yet he had allowed one delay after another before he departed the inn. Thus, when he gained his vantage beyond the dock on a well-traveled road, it was too late to see her arrive and board the ship that sat low in the water for the cargo in its hold and passengers thronging the deck.

As Warin and Séverine were not among the latter, would they come above deck before the vessel began its snaking journey from river to sea? If so, by then would they be too distant to determine which figures were theirs?

No difference would it make, and yet he wanted...

He closed his eyes and, in the darkness against which sunlight pressed, let Séverine in again—the slight height and breadth of her, sorrow and hope of her, touch and feel of her, longing and love of her. Then came memories of Warin of the night past—his forgiveness, encouragement, belief what was impossible was possible. Were it, that possibility would soon be on the other side of the sea.

His mount shifting beneath him, Hector opened his eyes. Seeing the ship's crew move more vigorously in preparation to release the moorings, he patted his horse's neck. "Soon we go," he murmured then once more searched for sight of Séverine and Warin.

"I am not there, Brother."

Hector snapped his head around, stared at the blond

Wulfrith who *should* be there. "What is this, Warin?" As his brother guided his horse alongside, a different question struck, and its answer—were it so—caused anger to replace surprise. "She is alone aboard ship?"

Warin drew rein. "She is not."

"Then who escorts her?"

"None."

"What?"

"She needs no escort, Hector—at least not this day."

Lit with understanding, the strain in hands alerting him to fists, Hector said, "King Edward expects her to be on that ship."

A corner of Warin's mouth rose. "'Tis too late since she is at The Tower waiting for one who has decided not to participate in denying his brother—and her—happiness."

"Warin, you cannot—"

"And yet I have." He dismounted and unfastened his pack from the saddle. As he came around, he tossed back the flap and withdrew a purse that held coin and the letter that was to provide Séverine funds.

He halted at Hector's stirrup, extended it. "Either you deliver these to the lady when you escort her to France, else many a beautiful gown they will afford the wife of the Baron of Wulfen."

Anger again, though of lesser depth, Hector ignored the purse.

Warin sighed, turned to his horse, and hooked its strings on his saddle's pommel.

"Warin!"

He shouldered his pack. "As that ship waits on me, and the coin paid the captain will not stretch much further, I leave my horse in your care so it may convey Lady Séverine from The Tower—that is, if you are too stubborn to take her up before you."

"You are a dreamer!"

Warin set his head to the side. "'Tis long since I was accused of that. I think I have missed it." He frowned. "I have thought that for how much pain one risks in loving, perhaps one ought never. But that is hardly courageous and far from worthy of a Wulfrith." Once more he stepped near, this time set a hand on Hector's arm. "Pray, make something good of this so it may be my apology to *you*," he said, then strode toward the dock.

It took Hector a moment to open a throat so closed it felt a hand around it. "Warin! When you have concluded matters in Calais, you will come home?"

His brother turned and, walking backward, said, "I shall. Now go to her." As though sensing continued resistance, he added, "If Edward is a barrier, it is because you allow it though you are owed a great reward. If still you do not wish to claim that reward by joining the order, redeem it another way." Then he was running and soon the last up the gangplank.

Turning over what had passed between them, Hector watched the ship grow distant as it navigated the river and other vessels, then raised an arm that was answered in kind by the one at the rear railing.

"Godspeed, Brother," Hector said, then took the reins of Warin's horse. Though tempted to ride to The Tower, since it was a waste of time that could cause further heartache, he bypassed it.

Tower of London

SOMEHOW HE HAD ESCAPED.

Now the day that had dragged toward noon, across which

Séverine paced inside and outside her tower, no longer dragged. The garrison was alert as likely they had not been when Sir Sinjin found a way past them—*if* he had.

Jonesy, once more keeping watch over her in the upper chamber, had assured her she was no longer a prisoner but must be kept out of the way of those searching for the knight who might merely bide his time before shedding these walls.

Though the escape distracted from her waiting and the uncertain conclusion something had prevented her ship from sailing that would mean another night here, the distraction was not welcome.

She liked Sir Sinjin, and now feared more for the future of the knight who could have been freed after one more bloody win. When earlier he mentioned devising an escape, it had been no passing nor jesting comment. She could not know whether he had referred to this day or if every day he sought an opportunity to gain his freedom, but were she to once more yield to emotions in this chamber, he would not suffer them.

Séverine turned from the window beyond which men-at-arms scurried like ants and barked orders like dogs. She picked at foodstuffs, sipped wine, paced the floor, and jumped when a knock sounded.

At her bidding, Jonesy appeared. "Your escort is outside the walls, my lady. Though none are to enter nor leave the fortress, the constable will make a way for you."

Then her ship sailed later than expected, meaning at least one dread night on the sea.

Little was spoken as he carried her pack through the inner ward and past every barred gate raised for her that evidenced the likelihood Sir Sinjin remained inside.

At the final gate bordered by the vast moat whose water was provided by the Thames, Jonesy passed the pack to her. As she joined it with the bundle in her left arm, she asked, "What will come of Sir Sinjin?"

"Perhaps better asked what will come of his guard," he said wryly.

"But the knight was with the constable."

"He was, though that may not have been so when he escaped, and for how often his guard indulges in wine..." He shrugged. "As for what will come of Sir Sinjin, no good if he is captured outside these walls, little good if captured inside. When our king learns his favorite approver has demonstrated The Tower of London is less secure than all the world believes, the supreme tolerance shown that northerner may find its end."

"Supreme?"

"Aye, where that noble is concerned. I cannot speak to it more than that, but know ours is a good king, my lady. As with most, he can be moved to revenge when wronged, but greater his capacity for forgiveness—and not only for the wisdom of such but godliness."

After Séverine's experiences with Edward, more she believed that than not, and it gave her hope tolerance for Sir Sinjin's defiance would extend a bit further.

Jonesy patted her shoulder. "I wish you a good life, my lady."

"I wish you the same."

He motioned for the final gate to be raised that would immediately lower behind her, keeping inside those the king was not willing to release, including the lady who had called *craven* on the day past.

Hoping whatever Lady Adelaide had done that made some believe Edward cut out her tongue was not so terrible she would be imprisoned forever, Séverine stepped before the riveted bars.

As more chains clattered, she peered at four soldiers standing shoulder to shoulder at the causeway's end. None having been stationed there upon her arrival, Sir Sinjin must be responsible.

Moving her gaze beyond to a group of riders on the winding dirt road, her search for Warin yielded naught—that is, of him. The riders were distant, but not so much she was unable to recognize it was they who had escorted her to London. And neither was Hector among them, in his place a riderless horse surely meant to convey her to the dock.

Where were the brothers? Had something—?

Thoughts snapping back to Hector fighting to gain her freedom, her breath caught. He had not appeared badly injured, but some wounds were sly, revealing their severity only when one was vulnerable.

Fearing him abed, Warin in attendance, and their men tasked with delivering her to the ship, Séverine's heart pounded. When the rising gate reached the height of her ribs, she ducked beneath and hastened over firm planks.

The chains ceased their clanking, and when they sounded again in lowering the gate, the soldiers ahead parted. It was then she saw what the wall of them had hidden—or nearly so since, had she looked closer, above one of the peaked helmets she would have glimpsed the top of a silvered head.

Séverine stopped and, vaguely aware of the thump of her pack and bundle on the planks, searched the face of the man who stepped onto the causeway. His expression was not grim, but it was solemn.

When he halted five feet distant, she asked, "Warin?"

"My brother is well."

She sighed. "Then why are *you* here? What has happened?"

"*You* happened, Séverine—over and again as if ever you were meant to."

Thinking it impossible lost hope was found, she said, "Either I misunderstand or my hearing is not as recovered as thought."

"Just as you hear well, you understand." Movement at his sides revealing he opened closed hands, he said, "I believe you love me."

Without hesitation, she nodded.

"Then we are halfway there, Séverine."

"Are we?" she whispered.

As if reconsidering something, he looked away. When his eyes returned to hers, they were nearly as fierce as when he wielded a blade against Sir Sinjin. "Having prayed Warin and you are right—that I am not meant to be alone—I shall deliver us the rest of the way providing you are willing to risk life with me."

Was it possible she who ought to be bound for France and ever parted from him and Mace was being offered marriage?

"Séverine?"

Determinedly keeping her feet planted, she said, "Whatever the Lord gives me of life with you is far better than life without. So what risk that?"

The relief in his smile nearly made her run into his arms as she ought not with so many watching, but when he said, "Then as I am yours, you are mine," she sprang forward and he caught her up.

They held long, then she tipped back her head. "I believe *you* love me, Hector of the Wulfriths."

Eyes more alight than ever she had seen them, he said, "Even the mess of you, my lady, though of course henceforth we must give Edward as little cause as possible to regret yielding to Queen Philippa."

"The queen?"

He lowered her to her feet. "She supported redemption of

my reward for aiding their son not with membership in the order but marriage to a lady of France."

She frowned. "For this I was not delivered to the ship earlier?"

"Aye. Though I came to the port to see you away, Warin had other plans. He told it was too late to collect you, and he would go alone to Calais to finish his business. Before the ship sailed, he encouraged me to redeem my reward for something *I* wanted. I nearly came to you then, but to be certain you were within my grasp, first I went to Westminster." He glanced past her. "The timing could not have been better since Edward's generous mood would have been far from that had he known of the escape."

"Sir Sinjin may yet be inside the walls," she said, then asked, "Did I cost you more than membership in the order?"

His smile faltered. "The king wants a Wulfrith heir and soon."

She understood his unease, and more since he had prefaced the offer of marriage with the reminder it could risk her life. "Then God willing—and I believe He is not unwilling—a child we will make. For us."

"There is one other thing Edward wishes."

Warily, she said, "That is?"

"To borrow *The Book of Wulfrith,* of which he has long heard. However, since once a book on loan enters his library it is wont to stay, I persuaded him to avail himself of Stern's hospitality when next he travels his realm. There he may pore over the text in the company of Lady Héloise who will further his knowledge of what is within the pages."

"I am glad of it."

"Until he and his entourage come calling," he said. "As you will be the lady of the castle, he will keep you busy."

That part of being his wife had not occurred, and it intimidated beyond duties for which she was unprepared. "But Lady Dangereuse runs your household, and I would not—"

"She knows the way of things, Séverine. Once she has acquainted you with managing Stern, she will find something else with which to occupy herself."

"I do not wish to make an enemy of her."

"You will not. It may be difficult in the beginning, but she will be glad her brother has found happiness."

Tears wet her eyes. "I thought this day among my worst. Now I think I could not be more joyous."

He raised an eyebrow. "Does my betrothed issue a challenge?"

"Betrothed," she breathed, then jumped to her toes and offered her mouth. "No challenge needed, Hector of the Nine Worthies—*my* worthy."

EPILOGUE

Stern Castle
Summer, 1352

She could have wed in one of several gowns acquired this past month, but Fira had pressed her to speak vows in that of purple cloth.

Lady Héloise had appeared more thoughtful than disapproving, while beside her Esta had nodded.

Dangereuse had shrugged and resumed correspondence she would soon relinquish to the lady who was to be her sister-in-law.

Ondine had shaken her head and proposed the gown *she* had fashioned, one that would be scandalously sheer were it not made of layers of her favorite material. Though that ivory creation had not been under consideration, Séverine had donned it, albeit in the nuptial chamber *after* shedding Lady Annyn's gown.

Now, following a wedding feast attended by Mace and

absent Warin who had yet to return to England, Séverine's husband circled her amid the light of a dozen candles.

"Hector!" She turned her head to follow him out of sight, opposite to return him to sight.

Lips twitching, he halted before her. "Obviously, a gift from Ondine."

One that did not rival that received from the king—return of the dagger of Maël D'Argent and tidings Colbern and Le Creuseur were banished from England.

Glancing from her husband's undertunic that bared his lower legs to what she wore that looked more a lovely dense mist than a garment, Séverine said, "Ondine made it, and though I did not think it a fitting wedding gown, it seemed appropriate for the night."

"For the short time you shall wear it," he rumbled.

"Only a short time?" she teased.

"Dearest Séverine, I did not think you terribly overdressed when I entered, but now I am near..." He pulled a tress through his fingers. "...methinks your hair covering enough."

Face warming, she said, "For my shoulders and back but not much beyond."

"And not for long." He raised her left hand on which he had placed the ring worn by every bride of a Baron of Wulfen since Lady Annyn's mother-in-law. In light of its most recent past, he had told his grandmother he would have a new ring made for Séverine. Lady Héloïse had responded by summoning her grandson's betrothed and commanding her to support the tradition.

Séverine had, though not to avoid her displeasure, and only after she and Hector spoke in private. She had told him she saw the ring as merely something fashioned of metal and stones, that no matter whose hand it fit in the past and would fit in the future, it but symbolized what was between one bride and one groom. However, if he believed ever it would trouble him to see it on her finger, she would have him commission another that would be as dear to her even were it of iron and naught else.

Now, brushing a thumb across the large sapphire encircled by small rubies, he raised his eyes to hers and said, "A perfect fit."

So it was, and not because there was no need to alter its size.

As beautiful ache convulsed a heart growing larger in love with him, Hector carried her hand to his mouth and kissed her fingers. Then he turned her wrist up and touched a looped button beneath which her pulse leapt. "May I, Wife?"

A shiver coursed her. "You may, Lord Husband."

She had thought it would take longer to unfasten all the buttons on both sleeves, but despite how indelicate his hands and fingers, they were deft. And neither was he troubled by laces whose crossings he loosened while kissing her neck and shoulder.

Every place he touched incredibly alive, every place he had yet to touch longing to know his calloused fingers, the soft and firm of his lips, and the rasp of his beard, Séverine felt as if she had overly imbibed during their wedding feast—so much she had to grip his tunic to keep her balance.

When his hands on her stilled and he lifted his head, she gave a murmur of protest.

"Two hundred years," his husky, wine-scented words swept her face.

She raised her lids and, finding his eyes nearly all pupil, guessing hers were as black, said, "Two hundred years?"

How she loved his smile—almost as much as his kiss. "Since a Baron of Wulfen took a wife who stole inside a fortress exclusive to men, next the fortress of his heart."

Fira had expressed something similar in persuading

Séverine to wed in her predecessor's gown, but it did not compare to how it was worded by the man with whom she would spend her life.

"Hector," she said across a small sob.

"Séverine," he said, then gruffly, "Raise your arms."

"Do I fall, you will catch me?"

"Always I will catch you."

"As ever the valorous one does," she said, "and I wish to do for you."

Something not of the moment crossed his face, and with what seemed urgency, he said, "You do, Séverine. Stay my side, and always you shall."

Still he feared losing her as he had the others. Unable to promise him anything beyond her own heart, she said, "Even God will have to pry my hands from you, and every night I shall pray it is as a very old lady." She smiled, and upon the return of his smile, raised her arms.

When the gown floated to the floor and his eyes were all over her, she said, "Raise *your* arms."

When his undertunic joined the gown and her eyes were tentatively upon him, he said, "I love you in heart, Séverine Wulfrith."

She stepped between his feet, set a hand on his chest and the other between her breasts. "As I love you."

He lowered his head and, gently coaxing her lips open, moved his hands to her hips, the small of her back, and up her spine. "Your skin is so soft."

She slid her hands up his muscled shoulders. "Yours is not, and how it thrills."

Less gently her husband kissed her, then he swept her up and carried her to the nuptial bed.

Dear Reader,

Thank you for joining me on my writing journey. If you enjoyed the first tale in the 14th-century Age of Honor series, I would appreciate a review of VALOROUS at your online retailer. A few sentences is lovely. A few more, lovelier.

Up next is the tale of Lady Ondine, something of a reversal of Beauty and the Beast. Something... An excerpt of BEAUTEOUS is included here.

Blessings ~ Tamara

Author's Note

Dear Readers,

Since I wrote *Baron of Godsmere*, the first book in The Feud series, I've been fascinated with one of the most significant conflicts of the Middle Ages known as The Hundred Years' War. Of course, contemporaries did not name it that, having no idea it would last over a century.

Though there was much to the hostilities between England and France, for the backdrop of *Valorous* my focus was mostly on the English king's attempt to recover the French lands of his ancestor, William the Conqueror, and the King of France's determination to seize the remainder of his royal vassal's lands. *Was* it an age of honor? No. But on that teetering stage made more precarious by the pestilence that swept the known world, were men and women who sought the honorable amid the dishonorable, among them my fictional—and certainly flawed—Wulfriths.

For readers of the Age of Faith series, you will recall Sir Elias de Morville of *The Raveling*, the 12th-century poet knight who began *The Book of Wulfrith*. It was thrilling to finally bring to life his chronicle of the family he esteemed. As for readers of the Age of Conquest series, in *Valorous* you'll recognize mention of some of its characters and the missives in the cask that appeared in Sir Maël and Lady Mercia's tale, *Heartless*. Though the first missive was included in its entirety here, I summarized the second due to its length that could be unclear to those unfamiliar with the 11th-century series.

As ever, thank you for coming alongside me on this wondrously long and winding journey.

Godspeed ~ Tamara

BEAUTEOUS: BOOK TWO EXCERPT

PROLOGUE

Barony of Wulfen, England
January's End, 1349

"I war, I war," she whispered. "Heavenly Father, I war."

"His suffering is done, Ondine," spoke the one she could not bear to look upon where he lowered to the mattress beside her. "Now drink."

So she could prolong her own suffering? So she could watch the suffering of others destined for the hunting lodge the same as she and the squire? So she could hate longer, not only this brother but herself?

Pressing lips in defiance of the cup Hector set against them, she held burning eyes to the two on the opposite side of the timber room—the young man first to succumb to the pestilence at Stern where he lay unmoving beneath the sheet drawn over him, and the kneeling physician who sought to pray into heaven what had fled a body so ravaged it was barely recognizable.

Blessedly, entirely unrecognizable to her brother and her were the squire's final words. Despite the absence of a priest to shrive him, had they been of confession? If so, would the physician share them with Hector?

"You must drink, Ondine."

Longing to cast some portion of her punishment at her brother—to strike with cruel words and hands that ached to scratch her skin—she continued to refuse him her gaze. Then turning her pained head on the pillow to look nearer on the two opposite, loudly she beseeched, "Lord, I war!" She coughed, drew a wheezing breath. "How I war..."

"Almighty," her brother also entreated, voice so strained it did not sound his, then he said firmly, "Drink!"

Refusing to look away from the dead and the praying, she croaked, "Why? It will not ease your...conscience."

Hector had been tense before, but as the Lord refused to aid in tempering her tongue, now he was so rigid a blow might split him down the center. Still, he was gentle in shifting her higher on the pillows and once more pressing her to drink.

Were those the worst of his new offenses, perhaps she could have closed her eyes and allowed what had taken Squire Briant of twenty years to take this lady of ten and six. But with obvious intent, her brother turned his body to block her view of the first casualty of what his hubris had brought into their home.

God help him, he went too far!

And God help me, she thought. Not only did she thirst, but anger demanded of her what she had too little breath and strength to waste.

Flinging up a hand Hector had wrapped in bandages to

keep her from tearing at things rising from beneath her skin, she knocked aside the cup. The warm drink of honey and herbs splashed the space between them, ending its flight against his tunic and the cloth covering his lower face that the physician believed aided in keeping the evil from entering the healthy.

Hearing the cup clatter to the floor on the opposite side of her cot, wanting her brother to be far from gentle so she had more cause to hate him, Ondine swept her gaze to where he sat like stone. "He is dead," she put between chattering teeth. "Dead! And soon I follow."

He jerked as if dealt a fist, causing the silvered dark hair on his brow to shift. "You will not, Ondine!"

She did not think it possible to laugh, and perhaps she did not since what came out of her was so absent music it would frighten were she not wading in things more terrible than a sound.

"I shall," she hissed, then recalling what many named her that she needed no mirror to confirm was lost, added, "Just as beauty flayed from me, life taken by death circling and… choking the moat around my sickbed."

"Cease," he growled and started to draw her to him.

It surprised she wanted to be held and comforted thus—and there the war within Ondine Wulfrith. Determinedly defecting to the other side, with bandaged hands she slapped and punched, but to no effect. Easily he deflected all and ended her assault by capturing her wrists.

She whipped her head back to spew more words and once more make stone of him, but what she saw made stone of her. She had thought her flailing ineffectual, but if the drink-splashed cloth now down around his neck had kept the evil from him, her exertions had proven of great effect.

Fractured heart threatening to shatter, she strained away. "The cloth, Hector!"

He pulled her in the rest of the way, releasing her wrists once her arms were pinned against his chest and fixing her there with an arm around her back.

Unable to grip the face cloth through her bindings to push it up and prevent the ill from entering him, she dropped back her head. "Pray, cover yourself!"

He lowered his chin and, moist green eyes peering into hers, said, "I am sorry for what I wrought. All my life I shall be."

"The cloth!"

Cupping the back of her head, he urged it down and pressed her face against her useless hands. "All my life, be it one more day or thousands," he murmured.

She longed to argue further, to persuade him and the physician to leave this dying woman and save themselves, but the strength scraped together was spent. As she sank into him, through a haze she heard someone who sounded like her crying softly between whispered prayers that all this end with her.

It did not. Though for days she was barely present, this she knew—the three in the lodge grew in number. Hector's pregnant wife entered here, followed by their second brother's wife, then their sire, next castle folk.

Though the Great Mortality had been late in coming to England and extending its tentacles to the Barony of Wulfen, it had come—and shown biding its time was no great inconvenience.

CHAPTER ONE

Stern Castle, Barony of Wulfen

November, 1352

Visitors at Wulfen, and of good regard for being permitted to dismount in the inner bailey before the donjon rather than the outer bailey at the stable.

Wishing she had not been so quick to cast off her gown following her outing with the owl, Ondine turned from the table where she completed her ablutions with towels and a basin of perfumed water and hastened to the postered bed draped with swaths of nearly sheer cloth.

She snatched up her robe, thrusting her arms in the sleeves as she crossed to the nearest window, cinching the belt as she skirted a chair.

Though tempted to whip back the shutters so she not miss those below entering the great hall, lest creaking hinges reveal the observer, she eased open one and was caressed by a mildly warm breeze.

Pleased her windows had yet to be fit with partially transparent panes to avert the cool of autumn and chill of winter, slowly she leaned forward to prevent any with a well-developed sense of the unseen from looking upon her bared face.

Below, in the company of Stern's captain of the guard and three men-at-arms, were four horses whose warriors had dismounted. However, the fifth horse retained its rider, and that man of dark brown hair was of note for manacled wrists, and more so for how short the chain linking them.

Dangerous then, but not terribly so. Otherwise, he would not have been permitted to enter the inner bailey, perhaps not even the outer. But after looking closer on his escort, Ondine revised her conclusion. As revealed by what was emblazoned on tunics worn over fine armor, here were King Edward's men. Regardless of the danger their prisoner might present, they had been admitted to the inner bailey, none gainsaying those who determined the manacled one should accompany them to the donjon.

So who was the man likely bound for London to answer to one who may or may not be his king? What had he done? And what would be his punishment?

"Come down, Daschiel," commanded the knight before the steps whose balding head evidenced middle age or greater.

"Daschiel," Ondine whispered in search of familiarity with what she guessed a surname as she watched the prisoner lean slightly back and swing a leg over the horse's neck. Thigh met thigh and, with a thrust of hips and rattle of manacles, he came down the saddle's side and landed booted feet to the ground.

More metal links sounded as one of the king's men stepped forward. When he went to his haunches before the prisoner, Ondine saw he held another set of manacles, the chain between these longer. And a good thing since otherwise the prisoner would have to be carried up the steps. What was not good despite the entertainment of great curiosity was he should be so dangerous it was necessary to bind hands *and* feet.

Had the Baron of Wulfen been at Stern, likely he would have denied the prisoner entrance to the donjon regardless of offending the king's men and, in turn, the king. But he would do it only in consideration of the comfort of the women and children of his household since Stern's garrison would have no difficulty protecting its charges.

In Hector's absence, doubtless their eldest sister had taken measures against exposing her young son to one so villainous he might be a murderer. Were Dangereuse standing just inside the doors with their new sister-in-law, it was only because she had sent Sebastian abovestairs.

Such ruminations were nearly Ondine's undoing. Peering

down at the prisoner who looked upon the one fitting irons to booted ankles, sooner she should have seen the rise of his chin and slide of eyes up the donjon.

Glimpsing an attractive face she had not known was fit with a beard whose russet color contrasted with brown hair, she lurched back to ensure her face was not seen. Albeit once its beauty might have exceeded the attraction of his, never again.

She teetered against the chair she came up against, emptied her breath, and dropped onto the seat. Hating she trembled as if seen by eyes that could have only caught the movement of one who spied on him, she bent forward, pressed forearms into her thighs, and clasped hands that were now her greatest beauty—graceful, long-fingered, unmarred. It was nearly the same for her breasts, abdomen, back, and feet, their blemishes so slight they were more felt than seen. But the rest of her...

Ondine pried her hands apart and studied them to assure herself naught had changed. Then she fingered scars on her neck and face that would be worse had Hector not so securely bandaged her hands that even the tear of her teeth had been unable to free fingers tipped with destructive nails.

Feeling a tug at her center—a warning memories dug in and, given the chance, would drag her back to those cruel weeks—she said, "Nay, I am here." She shoved to her feet. "Here. Now. The present moving toward..."

She moistened her lips, nodded to give herself permission to speak what once she had thought lost to her and still felt foreign though day after day she went through one end of it and came out the other. "...the future, whatever that may be."

Below, the great doors closed, evidencing the visitors had made it up the steps and entered the hall where they would be greeted by the womenfolk of the trainer of England's worthiest knights.

Ondine longed to join her family who satisfied their curiosity over the king's prisoner, but it was hard for her to stand before the unfamiliar—worse, strangers. So much easier to go to the upper room and while away time in the company of her owl who was near to gaining his freedom.

"Easier were you not a Wulfrith," she scorned, then preferring to be faceless than faint-hearted, crossed to her clothes closet.

Recalling the attractive face glimpsed, she reached for her favorite gown fashioned of layers of pale blue gossamer cloth to render it impenetrable to the eye, hesitated, then dropped her arm to her side.

As her first consideration in choosing a gown had been the man in chains when it ought to be what pleased one whose life was mostly a lonely and unloved one for an inability to wed and become a mother as longed for, she pulled out a gown of dark green wool whose bodice and hem were finely edged in fur. It was lovely—more, practical and proper.

On the morrow she would be fanciful again, but should Stern's visitors join the Wulfrith family and their retainers at meal this eve, the greatest curiosity she would present was that of one who veiled her face and hair as if in mourning.

And in her own way, she did mourn. Still.

THE BARON OF WULFEN was not in residence. And that was not a bad thing since it was his wife with whom Sinjin had a favorable acquaintance. Not that he and her husband were of foul acquaintance, but they *had* met at swords six months past— one out of choice, the other necessity.

For the baron's victory, he who was publicly called only by his title and surname *Wulfrith* had gained the life and freedom of Lady Séverine whom he had wed and got with child. For Sinjin's efforts in fighting for a miscreant supposedly incapable of engaging in trial by combat, all this warrior had gained was minor injuries.

And yet his only regret in being defeated by so worthy an opponent was he remained a prisoner at The Tower of London. Fortunately, that he had quickly remedied. Unfortunately, his escape of inescapable walls had been temporary.

But temporary need not remain that, he assured himself as he looked around Stern's hall from atop the dais where Lady Séverine had seated him at high table though his escort tried to discourage her from honoring him by requiring two king's men on each side of their prisoner. She had wavered, then displaced family members and three household knights to accommodate all her visitors.

God willing, soon Sinjin would effect another escape, but it would not be from Stern Castle. As much as he liked the detour he had suggested after a spooked horse threw one of his escort, requiring a physician set the man's broken arm to increase the chance of it serving him well again, this was merely diversion.

Come the morrow, mounted and absent the added precaution of chained ankles, once more he would expend much thought and effort on ensuring days hence he was not knocked to his knees before the king who might decide to wipe clean whatever remained of his debt to Sinjin Daschiel. And considering all, Edward would be justified in believing it mostly paid in full.

The sudden lowering of voices indicating the evening meal would soon commence, Sinjin leaned forward to peer past Lady Séverine and the baron's grandmother to the priest who had risen from his chair.

Beginning to raise his hands, the man stilled and frowned at something that captured his attention. Then cheeks deflating with exhaled frustration, he motioned forward the one Sinjin's seeking eyes landed on—a lady in a fitted gown of green who stood before the stairs off which she had come in time to interrupt the blessing of the meal.

A dark veil covering face and hair as if in mourning, nothing else could be known about her beyond her height and lovely figure—until she answered the priest's summons. She did not glide, that being impossible for a creature not of the water, but nearly so as she crossed the hall.

Though torchlight penetrated enough of the veil's loose weave to occasion a glimpse of fair skin and glimmering eyes, it could not be known what she looked upon. And yet he sensed he was framed again and again in those tiny openings.

Vanity, his sire would name it, but it was not that. It was sensation, the same felt while the second set of manacles was fit outside the donjon. But was the one who looked down upon him then the same now peering up at him at high table?

When her destination proved a lower table nearest the dais where sat those displaced by Stern's visitors and room was made for her between Lady Séverine's sisters-in-law, Sinjin was certain the veiled one was a close relation.

She stepped into the space opened for her but remained standing, doubtless knowing the priest would resume what she had interrupted. He did, and when all rose as commanded, asked the Lord to bless their meal and the men and women present as well as absent. Then those gathered here sat to receive the squires who appeared and washed their hands in advance of the delivery of pitchers of drink and platters of viands.

As Sinjin was seated between the king's men and had naught to say to them that was not already spoken during their southward journey, the only good of the meal was excellent wine and fine fare. Or so he told himself amid musings over the veiled lady who, though she ate and drank little, gracefully did so under cover of the veil when not conversing with Baron Wulfrith's sisters, Lady Dangereuse of silvered dark hair more striking than the baron's, and Lady Fira of wildly freckled face and abundant red-blond hair.

Sinjin did not think it imagined he often fell beneath the regard of one who intrigued. Indeed, so certain was he that he began offering one-sided smiles when swept by the sensation of her. The first few times he was rewarded with slight startles, but thereafter none as if she was no longer interested in he whose wrists were so closely bound that one followed the other in delivering food and drink to his lips. It was possible she looked elsewhere, but he did not believe it.

Again his sire would name it vanity, and perhaps it crossed that line, but the sensation persisted.

When Lady Séverine called an end to the meal and invited all to relax over conversations and games while the hall was set aright, Sinjin was further impressed by her air of authority that had not been evident while both were imprisoned at The Tower of London.

As concluded upon his arrival when she greeted him with enthusiasm and introduced him to her in-laws and knights present in the hall, the French lady whose country remained at war with England was accepted by her husband's family and people. Thus, more smoothly the way was paved for one who, in less than five months, would gift her husband a son or daughter as none of his first four wives had done.

Moments later, she surprised in appearing beside him as he descended the dais with a clatter of chain, and further surprised in sliding a companionable arm through his. "Sir Sinjin—"

"Not allowed, my lady," warned the knight coming behind.

Ignoring the man whose arm her physician had set and secured with a sling, she tilted up her face. "Sir Sinjin, by invitation of Baron Wulfrith's grandmother, will you join us at hearth and regale us with your exploits since last you were in London?" That was said for all, then quietly she added, "Too, I would see to its end our last discussion, that which was interrupted and yet troubles me."

Before he could recall what it was, the aged knight ahead turned, halting their progress. "He will not join you at hearth, my lady. As soft confinement is no longer due this enemy of our king—who you would do well to remember is now *your* king—Sir Sinjin has been shown enough courtesy. Now loose him so we may avail ourselves of a good night's sleep to sooner resume our journey."

Knowing Sir Orton to be of poor temperament for having recently lost his wife as confided by one of his escort, Sinjin said, "My lady, much gratitude to Lady Héloïse for the invitation, but—"

"Non!" she said in her language as if to emphasize the French of her and, holding her gaze to Sir Orton, continued, "This is Wulfrith hospitality due a man I hold in good regard and—"

That one lunged. As movement all around evidenced Wulfen's defenders were prepared to act against any who aggressed on their lady no matter to whom the offender answered, the aged knight's hand closed over hers on Sinjin's arm.

Being very aware of her pregnancy and his chains limiting his ability to protect her ahead of the arrival of Wulfen's knights, Sinjin turned into her to shield her and break the knight's grip. He believed that would suffice, but lest he was wrong, thrust his left elbow behind and up into the face of the king's man.

"God's teeth!" growled the one of broken arm as Sir Orton bellowed and stumbled back.

As cries and gasps resounded around the hall, what could have become chaos was averted by Wulfen-trained warriors who, hands on swords, placed themselves between the king's men and their lady and Sinjin.

"Order!" commanded Stern's senior household knight as he took his lady's arm to draw her away from the prisoner. "Order!"

Resisting him, she raised her face and rasped, "I did not mean to make it worse for you, Sinjin. Pray, forgive me."

"No worse, dear lady." He managed a smile. "Indeed, better since these days have been tiresomely uneventful."

"But what they will do to you when—"

"Their orders are to return me to King Edward whole of body. Be assured, with little more than grunts, this warrior can endure any pettiness worked on him."

"Pray, Lady Séverine, loose him," entreated Baron Wulfrith's man who knew to handle gently the mother of his lord's unborn child.

She hesitated, then did as bid and was pulled away.

As Sinjin turned to Sir Orton and two others of his escort, the former gripping a hand over his bloodied nose as he threatened the defenders of Stern, the knight of broken arm stepped near. "Almighty, Sir Sinjin, did you have to do that? You know he would not have harmed the lady."

As the man's commander was urged toward the hearth to be tended by the physician, Sinjin glanced at one he rather liked, and not only for a good pinch of Scots blood amid the English. "Not intentionally, Sir Wallace, but as you know, often those who place themselves between predator and prey are unintentionally harmed. And 'twas not only the lady I defended but her babe who may one day train up warriors for King Edward the same as his sire and sire before."

The man gave a groan of long suffering, then a grunt of sudden enlightenment. "When you answer to our sovereign for this—and you will—tell it just as spoken here, Sir Sinjin. Hard to argue you should have done differently."

"Careful," Sinjin said as he sent his gaze around a hall quickly recovering its order, and not only for the presence of household knights. The heretofore watchful Lady Dangereuse of dark hair more silvered than her older brother's had slipped into the shoes of Stern's new lady who conversed with her senior knight near the great doors. Likely this sister had filled those shoes before the baron remarried, and now as she issued commands to servants and retainers, so comfortable did she appear, it would not surprise if she regretted yielding her place to Séverine.

"Careful?" Sir Wallace said warily.

Sinjin looked to him. "Aye. Do you show me too much consideration, I may turn it to my advantage as I did that of my guard at The Tower of London."

The man's frown deepened, then he made a sound of disgust and drew the prisoner to where his fellow knights remained bounded by Stern's defenders the same as Sir Orton who was being treated by the physician across the hall, likely for a broken nose.

"Grant me a kindness and settle in," Sir Wallace said, "and once we are abovestairs, do not rise to my commander's baiting, eh? Poor guests we have made already, and of no good account do our hosts deem it necessary to summon their lord who ought not be distracted from making warriors out of snotnosed boys."

Especially since it was told Baron Wulfrith had recently

returned to Wulfen Castle following a visit to his wife, Sinjin reflected. "Granted," he said and silently added, *This night*. If it served him not to settle during the morrow's ride he would not. And would pray the king's men—especially Wallace—were not severely punished should their prisoner once more seize freedom.

Shortly, movement toward him and his escort drew his eye to Lady Fira who had tried several times during his introduction to the Wulfrith ladies to engage him in conversation. Not because she was attracted to him, he was fairly certain, having enough experience with making the hearts of ladies jump to know her interest traveled a path that went the long way around the heart. Likely he was more an object to be examined all sides, and once curiosity was satisfied, placed on a shelf to gather dust.

It amused him. And then it did not, for coming behind the young woman was the veiled one whose hem skimmed the rushes rather than bounced across them as did Lady Fira's. Not amused at all, for now he was the one thinking to make an object of a person.

"Ladies, the night is near done," said a household knight. "Best you go abovestairs and gain your rest as shall Stern's guests once the physician has finished with Sir Orton."

"Ah, but 'tis early yet," said Lady Fira. Halting, she settled a smile on Sinjin. "Having looked near upon you, Sir Knight, I believe 'tis true what was told, but—"

The shift of his gaze past her shoulder silencing her, she looked around and startled as if she had not realized she was followed. "Oh! You have not met my sister."

As believed, of close relation, and now known to Sinjin was the baron had three sisters and at least one brother, Sir Warin having attended their trial by combat.

"'Tis not unusual for her to come late to dinner." Lady Fira returned her regard to him. "So do not fear it has anything to do with you."

"I am much relieved," he said as that lady halted alongside one who was surely younger. Catching the glitter of eyes behind the dark veil, he dipped his head. "Sir Sinjin of the Daschiels, my lady. You are called...?"

She made him wait on a voice he hoped a match for the grace with which she carried herself, and just when he thought her sister would be the one to answer, she linked her hands at her waist and said, "Ondine Wulfrith."

Though her given name seemed a perfect fit that made him wonder if her face was as well, there was less grace—and much accusation—in her next words. "*Lady* Ondine who requires no introduction to he who tried to slay my brother. And failed."

As he had little cause to be ashamed of that contest, it was not what made him stiffen. Rather, the tightening of his muscles supported the determination not to offer a defense not owed her. But just as Lady Séverine had found a welcome champion in Baron Wulfrith, Sinjin now found an unwelcome one in Lady Fira.

"Ondine, you know that as an approver Sir Sinjin was required to fight for others at our king's pleasure, and he chanced death to prove or disprove the charges of Séverine's accuser."

"So he might gain his freedom," the lady said, "uncaring that had God been unreceptive to prayers that day as we know He can be, not only might our brother have died but Lady Séverine. Then as the villain for whom this knight fought would not have been exiled, still that knave would be working his ill in England."

"Ondine—"

"Your sister is right, Lady Fira," Sinjin said. "Had I prevailed in the absence of the Lord's intervention, that could have been the result. And a great and terrible injustice."

They turned their heads back to him. As the surprise of only one was visible, he nodded at the lady he could not read. "Much gratitude."

"For?" she clipped.

"Your faith in this warrior."

Fira understood immediately, as evidenced by a playful chirp. Since it could not be known if Lady Ondine also understood, he waited for some semblance of a response. When none was forthcoming, he knew he should speak elsewhere, but he wanted to know more of her, and rousing her seemed a good means of doing so.

"Though I cannot own to being Wulfen-trained, Lady Ondine, I am exceedingly proficient at arms, especially when not chained." He gave another one-sided smile. "Indeed, so well matched were your brother and I that the slightest alteration of one of my swings could have seen the contest go my way." He raised his eyebrows. "As it can be no easy thing for a proud Wulfrith to acknowledge the excellence of one not of Wulfen, I am encouraged by your high regard, especially considering these circumstances in which I find myself."

Had she not understood earlier, she did now, and though still she did not respond, he sensed much displeasure.

"Well, then..." Fira drawled as if uncomfortable with her sister's silence, then brightened and stepped nearer Sinjin. "I know my brother cut your face, but as 'tis hidden beneath your beard"—she tapped the center of her chin—"here I am told, would you not at least give a good account?"

Thinking he could not have heard right, though almost certain he had, he said, "At least, my lady?"

Pulling from her bodice spectacles that evidenced her near

vision was wanting, she said, "At best, I would look upon it if you are well with me parting your whiskers."

He laughed and, sidelong, saw Sir Orton jerk his chin out of the physician's grasp to observe his prisoner. Deciding to ignore Lady Ondine, Sinjin angled toward her sister. "I do not know I am well with that, Lady Fira, nor do I believe your brother's men would be, but do tell of your interest in something so personal to me."

She stood a bit taller. "As I am to be my family's tale-giver after my grandmother, I record important events in the lives of the Wulfriths. *That* your contest with my brother was, and more so for the victor coming out the other end with his fifth wife." She grinned. "And ere long, his first child."

Even more Sinjin liked this Wulfrith sister. Were she some years older and he not at odds with her king whom he struggled to accept as his own, he might seek a match with her. "Alas, my lady, you must settle for a good account lest what was averted here circles back and cannot be averted again."

She dropped the spectacles down her bodice, gave a little sniff. "So?"

Liking the ease of their exchange that could prove his last enjoyable distraction from what would come should his escort succeed in delivering him to London, Sinjin cleared his throat. "What your brother told—"

"Not him," she interrupted. "Though he knows the importance of recording our family's history, near always other matters occupy him. It was our new sister-in-law who told us."

Of course it was, Sinjin thought and, with teasing, said, "Regardless, it is true this knight was marked such that now he keeps a beard as much for the warmth and ease as to hide disfigurement."

She caught her breath. Though there was slight sound and movement from her sister as well, the stubborn of Sinjin who did not want to be intrigued by one who disliked him continued to discount her presence.

"Disfigurement?" Lady Fira exclaimed in a slightly choked voice he would think indicative of taking offense were he speaking of one other than himself. "It cannot be as bad as that."

With a rattle of chain, he raised his hands and set a finger to the bottom of his bearded chin, then tapped it up to the dip beneath his lower lip. "As much is relative in life, Lady Fira, one ought to take into account the starting place. Though once many a maiden would have said this knight was as fine of face as figure, especially absent a beard, were I to shave these whiskers as was necessary to stitch my flesh, you would see that is less true than before."

She frowned. "Even so, you would not be unsightly as you make it sound."

Disliking the dampened mood, he chuckled. "You are right—not unsightly. 'Tis only my chin, not all my face, and I am fortunate Baron Wulfrith's blade did not also scar my neck—or worse."

Considering him, she set her head to the side. "What other marks did he leave on your body?"

"Likely as many and similarly situated as those I dealt him. But again, not truly unsightly, especially for a warrior who can count up the scars on cold winter nights and be encouraged."

"Encouraged!" At last, more words from Lady Ondine, albeit in a tone suggesting disbelief dragged through the manure of disgust.

He shifted his gaze from the wide-eyed young woman to the veiled one. "Encouraged, indeed, by all he has survived in a profession that bodes ill for one who wishes to reach a good old age. Too, though ladies find no value in their own bodies being marked thus since they are taught fair, unblemished skin more easily captures a man's eye, many revere the scars of a warrior for their proof of battle prowess rather than deem them distasteful."

Sinjin thought that well enough reasoned to pacify the veiled lady, but she said coldly, "You are right, much is relative, Sir Sinjin. I do not like bloodletting, but I can accept it when it is done by one who fights for the side of right to defeat one who fights for the side of wrong. Good eve." She turned and, with less grace for an angry step, crossed toward the stairs.

He was so intent on her he would have watched her all the way out of sight had not Lady Fira made a sound of distress.

He returned his attention to her. "I tend not to sit well with people, and I know I could overcome that with more effort, but I did not mean to offend your sister."

"I know that, and she does, Sir Sinjin. 'Tis just that she is..."

"...in mourning." He nodded. "Ever difficult to lose a beloved one."

Her mouth popped open, and he thought she would correct him, but she hesitated, then said, "Great her loss."

Guessing Lady Ondine was widowed the same as it was said of the eldest sister, Sinjin entertained the superstition whispered about that the Wulfriths siblings had fallen under a curse when their sire took as his second wife a woman so ill-suited as to be scandalous.

Ungodly superstition, he told himself, then said, "My sympathies."

Lady Fira curtsied. "I thank you for providing the length and placement of the scar, Sir Sinjin. Now I hope for you a good night's rest and, lest too soon you depart come morn, wish you Godspeed."

"A castle full of intriguing women," Sir Wallace said low as she hastened opposite.

Sinjin considered the stairs that had swallowed the veiled

one while he was not looking, then shifted to the other ladies who conversed at a good distance from the hearth, ensuring Sir Orton could not listen in—Séverine, Dangereuse, Fira, and the elderly and somewhat imperious Héloïse.

Quite intriguing, he silently agreed, then mused Baron Wulfrith's wife was a fitting addition to those of Castle Stern. And again was glad God had given the victory to the one who became Lady Séverine's husband though it had brought Sinjin to this.

Of course, now that lady is out of harm's way, Lord, might You side with me? he sent heavenward. *Make a way for me out of captivity? Give me reason to remain free that will calm this roiling to which there seems no good answer?*

"Now to our rest," Sir Wallace shunted aside thoughts of the morrow and all morrows thereafter, then jutted his chin at his advancing commander whose nose was heavily bandaged. "And pray, forget not the kindness granted me, Sir Sinjin. Give him no cause to deny us all a good night's sleep."

"I vow only to defend myself should it be necessary," Sinjin said and, as he followed, silently added, *This night only*.

Dear Reader,

I hope you enjoyed this excerpt of BEAUTEOUS, the second book in the Age of Honor series. *Watch for its release Summer 2022.*

PRONUNCIATION GUIDE

Achard: AA-shahrd
Adelaide: AA-duh-layd
Annus mirabilis: AAN-oos Mee-RAH-buh-lihs
Amaury: AW-moh-ree
Barra: BAHR-uh
Caen: KAHN
Calais: KAA-lay
Chanson: SHAHN-sahn
Colbern: COHL-buhrn
Crécy: KREE-see
Creuseur: KROO-zuur
Dange: DAHN-zhuh
Dangereuse: DAHN-zhuh-ruuz
D'Arci: DAHR-see
D'Argent: DAHR-zhahnt
Elias: uh-LIY-uhs
Esta: EH-stuh
Fira: FIY-ruh
Fitz Gére: FIHTS ZHAY-ree

PRONUNCIATION GUIDE

FitzSimon: FIHT-Sih-muhn
Fléau de l'Anglais: FLAY-oo duh LAHN-glay
Godfroi: GAWD-frwah
Guarin: GAA-rahn
Gytha: JIY-thuh
Hector: HEHK-tuhr
Héloise: AY-loh-weez
Ingvar: EENG-Vah
Les Neuf Preux: lay-NUUF-pruu
Louis: LOO-wee
Mace: MAYS
Maël: MAY-luh
Mercia: MUHR-see-uh
Moreville: mohr-VEEL
Odo: OH-doh
Ondine: AWN-deen
Owen: OH-wihn
Oriflamme: OH-ree-flaam
Percival: PUHR-sih-vuhl
Philippa: FIHL-ih-puh
Plantagenet: plaan-TAA-juh-neht
Ravvenborough: RAY-vuhn-buh-ruh
Rémy: RAY-mee
Robine: rah-BEEN
Roche: ROHSH
Sévère: SAY-vehr
Séverine: SAY-vuh-reen
Sinjin: SIHN-jihn
Stern: STUHRN
Villeneuve-le-Hardi: VEE-luh-nuuv LAHR-dee
Warin: WAH-rihn
Wulfen: WUUL-fehn
Wulfrith: WUUL-frihth

PRONUNCIATION GUIDE

PRONUNCIATION KEY

VOWELS
aa: arrow, castle
ay: chain, lady
ah: fought, sod
aw: flaw, paw
eh: bet, leg
ee: king, league
ih: hilt, missive
iy: knight, write
oh: coat, noble
oi: boy, coin
oo: fool, rule
ow: cow, brown
uh: sun, up
uu: book, hood
y: yearn, yield

CONSONANTS
b: bailey, club
ch: charge, trencher
d: dagger, hard
f: first, staff
g: gauntlet, stag
h: heart, hilt
j: jest, siege
k: coffer, pike
l: lance, vassal
m: moat, pommel
n: noble, postern
ng: ring, song
p: pike, lip

PRONUNCIATION GUIDE

r: rain, far
s: spur, pass
sh: chivalry, shield
t: tame, moat
th: thistle, death
t~h: that, feather
v: vassal, missive
w: water, wife
wh: where, whisper
z: zip, haze
zh: treasure, vision

GLOSSARY

BLIAUT: medieval gown
BRAIES: men's underwear
CASTELLAN: commander of a castle
CHAUSSES: men's close-fitting leg coverings
CHEMISE: loose-fitting undergarment or nightdress
COIF: hood-shaped cap made of cloth or chain mail
DEMESNE: home and adjoining lands held by a lord
DONJON: tower at center of a castle serving as a lord's living area
FEALTY: tenant or vassal's sworn loyalty to a lord
FORTNIGHT: two weeks
GARDEROBE: enclosed toilet
GIRDLE: belt worn upon which purses or weaponry might be attached
KNAVE: dishonest or unprincipled man
LEAGUE: equivalent to approximately three miles
LIEGE: superior or lord
MAIL: garments of armor made of linked metal rings
MISCREANT: badly behaving person

GLOSSARY

MISSIVE: letter
MORROW: tomorrow; the next day
NOBLE: one of high birth
NORMAN: people whose origins lay in Normandy on the continent
PARCHMENT: treated animal skin used for writing
PELL: used for combat training, a vertical post set in the ground against which a sword was beat
PIKE: long wooden shaft with a sharp steel or iron head
POLTROON: utter coward
POMMEL: counterbalance weight at the end of a sword hilt or a knob located at the fore of a saddle
PORTCULLIS: metal or wood gate lowered to block a passage
POSTERN GATE: rear door in a wall, often concealed to allow occupants to arrive and depart inconspicuously
QUINTAIN: post used for lance training to which a dummy and sandbag are attached; the latter swings around and hits the unsuccessful tilter
SALLY PORT: small hidden entrance and exit in a fortification
SENNIGHT: one week
TRENCHER: large piece of stale bread used as a bowl for food
VASSAL: one who holds land from a lord and owes fealty

Also by Tamara Leigh
Available in Ebook, Paperback, and Audiobook

INSPIRATIONAL HISTORICAL ROMANCE

AGE OF CONQUEST: The Wulfriths
AN 11th CENTURY MEDIEVAL ROMANCE SERIES

MERCILESS: Book One Amazon

FEARLESS: Book Two Amazon

NAMELESS: Book Three Amazon

HEARTLESS: Book Four Amazon

RECKLESS: Book Five Amazon

BOUNDLESS: Book Six Amazon

LAWLESS: Book Seven Amazon

DAUNTLESS: Book Eight Amazon, iBooks, B&N, Kobo

AGE OF FAITH: The Wulfriths
A 12th CENTURY MEDIEVAL ROMANCE SERIES

THE UNVEILING: Book One Amazon

THE YIELDING: Book Two Amazon

THE REDEEMING: Book Three Amazon

THE KINDLING: Book Four Amazon

THE LONGING: Book Five Amazon

THE VEXING: Book Six Amazon

THE AWAKENING: Book Seven Amazon

THE RAVELING: Book Eight Amazon

AGE OF HONOR: The Wulfriths
A 14th CENTURY MEDIEVAL ROMANCE SERIES

VALOROUS: Book One Amazon, iBooks, B&N, Kobo

BEAUTEOUS: Book Two (Summer 2022)

THE FEUD
A MEDIEVAL ROMANCE SERIES

BARON OF GODSMERE: Book One Amazon

BARON OF EMBERLY: Book Two Amazon

BARON OF BLACKWOOD: Book Three Amazon

LADY
A MEDIEVAL ROMANCE SERIES

LADY AT ARMS: Book One Amazon

LADY OF EVE: Book Two Amazon

BEYOND TIME
A MEDIEVAL TIME TRAVEL ROMANCE SERIES

DREAMSPELL: Book One Amazon

LADY EVER AFTER: Book Two Amazon

STAND-ALONE MEDIEVAL ROMANCE NOVELS

LADY OF FIRE Amazon,

LADY OF CONQUEST Amazon,

LADY UNDAUNTED Amazon

LADY BETRAYED Amazon

INSPIRATIONAL CONTEMPORARY ROMANCE

HEAD OVER HEELS
STAND-ALONE ROMANCE NOVELS

STEALING ADDA Amazon

PERFECTING KATE Amazon

SPLITTING HARRIET Amazon

FAKING GRACE Amazon

SOUTHERN DISCOMFORT
A CONTEMPORARY ROMANCE SERIES

LEAVING CAROLINA: Book One Amazon

NOWHERE CAROLINA: Book Two Amazon

RESTLESS IN CAROLINA: Book Three Amazon

OUT-OF-PRINT GENERAL MARKET TITLES

WARRIOR BRIDE 1994 Bantam Books (Lady At Arms rewrite)

VIRGIN BRIDE 1994 Bantam Books (Lady Of Eve rewrite)

PAGAN BRIDE 1995 Bantam Books (Lady Of Fire rewrite)

SAXON BRIDE 1995 Bantam Books (Lady Of Conquest rewrite)

MISBEGOTTEN 1996 HarperCollins (Lady Undaunted rewrite)

UNFORGOTTEN 1997 HarperCollins (Lady Ever After rewrite)

BLACKHEART 2001 Dorchester (Lady Betrayed rewrite)

www.tamaraleigh.com

About the Author

Tamara Leigh signed a 4-book contract with Bantam Books in 1993, her debut medieval romance was nominated for a RITA award, and successive books with Bantam, HarperCollins, and Dorchester earned awards and became national bestsellers. In 2006, the first of Tamara's inspirational contemporary romances was published, followed by six more with Multnomah and RandomHouse. Perfecting Kate was optioned for a movie, Splitting Harriet won an ACFW Book of the Year award, and Faking Grace was nominated for a RITA award.

In 2012, Tamara returned to the historical romance genre with the release of Dreamspell and the bestselling Age of Faith and The Feud series. Among her #1 bestsellers are her general market romances rewritten as clean and inspirational reads, including Lady at Arms and Lady of Conquest. In 2018, she released Merciless, the first book in the Age of Conquest series, followed by seven more unveiling the origins of the Wulfrith family. And now—VALOROUS, the first book in the Age of Honor series chronicling the 14th century Wulfriths.

Connect with Tamara at: www.tamaraleigh.com, Facebook, Twitter and tamaraleightenn@gmail.com.

For new releases and special promotions, subscribe to Tamara Leigh's mailing list: www.tamaraleigh.com

Made in United States
North Haven, CT
19 April 2022